About the author

Geoff Nowell is originally from Eccles, near Manchester, which is known to have lost at least two people at the Peterloo Massacre. From a young age, he has enjoyed writing fiction, not to mention learning about history. Learning about Peterloo at quite a young age left him speechless, with such a monumental and epic event having happened on his doorstep. He has been actively involved in annual projects commemorating Peterloo and those marking the event's bicentennial in 2019. This is his first novel.

1819: DARK ANGELIC

Geoff Nowell

1819: DARK ANGELIC

Vanguard Press

VANGUARD PAPERBACK

A CIP catalogue record for this title is
available from the British Library.

ISBN 978 1 784659 23 3

Vanguard Press is an imprint of
Pegasus Elliot MacKenzie Publishers Ltd.
www.pegasuspublishers.com

First Published in 2021

Vanguard Press
Sheraton House Castle Park
Cambridge England

Printed & Bound in Great Britain

Dedication

To our Great Martyrs of Liberty; to the Injured; to the Protestors.
Their cause absolutely central; their calibre legendary.

&

In memory of Bob Ainsworth

(1949-2019)

Acknowledgements

First and foremost, many thanks to my parents. Their constant help and support have been massive and are very much appreciated. Thanks to Martin Gittins, for his help in answering numerous questions. Thanks to Niall McGuinness for his expert proof reading and patience with me! Thanks to museum staff for answering my questions on the period this novel is set in. Thanks also to Chris and Keri, for their support and encouragement of me as a writer.

Author's Note

Firstly, I hope you enjoy this. Now that's out of the way, I want to say something before it begins. This is historical fiction, based firmly on real events. Some may even say it's a revisionist novel. I won't contend that if they do. Some of the events and characters were real. I hope I've been respectful to them, while trying to harness them to tell the story. It's very important to me that this novel is read into in the right way. It is not anti-anything. Some may read into it that way, but I implore you to trust me that it isn't targeting anything or anyone contemporary or outside of its historical context. It is not pro the left, right, centre or anything else. It is purely a tribute to the sacrifices of our people for Liberty.

The novel is about the Reform Movement and the Peterloo Massacre. That event will feature at the end, but most of the novel is set in the six months or so leading up to the massacre. History, is of course, sadly, littered with great injustices, of many different kinds. For many of us even today, they affect us deeply. The Peterloo Massacre was one which took place in the UK. An unprecedented mass-gathering of over sixty thousand people took place on St. Peter's Field, Manchester, on the 16th August 1819. They were there for a political meeting and after a picnic. It represented a huge waypoint on the UK's long and arduous journey to democracy. Those who attended saw their peaceful campaign tarnished by what I've no shyness in describing as a latter-day feudal regime run by tyrants. It was an attack by the state on their own people, our own people. The aim was to crush the stand they were making for civic liberty. Indeed, injuries were inflicted and lives were lost. For those who survived, the day would have stayed with them forever, and no doubt would have been a stain on their souls. With that in mind, it's worth mentioning that my novel features a *lot* of fantasy. Now, of course, I firmly understand the actual events portrayed in this novel would obviously not have featured any fantasy at all, no matter how seriously I present it. I DO NOT intend the fantasy elements, or the path the narrative takes in this novel, *to mock or belittle the tragic facts of what happened at the Peterloo Massacre.*

The Peterloo Massacre was the culmination of a period of campaigning by the disenfranchised, wanting to secure the vote and the precious citizen rights which came with it. These early campaigns were the foundations of freedom and democracy in these United Kingdoms. The campaigners organised themselves as the Reform Movement, who wanted to change the way the political system functioned, along with society itself, without resorting to a revolution. (Nevertheless, they represented a very radical form of thinking.) They easily transcended their outdated social status, identifying and aligning themselves with Enlightenment ideals and those of the French Revolution: Liberty, Fraternity and Equality. Most Reformers were working-class cotton workers, but from them, and the Chartist Movement, which came later, so many of us can trace the origins of our modern-day liberties back to these people, wherever we view our position in society today. These campaigning folk in the nineteenth century (and some of the eighteenth) started the freedom we have now to be ourselves, and do what we want with our lives.

Coming from right near Manchester originally, it affected me deeply when I first found out about this monumental event in history, having taken place in my own backyard. It continues to and always will. Recently, lots seem to have been done to remember these Reforming heroes of 1819, and to raise awareness of what they stood for and their sacrifice. Especially with the bi-centennial commemorations last year.

I want this novel to be viewed purely as an epic tribute to our forbears' heroic campaign for freedom, and hopefully it will be. Also, I hope this novel will inspire people to find out more (if they don't already know) about the Peterloo Massacre and the part played in securing freedom in the UK by these early protestors. One question I will ask readers: do they think my novel brings *artistic* justice to the great injustice that was the Peterloo Massacre?

Geoff Nowell
February 2020

Prologue

The year is 1419. Darkleigh, Lancashire. The famous but unassuming vill sat peacefully as it always did. The mid-evening sun retreated from the landscape, leaving the vast valley and lusciously glazing the hills. A gently billowing wind combed the otherwise silent valley, representing the only noise. It was the kind of evening which smelt of fond memories, nostalgia, sorrowful farewells, unrequited desires and regrets. Basically, it was the end of an era. The last former tenant of the manor turned to see his home vill one final time. A tear dropped from his eye and watered the grass. He had seen his home vill and manor like this many times. So crisply peaceful and modestly immaculate. But before the dawn of the present week he had known it to sleep and rise peacefully again in celebration of a saint's day or festival. But this was the last time he would see it in this or any other condition. His manor had not just been his lord's grand possession, but a beacon which had expressed how his lord and his people saw the world. And what a grand world the de Darkleigh family had made within the majestic pinch of earth which was their manor. But now that was gone. For a moment, the sigh the young tenant made seemed to echo across the valley. The last breath of human life left the landscape, and it was totally deserted. Almost.

All the tenant's houses were empty and listless. The individual decorations, which had adorned their timber and thatch, had been stripped bare from them. The many-coloured strips of land the tenants farmed lay there like stained glass. The vill square with its stone buildings stood motionless. Even the Guildhouse and the tavern *The Phoenix,* normally colourful hubs of merry activity, gave off an air of resignation. The armorial shields had been removed from the Guildhouse and this added a layer of sadness to the scene. Beyond the Guildhouse, towards the northern most hills, which ensconced the valley, was a small hill which rose before a brook which drifted across it, and atop of this was St. Darren's, the local church. As the late shafts of sunlight caught its stained-glass windows, it glinted in the landscape and the bronze stone and slate stood assertively defiant, almost knowing what was to come, awaiting it with divine calm. Across the brook, and some distance from it, was another hill isolated in the valley. And on top of this second hill in the valley was the local manor house. The smallest of castles, it was wide and centuries had stained the stone dark brown. It was clear that this was the seat of the lord of the manor. Despite its boldness, there remained something inviting about it. Its rugged dark stones almost called out to weary backs. For those who gained pleasure from touching, this tiny castle demanded to be stroked. Admired, adored. The de Darkleighs had gained so *much* admiration since they'd founded the manor. And from one of its towers, there still flew the family standard of the de Darkleighs. It was a phoenix rising from the ashes of a castle. That image would have been to an onlooker in the know disturbingly imminent. A door which led to the battlements opened, piercing the silence with a clattering echo. Tilly, the castle chambermaid, ran from it along the gangway between the battlements. She seemed concerned, but firmly in control. She was followed by the castle's Sergeant-at-arms, John Halgh.

"John, they're coming. I've just seen Michael signal for it," she said with urgency.

John nodded, unsurprised.

"Aye," was all he could say.

"What in hell are we going to do now?" Tilly said, starting to sound distressed.

John sighed.

"Whatever the master wants. I know what I'd like to do, though."

"So do I," Tilly agreed.

"Don't know if he'll let us, that's the problem," John said, cynically staring down the valley.

"This is so wrong. Dalbern's got no right to attack the master's home manor like this," Tilly declared, angrily gesturing to the deserted vill.

"I know, lass, I know," was all John could say in reply, looking sadly at the ground.

At that moment, a trap door on the gangway flew open and out jumped a figure, which made both Tilly and John restrain their emotions.

Standing there was someone wearing a black and green tabard and the same colour scheme for his winingas. His long, crow-black hair caught the wind. It was their lord. Sir Clarence de Darkleigh, seventeenth lord of Darkleigh, owner of the castle.

"Both of *ye* should be gone by now. I shall not lose one person to him!" he said with measured authority.

"We can't leave ye, Sire," protested Tilly.

"Surely someone should stay here with thou, Sire. It would be a terrible crime to leave thou on thy own," John added.

"Both of ye, be gone!" he commanded.

Tilly started to cry. John hugged her and couldn't bring himself to look up, his pride and joy drained away. When Sir Clarence saw this, he felt a twinge of guilt.

"Forgive me, friends. But I *shall* be assured of thy safety. It is my last wish for my closest servants, my closest friends," he said softly.

"Don't send us away, Sire, please," John pleaded.

"John, there shall be none..." but just then a ray of ruby-red light shot at the chest of the astonished Sir Clarence.

Looking across to St. Darren's on Church Hill, he immediately recognised the form of his old friend Michael the priest, rector of Darkleigh, catching the retiring sunlight with something and directing it unto him. Attention gained, he looked curiously at the object emanating red light, which Michael held in his hands. But he knew also that this was the signal which told him that his closest friends would not be able to get away in time. This confirmed Dalbern was on his way. He would have to honour their wish to stay.

"All right," he said, taking John and Tilly in his arms. "Here is our plan. When it is done, ye must swear on thy lives to follow the rest of us to Yorkshire and safety. The bailiff hath thy possessions listed on his scroll."

John and Tilly nodded with renewed enthusiasm.

"So..." Sir Clarence began.

Even though the long tenure of his family and the rich, proud legacy they had created was coming to an end, he still had his famous glint in his eyes.

Lord Dalbern rode relentlessly towards the southern hills, beyond which lay Darkleigh vill. With him were around sixty of his most ruthless warriors, which made up the core of his personal retinue. And a snarling, arrogant bunch they were.

Tyrewell, his closest confidante asked, "And thou canst be sure, Sire, that he will be the only one left?"

Dalbern nodded. "Indeed. My scout reported that he had ordered at his court the whole evacuation of the manor, to be complete within a week. He oversaw it. But trust me, he is far too stubborn to leave himself. Too much in love with his family's own legend. If I'd have even suspected that he'd have kept a reasonable force to defend his manor, then I'd have brought my whole army. This is what the Darkleighs do, you see, they cling."

They rode on, sheltered from the spectacular evening sun. Soon, they passed through the hills and came into the valley. Immediately impressed upon by the width and depth that now imposed itself on them, they ignored the pacifying beauty of the vintage sun and rolling grass, and they carried on to the centre of the vill.

Darting down the main track, Dalbern and his band kicked up an angry trail of dust, with their attention firmly trained on the two small hills at the head of the vill. They pressed on, past all the former strips of land the tenants tilled. Within the space of a few minutes, they slowed their pace as they trotted into the vill square. Dalbern regarded the square with suspicion, even though he believed that he and his enforcers were safe.

"Darkleigh! Come out, Clarence! Face me!" Dalbern bawled around the square.

When silence was returned, he scowled and motioned his entourage on.

"Ha, Clarence is obviously too cowardly to come out and face us. I thought as much. He might be a great jouster but he hasn't the knack for battle in the real world!"

Dalbern managed to quell his nerves with that bravado. His lieutenants laughed in encouragement of their leader's bragging. As they were making their way across the square, two shadows flickered between the stone buildings that dotted its perimeter. They dashed and darted with such speed that Dalbern and his band scarcely noticed them. Then, from

16

out of nowhere, there flew two arrows, one after the other, which knocked two of Dalbern's lieutenants off their horses. They proceeded to writhe around on the floor in agony. Taken unawares, Dalbern and his party swung round.

Tyrewell cried, "Ambush!" and they rode off at speed towards the Guildhouse at the far end of the square.

In the shadows, Tilly kissed her bow affectionately. She was pleased to be serving her master still, despite what today spelt.

When Dalbern and the rest of his group reached the end of the square, his band filtered out between the buildings. This led them into the shade. Down the narrow passageways they galloped, knowing that they were in a strange vill and that someone else, someone who was concealed, had the upper hand. As they left the rear of the buildings, they made a fresh gallop to Church Hill. Then they felt their horses slowing, then floundering, as their progress ground to a halt. Below them, they saw that their horses had become stuck in a huge trench of mud, as wide as it was long. It had not looked wet which is why they had crossed it, unconcerned. Behind them on their right-hand side, down another narrow, darkened passageway, John had a giggle at the miscreants who had come to meddle with his beloved master. Eyeing his spear and a large jug which had been responsible for this handiwork, he scurried away to meet up with Tilly.

Frustrated, Dalbern urged his warriors on, and they dismounted and trekked through the mud as fast as resistance would allow them. Sixty-odd warriors trudged angrily past Church Hill. When they passed it, Castle Hill was in plain sight.

"This is it," Dalbern said to his closest confidante.

"Let us hope they hath no more traps for us, Sire," Tyrewell said with some apprehension.

Then, slicing at the wings of the ranks which had loosely formed up around Dalbern, came a hail of arrows. His warriors fell like dying embers as all Dalbern could do was flail around.

"This way, Sire," Tyrewell said, directing his master to a clump of bushes where he intended them to take shelter.

As Dalbern and his louts either fell or scattered, some time had been bought.

In the churchyard at St. Darren's, Sir Clarence looked gratefully over to his two friends atop his castle. Having said their emotional goodbyes beforehand, he expected them to follow his instructions of running after they had succeeded in keeping Dalbern at bay. Which they did. Relief filtered into him at this. Watching these violent events with a clergyman's disapproval, Michael the priest looked towards his lord and friend. He had known Sir Clarence all his life. He had baptised him and watched him grow to become a great knight, a bit of a maverick and a worthy successor to his father in his family's line. And it came down to this, a last battle with the wicked Dalbern, a lord whose greed had taken him — then others. Sir Clarence's defeat of his forces had had the kingdom delighted, but now Dalbern wanted revenge, after a humbling defeat by Clarence.

"Sire, all I canst do now is to wish thou the best of fortune. May God keep thee."

"And ye, Michael," Sir Clarence responded. "In whatever way thou canst, I know thou shall make us, all of us, rise again. Just like the phoenix."

Michael nodded through watered eyes. Wishing each other God speed one final time, Sir Clarence ran to the end of the churchyard and mounted his treasured horse, Azlight. Then he came thundering out of the churchyard and down Church Hill, towards where a confused Dalbern and the remainder of his thugs were staggering about.

"Well, well. Here he is. The greatest knight of our age uses his petty servants to take out my closest friends," Dalbern greeted sarcastically.

"My friends are not petty and thou hath none, Dalbern. Only hangers-on," Sir Clarence replied.

"Believe me, I shall not be the one hanging by the time this is over," Dalbern scowled.

Sir Clarence smiled sardonically.

"No, I do not expect thou will," was all he said.

After what was an uncertain pause for Dalbern and his crowd, Clarence charged amongst them, cutting them down with simple strokes of his sword.

Panicking, Tyrewell shouted, "On our lord!"

The thugs who had escaped Clarence's sword clustered round

Dalbern and held their weapons out, so that they resembled a mound of earth with weapons sticking out of it. Clarence duly dismounted Azlight and told her to run to safety. He knew this was the end. But an end which would see him go down having taken with him the worst villain his age had seen. Clarence purged everything in preparation to meet God, with Dalbern by his side in chains.

From the surrounding hill he had now retreated to, Michael reached inside a bag and stroked a smooth ruby-red object. Raising half of it out, he passed a picture of a dragon over it. Clarence waited for the phalanx to reach him. There he stood, poised like a wild animal, his sword at the ready. However, the phalanx abruptly stopped when they spotted something of the weird variety in the sky above them. A mass of red mist eerily floated through it. Neither they nor Clarence had seen this before. They kept watching as, slowly but surely, the mist wrangled itself into a discernible shape and form. It wasn't long before it had clearly formed into a dragon. The phalanx became loose as Dalbern, too, ogled the strange phenomenon. Then, the mist moved, with the intelligence and intent of a living creature and dived towards the patch of earth where the castle was. This caused some of Dalbern's louts to scatter and retreat. But then, to Michael's horror, the great dragon opened its mouth and breathed a huge volume of fire down towards the earth. It instantly set the ground between Church Hill and Castle Hill alight, assailing many of Dalbern's thugs. Clarence, untouched, ran inside the open gate of his castle. Dalbern was floundering but followed him in on his own.

Confronting him inside the courtyard, Dalbern growled. "Thou think thou could stop me from doing my will, do thou? Thou, a mere knight of a token realm!"

Clarence smiled. Thanks to the fire, he knew Dalbern's fate would be sealed for sure now.

"Hmm. My realm is a great token. One which no noble has perhaps had before. One from heaven," Clarence stated through sure lips.

Scowling, Dalbern sliced at Clarence with his sword. Clarence neatly dodged and countered all Dalbern's angry thrusts with his own sword. Up on the hill side, Michael was praying, imploring what he had used against Dalbern's warriors to stop. But the dragon reared up again, and looked down at the castle. Dalbern threw himself at Clarence again, to deliver a mighty thrust, but Clarence saw the space and ran him through. With a defeated scream, Dalbern sank to the ground. Clarence was relieved it was over. A tyrant was defeated. Gone. Then he went to look to the heavens with thanks, but instead found himself staring up into the mouth of the dragon, whose fire blazed down on him and engulfed the castle. Michael slumped on the hillside. He wanted to call out but found even his very voice stifled. Unable to express agony, it flooded through him in waves. The dragon then faded out in the same way it had arrived until not a trace of red mist remained.

They found the charred remains of Sir Clarence's body the very next day. They interred it at St. Darren's, with John, Michael and Tilly the sole mourners. It was the most solemn occasion of their lives. None of them had ever thought that just the three of them would be standing over their master and friend's tomb. They remembered him and everything he had been to them. But the sad, sad end of the noble line of de Darkleigh had come. Dalbern's body was not found, but there was no way, in their eyes, he could've survived the blazing fire of the dragon. They found Azlight, who sensed her master was missing. After consoling her, they rounded up all the horses belonging to Dalbern and his party, and together with Azlight, escaped with them over the Pennines to safety. Michael was the last to go. He looked out over the vill of Darkleigh one more time. Bowing his head, he sighed with sadness and turned for his friends.

***

In a chapel on a quiet Lancaster street, Michael sat, deep in his sense of contentment. A few months had passed since he, John and Tilly had left Darkleigh. The dreadful things which had preceded that event would be with him forever. But now he had migrated up to the county town and was now living a quiet life, speckled with many spectacular displays of the divine Lord's power. At his table he sat, sighing happily as he finished his writing. Admiring his calligraphy, he regarded the way he'd illustrated his manuscript with a picture of Lancaster Castle.

"In the genesis of our shire, lies the power of our people," he spoke with proud tones.

Locking the manuscript away in a chest, he left the chapel, smiling to a monk deep in study on his way out. It was time for the tavern.

Chapter One

The town of Darkleigh bustled away in the midst of a spring day. The valley it sat in was laced as far as the eye could see with row upon row of intricate streets, lined everywhere with cobbles, terraces and ginnels. They were fixed ruggedly to the valley in place of where there had once been wide-open fields. Punctuating the swell of these copious brown dwellings were numerous industrial buildings. Vast and box-like the mills stood, their long, narrow windows occasionally catching the sun as it pierced through the considerable smog, glinting back at it cynically. There were also the massive chimneys which stood like obelisks over each mill or factory. The source of thick smoke, which in turn provided the smog, announced the primacy of each and every mill in the same way that steeples did churches. The new industrial nature of the town had really imposed itself on the landscape. But, of course, this had happened pretty much everywhere during the last century. With the advent of industry, so, so many towns in the North and elsewhere had had to incorporate the heaviness of the age and all the changes it brought to them. So Darkleigh was far from alone in what it had become. Looking down to the town from the hills on the south side of the valley, there sounded like there was an eternal buzz hanging over the town; there was, and this buzz by and large came from the looms which never seemed to cease, day or night. The coarseness of the by-products produced by the mills, particularly the smoke, would waft over and reduce even the hardiest person to a coughing fit. Despite this though, there was something else that rose from the town. An indescribable feeling of glory and determination which cried with pride from the dense rooftops of the houses and mills. Despite the hard press of industry, a very noble and optimistic vibe sprung from the town. A vibe of defiance. It was self-aware of its sufferings but refused to define itself by them. For in this afflicted town, many things were growing. Amongst them a new sense of beauty, and a re-born sense of courage.

In the town's largest mill, Shackfield's No. 1, there were a massive eight floors. Folk called it Shackfield's Top Hat, in reference to its owner, Squire Shackfield's hat. Rumour abounded that the profits he gained from No. 1 were used to buy himself a new top hat every month. Most folk were lucky to get a new one every couple of years. Lying roughly in the centre of the town, several hundred yards away from the square, it dominated the skyline for miles around, and could be seen from any direction on the hills. It so happened that a young woman worked there, on the fifth floor. Her name was Mary Rishworth. And today, she was experiencing a day like every other — mounds and mounds of grit, grind and pure hardship were building up on her. Her mind intent on keeping to the rhythm of the loom, all she could think about as she worked was warp and weft. The relentless clatter of the shuttles pounded her ears and helped reduce her thinking to all that was necessary to sustain her existence. She had grown to ignore the ringing she heard afterwards, out on the street. She knew she would have to wait till she got home to have a conversation that didn't need the animated mee-maw chatter adopted in the mills. With her shawl pulled tight to her, the trusty and beloved garment felt like something of a shield. Peering through the film of dust that lingered in the air, Mary made out all that she needed to: the profile of her loom. In and out the shuttles clattered, followed by her, continuously replacing the yarns. Then came the horrible moment of every minute: the kissing of the shuttle. Quickly, she used her tongue to pull the thread through the shuttle's eye. An unpleasant tickle at the back of her throat followed. Re-inserting it, she waited for the process to begin again. Despite the rawness of her situation, she had crafted out a fine art of coping with it. One that ensured she could keep up. She remembered the soldiers at Waterloo and took pride that she too could cope with extremity. For no matter what the mill threw at her, she knew that she had developed a ruggedness. And, in turn, despite that, she took an even deeper pride in keeping enough ladylike-ness not to turn over-rugged. In fact, Mary often wondered what life could be like if things were better. For if the mills were more accommodating, then no doubt the life of a weaver would be a prized possession. Mary and many of her friends took terrific pride in what they did. She had worked there since as long as she could remember. Since she was six, her mother said. It had become a part of her, as it had for countless others. They sometimes saw what they produced, a rare event which brought them to tears. Beautiful clothes and textiles, worn the world over. The finest quality, too. Mary always felt the joy of seeing a finished garment, much like a sword smith must have done when he produced a sword in the old days. The only difference was he would have seen every sword he made in its entirety. Mary hardly knew a woman who hadn't picked up a shuttle and worked as a weaver. She felt part of something now, like a legion. Maybe like soldiers did in the army, and sailors in the navy. But although Mary and her friends had no fight to fight, it didn't stop them from being conscious of what was happening to them. There was a line behind which people kept polite graces, but you daren't cross to the other side. That was the divide between yourselves and the mill owners. For they held a lot of power, and the ruling classes propped it up for them. Aye, Mary and her friends knew there were ills in the mills, but the greatest ills were in something that shouldn't have existed by then. Something bigger, something invisible. Something that worked unseen to keep you at bay. Something that took great pleasure in quashing new ideas with pompous savagery. However, for now, Mary was firmly focused on work. Earning her weekly wages was her main goal.

Sometimes during the course of her shift, Mary would notice the occasional ray of sunlight dazzle the dust. She loved this majestic sight. As it brightened then faded away at intervals, it brought her some solace, as well as enchantment. She and her sisters called them the 'Angel Beams'. This caused her to look out of the window and see as much as she could of the world taking place. She'd look as much as she could across the rooftops and think about all the other embattled souls, just like her. She'd sigh a prayer for them and sometimes blow a kiss. She'd stare down the streets and down the ginnels which felt eternal in their extent, leading to a noxious infinity. Despite the dirt of industry, Mary loved her town. It was like a labyrinth of streets and ginnels, where you could wander for hours in wonder, even in a town the size of hers. The acute sense of homeliness made her feel wanted, even by the very bricks and cobbles. It was like every town nowadays was York — without the walls. Eventually you would find your own niche and become a great fixture there. She'd gaze up at the hills and wonder when the streets ran out so she could climb them. Then she'd see the sun piercing the smog, peeking out from behind clouds, and felt reassured. It was like that with rain as well, though. She felt so strangely comforted and secure when the rain came pelting down. She'd look out of the window then and try her best not to become enticed with the shimmering rooftops, flashing silver as the huge face of the clouds hovered directly above them. The patterns the rain often made intrigued her too. The elaborate little dances they made as they met the surface. Lovely redeeming, cooling rain. The complex mass of clouds that came during rainy days told some kind of epic story that Mary had never been able to fathom, with all their shapes, blurring and movement. But she was glad that a story like that was told in the skies above her town. Mary had heard of theatres but had never actually been. She'd always wondered what it would be like to go, and lusted after it. But as she said to her friends and family, the drama here's either at the mill or in the clouds. (Ideally she preferred it in the clouds.)

Mary regarded the latest ray to come in, and let herself linger on it for a few moments. Then an overseer walked by a few looms in front of her. With her eagle-eyes noticing him, Mary quickly diverted her gaze back to her loom, and then towards the warp thread at the back, portraying her concentration as unbroken. Her tactic worked and the overseer's suspicion vanished as he rolled his eyes and continued on his way. Mary had had a few run-ins with him in the past, and had long-since developed ways of 'beating the gaze'. Strategies to trick the overseers, who were craftsmen when it came to looking for excuses to persecute workers for what it suited them to pass off as laziness or shoddy work.

At one point during that shift, something extraordinary happened. Noticing some 'Angel Beams' coming from the window, she looked towards its source. The sun was indeed shining outside. However, in the space of a few moments, she felt herself go numb, a similar feeling to being intoxicated. Mary couldn't fathom this as she only ever drank to keep herself hydrated. But not only that, the light outside the window had disappeared. Now there was just inky darkness, with the sun beam a swirling array of gold pieces. The more she looked, the more she felt enticed by them. Mary felt the work of her hands slow down and worried about what was happening to her, and when the overseer would see. But her worries soon evaporated and all concern left her as she felt herself drift up into the air and towards the newly darkened window. She knew that she shouldn't be floating through the air but she was, and she was becoming less and less self-conscious of it. She did manage to look around at all the other girls, tacklers and piecers, but they just carried on, absorbed in their work, not even noticing what was happening to her. Mary felt surprised at this, and was able to sneak a glance at her own loom for a couple of seconds. Standing in her place was another weaver, her height, doing her work for her. Mary wanted to call out to her but she felt that she couldn't. She felt her voice softly fade. The weaver at her loom turned her head slowly to Mary, as if casually noticing her. All Mary caught was the briefest of glimpses, but it was enough for her to make out a scratched grey colour where a face should be. She was herself scared, confused and intrigued all at the same time by this. Then something gently brought her back to face the window, and as she got closer, she was worried that she'd crash into it. Mary couldn't remember the impact; things just went blank as she made contact with it.

The next thing she knew she was outside the mill, floating pleasantly through thin air. She could see the red-brown tint of the bricks cutting something of a dash against the deep purple sky. She saw her window, recognisable from the candle she had on its ledge for the night shift. The window was a vividly warm yellow colour. To Mary, this suggested rampant activity, but she could make out nothing behind it. All the other windows were yellow but dimmer. After she realised that she was floating through the air, she fell to confusion again. But the farther away she got from the mill (which was now a very curvy shape) the less she cared. It was only now she noticed that she was completely relaxed, like she was sleeping but awake at the same time. All the pains and traumas of work had left her. She felt renewed. Then, all of a sudden, she changed direction and began to slowly slide down vertically. With this she saw that the darkness of the night sky had quickly peeled away, and its veil was lifted to reveal Darkleigh as she had always known it. But there was something different about it still. Its buildings, roads and streets were exactly the same, but there was no smog. In the smog's place was a very golden spring evening. The retiring sun caught the sentimental hues of the mills and terraces warmly and sympathetically. This stirred up a feeling of contentment in Mary, the richness of which she had never felt before. She came to rest on the cobbled road, which led into the north of town. The slight clunking of her clogs was the only sound. It was then she realised that there was not a speck of dirt, or rubbish about. Her town was immaculate. Inner confusion was replaced, probably for the first time in her life, by a feeling which made her feel so right with the world. Pausing for a moment to take in her newly furnished surroundings, she then felt herself lift slightly off the ground before whizzing off at a manic speed. Seconds later, she found herself in the town square, in front of *The Phoenix,* Darkleigh's oldest tavern. Its medieval construction showed this. Coming from inside the tavern, she could hear the warmest sounds of merriment. Her insides slowed down at this. Just these sounds made complete sense to her. There was familiarity in what she heard. This made her eager to go and put faces to names. When she approached the door, things just went blank again. Then she found herself inside. There was no one in the main bar area. This didn't surprise her as she had heard the happy natter coming from the vault. She walked further up and turned to the right. No sooner had she done this than things went blank, again. This time Mary knew what to anticipate. She found herself in the vault, in the middle of the floor. The sides were lined with people, all kinds of folk who she knew from town, her childhood and the mill. Her mother and sisters were there, too. She could hear musical instruments playing and people clapping in rhythm. She knew what to do. She thundered into a dynamic dance, with her clogs hammering the wooden floorboards in time to the music. The crowd adored this and the cheering and clapping became more intense. Mary could feel the effort she was putting in, but curiously no exertion. It was as if she were a flowing piece of silk, evading being tied into a knot. With a flourish, the music and her dance ended at *exactly* the same time. Looking up, Mary accepted the plaudits graciously. Mary was an accomplished dancer. Everyone in Darkleigh knew that. Looking at her proud mother and sisters, Mary felt a strong streak of happiness run through her. Then amongst the cheers and clapping, she noticed someone in the corner. This person was in a dark cloak and was clapping softly. A hood obscured his face. He was evidently unnoticed by everyone else. Mary received nothing sinister from him though. In fact, she gained a sense of familiarity from this person, who she sensed was male. Intrigued by him for several moments, she let his presence register and then went back to taking in the whole vault. At this point, she felt such a oneness with herself that she had had glimpses of in the past, but had rarely been soaked in, as she was now. However then, it was as if the whole thing sped backwards, the process completely reversed in a rude blur. A moment later she was back at her loom, checking the weft, replacing the weft as she always did, as if she'd never left it. Then the bell sounded, to signify a change of shift. Disturbed, she saw her friends and colleagues finish in the normal manner, not noticing her apparent return.

Neither did the overseers, who just walked around saying, "Come on, ladies, sign off, make way for the next shift."

Mary looked towards the window, which had provided the portal for her adventure. Her mouth wide open, she didn't see her friend Bertha approach. Bertha shook her gently.

"Come on, Mary, I didn't know you loved that loom so much."

"Reet," was all Mary could say.

Mary switched her machine off, signing off on an even keel. Then, tightening her shawl, she followed Bertha and the others straight out of the mill and into the open air of the town.

Chapter Two

As Mary and her friends made their way out of the mill's vast yard and walked out from underneath its shadow, they joined on to one massive herd of folk walking back towards the town, their clogs clopping collectively on the infinite cobbles. The smog had lifted somewhat. Work had abated for no one, but as they looked skyward and saw the broken grey clouds and the blue sky behind it, they were taken aback by how sincere it seemed to return their gaze. Family and festivals dominated the talk between folk as they strode, plus the gossip that some treasured. The girls' target was the town square, as they knew that an event of importance was taking place there today. That event sent shivers down everyone's spines, even the well-to-do and those in authority. But they were shivers of change, felt by most reasonable folk. For them, these shivers heralded excitement. For today, the square was playing host to a Reformers' rally.

Outside the Guildhouse the hustings stood, with a huge throng of folk crowded before it, listening intently. Standing atop was Joe Duckworth, local hand-loom weaver and known radical. His profile in the town was well-known, and respected, given the articulation with which he spoke, and the diplomacy with which he represented the Darkleigh Reformers. But he had passion for his cause. And it beamed through in his oration. Standing astride of him on the hustings were his wife Laura (a very astute woman who always had time for folk) and several other senior members of the local Reform club, amongst them the very diverse friends of liberty of the town; shopkeepers, weavers, printers, spinners and shoe-makers.

"And so, my friends, what has it all come to?" he boomed charismatically.

"Our great victory over Napoleon, what an achievement! How we all fought. How we were all lauded as heroes on the battlefield. Then we came home. And what awaited us at home? A hero's welcome? I tell you what we came home to: a crippling economic depression, where the ones of us lucky enough to have jobs in them terrible mills are slowly ravaged to death every day in return for a pittance that barely keeps us and our families alive, just enough for us to trudge to the mills the next day for it all to happen again. And everyone suffers. Everyone. The ones of us who sell their wares to the rest of us all are being deprived of the custom which this post-war depression has brought. They too are slipping further towards destitution. We are all assailed by the same sharp Devil, make no mistake. The Corn Laws plague parliament. No corn for us, just them with too much brass than sense!"

The crowd were hanging on his every word, cheering at the points of emphasis.

"But maybe worse is despite everything we did for each other on the battlefield, in the name of toppling tyranny, from whatever walk of life we came from, we still live at an appalling distance from one another. Toppling tyranny, eh? I myself think it was a slogan to get us through the war. And nothing more!"

The loudest cheers of agreement sounded, booming out around the square, attracting the attention of those scurrying to and from places behind it. It was at this point that Mary and her friends arrived, joining the crowd.

"What does solidarity, comradeship and brotherhood mean when we can't even vote? When by and large we're treated like serfs? When the damn country's still run with a feudal system? This country travels far when it likes, and leaves behind what's convenient for it to do so. We are not their enemies but their compatriots, perhaps even friends. But to them, we are foreigners in our own country, *their* own country. And our sole purpose is to live and die at our lord's behest, for the needs of the economy he backs. My friends, surely you will agree with me when I decree that there is only one solution for this wicked dilemma. There must be lords no more. They shall live on, on their grand estates, of course, but with no power to lord over us, ever again. We may have defeated the French, but doing a few things as they do wouldn't be a bad idea. It is time to tear back if we have to, the veil of archaic tyranny to let the light of liberty in over our land. Our birth right — liberty, fraternity, equality and peace. Nothing less!"

At this point, a massive cheer sounded out and didn't seem to die down for half an hour. Laura and Joe's friends on the hustings clapped proudly. They couldn't stifle their pride of him with his eloquence, even though it was in favour of something that bypassed trivial egos.

In the crowd, Mary said to Bertha, "Well, that's telling them, isn't it?"

At that exact time, in what seemed like a place a whole world removed from Darkleigh, there scurried frantically a group of blokes, in all directions, desperately posting bills in the town of Manchester. The bills read:

Friends of Reform

From wherever ye hail in life, whether ye weave or sell trinkets for a living, wherever ye art from, ye are all invited to take note that in this very city, the agitation of the great giant is gathering pace. And when he awakes he must use reason rather than his fists to bring about the noblest goal that this land has ever had: Liberty.

To that end, be advised that a mass meeting will be taking place in Manchester this very summer, the greatest industrial city in the world. For amongst the machinations of industry that hath hitherto changed the world, there grows another yearning to change it again. The nature of the change? Justice.

Your attendance at this meeting is massively welcome, given the message it will broadcast. Please continue to check thy trusted newspapers such as the Manchester Observer for the date which will be set, along with more details.

Long live Liberty!

The men posting these bills were there and gone in seconds, like will o' the wisps. Like phantoms they streaked, slapping the bills onto shaded brick walls and those out in the open, the latter requiring the most daring. They were then sloshed with solution to make them stick. The mighty ginnels and cobbles of Manchester denoted a kind of cousinhood with most of the surrounding towns, but their scale in Manchester was colossal. The scope of where they were gave these plucky men their gumption, as things had taken place in Manchester since the second half of the last century, and things were now coming to a head. They knew it, which is why they were out. Observers knew it, and pondered what to do, which side to pick. The authorities knew it, and deep down they knew that this day had always been coming. As the street lamps of Manchester flickered and frayed, one of the bill men spotted a couple of special constables, snooping about.

"Hey, lads, Nadin's mob," he hissed, gesturing towards where they stood, outside a tavern.

Immediately, heads turned and the last bills went on, with the equipment they'd been using going under their jackets.

"This way," the lead one of them said, and all six ran after him.

The special constables couldn't fail to hear the sound of retreating clogs and went to investigate. As they made their way down the ginnel where the bill posters had been, they hovered in apprehension, given the intermittent light. Then, glaring at them were the posters. One of them scoffed and gestured to his pal, who gave off an equally disgusted snort, trying perhaps to hide his dominant emotion — fear. These bills had been placed purposefully there, opposite the exits to a warehouse. In a few hours, the workers would spill out and be confronted with these, so they tried to tear one off. However, looking down the ginnel, they realised that it was covered with these posters, which stretched right down it as far as the eye could see. They felt defeated. The men who'd been posting the bills had since escaped into the shadows, and anonymity. The bill-posters were now back at the tavern cellar where their secret base of operations was. In each of them, a glowing feeling that this war they were in with their *own countrymen* was slowly being won.

Back in Darkleigh, the crowd changed shape as the rally finished. Joe Duckworth was speaking to the local magistrate's son, Harvey Tabway.

"Well done, Joe, another rousing speech, but one that didn't excite any bad passions," Harvey complimented.

"Well, it wouldn't have been possible without you, would it?" Joe pointed out.

"Well, it's always our pleasure to allow our people to express themselves freely, providing it is done in a respectful manner. And yours always is, I'm glad to say," said Harvey.

"Please, convey my grati... our gratitude, to your father," Joe thanked.

"I will," Harvey promised.

"If only all magistrates could be like him," Joe mused.

"Well, we know you, all of you. We know our own people, and we want only the best for them. Of course, politics isn't the job of me or my family, at least not in our official capacity. So I'm afraid, on that score, all I can say is good luck. And God speed."

With warm, satisfied smiles, the two young men shook hands.

As Laura Duckworth climbed down from the hustings, she saw Mary, and the pair waved to each other. They strode over and met between different groups who were breaking up after having been one for the rally.

"Hey up, Laura, you're reet gradely today," Mary noticed.

"Well, I suppose I have to be on a day like today, don't I?" she laughed.

"Being Joe's wife comes with a hefty price sometimes, but he's reet worth it. I did reet' well when I chose him."

"And he you," Mary reassured.

Laura didn't return that, she just smiled modestly back at her friend.

"Joe says he values my opinion but sometimes I just feel like I'm just there to look gradely, all tarted up all the time." She frowned.

"Hey, there's plenty more to you than meets the eye, Laura." Mary winked.

"We *all* look to you. Not just the women. You're like the Queen of the Reformers."

"Well, I've sometimes opened my mouth when Joe hasn't, at my own peril, told it like it was," Laura began to concede.

"You've told it how it is, offered other things and led us to them in the past. And long may that continue," Mary added.

"Thank you." Laura smiled.

Both Mary and she joined hands as everyone headed for the taverns.

Chapter Three

The Sunday of that week saw Mary and her family in church, along with most other folk. Crammed into their recently built Methodist church, they all sat pretty, clad in their Sunday best. The sun streamed in through the windows overhead and made the wooden pews and pulpit glow sedately. This was part of the reason why Mary felt so renewed in church. There was just something magical about it, which had the effect of re-invigorating her. Sometimes she found it hard to follow, when the minister preached, but she found the stories of the Bible inspiring. Sometimes though they were upsetting, other times fantastical. But whatever the readings and sermons were about, she always felt the feeling. And that was what counted most importantly. And what a lovely, rich, indulgent feeling it was. One of the few genuine pleasures that weavers like her could have. Mary knew also that the week to come would grind her back down, placing her in need of church, re-building her craving in an agonising way. After heading to the tavern on Saturday night if she wasn't on the night shift, she would enjoy a drink, a laugh and a dance with her friends. Then there would follow a glorious Sunday. Beginning with a frantic rise to be sure that they would be on time, this was followed by some breakfast, sometimes a bath, and then a giggling walk to their church, which lay in the western part of the town. Distinctive as a Methodist chapel, its white exterior sat beamingly next to the usual collection of oranges and browns, attracting many a thoughtful glance from an uneducated eye. Then, there would be a warm welcome from the minister and his wife on the door. Following this would be prayers, singing and readings. Maybe an interesting sermon. Mary loved it. Her mother was happy when there, and her sisters pretended to look awake. But today, the minister, Eric Fields, was narrating quite an epic sermon.

"And so, my friends, the day of the apocalypse, when all we know and hold dear shall vanish from before our eyes, replaced by the Devil's terror and chaos!"

The minister's ominous warning boomed throughout the church, into the furthest reaches of the rafters while most folk just sat there entertained. Some secretly hoped for it, as a break-up to the rhythm of the none-lives they led. Mary enjoyed hearing him say it, but was quite disturbed when she saw the stained-glass window to the left of the pulpit. As the minister's words echoed in her mind, the pictures in the stained glass clearly changed shape radically before her eyes. 'Terror and chaos' his voice echoed around her mind, as she saw the figures in the window take on the forms of soldiers, pursuing their enemy. Wearing their distinctive red coats, they snarled cynically as their muskets slashed and banged. 'All we know and hold dear shall vanish from before our eyes' the echoing voice came again inside her. Mary was chilled by what she heard next, as the soldiers' cries were accompanied by screams and a general sound of alarm, a great commotion. Mary was confused as she knew redcoats to be British soldiers, of course on her side, fighting for her country. She had known some lads at the mill to be soldiers, returning from Waterloo with a myriad of stories. What these soldiers were doing in amongst the sounds of screams and general fright was beyond her. She would have expected to hear the opposing shouts of the enemy. But, as quickly as this vision had arrived, it faded. She was now staring back at the window as it was, with a saint and a pilgrim smiling out onto them. She reacted to this with surprise, rolling her eyes and hearing the last words of the minister who then brought his sermon to a close. Church was, for that day, almost over.

After church, Mary and her family were joined by her friends when Mary went to archery practice. This was something she had excelled at from an early age. Some had said it weren't proper to have a lass arch, but others thought she cut a romantic dash, being an archer with her shawl off and hair flying in the wind. Either way, both camps had soon gathered respect for her abilities as an archer. Mary had begun archery with her father just before he died. Mary had always wanted to carry on passionately. She saw it as a part of her father that lived on in her. Her mother understood this, as Mary had told her that in secret, but her sisters were just pleased to have a sister who was locally famous for being good at a lad's sport. And Mary was the pride of her local club, the Darkleigh

Archers, whose history stretched back to the middle ages. She had won numerous awards competing against clubs from other towns down the road. Everyone knew her for it, and her down-to-earth, approachable attitude made her popular with everyone. Even the overseers at Top Hat were known to keep extra distance from her. Today, she stepped up and shot all three of her arrows onto the bullseye of the butts, right at the opposite end of the field. The club cheered this enthusiastically. After, she went inside while the other members carried on, trying to emulate her. The temperature was higher than normal, so she hoped to make the most of the shade the old wooden club house provided. In there, she found Bertha, Unity and Anne from the mill, hiding behind the beer kegs.

"Ooh, hey up, Mary," Bertha called.

Mary raised an eyebrow when she saw where they were.

"Ooh, hey up, girls, what're you doing behind there?" Mary responded.

"Ssshh," Bertha went, making out as if she were desperate not to be heard.

Mary then knew that she was probably up to one of her pranks. She was notorious for them. Keeping her eyebrow raised, Mary walked over and stated in no uncertain terms that she wanted to know what was going on. But instead of a giggle, Bertha stayed sincere.

"Mary, I'm so glad I saw you. We need your help. We've all been dared to do something pretty daft."

Mary rolled her eyes and walked away. A prank. She knew it.

"No wait, Mary, please don't leave. We're not brave enough to do it on our own see."

Mary stopped short and didn't turn. Bertha grasped at this opportunity.

"You know the girls on the floor below us, well, they've dared us to go to the old castle, to see if we can find the ghost that's meant to haunt there. Course we think it's a load of daft crackers, but we don't want 'em to think we can't do it."

"Well, if you think it's a load of old cobblers, why bother doing it at all then?" Mary said cynically.

"Well, the girls on the floor below us at Top Hat think it's a big deal. If they did it, it'd be like they were lifting the Holy Grail. So we want to go there and show them how daft they are to believe it."

Mary turned round and fixed an impatient glare on her friend.

"Aye, but as I said, if it's a load of old cobblers, why can't you just do it yourselves? If you know it's not real, there's nowt' to fear."

"Well, you see, Mary, it's not the ghosts we're worried about," piped up Unity. "It's the dirty old buggers that folk see there sometimes."

"And we can't ask us rosebuds or they'd laugh at us," explained Anne.

"What about your fathers?" Mary asked.

The girls were sceptical.

"Ooh, Mary, you don't tell your father things like this, he'd have us over his knee," Bertha exclaimed.

"You know going to a place like that you're facing all kinds of dangers. It'll make the mill look like a dip in the lake. You're daft for putting yourselves in danger for that alone, girls," stated Mary.

"What, with the dirty old blokes?" Bertha asked curiously.

"Aye, not only them, but they'll be the least of your worries. You could fall down where you can't see the path. Trip over tree roots. Fall down a shaft from an old building, God knows."

There was then a pause between Mary and her friends.

"Well then, that's even more of a reason for you to come with us, isn't it?" Bertha appealed.

"We asked you because you're the one who's the bravest, Mary. You know how to sort everything out if we run into trouble. We can't, we're hopeless. So come with us. Please."

For some reason, Mary found herself reluctantly trekking up the town towards Church Hill. Bertha, Anne and Unity had all given her hugs when she'd agreed to come. Now, they weren't talking about it, they were just grinning with gratitude. But this was the effect brave Mary had on folk. She had courage, some would say too much than was safe for a woman, but she didn't let that bother her. Mary had her fair share of admirers for her daring and good looks. Traversing the streets they went, passing many silent mills, just standing there dormant of a Sunday, waiting to be fired up the next day. Not before long, they came to Church Hill, which told them they were reaching the outskirts of the town. The old manor boundaries went on for a while yet, but the town that had grown since the advent of industry was thinning out. This was noticeable as buildings were becoming less and less dense. Mary looked up at St. Darren's, which was Church of England. It was one of a few medieval buildings which still stood in Darkleigh, the others being the Guildhouse, the Phoenix and her archery club's lodgings. It looked to her like something out of a book of legends. With its bronze-coloured stonework, curved lancet windows, weathered wooden fence, and multitude of headstones, she wondered about it, and the whole development of the town it would have seen. She had been in a couple of times when she had been younger. She vaguely remembered seeing lots of banners up in it, along with several tombs which had scared her to death at first, then spellbound her in time. It was a proper medieval church, which still stood. But today, she and her friends just let the sun catch it as they strolled by. As they cleared Church Hill, they saw the bridge over the stream and beyond it Castle Hill, which was deeply wooded. If there were remains of anything in there, they were now firmly obscured by the layers of the woods, which had grown on top over the centuries. Just about escaping the pallor of industry, the woods were really flourishing. To many, Castle Hill was just a name for a hill that lay just outside the town, not giving its original purpose any thought. The four of them came onto the bumpy ground before the stream, and struggled slightly up it. Mary knew that it would probably be a measure of what was to come, inside the woods. Anne and Unity squealed with delight as they crossed a wooden bridge.

"Ooh, it's like we're fair maidens crossing the bridge into the lord's parkland," romanticised Anne.

Mary didn't react. Bertha smiled, knowing how much this little trip meant. They crossed the stream back onto the bumpy ground on the other side. Looking up, they saw it loom massively over them. The tall, thick woods: green on the outside, dark inside. The girls looked to Mary to take the lead.

"Bertha's the lead, she looks as if she's the ring leader here," Mary said, resigning before accepting.

"Don't worry, I've got you covered," was all she could follow up with.

So, they began their slow trudge into the woods, leaving the light behind and entering their dark majesty. They found it cool inside, which was a pleasant sensation. In fact, Mary received a real sense of calm there, nothing like the hazard trap she had warned about. The woods were full of flora arranged randomly as nature had decreed. She enjoyed it. Though she didn't tell the others, as she was determined not to join in with their daftness. Overhead the many, many trees arched, as if to guard from the outside world. The deeper they went, along paths covered only with leaves, the girls completely forgot about their lives outside. It felt like they were a million miles away from Darkleigh. None of them spoke. They were too taken with the place to utter a thing. Mills may well have only been someone's surname as far as they were concerned now. Mary only paused for a moment to wonder if what she had read about woods in legends were true — that they did indeed cast a spell on you. But if this was a spell, then it was certainly one with good intentions. Inevitably, they did have to cross a few fallen trees, which they did slowly, to prevent falls. And they did this with laughter, rather than screams. Mary still said nowt', but she too was very happy with the whole adventure. At one point, Mary thought it best to approach Bertha to ask where the castle was in there. But she didn't do this, wanting the walk to continue. She needn't have said anything anyway, as then, they eventually reached the summit of the hill. And through the thicket of trees, they saw what looked like an old castle. Small but definitely a castle. All four of them stopped short. There it was, the old Darkleigh castle of legend.

Chapter Four

"Is this it?" Anne asked.

"Aye, must be. And we've made it, girls," Bertha said.

"We've got to get in yet," Unity reminded them.

To everyone's surprise, Mary led the way. Closing her eyes, she pushed through the thicket, hands up close to guard her face. She then heard the other girls behind her, gingerly coming along. While her eyes were closed, Mary heard the faint echoes of a battle taking place: cries, clashes of swords, the sound of storming. Somehow she fought through it, continuing her progress through the branches, pushing past them. She had come to reason that her experience in church this morning when she saw something that wasn't there, just meant that she'd been a bit delirious. She knew that now, and likewise what she heard now wasn't happening and couldn't be real. She had heard that delirium affected weavers. She had never known when it would come for her, and she had forgotten about it, as there was enough to worry about in the mills, but now it was as if it had. She just stayed calm and pressed on. She stumbled out of the bushes and almost fell head first into the solid stone wall of the castle as she opened her eyes. The other girls, seeing her example, weren't far behind. All four of them stared up at this castle that few of their era knew even existed, despite being a ruin. A relic of a past age. They were like awe-struck bairns gazing up towards the battlements. The dark stones had been tarnished with age but still stood there mightily.

"So, the question is, girls, how do we get in?" Mary asked.

Everyone looked at her, surprised that she had been the one to ask first.

"We could try the front door," Bertha said naively.

Unity was closest to what had been the gatehouse.

"Aye, good idea, Bertha," she said, pointing to it sceptically.

Bertha and Anne walked over to her, only to see that a portcullis buried in weeds and foliage barred their way in.

"Ooh heck, I didn't think it'd be like that," Bertha squeaked, quite embarrassed.

Anne and Unity frowned. Mary didn't react, but instead looked down the wall of the castle. She spotted a very rough-looking spot where the wall met the earth. She said nothing but grabbed a large branch that had fallen off a tree and started stabbing away with it up against the wall. Her friends looked at her as if she'd just gotten out of bedlam. Within a couple of minutes, the sound of crumbling stone was followed by the sound of relief as it gave way.

Bending down, all Mary said was "Ha" like when a tackler mended looms.

"Come on, girls, we're in."

Her friends were still gobsmacked.

"What've you done there, Mary?" Bertha asked.

"I've found us a way in. If it's been deserted for centuries, I don't think anyone'll mind that I've just burrowed me' way in," Mary explained.

"Mary, that looks as if it could be a bit... unstable," Unity commented.

"Oh aye, we knew that from the outset, didn't we?" Mary said with an eyebrow raised.

Mary disappeared inside the hole she'd just crafted. The other girls were in disbelief and then Bertha quickly followed Mary, joined soon after by Unity and Anne.

The hole went down underneath the castle somewhat, providing a well for some of the stone which had fallen down to let them in. Crawling through this hole was exciting for the girls, and seemed to last a long time even though it was only no more than a six-foot gap. But when they arrived on the other side and pulled themselves up into what had been the castle courtyard, they fell instantly enchanted. The lure of uncertainty and excitement merged in them, and the rawness of that feeling lent its presence to something which was for them, almost totally alien. Some of them had seen old Tudor manor houses before on wakes week excursions, but never a proper medieval castle. This, they knew, was a part of Darkleigh, which had existed before them. But the more they heard the echoes of birds flying to and from its battlements, and the more they regarded the silent hollowness of the walls and keep, the more they felt saturated in this other world they had entered.

"Ecky thump, where are we?" Anne whispered.

"This is it," Bertha stated.

"This is our castle, girls. And we've discovered it."

Mary raised a humorous eyebrow at that.

"Think we'll see the ghost?" Unity asked with a smile on her face.

"Well, I think we should explore," Bertha said. "See if we can find the scariest part."

Mary had resorted once more to saying nowt'. Unity and Anne went off, giggling happily to each other. Now they were there, they knew that they'd win the dare. Bertha and Mary walked close to each other.

"How did you know to do that?" Bertha asked, referring to the hole Mary had made.

"They used to dig underneath back in the day, then set fire to it, like when they were having a siege. And slowly but surely the wall burnt away and they had a way in. I reckoned that that's what'd happened with that bit I spotted. It had started to crumble away but obviously not caved in until…"

"Mary Rishworth stepped up with her no-nonsense stick!" Bertha laughed.

Under normal circumstances, Mary would have laughed too, but outwardly she was reserved with her enthusiasm.

The girls explored the old castle as best they could, drenched in euphoria. Nature had long since taken the castle, riddling it with ferns, bushes and trees. But this just added to the lure of the place, which had wasted no time in seizing the girls' imaginations. Eventually, Bertha had pushed what remained of the keep door open and gone inside. Mary had chastised her, reminding her that they hadn't yet seen a ghost and wouldn't because there was none. Bertha had shot an innocent look back at Mary in response to this, the kind a bairn does when its mother warns them before they play out. Anne and Unity had blindly followed her. Rolling her eyes and sighing, Mary stormed after them. But her huff soon faded as she too became even more taken by the interior of the castle they were now in. She just glared about the place in silence after her friends.

There was a spiral staircase in the foyer which hugged the keep's inner walls. The staircase and stone walls were slightly lit by a streak of light whose origin was difficult to see. On every landing there was a wooden door, bolted with studs, which was decaying after years of disuse and weathering. The girls speculated as to what lay behind them, and, more to the point, what their rooms were used for in the past. Eventually, they came to a floor where the door had rotted away completely. The room was invitingly wide-open, with quite a bit more light streaming into it than had led them there.

"Ooh heck, let's get in here!" Bertha said giddily.

"Come on, Mary, look, there's no door," Anne said, stating the obvious.

Mary found herself ignoring her friends and walking in of her own accord. Inside, the room was quite vast. At the back, there was a wooden platform which ran the whole length of the back wall, up until two darkened doorways, which stood either side of it. At the front and sides were big gaps which had once housed neat windows, which allowed the light in. The girls could see quite an expansive view of Darkleigh from it, albeit through the trees.

"By heck, look at this place. Bet this is where the lord of the manor sat back in the day. I reckon he knighted people over there!" Bertha mused.

The girls giggled, all except Mary, who was still looking round, absorbed in the place.

"This day is the best I've had in years, I mean, look where we are!" Anne declared.

"Aye, it's been reet good for a laugh, but we'll need summat' to show them girls on floor four that we've been here," reminded Unity.

"Aye, we will. How 'bout that shield?" suggested Bertha, pointing to a shield hanging over the stage on the back wall.

When Mary saw it, she was taken. It was of a phoenix rising from the ashes of a castle. She had seen that emblem in Darkleigh numerous times, but here it was exactly the same design as the one on the *Phoenix* tavern's sign. Her friends didn't seem to notice it, but she did. She found it a little eerie, somehow.

"Aye, we'll get that later. But first, I think we should summon the ghost, don't you, lasses?" Bertha prompted.

All the girls huddled together, with Mary still eyeing the somewhat faded shield, whose design she knew so well. She didn't want to admit it, but she yearned to find out more about this place.

Before long, the girls were sitting cross-legged on the dusty stone floor, tightly packed, with their hands joined. Eyes closed, Bertha started asking the questions.

"Hello, spirit, we mean you no harm. We're from the town that sits beneath this hill, beneath this castle. We want to find out more about you. We feel we should 'cause we're all Darkleigh born and bred. Can you show us you're here?"

"Ooh, Bertha, I'd be lying if I didn't say you sounded a bit daft!" Unity whispered through a giggle.

"Sssh, Unity! Take this seriously, allreet!" Bertha hissed back.

"Sorry about that, spirit. I've introduced us and why we're here. Can you show yourself to us, please? We'd love to learn more about you."

Silence. The girls sat there in complete silence and were met with it. Anne squinted an eye open, as if to prompt Bertha. Bertha then changed tack.

"We've all heard the legend. We know you were a great warrior who came from here. We want to see you, and talk to you 'cause all our mates who work on the floor below us at the mill reckoned we were too scared to come here. So, great knight, please can you come and show yourself?"

A long, tense pause. Then the oasis of silence took over again.

At about that time, somewhere in a dark place, something old, and something primal awoke. It wasn't awoken by a human hand, or even nature's fair call. But something that had bided its time for centuries. And now it was being sublimely unleashed. A ruby red glow slowly flashed through the pitch darkness. Moments after, almost as if in celebration of its rising again, it launched a pulse, that spanned the whole of its limit. The pulse had no shape or volume but still great effect. Touching everything in its path, it made flocks of birds scatter in delight. It turned the heads of whole herds of cattle. Its force was felt down every valley and over every moor. All but the drudgery of humans was touched by it. The ruby red glow flickered again, then died down. It knew that soon, its time would come.

In the castle, the bored girls slowly felt something vibrating from underneath them. Only very slight at first, they all raised their eyebrows as they came to notice it. They said nothing to each other, as they were now confused. The vibration gathered pace, and soon became a moderate shaking. Anne giggled, but the other girls pushed themselves out of the circle they had been in as the shaking increased. As it got louder, and as pieces of stone came falling from the ceiling, it became clear that the whole castle was shuddering violently, as if it would come crashing down. The girls, (apart from Mary), started screaming.

"Oh heck, what's happening?" shrieked Anne.

"Come on, girls, grab hands, let's get out of here!" ordered Bertha.

Mary used a stance that gave her some stability as she forced herself, with difficulty, to remain calm. Unity fell forward, caught by Mary.

"Ooh, Mary, I'm so scared," she said, almost crying.

"Easy, Unity," Mary replied.

Bertha and Anne were falling over each other trying to get out.

"Come on, girls!" Bertha shouted at Unity and Mary.

But Mary looked up, to see something fall down from the ceiling and land right next to her. It was a small, gold-coloured object. Steadying herself, while keeping a reassuring arm round Unity, she picked it up, unnoticed by the rest of them. And in that moment, the terrible shaking stopped. Silence and stillness returned. The girls, including Mary, were now shocked. Mary had no idea, other than impulse, why she had picked up the object. Unity had by now made her way over to Anne and Bertha, and they were in a big embrace. Mary could only stand there, gazing at the object she hadn't even properly observed yet. Holding it up close to her, she saw it was a ring, with a small engraved image of a phoenix rising from the ashes of a castle. Her confusion increased.

"Come on, Mary, let's go," Bertha said behind her with sincerity.

Mary turned to her friends and dropped the ring. But with this, the mighty shaking returned. Screaming, Mary's friends stumbled and grasped on to one another in a frantic attempt to stay on their feet. As the screams of her friends paled into the background of noise Mary could hear, she focused her attention on the ring again. She wondered. Reaching down, she gently tapped it and although nothing happened, the single act of this slight touch gave her something of a halo. So, anchoring herself with the ground, she picked it up cleanly off the floor. And the shuddering stopped. Instantly.

"What *is* going on?" Anne asked, distressed and confused.

Mary wasn't in a position to answer. Neither were the rest of them. Right now, she felt she couldn't spend any time assessing what had just happened.

So she just said, "Right, girls, stay close and keep walking. Nice and steady. We're going to get out of here."

Her shocked friends were only too happy to trust her as they left the room, and the castle.

Chapter Five

Sir Clarence de Darkleigh came to, sitting on the stage on his throne in his castle's great hall. He slowly twitched and became aware of his faculties. It felt like he'd had a very long, wholesome sleep. With that, he felt a sense of freshness and satisfaction. These were perfect for the new day he'd awoken to, which smelt of bright optimism. Indeed, the moderate heat of a spring day shone outside and the drapes and banners of the court swayed gently like maidens in dresses, responding to the cool breeze which filtered in. Smiling, Sir Clarence stood up and decided he would begin whatever day he had awoken to with some dancing. Climbing off the stage, he walked into the centre of his court. Making some simple patterns, he frolicked about with joy. Gradually, his dances became more complex and quicker. During this time, he became so impressed by how fluent he moved, how he didn't seem to fatigue and how effortless his exertions were. Today, he concluded, was a truly optimistic day! He performed the maying dance native to his manor and applauded himself in delight. Next, he decided he would check the tenants who produced honey corn, a local delicacy, something both he and they were proud of. However, then he came to notice, for the first time that day, that he was the only person in attendance in his great hall. So he called for the first person who usually came to hand, one of his most trusted. This was his chambermaid, Tilly. Moments passed, filled with the same crisp silence. So he called again. At this time of day, Tilly wasn't usually that far away and always came when her master called. But again, nothing. So Sir Clarence quickly went to investigate in the maids' quarters and then his own bed chamber — but found nothing. This unsettled him because not just Tilly, but no servants were about, as they should have been. This was strange. Taking the spiral staircase down to the main door of his keep, Sir Clarence briskly pushed the door open and looked about him. Not a soul. Just the gentle rolling roar of the wind, whose subtlety was a comfort for him. However, he would have preferred the scene to be supplemented by folk he knew.

"John," he called, to his Sergeant-at-arms.

Only echoes returned to him. Perhaps John was in the guardhouse, and would be able to shed light on why the castle was so deserted. Making straight for the guard house, he listened for the sound of John's voice, speaking to the warriors-at-arms he marshalled. No such voice came though, and on using his master key to open the door, the guard room lay still and empty. Sir Clarence began to feel disturbed by that point. Taking a step back, he then proceeded to scour the castle, not discovering a soul. This was the queerest day he had experienced for a long time. He then exited his castle via a door in the gatehouse. His mind was now firmly on meeting with his old friend Michael, the local priest. He would know what was happening for sure. Despite the massive confusion simmering beneath, Sir Clarence still maintained an aura of calm, second nature thanks to his knightly training. This skill had been refined by his family for generations. Michael had always had a reassuring effect on Sir Clarence, so the young lord was sure his inner confusion would soon evaporate.

While striding over to Church Hill, site of the parish church of St. Darren's, Sir Clarence couldn't help but feel a sense of completion not just within himself, but within Darkleigh too. For everywhere he went, his manor was total in its perfection. In the way it smelt, felt and looked. There weren't any sounds other than the wind, which added to the sense of peace, which now filled the place. Climbing the hill where his friend's church stood, Sir Clarence was pleasantly surprised not to find the climb a bother. Entering via the wooden gate and making his way through the churchyard, Sir Clarence knocked on the porch door, but to no avail. Next, he tried the concealed door in the transept. Silence once again. Sir Clarence was then pitched into a dilemma: should he try to find out where everyone was, or should he enjoy his vill in this oddly fine state? He chose the latter, surrendering his former concerns.

Around in circles he must have walked, watching first the lush grass slice skyward. The sheer blueness of the sky was what struck him next, backdrop to the patient hills which enclosed the vill. They just stood there, a deeper shade of green, cutting a contrast against the sky and its fuzzy sun. There was a certain purity about the sky and the hills that day which mirrored the vill's tranquillity. Around the square he went. Coming first to the Guildhouse, he saw the sleek cuts of brown timber that held it together at intervals amongst the sandy stonework. He saw the windows of dark stained glass which provided the Guildhouse's well-known mystique. For a fleeting moment it occurred to him to knock on the door at the front, to see if anyone was in and if they could explain his deserted vill to him. Then he retreated into his wondering enjoyment. He then walked across to the vill tavern, *The Phoenix.* There was something about an empty tavern that utterly arrested him to the extent that he felt spellbound. The stillness and silence to him represented something which lay dormant. He had had many a wonderful time with his people in *The Phoenix*; it was almost as if it produced a greater thicket of energy than his court or even St. Darren's. Memories of a great tradition of his manor erupted in his mind: he remembered bringing the stag's antlers down off the hills, and sometimes the moors beyond them. Every year they were hidden, and every high summer he and a party of his tenants went out to find them. Legend had it that if you saw the ghost of the stag the antlers had belonged to, the manor would be plentiful forever more. No one had ever seen that though, other than the odd drunk. However, he saw himself in *The Phoenix* drinking horns of ale with his tenants, parading the antlers for all to see, surrounded by the families of the manor. Sir Clarence gazed at himself, pitched in complete joy. What a scene. But the more he allowed the memories of that to filter through, the more distant from them he became, as if they were becoming unattainable. Sir Clarence felt strange at this. Then he remembered that the vill he called home was deserted. Then he remembered his last memories before waking up. They had been of him in battle with his arch enemy Lord Dalbern. He remembered how Dalbern had chased him all over England in a relentless pursuit after he had foiled one of Dalbern's evil schemes. He remembered how Dalbern had threatened to raise a small army against him. He remembered evacuating the manor and sending his people off to safety. And then once more, he remembered the battle at his castle with Dalbern who had come up to try and seize his assets. Then he remembered the absence of his servants and friends.

"Tilly! John! Michael!" he called despairingly back to his castle.

His calls became echoes, and in distress, he ran into the centre of the vill square and looked all around him. Then he noticed something very small but very distinctive glinting on one of the hills south of the vill. He saw it glint again, almost as if done deliberately to get his attention. The glint had been white and as the distress dried up within him, it was replaced by curiosity. So he decided to pursue it.

Walking right through the centre of the vill down the dusty road, which led south to the lower hills, Sir Clarence noticed the dwellings of his people. They too were in keeping with all else he had found at his castle and in the vill centre. The timber cottages and stone farmhouses scattered around the valley were neat and appeared pristine. They were normally in good condition, given the dedication of his tenants, but today they continued the theme of shrill silent perfection. The more he walked along that road, the better he felt. He began to feel quite tired, the way he usually felt before he retired to his bed chamber. But alongside this was the feeling that he was closing in on answers. Today of all days, he needed them. Sir Clarence didn't notice the thick low cloud that descended like barding over his vill behind him. He didn't look back, even when he reached the hill and began to climb. He had one aim in mind, to reach the area of the hill where he had seen the glinting object. Beginning his climb, he found the steepness of the hill quite easy to cope with. His progress was continuous and flowing, which made him feel well. After a short while, after climbing over the many bumpy crags the hills played host to, he arrived half way up Falixstone hill, where he had seen the glint. Thirst now replaced fatigue and he came to the outcropping where he was sure the glint had been. All the time, he had not been aware of the massive, thick clouds that had formed behind him, which now covered the whole valley. Arriving at the spot, he looked about it, searching for whatever it was he had seen. However, there was nothing. Nothing but the grass-coated plateau he stood on, which eerily greeted him. However, he didn't let this affect his focus. Remembering his knightly training, he breathed and remained calm. He noticed that his breathing wasn't as he'd always felt it normally. It was at that point that he saw the glint again in the corner of his eye. This caused him to spin round and confront the vast valley which his vill was set in. The blanket of cloud had completely dispersed and in its place was what he knew was Darkleigh, covered in a massive plethora of buildings that was completely foreign to him. All of them were a rusty orange colour, with plenty of browns and bronzes in the swirling mix. It was like seeing behind the city walls of York, only bigger. But Sir Clarence knew this was Darkleigh, for sure. The surrounding landscape hadn't changed. And from this position he could easily see the square, with the Guildhouse at its head and *The Phoenix* tavern to its side. Beyond that he saw St. Darren's, exactly as he had left it earlier that day. But beyond that was Castle Hill, now consumed by woods. At that very moment, he felt his heart sink and flake away inside him. Then several memories which led him to the threshold of the answer to his confusion surfaced. The red mist, the despatching of Dalbern, the dragon with its fiery breath — Sir Clarence looked out over his old vill. He saw the long brown obelisks belching smoke, he heard the rotating clanks coming from massive rectangular castle-like structures. All this was not of his land. He took a dagger from inside his jerkin. Then he swiftly stabbed himself. But he felt nothing. At first he suspected leprosy, but he knew that it had died out in England long before he'd been born. And when he withdrew the dagger from himself, there was no blood, no nothing. Then realisation took a firm, firm grip on him, as he dropped the dagger and sank to his knees, letting out the shrillest of screams that echoed all around the valley, causing many a flock of birds to flee the hills and the dogs of the valley to turn to the hills and bark with a vengeance. For of course, Sir Clarence knew he was dead.

Chapter Six

Mary was struggling. Her breathing had become even heavier than usual and she was not able to keep pace the way she usually did. Keeping pace with her loom was a mightily stretching task in itself, but with the disturbing events at the castle, the whole thing was teetering on the brink of collapse. Then she thought she saw a warp thread snap. She was beginning to feel desperate. She could feel her weekly wage drying up in the face of fines — maybe worse. She knew that more times than were rare, overseers had their wicked ways with a lot of girls who worked in the mills. Mary had always wondered why such crude, callous men were employed in serious operations like these. She had worked out that there was one answer: profit. Forcing herself against the strain, she managed by inches to pull her work through, and everything again returned to an even keel. Then she found herself crouching down, strength having left her. Wave after wave of anxiety poured through her. It was then she saw the unmistakable silhouette of an overseer, plodding his way through the dusty air. Mary knew him. Folk said he was the worst one there was, given his reputation with his rod — and with girls. Summoning her composure, Mary's eyes daggered as she dragged herself to her feet again.

Then she heard the inevitable shout of "Oi you, what were you doing slouching? Squire Shackfield paying you too much is he?" Mary shot him an icy look over her shoulder. "Don't you give me that look, lass, all that arrogance will end badly for you!" he warned.

Mary slowed herself down. Warp and weft, warp and weft, Mary embedded her mind back into the old pattern of uncompromising efficiency. Despite this, the overseer, named Melling, didn't approve. He briskly walked over to her and was about to shout his gob off when something else in the dusty spaces between the looms caught his eye. Mary noticed his apprehension and wondered whether it was nothing but a trap so that he could eject her for not paying attention. But instead there was another shape in the dust. A dark brooding shape from which Mary received only warm feelings. Melling was staring at the shape, mouth open, aghast. The shape stood there still, expectant of something. Mary could tell it was a person but she couldn't see the face of whoever it was. She looked back at Melling, but he had already walked off in fright. Looking back, Mary saw the shape of the person had vanished. Wondrous, she carried on with her work.

Sir Clarence's ghost was back at his castle, smothered with the shocking truth he had just found out. Sitting in his now derelict great hall, head in hands, he saw in his mind the perfect formation of his memories. Thanks to his knightly training, he was just about able to stay calm, but the terrible fact was that now he knew he was dead. That thought locked itself over him as he tried to lose consciousness, but failed. He had found himself back at his castle after turning around on the hills to see Darkleigh as it was now. The time in between those moments and now was just a blur. He remembered falling forward in surrender, knowing that he wouldn't die again so it wouldn't matter. He had sped through the air at an alarming pace, right down the length of the valley, to somehow re-enter his castle. He remembered before waking up that day on his throne how he had evacuated his manor after the villainous Lord Dalbern had chased him right through England, desiring revenge. He remembered the final battle which his closest friends had helped with, before being told to flee themselves. He remembered despatching Dalbern and the fire enfolding him. Sir Clarence knew what he was now, and that pierced him with a very acute feeling of sadness. His castle did occupy a certain sedateness now, the kind you'd find in many derelict sanctuaries, but unless there were other friendly ghosts hanging about, he would continue to be alone. And if able to communicate with him, the living would run in fear. Alone in his once-thriving, dynamic great hall with its welcoming decadence, he sat. And he knew not what to do next. That was the worst part of it. Out of silence, Sir Clarence heard what he thought at first were gusts of wind, whisking in through where the windows had once been. Then they changed form, slightly. They became whispers, human whispers. Instead of scaring Sir Clarence, he enjoyed the silkiness of their tones, combining beautifully with the coolness of the wind to induce a definite state of relaxation in him. These whispers responded, and swirled up around in front of Sir Clarence, gaining confidence as they became gradually louder. As the whispers intoned all the more, a now-reclining Sir Clarence came to sit bolt-upright, recognising the voice they carried. For he was certain it was that of his old friend, Michael. The manor priest who had baptised him, the priest who had blessed him and his friends before they set off to battle, the person his parents had known and trusted with his education.

"Sire," the voice gently rasped, trying to establish contact. "Sire," it came again.

"I hear thou, I hear thou," Sir Clarence replied, desperately wanting a conversation to start.

"Hello, Clarence," Michael's disembodied voice said affectionately.

"Michael, is that thou?" Sir Clarence asked.

After a pause, it answered, "It is."

Sir Clarence's whole countenance lit up with delight. "Glad tidings to thou," the knight greeted.

"And to thou, young squire, and to thou," Michael chuckled.

Sir Clarence smiled at Michael calling him that, something he'd done even since he had grown up and been knighted.

Sir Clarence opened the conversation. "Michael, I know what I am now. A ghost, a spirit. I woke up yesterday to find my manor pristine but deserted. Then it all faded into what Darkleigh hath become. To begin with, I cannot comprehend that. But my biggest question is why hath I cometh back now? It hath been a rude, crude awakening, my old friend, and a cruel one at that. But why now, and for what purpose?" Sir Clarence wasted no time in stating his concerns plainly to his old friend, as this unique conversation demanded.

Coming to his proverbial rescue as he had done so many times in life, Michael answered, "Do thou not want to spend some time learning about thy new existence as a spirit before thou find the reason for what thou ask?"

Sir Clarence knew there was a purpose to his friend's cryptic response. He recognised it from life. "To be honest, Michael, the thing I want most is to go back. My mission on earth was completed. Dalbern was defeated, God witnessed this, and I earnt my eternal rest." Even though Michael wasn't seen, Sir Clarence could see him nodding understandingly.

"And sleep thou will, after a short time," Michael reassured. "But to reach that point, dear Clarence, I urge thou to take heed of thy new abilities. Because they will lead to thy eternal rest again."

"How?" Sir Clarence said.

"Well, try seeing with thy eyes closed. Try running like a thousand horses. For heaven's sake, try walking through walls. And when thou wishes to not be seen, retreat into thyself as thou didst when alive."

Impressed with Michael's advice, Sir Clarence then asked, "And what about thou? Why canst thou not show thyself and come with me?" He felt Michael's gentle smile again.

"I am there with thou. Within thou," Michael assured.

"But why canst thou not…"

"All in good time, young one. All in good time," Michael softly intoned. "This is daunting. But thou shall not be alone. My best words of advice are to seek out what is thine. Use thy new abilities to seek out what is thine and this shall lead thou to sleep once again."

Sir Clarence glanced towards where Michael's disembodied voice was coming from, enraptured with wonder. "It is a great shame that we hath not spoke in heaven, dear Michael. It would hath been good to see thou and everyone else."

"Everyone else is fine, young knight. Believe me. But hear this: thou hath returned for a reason. So make it thy mission to grasp what is thine by divine right. And when thou dost, thou will take thy place in heaven back."

Sir Clarence felt pure inspiration flow through him. But this didn't mean that the confusion lifted. "But, Michael, dear Michael, tell me why this is. I hath had the life of a spirit thrust upon me…" He felt Michael start to retreat.

"God speed, young squire," were Michael's last words to him as his voice died away.

"But, Michael, do not go…" shouted Sir Clarence desperately, but then the atmosphere in his former great hall fell flat and returned to how it had been before, when he was despairing.

It took Sir Clarence a few moments to refocus, in his ghostly state.

But when he did, he repeated once in his mind Michael's instruction to seek out what was his. Then he rose with speed and went over to the window. Looking out across his heavily urbanised old vill, he let his mind relax, lying fallow. Why, he didn't know, he just had an intuition to do it. He was astounded by what he could hear: the hum of a hundred conversations, all happening together. The clanking in workshops, the manic buzz of the looms in the mills. He focused on certain noises in particular, a mile out into the valley and heard a daughter talking to her mother about her little rose bud. That made him smile, but more so he was intrigued by how extensive *and* precise this new ability of his was. Michael was right — it was worth finding out how to use them. After leaving that particular conversation between a mother and her love struck lass, he decided to let his mind lie again, by relaxing as he did during life.

Then he heard himself repeating, like a prayer, "Seek out what is mine" over and over again.

Sir Clarence closed his eyes, all the time trying to stretch out with his imagination to find whatever it was that could be his now. When he opened them, he found himself looking down at his fingers. All but one of the rings he had worn in life were there. These included his knight's ring, but *no* lordship of Darkleigh ring. Looking out across the valley again, it was almost as if Sir Clarence blinked — and saw through different eyes. For this time, he could see into houses for miles around. Their brick facades peeled away like burning scrolls, and he became embarrassed at seeing people taking baths, getting undressed, etc. But he remembered his prayer to seek out what was his in his mind again. And at that moment, some distance into the town, he saw another glinting object in someone's house from afar. It had a yellow glint this time. Sir Clarence moved his focus through the town, pushing past the myriad of brown brick terraces and not so far away from one of the box-like castles with its own smoke-belching obelisk. This arrested Sir Clarence's attention severely. Focusing in on it, the image of this house became larger and more vivid. He could now see that this glinting was coming from the bottom of a box. He wondered whether this glint belonged to the same thing he thought he'd seen on the hills before he had realised he was deceased. He could see a young woman, the age he was when he had died, talking to another young woman. She had a strained, apprehensive look on her face. And sitting beneath her, he could see now in the box, after focusing deep, was his ring of lordship. 'Seek out what is mine' he thought to himself triumphantly.

Chapter Seven

Mary went straight to bed that night after getting home from the mill. Her mother and sisters had noticed her silence at tea. When questioned, Mary gave the explanation that she had seen a shuttle fly out and strike a girl in the face, injuring her badly. It had been the worst incident of its kind she'd ever seen. Mary's sisters were satisfied with this, but her mother only half so. For she knew that Mary had seen that more than enough times than she could remember. Although sad and often tragic, that was life in the mills. It usually took a lot more than that to shock Mary into silence. But as it had been the worst she'd ever seen, it was just about convincing enough to tip her mother's watchful mind over into belief of what Mary told her. For her mother had seen some vicious things in the mills, and only the very worst had been able to stay with her from time to time.

Mary settled down quietly to bed after, followed by her sisters. Shortly after she had closed her eyes, she fell into a deep sleep. She could feel the relief drench her as she lost consciousness. The deeper she slept, the more she could feel a sense of security and insularity build up around her. Mary wasn't usually one to even have dreams, let alone recognise her feelings as she slept. As she slept, there appeared in her dream something akin to frosted glass. She wasn't able to see through it. But she did see a faint shadow start to form behind it. Mary became compelled by this. For the first time in a long time, she actually became aware that she was having a dream. She struggled to make out what it was so decided she would pay closer attention. And the silhouette was getting gradually bolder. Trying to reach out through the frosted glass, she was frustrated as it became apparent she couldn't. Then she remembered that she was dreaming, which told her that, of course, she was lying in bed, resting. That explained why although she wanted to get closer to the glass, she wasn't being allowed. So she decided to let whatever was happening unfold. As she let go, the shadow's growth stagnated. The effect of the frosted glass began to thaw. This happened slowly but surely and instead of a climax building, she felt an even deeper sense of security affect her. In the vision in front of her, there now was a young fellow, about her age, dressed very oddly, it had to be said. Mary only had time to study him for a fleeting moment, registering just the criss-cross pattern on his boots and the massive buckle which sealed his jacket, before she found his whole head and shoulders staring vacantly into the space which was now central to her dream. Now she could see his face vividly. And her breath was taken by him. He had long, black hair, with some curls at the ends. His skin was very white and his eyes crafted in perfect oval shape. His other features were smooth and sleek. Mary ogled him, which embarrassed her, but at the same time, her dream state prevented her from stopping. He didn't seem to take offense though, as he then directed his gaze to her, wearing on it the warmest of smiles.

A lone, large wagon careered over the hills towards Darkleigh, with a lusty haste about it. Drawn by two horses, its sides were marked by a crown and the letters 'GR' which showed it was on official business. Inside it were a squad of trainee special constables from Manchester. They looked about themselves, chatting idly and full of their own conceit, believing they had made it as the elite class that year. Someone who had had a hand in their training was with them. His name was Joseph Nadin, Deputy Chief of the Manchester Special Constables. His name had taken on a new function as a harsh tone, a word to describe the tyranny which Manchester and many of its neighbours endured. Joe Nadin had had limited success as a cotton spinner early in his life, which had allowed him to enjoy the wonderful fellowship that existed between members of that profession. However, that was before the rot set in. Rightly or wrongly, he had become a grass, letting his employers know about the small indiscretions of his fellow workers. Sometimes reporting these had been justified. Other times he often told on them solely for his own benefit. Like the time he told his employers about a group of his mates who were forming a secret spinner's society. A grateful employer had them all sacked, and Nadin had been given a purse for his information. It was this kind of behaviour which sparked a taste for seeking power over others. And with the massive frame he'd been granted in life, he looked for somewhere that he'd find power in abundance. That place turned out to be the law, in the shape of the Manchester special constables. Although not a military position, they had presented to him a chance to carve out a career founded on authority. Naturally, Nadin seized this opportunity. He only too well enjoyed hiding behind higher authority and pretending to understand the pompous splendour that went with it all. With his utter ruthlessness, he had shot through the ranks like a cannon ball aimed to the heavens. Threats, beatings, intimidation, blackmail, all these different strategies and so many others had become part of the way he went about extracting confessions and getting results, which his superiors adored him for. In fact, the select committee of magistrates (his superiors) were not feared anything like as much as he in Manchester. Many of the folk of Manchester called him the town's 'real ruler'. And he needed no iron rod but more of a heavy steel pike to rule by. Now deputy chief of the special constables, Nadin adored his position with arrogance, leading his special constables with a pretence of nobility. In recent years, Nadin's main thrust had been to be an instrument, used by the authorities to crush Reformers. These were folk who wanted to achieve in Britain what the French had done in France, just without the bloodshed. In short, they wanted liberty. Those in power, however, saw this as an attempt to subvert and undermine church and state. So in the Reform movement's hotbed of Manchester, Nadin was only too well aware that his position was the establishment's fulcrum against the thousands wanting change. He knew of his feared reputation and lofty position, but cowered when he thought of the enormity of what he and his superiors were seeking to put down. Today, he had opted to supervise the final stages of training of a fresh batch of new recruits who had impressed. Now he would use this 'sortie' to see if they had the real mettle to emulate his standard.

"Right, now, lads. Where we're going now, they think 'cause they're out in the sticks, they're immune to the law. You wouldn't believe how many reports we've had of *open air* meetings canvassing for that bloody Reform movement. And the local magistrates have turned a blind eye to it! So we're going to pay them a visit and sort them out. Show the local authorities how we deal with the likes of these scum in Manchester. Right, lads?"

"Yes, sir," his little prodigies barked promptly.

Mary wanted to speak but didn't know what to say to this handsome fellow who was now beaming at her, causing her to feel completely at ease, for the first time for as long as she could remember. In fact, the feeling of comfort was so unreal, Mary started to retreat, knowing it was a dream. However, luckily, the dream wouldn't let her go.

It was the young fellow who spoke first. "Hello," he smoothly intoned.

"Hello," replied Mary.

"How dost thou feel?" the fellow asked next.

Mary was taken aback. It sounded like he was speaking the old way, which she had heard in plays at festivals. But no one spoke like that in conversation any more, not often anyway.

Trying unsuccessfully to stifle a laugh, she said, "Aye, I'm reet good. I've never felt this well before." The fellow smiled at this, pleasantly surprised that he'd had that effect on her.

"What is thy name?" was his next question.

Mary strained slightly to unravel his words, in line with the old way he spoke, but she knew within a moment or so to tell him, "Mary."

He nodded a greeting at this. "Blessings, Mary."

"And to you," Mary returned, touched by his good nature.

"My name is Sir Clarence de Darkleigh, seventeenth lord of the manor of Darkleigh."

Sir Clarence had introduced himself in the calmest of fashions. Land owners normally didn't. They normally announced it with pomp. But with the way he did it, he breathed reassurance into Mary's heart. It was only then that she realised who he was.

"I think I know you. Well, not you yourself, but I think I know who you were," Mary told him. Sir Clarence's face waited with calm expectancy. "You were a knight, and part of the family who used to run Darkleigh, weren't you?"

Sir Clarence nodded with a gentle smile, contented in that she had realised who he was. "There's a lot of stories about you and your family. Some say they're too good to be true, because your family were very special in what they did, and the nice way they treated folk."

Sir Clarence nodded with happy satisfaction. Mary then noticed she was talking like a bairn would to someone they looked up to. But Mary had heard all the awe-inspiring stories about the de Darkleigh family and she still leant towards hero-worship on occasion. Sir Clarence, listening to Mary, was glad to hear that the accent and dialect of his people hadn't changed in the probable centuries since he'd been away.

"And shall I tell thou something?" the knight asked. Mary nodded enthusiastically.

"All the good stories thou hear, they art all true."

Mary's eyes lit up with inspiration. "You were real and what you and your family did were real," Mary stated. Smiling, Sir Clarence nodded to confirm.

"Sorry, I'm just a bit struck by all this," Mary said, realising how daft she must have come across. "It just feels so odd, but in a good way. I mean, it's a rare event to be visited by a really legendary person from your home town." But once again, the knight smiled kindly.

"It is wonderful for me to receive this kind of reception, even in death," he said.

Mary's emotions changed tack. A tear formed in her eye. "You're a… spirit?" she gingerly asked.

"Yes," Sir Clarence confirmed, nodding his head calmly once again.

Then, Mary felt a deeper twist within her. She remembered her jaunt to Castle Hill the other day, and her invasion of the very place this deceased person once called home. And what's more, she knew that he would know. "I'm sorry…" Mary then quickly said.

"What for?" Sir Clarence asked.

"I'm… I'm sorry for what I did the other day. I know that even though no one owns it any more, I think, it's still your home and we broke into it, and I only did it so my friend Bertha could win a bet, 'cause them girls on the floor below us are reet daft and…" But Sir Clarence raised a subtle finger to his lips.

"Slow down, my dear, slow down," he said, as if he were speaking poetry. "Hath no fear. I hath not chosen to appear before thou because I am angry with thou. There lies nothing in our castle any more other than broken memories and lots of rubble."

With this masterful intervention, Mary regained her calm. "No. It just so happens that God hath chosen this point in time for some reason, for me to rise again and walk the earth in spirit. Why he hath willed that,

I doth not know. But what I do know is that I need to return to my slumber as soon as I can. This is where I require thy help." Mary was captivated; feeling needed by a legendary person from her town made her feel so special, so privileged.

"My help?" Mary asked innocently.

"Yes..." Sir Clarence began but his words were drowned out by constant, rhythmical thuds on what Mary could tell were cobbles.

"Sir Clarence!" she shouted, in despair at losing this wonderful conversation and the feelings it had brought with it.

But the knight's image was already rippling away, as when a reflection is disturbed in a pond. Then the clattering sounds came again, and the whole image rudely blurred, as she woke to the dust, darkness and silence of her family's sleeping room. Sitting up in her bed, she heard the sounds of horses' hooves dying away as they made progress down a nearby main road. She felt a strong feeling of disappointment, as she knew that she had been enjoying a very wholesome dream. However, she could only remember little shards of it that lay in her mind, even though she had just been having it seconds ago. She remembered the compelling tones of a medieval voice, the image of a handsome-looking fellow with dark hair, and him saying that he wanted to sleep again. And the last thing she remembered was the Phoenix crest, which featured on shields in St. Darren's, and the sign on the oldest tavern in the town. All these things connected in her mind. It was then she simply *knew* what she had to do: return the ring to the castle. She looked across at her box of things and made a decision.

Chapter Eight

Mary was out. Before breakfast, before her shift. She had snuck out with extreme skill, not disturbing a thing as she left her house. Tip-toeing past the beds of her mother and sisters and slowly, deliberately turning the key in the doors which led to their rooms. She had one opportunity to do this, and she had decided that it would be done before breakfast and forgotten about forever more. She was haunted by the dream she'd had. On the one hand, she remembered feeling like she'd never felt before because of it: safe, enchanted, even powerful. On the other hand, it had motivated her, out of massive fear, to do what she was going to do now. On her own, Mary strode right through town towards Castle Hill. The tapping of her clogs created an innocent, lonely sound as folk slept. The grey mist was light, ready to hail a new day. Mary knew that day break meant she had to be back.

The wagon Nadin and his trainees had been travelling in had stopped in the town square. When folk would get up, there would be closed curtains, nowt' said and a few secret winks. Inside, Nadin briefed the somewhat privileged men who were on the verge of graduating as special constables.

"The particulars of today's objective are to investigate for signs of treasonous activity in the local taverns and shops. These are mainly concentrated around this square. However, there are some more in the streets that branch off it. Your task is to question the owners of these establishments to see if they are allowing any of these secret meetings to take place. Maintain a low profile, but you are free to use *any* means necessary to gain confessions. Remember, we're dealing with people here who think they're entitled to do as they please to undermine the sovereignty of our great king. Understand?"

Again, the trainees answered resoundingly. With that, the squad disembarked the wagon and went off in twos to conduct their investigation. Nadin walked off towards the end of the square to observe their progress. He fumbled in his pocket for tobacco but found nothing. He snorted with disappointment. Other than he and his lads, there was no one about. He sighed a bored sigh as he slouched against the *Phoenix* tavern. It wasn't long though before he noticed the slender figure of a young woman making her way down one of the streets that ran parallel to the square. She was walking at a brisk pace and was visible as she passed between the buildings that faced onto the square. This grabbed Nadin's attention and stirred his predatory little mind. What was she doing out here at this time of the morning? Maybe she'd just been to a Reform meeting. Maybe she had just finished a shift somewhere other than a mill. Intrigued, Nadin sensed an opportunity. He quietly left the square.

Mary strode through town single-minded. Her mind was clear, rather than rhythmical as it usually was before work. She just wanted to walk through the ginnels, unseen, quietly before folk started pouring out of and into the mills. Then she would disappear under the leafy cover of Castle Hill and wade her way through the great thicket to the castle. There she would throw the ring back into the grounds of the castle, which would mark the end of this whole episode, which could then be forgotten forever. Briskly striding, she was satisfied with her progress. She saw the last few buildings behind the town square give way on her walk to reveal Church Hill. She was glad she'd got this far in quite a short time.

Crossing the stream after Church Hill, she paused for a brief moment to look up into the alluringly dark woods that dominated Castle Hill. Taking a breath, she began to press herself up the hill.

"Oi, you girl!" a gruff, angry voice cried behind her.

Turning quickly, Mary saw a large, hulking figure some twenty yards away from her. His thickset head carried a disgruntled frown and his frame stood in a domineering stance. These features struck Mary first. Then she realised that he could well have been following her, with the expert skill of a wild animal stalking its prey. Then she noticed his fatigues. They were dark and the livery indicated a special constable. Mary had heard of these in Manchester. They had a sickening reputation. And with that realisation, she froze. His voice had sounded accusing. Mary prepared to explain what she was doing in the most reasonable way possible. But she wasn't given a chance.

"What's a pretty girl like you doing out on your own at this time in the morning?" he boomed.

"I come up here to enjoy the fresh air," Mary said in a calm, level voice.

"You work in a mill?" was his next question.

"Aye."

"Which one?"

"Downsight."

The special constable nodded. "And where's that?"

Mary knew where the mill was but she had never been inside.

"On the edge of town, in the west."

"It's going to take you a while to get there, isn't it? I'm guessing you're on shift soon."

"I don't mind the walk, keeps me banted," Mary said, not giving any vulnerability away in her voice.

The big fellow chuckled sceptically. "You know, in my normal jurisdiction a girl out on her own at this time in the morning's usually just finished her shift. In a ladle-house."

Mary raised an eyebrow at this. "Ah well, that's your jurisdiction," she half-scowled.

"Oh, believe me, my dear, my *jurisdiction* extends anywhere and everywhere in this county, given that I received my commission from his excellent lordship the noble William Hulton. Now, if it's not already obvious, I can see right through you. So, it's now become my duty to arrest you for soliciting. However, if you give me a sample of your professional capabilities, free of charge, then we can forget mine. You see, my lads are completing their training today, and I feel I need to treat myself for my part in that. So what's it to be?"

Mary had been rendered speechless, listening to what was obviously a monster wearing an official uniform.

"You, leave me alone, you filthy great mawkin," she sneered.

"Oh dear, sounds like the choice is made. Not many girls in your position want it both ways," he said, advancing towards her.

Mary backed off, not believing at first that he was serious. He quickened his pace, and Mary turned and started to run. He followed her. She heard the clump of his boots on the craggy ground get heavier and more frequent. She gasped as she knew he was going to chase her to get what he wanted. She didn't see some bushes rise to meet her which caused her to stop short. She turned round quickly to see the huge fellow bearing down on her. Mary dropped and kicked him right across the shins. That caused him to recoil somewhat.

"Argh, argh," he cried, aggravated that Mary's cleverness had put him down.

Mary tore up the hill as quick as she could, determined to lose him in the thicket, somewhere she was sure he couldn't navigate. But she stumbled and that gave the fellow time to catch up, pinning her to the ground. For a moment, all sound ceased. The activity of that moment ceased. No birds flew, no branches swayed, no leaves rustled. Mary could only summon all her courage to prepare.

"You know the reason why a lot of girls find their ways to houses of ill repute is 'cause they're laid off by your masters. You know, the mill owners? Them whose hands you eat out of? Aye, them girls may not be the cleanest of the clean, but they're reet finer people than you could ever be," Mary said, telling him straight.

"You seem to know far too much about politics than what's healthy for someone of your station, especially a woman," the fellow said, loading his weight onto her.

Mary snarled in defiance. "Oh, believe me, we know it all. And you bloody know it."

"Well, well, sounds like we've got a Reformer in our midst. That means I can add treason to your charge sheet as well as soliciting. You should've bargained, my love."

"What's your name?" Mary demanded.

"Chief Constable Joe Nadin, Miss, at your service," he replied, salivating.

Mary braced herself for what was going to come, and whatever she could do. In that moment his eyes bulged down at her breasts, poised like a wild beast. A painfully fast dash of coldness cut over the top of Nadin and Mary, disturbing both of them. A fraction of a second gave Mary just enough time to make out a boot, kicking Nadin's head. It had criss-crosses on it. Mary's eyes widened.

"Argh," Nadin screamed as he flew back and off Mary.

The kick itself was bad enough, but the icy cold which had come with it was what put Nadin well and truly down. Mary sat up and watched what happened next with a drooping jaw. Nadin drew his cosh with a delayed haste. Mary didn't see her deliverer at first, but something rustled in the tree tops close by, before diving on Nadin with the speed and ferocity of an avenging angel. This time it was Nadin's turn to be prey — to something of a human crow. The figure struck at Nadin's cosh with what looked like a sword and Nadin went to grapple with him, but the same chills from before affected him, undermining his struggle. The figure jumped off him and stood, poised with a sword in his grasp, ready for combat. This image gave Mary her first clear view of him. Instantly, she recognised him as being the fellow from the dream she had had the previous night. Panicking, Nadin grunted aggressively as he lurched towards Mary's rescuer with some massive chops. But the fellow deflected each one of them with unreal speed. A parry at the end of a series of slices from Nadin sent the 'chief constable' off balance, and he stumbled. The fellow then tapped Nadin's wrist and his cosh flew backwards. Nadin was almost crying through shock, exertion and being chilled to the core by something he had never encountered ever before in his life. As he retreated after his weapon, the fellow bladed him up the bum, which caused him to fly faster away from them. Grabbing his cosh, Nadin took on a quite comical shape, legging it away from them, nearly in tears. The fellow whom she recognised from her dream looked at her with a concerned, sensitive face. Mary knew this meant he was asking if she was all right. She smiled back with a nod, and he slowly approached her. Pointing to his finger which was wrapped by a gauntlet, he returned her smile. Mary couldn't believe what had just happened, let alone him knowing why she had gone there. She reached inside her shawl, took out his ring and handed it to him. Nodding his regards, all he said was,

"Thou art safe now. He shall not return."

Mary wanted to thank him with all her heart, but all she could manage was a nod herself. With that, he vanished into the thicket. Sound and movement ceased again for Mary. This time though, it was out of awe and wonder. Only then did she notice the lingering coldness which the fellow had left in his trail...

Chapter Nine

Now Sir Clarence had the ring, he had a firm idea of what to do. Making straight for Church Hill, he held it in his hand. The ring was solid and worthy in his hand, though because of his new composition as a spirit, he had to increase his denseness to be able to wear it. For it was not like the ghostly clothes he had which had become a part of his spirit's constitution. For Sir Clarence was only just beginning to discover a new ability he enjoyed as a spirit — that of being able to increase or decrease his denseness. An increase would lead to a better sensation of touch. Now a mere mass of cold energy, Sir Clarence knew he didn't need food or drink and didn't have to even sleep. He suspected that he was invulnerable. The encounter with the young woman — he had spoken to through her dreams the previous night — proved he could interact with the living if needs be.

Sir Clarence burrowed silently into the mound of earth which was Church Hill, seeing only compounded darkness, to reach where he reasoned his family crypt would be. Indeed, he landed in the crypt, at its entrance. This featured all the coats of arms on it, with a gate that resembled a portcullis in the centre. He walked through and down a short flight of stairs before coming face to face with the rows of his deceased ancestors. He looked forward to seeing them again when his work there was done. He had also decided on a name for the ability which allowed him to see and hear into the fabric of life beyond walls and distance. He had named it his second sight. For when he had lived, that is what witches and soothsayers had called their ability to see and hear ahead. And it was to this ability he turned, to see in the deluge of darkness that covered his family's crypt. It picked out perfectly the details on all the tombs. Sir Clarence was quietly disappointed that this ability would be short-lived. He bowed his head and made his steady walk down the aisle to find where he was. Above the tombs lay a myriad of items, including some donated by their people as grave goods at funerals. One of these included a scythe, a poignant illustration of the good relationships Sir Clarence's family had had with their tenants. Up the aisle, an archway led to a chamber which contained someone Sir Clarence remembered as 'The Progenitor'. This was the very first Anglo-Saxon lord of Darkleigh, founder of his family's manorial dynasty. It was a chamber which had an effect on those who entered. Sir Clarence, through his second sight, caught a glimpse of the old-school Anglian armour, along with a sword from the age which stood on top of the tomb, circled by a row of drapes and tapestries. Sir Clarence acknowledged it but continued on his way, the main goal, of course, being for him to sleep again. Passing by so many tombs of his ancestors, including several other chambers for crusaders and those who had fought in the Hundred Years' War, he saw some names inscribed in Latin which he recognised as being those he had known in life. Nodding his head again, he went on emotionally. But two tombs stopped him in his tracks. For they were the tombs of Hannah and Roger, his parents. Kneeling beside them, he placed his hand on the smooth, dusty surface of his mother's tomb and tried to summon a connection. Love was still felt, even though there was only this of them now. He didn't remember meeting them while he had been deceased. Standing, he blocked off his second sight and stroked his parents' graves in turn, bidding them tribute. Lady Hannah and Sir Roger had been such wonderful parents and a great inspiration to him. So for a while, he basked in this flourishing connection that was still there.

Sir Clarence turned to the side, coming face-to-face with his own tomb. He frowned slightly with the realisation that his own mortal remains were interred there. Taking out his manorial ring, which had proved his former lordship of Darkleigh, from a pouch, he held it there before his eyes, slowly rotating it in his hand. Then, with slow, deliberate action, he pushed it onto his left forefinger where he had always worn it in life. Then he stood at the end of his tomb and turned so he was facing away from it. Closing himself down completely, he surrendered in silent joy, falling back into his grave. Everything purged, with all feelings of concern falling away.

***

Sir Clarence came to, expecting to float with ecstasy into a bounteous heaven. Instead he saw darkness, which he found relaxing. However, an accidental blink caused his second sight to show him a harrowing image right above him. Above him were now worn away rags and a skeleton. Thawed and yellowed, it was becoming dust. Dry tears started to form in Sir Clarence's eyes. In life, his knightly focus would have prevented this. But his training, despite being deeply spiritual, had not prepared him for this. Sir Clarence could feel himself staring wide into the darkness. He wanted to scream as he had done on the hillside days before but was too gripped with terror to be able to. Plunging himself deeper down, he slid himself forward and shot upwards, out of the crypt, into the aisle above ground, and through the whole of St. Darren's and out, back towards his castle.

In Shackfield's No. 1, Mary's body moved with the mechanical regularity of the machine she operated. Years of experience had allowed for this. However, her mind was almost detached from her body as she worked. Even though, to her understanding, she was still aware of being at her loom, unlike her recent dreamy experience. But today, the loom made no labour or pain for her, as the wonder in her mind was so powerful, it caused her to numb the pain to the point of absence. Mary knew she had experienced a miracle. She enjoyed going to church but had always been sceptical about prayer. Now it had all clearly paid off. Looking out of the window, the block of stained white in the darkness, she thought about who her rescuer had been. What position did he have in the olde family who once lived at the castle? How had he known she was coming back to his castle with a ring which could well be his, or at least his family's? She had seen a real ghost, and because of it, previously redundant stirrings deep within her started to move. What they would latch onto she didn't know, but they were there.

Sir Clarence had returned to his castle, sitting in the darkened, empty and derelict room that had once been his bed chamber. There he sat, against the wall, trying to think nothing. He was just about getting by. He had spent the initial part of the time in his former bed-chamber trying to numb the shock of not returning to eternity. Now he was desperately trying to hold back the tide of despair. His meditative state provided a thin boundary between an empty mind and what was pressing him. Sir

Clarence did not give in and so tumbled instead into a panic which originated from nowhere.

The only words he could summon were simply "God help me".

In that very second, the falling ceased in his mind and the meditation abruptly ended. Eyes open, Sir Clarence now began to feel a sense of comfort, which was given off much like a signature, a flavour he recognised. The volume of this presence increased as out of the shadows stepped Michael, his treasured friend. Sir Clarence looked up, hopeful.

"Michael," he spoke, as if to announce his friend's coming.

"Hello, Sire," Michael replied, standing softly in his brown robes.

For a moment, the two just regarded each other, Sir Clarence not knowing what to say, and Michael looking benevolently on someone who had been as close to him as a son.

"Why?" Sir Clarence was the first to speak. "Why am I still here, Michael? Thou told me to claim what was mine, and I did. But still, here I am. Not at rest."

Sir Clarence could only say plainly to his old friend what had not happened since he heard his echoing tones inspire him to action days before. Nevertheless, Sir Clarence knew to anticipate a riddle. He was right, but it was a riddle that felt more like a revelation, which came like gold dust from Michael's lips.

"Yes, I didst say that. And thou went and found thy ring. Thou must surely see that as a fine achievement. However, when I said claim back what is thine, I meant that there is a great prize for thou to take, not just the ring," Michael said that with a matter-of-fact tone, which made Sir Clarence glare with shock.

"What didst thou say?" the knight said.

"Find thy great prize, young squire. It is thy right."

It was a riddle that both bamboozled and excited Sir Clarence.

"Michael, I am a spirit. As thou must be. I no longer live on this earth. My ancestral line is extinct, it seems. Several centuries may hath passed since I owned anything. Times are changed, things are likely different. Hath thou seen Darkleigh? If it is my old manor thou refer to then how am I supposed to regain this forest of castles, where our people used to till the land as if it were God's own occupation?"

Michael remained composed throughout all this. He just smiled gently. "Thou art right, Sire. Things hath changed. Massively. But I wouldst not tell thou this if it were not true, or not worthwhile. Believe me, there is a purpose in all this. I can only show thou to the first bend on the lane. In time, the identity of thy great prize shall present itself. I am afraid I canst tell thee little more."

Sir Clarence looked his old friend in the eye and knew that he must be right. There hadn't been much that Michael had been wrong about, certainly during Sir Clarence's lifetime. But the confusion remained in the knight.

"Right now, I implore thee, to gain friends who know this new world thou hath come to. Folk who canst guide thou and who thou canst cherish in return. Thou art invincible, Clarence. Hath no fear of anything any more. There can be no limit to what thou canst crusade. Just find friends, the true currency of life. That shall be thy first step towards thy prize."

Sir Clarence was left open-mouthed at this. His eyes were intensely wide at Michael's astonishing words.

"Canst thou not join me more often?" he eventually asked.

"I shall always be with thou. But get to know the living, young squire, and thou shall find that enormously rewarding."

Michael and Sir Clarence shook hands. Both enjoyed the fusion of their icy-cold constitutions before Michael nodded and gradually disappeared, leaving Sir Clarence in a thoughtful silence.

Chapter Ten

Joe Nadin alighted outside a very 'well-to-do' residence, six Mount Street, Manchester. Its ornate frontage complete with sandstone carvings imposed on even him. However, if being overawed was due to anything, then it was who he was going to meet. The meeting had been hastily arranged, more or less as soon as he and the trainees had returned from Darkleigh. They had been clueless as to why their renowned leader had sprinted into the square of the town in question, flushed and flustered. Their exercise had been terminated on the spot, with Nadin ringing the bell frantically to call them in. Nadin's distress had turned instantly to rage. The trainees knew to say nowt' at this. For today, Nadin was on his way to see his ultimate superior, William Hulton, chairman of the select committee of magistrates for Manchester and Salford. On the one hand, he was very embarrassed, as he had told Hulton that there was nothing he couldn't handle. But on the other, he desperately needed the help of Hulton, if he was going to get to the bottom of what had happened in Darkleigh.

William Hulton waited for Nadin to arrive with a manner that illustrated patience. He was looking out of the house's windows, across the area of the town of Manchester known as St. Peter's Field. He often did this, as he found his powers of command in quiet contemplation. On that day, however, he recalled all he had built in life. Namely his coal mines close to his family seat of Hulton Park in Westhoughton, near Bolton. He enjoyed not attending to matters regarding them, as he had, beneath his immaculate surface composure, nothing but resentment for those who worked them: his miners. They were to him but children, demanding more than their station required in life. They had a never-ending wave of complaints for him about conditions and how they were treated. But Hulton's resolute response to all their grievances was that they should be grateful to have jobs at all, which he claimed to kindly provide. No one forced them underground. They could seek equally fine employment in the mills or on the towpaths, to name but two. Mining carried with it a deadly risk, but that was the nature of such undertakings. Then his tack of mind changed to his bloodline. He was many things by virtue of his ancestry. He stood as chairman of the select committee of magistrates for Manchester and Salford. He took a tidy pride in keeping what he at least believed to be law and order in those tumultuous districts. His position as head of the committee had been gained in part via his former office, that being the high sheriff of Lancashire. For him, duty was a word that described only his lofty position in the makeshift feudal pyramid. Ah yes, aristocracy. He marvelled at the fact that his family had a real pedigree in his county. They had assumed control of Hulton Park in the twelfth century and had remained there ever since. His heritage ran as deep in the county as did the oldest trees and the most stubborn red roses. Many of his people admired his family for that alone, looking to them for guidance in various matters of local importance. However, what would have come to represent a hint of mutual affection was quashed by his upbringing. The divine order stood as it was and was not to be fraternised. Even in this great age of industry. Pouring himself a brandy, Hulton continued his wait for Nadin.

The guard on the door recognised him and let him in. Traipsing broodingly up the stairs, Nadin breathed in. He barely noticed the rich, immaculate carpet and lavish artwork as he ascended. Walking down a corridor, he felt something he'd not felt for years. The deep, sharp bite of genuine fright. Of course, he was scared daily, but relied on his brutishness to suppress it. Now, it was all coming to a very inconvenient head. This is because he would, for the first time, have to admit to Hulton that he was scared of something, something he couldn't handle. Almost tumbling forward, Nadin was greeted by a servant who came in off the corridor.

"Er, Deputy Chief Constable Nadin, to see his Excellency Squire Hulton," Nadin said, trying desperately to push his chest out.

The servant conducted him to the drawing room and left. Nadin knocked on as softly as he could manage.

"Come in," a ruling-class voice replied.

Nadin opened the door and entered. He quickly shut the door behind him and maintained a reverent distance from the sole figure in the room.

This figure was busy staring out of one of the windows onto St. Peter's Field below him, surveying everything as it was.

"Sir," Nadin began.

"Ah yes, Deputy Chief Constable Nadin, always a pleasure," Hulton greeted. "How can I help you today?"

"Well, first, sir, I'd like to thank you for your time. As you will no doubt be aware, it's not often that I need to come before you, other than to keep you updated on the excellent progress made by the special constables of Manchester."

Hulton recognised the flannel and said, "Yes, indeed, tell me, Deputy Chief Constable, what help is it you require?"

For a moment, Nadin was stunned at Hulton's powers of perception.

"Er, well, sir, you see a slight… issue arose on our recent exercise in the town of Darkleigh. One which your lordship may find quite, outlandish but, may I assure you, is nonetheless true."

Hulton had not turned to face Nadin the whole time he had been in the drawing room.

"Really, tell me more…" Hulton's voice continued with the same composure.

"Well, sir, the exercise was proceeding quite well, with my lads conducting their enquiries professionally amongst the inhabitants of said town. However, I myself happened to notice a group of lads of the town, exhibiting a loud and rowdy manner, walking past the square towards the town's edge where there are two hills. So, not wanting to disturb the important development of my trainees on their exercise, I proceeded to shadow this mob on my own. Eventually, they approached the second hill of the town, the larger of the two, which is when I stopped them. They could of course see who I was but didn't show me the respect that my office demands. When I asked what they were doing being rowdy at that time of the morning, they started gurning at me and throwing sticks. So, of course, I had no option but to draw my cosh. Of course at this, they scattered. But out of the trees came… something, which I can only describe as a boggart. It just descended on me, sir, with ungodly speed, slashing and bawling at me like bloody mighty. I tried to fend it off, sir, but the thing was inhuman. Nothing like I've ever encountered before. I don't even think our troops at Waterloo could've vested it. Aye, it had sharp teeth and claws. It overwhelmed me, sir. Which is why I retreated to the square in as quickly a manner as I could and terminated the exercise, as I didn't want my trainees to suffer from this monster."

"So," Hulton began, without a hint of surprise in his voice. "You're quite sure you encountered a boggart, are you, Deputy Chief Constable?"

"Yes, sir, if it was anything human, it'd have been in the New Bailey by now."

"Yes, I'm sure it would have been. I can always trust you, Nadin, to get the best results. I always have been able to and I always will, for sure. However, this… thing you encountered. Are you sure it wasn't someone dressed up for a festival perhaps?"

Nadin's heart sank, as this question revealed that Hulton didn't believe him, after sounding so understanding.

"Why yes, sir, I'm sure. Whoever it was would have been sluggish if it were a costume, and unable to move with the manic pace that it did. And like I say, sir, if it had been human, it'd have been in chains at the New Bailey by now."

At this point, Hulton spun cleanly around to face Nadin.

"Yes, but the salient point here, Nadin, is why are you letting this thing disturb you as it does? You will note that more and more people are ceasing to believe in boggarts and the like these days. And even if it is, then I doubt very much it is going to be an ally of his majesty's enemies. Just be grateful it didn't eat you," Hulton finished with a little smile of sarcasm.

Nadin saw his master study him like a painting. This always had the effect of making him feel uneasy. Nadin stared at the ground, as if in apology.

"Sir, I swear down to you, I wouldn't tell you this if it wasn't true."

"So what are you here to request?" Hulton asked again.

"I ask that I be granted more resources to tackle this problem in Darkleigh, sir. Perhaps some light field artillery and some troops from perhaps the local yeomanry. Compared to them, we only have a small number of men. And what special constables we do have need to remain here in Manchester, I'm sure you'll agree."

Hulton sighed.

"All this for a boggart?" he said.

"You're aware, sir, that the Reformers have a presence in Darkleigh? A quite rabid presence, allowed for by the laxity of the local magistrates of the area?"

Hulton turned completely serious at this. Something in his memory lit up at this. "Yes, I am. As a matter of fact, yes. And I expect that they are escaping justice unlike their counterparts in Manchester, are they not?"

"Yes, sir, that would seem the case," Nadin confirmed.

"Well, we can't let that happen, can we, Nadin? That damned nonsense about liberty, fraternity and equality just spreads like bloody wildfire. These people seem to forget that whatever they have is a gift from the king, dispensed by their social superiors. Yes, thank you for bringing this matter to my attention, Deputy Chief Constable. Very well, take whatever you need. There is surely no town outside Manchester more dangerous than that. It damn needs suppressing."

Nadin nodded his humble thanks to Hulton at this.

"Yes, the sterling efforts of our special constables here must be rewarded, they deserve to be listened to and taken seriously," Hulton continued.

Nadin looked at Hulton like a bairn being praised by his head teacher.

"Will that be all, Nadin?"

"Yes, sir, thank you," Nadin nodded.

"Very well," Hulton concluded, and his raised hand gave Nadin the signal to leave, which he did.

Hulton turned back to the window, to pour himself another brandy.

"Oh, Nadin," he called across the room.

Nadin froze, turning back instantly.

"Yes, sir?" he replied promptly.

"I do not suppose you noticed any, shall we say, distinguishing marks on your would-be assailant in Darkleigh, did you?"

"Er, yes, sir. He had an old-looking sword. The blade was double-edged and had a cross-guard on it. Had some kind of decoration on the hilt as well."

"I see," Hulton acknowledged, characteristically calm.

"Oh, and he wore what looked like a coat of arms on his chest. It had some bird on it, with fire… and a castle underneath."

Hulton's eyes widened. He had been disturbed. He was glad he had his back to Nadin to conceal his reaction.

"Right, thank you, Nadin. And till we meet next, down with the rump! Church and King!"

"Aye, sir, well said," Nadin responded and left.

Hulton turned a few seconds after he had heard the door of the drawing room close. Alone, he took his brandy and went over to his bookcase. He picked out one volume whose title read *Old Noble Families of Lancashire.* Putting down his brandy, he skimmed part way through the book until he came to a section entitled *Darkleigh of Darkleigh.* A boggart who wore the old arms of Darkleigh, in a town notorious for seditious activity. A town fallow for turmoil. Noticing the arms of a phoenix rising from the flames of a castle, he looked warily towards the window, deep in thought.

Chapter Eleven

It was a rare day when Mary found herself on her own in her family's sleeping room. Her mother and sisters were out as it was a market day. She just sat there, sewing and mending her bow strings. Her mind on nothing in particular, she felt quite resigned. Recent events led her to believe that there could be, and was, so much more to life. But now she had experienced it first hand, she'd decided to go no further. There was much more at work in this world than met the eye; but she didn't want to end up overwhelmed by it all. For she feared it would only lead her to an asylum. She couldn't cope with keeping even bigger secrets. That would drive her mad in itself. And she didn't want to end up committed. So, she had made a firm decision not to explore further, as she had considered doing. And now, things were serene. Other than the mill, life had become very calm.

Raising her bow to the light, it took a few moments for Mary to notice the sudden change in temperature in the sleeping room. It was only very subtle at first, then it developed into a definite streak, which came to dominate the room. She recoiled, scrunching herself up almost in response to what was happening. Things could get desperately chilly at times. However, the coldness normally lingered all day. Here it had just risen and risen within a short space of time. But that was just a simple precursor to what followed next. The room was darkened, but Mary saw several flashes of light a few feet above and away from her. They flashed several times deliberately, as if trying to get her attention. By now, Mary was scared. She put down her bow and sewing and was sitting back, bolt upright on her box. The flashing lights split open, being replaced by a long, cloud like substance. Strangely at this moment, the calm returned to Mary, but she couldn't fathom why. The faint white cloud appeared to crystallize before her eyes as slowly but surely, Mary noticed that it was forming into the shape of a person. Then the realisation came that she was being visited by a spirit. This had already happened to Mary recently and so she felt conditioned somewhat against it. Transfixed, Mary watched as the apparition shed its complete whiteness and started to take on colour. Black and magenta formed on it, and she could see that whatever it was, was dressed in criss-cross boots, gauntlets, jerkin and a tabard. On that tabard was an emblem she knew only too well: a phoenix rising from the flames of a castle. She began to suspect who it was as she waited for the last thing to form on the spirit — its face. Surely enough, the long black, curly hair returned, followed by the sharp features and pale white skin of her rescuer from Nadin. She felt familiarity at this.

"Hello again," she said.

"Hello there," the spirit replied. The spirit wasted no time. "Dost thou remember my name, dear maiden?"

"No, but I remember the dream I had that you were in, and what you did for me the other day. I should've said then. Thank you."

The spirit nodded kindly to her. "My name is Sir Clarence de Darkleigh, seventeenth lord of Darkleigh. And thou must be Mary."

Mary's eyes were blazing with complete awe. It took a moment for her to nod to confirm this.

"It is good to make thy acquaintance again," Sir Clarence said.

"Aye, and it's er... nice to see you again as well."

The two just sat and stood there, regarding each other like bairns ogling a sweet shop window.

"My dear Mary, thank thou for returning the ring. Thou do know that I am not angry about it, dost thee not?"

Mary nodded, impressed by the way she was untangling his old way of speaking.

"I had thought that that ring wouldst bring me peace, in the form of eternal rest." Mary listened intently. "However, I am afraid it hath not had that effect, alas."

Mary was upset at this.

"However, that misfortune hath helped unearth a fine purpose for me while I walk the Earth again."

Mary's complexion warped from concern to intrigue.

"Ooh, what's that?" she asked.

"I hath found out from communing with an old friend that to sleep again, I hath work to do, in the form of claiming something else which is apparently mine. Though that is all I hath been told so far."

"Why does he live up in the castle with you?" Mary said, wondering if there were now two ghosts in her town.

"Oh no, not exactly," explained Sir Clarence. "He comes and goes. Meditation somehow makes me feel closer to him though," he commented.

"Ooh, that sounds fun, I'd like to try it."

"Funny thou should say," Sir Clarence continued with a smile. "Mary, my dear, the reason I hath come to thou today is that I hath felt a connection with thou that I used to feel with people when alive. And to feel that again is beyond wonderful. To spend time with thou and teach thou meditation would be a joy. And to learn about this new world from thou would be a privilege for me in return."

Mary had not yet grasped Sir Clarence's meaning.

"What do you need to learn about this new world exactly?"

"Well, my dear, I need to grasp its customs, its ways of life, just what those ghastly things that belch smoke are, who is in charge these days and how the people of my old manor enjoy themselves... to name but some."

Mary was now open-mouthed at the needs of this spirit she had in front of her, given what he had been.

"And you think I'm the right person to help you with this?"

Sir Clarence knelt down to be at her seated level.

"Why yes, I do. Please, dear Mary, say thou will."

"You said you had a connection with me, but we've only met twice. I feel a connection with you as well, but, Sir Clarence, I must say, I'm not sure whether that's because of who you and your family were. You're really legendary people in this town. The kind we could do with now. But do you think we can trust each other after just two meetings?"

"Well, my dear, let me tell thou this. I am glad that thou think thou can believe in the legend of my family. So please, if it needs to be, let it become thy truth. God forbid the likes of that lout return, but if they do, thou and thy friends shall be safe, protected by my sword, which always used to protect this manor."

Mary found herself daring to believe in this knight, the first man she had felt she could truly, deeply trust somehow since her father.

"So you would look after us, if someone came to attack us?" was Mary's next question.

"Yes, of course. On my honour," Sir Clarence confirmed.

Mary was feeling a mixed state of excitement, gratitude and happiness in her heart at that moment, wondering if Christ's second coming would feel something like this. Of course, Sir Clarence was not Christ, but he was, as a hero, of yesteryear, returning to his people. Then, her mood soured as she thought of the possible consequences of becoming friends with a being like this. No doubt he would achieve great popularity amongst Mary and her friends. But at the same time he would make powerful enemies, in the form of Shackfield and many of his fellow merchant-class dwellers. What then? Would he claim whatever it was he was after? If so, what would that be? And he would have to find rest again very quickly lest he be harassed by the likes of Shackfield and those who supported them. Then there would be the backlash against her and her friends and colleagues in the mills. Maybe even her family. Shackfield and the rest of them would surely seek retribution. But something gripped at her mind, urging her to take this risk. She had always dreamed about the idea of being a schoolteacher, helping bairns to understand the world around them. Sir Clarence may not have been a bairn, but he still needed help, guidance, counsel. The grip turned into the burn of temptation. Looking back up to Sir Clarence, she said,

"Well, first things first. If I'm going to do this, I want to call you Clarence. If we're going to be friends, it's going to be Clarence and Mary, is that OK?"

Sir Clarence raised a confused eyebrow. He of course had always been used to everyone addressing him as sire or my lord. But then he understood. Thinking about the relationship he wanted to have with Mary, it was key that it should be a relationship between two equals, or not at all.

With a smile, he nodded surely and said, "Of course, Mary. Clarence de Darkleigh it is!"

He was impressed with Mary's courage. Maybe relations between nobles and tenants had changed in several centuries. Mary then explained her concerns to him.

"Clarence, if I'm honest, that'd be the nicest thing I could do with my life, to help you. But I'm worried, scared. You see, I know who you are, and it's reet amazing that we can talk to each other like this. But if you have to do what you say you will and protect us, which I'm reet sure you will, if needs be, what if Nadin and his cronies show up again when you've found peace? When you've gone up to heaven again? We're up here in the hills here like, but they'll come back. They'll be a bloody scrowe, and we'll have nowt' to stop it. I can't put me or folk I know, or my family in a situation like that."

The reality of this had now clearly dawned on Clarence, with optimism having fallen from him, replaced by guilt. Mary looked at Clarence, wanting a reply. For a while, none came. The silence provided an intermission which told Mary plainly that he fully understood the consequences. Clarence was reminded by this that he was no longer the all-powerful lord of the manor, and that now other forces held sway over his people. The feeling of powerlessness trickled through Clarence like a venom, nullifying him without leprosy, shackling him without chains. He saw himself out on the hills, close to where he had discovered himself to now be a ghost. He saw himself thrashing around. A mere individual, alienated in his beloved landscape. Then, he pressed into the earth, and the earth pressed back — with affection. Looking up and turning, he caught a brief glimpse of the town, which strangely occupied a middle ground between the old and new Darkleigh. Charged with inspiration, he found his vision ending as Mary's voice echoed,

"Clarence, Clarence…"

"Sorry, my dear," he replied.

"I need to know how we'd sort that out, if it happened."

Clarence looked down to his gauntlet and saw the manor ring on his finger.

"Mary, my sweet, listen to me. When it happens, if it happens, then sleeping again, whether I'm on heaven or earth will be a secondary concern for me. Thou see this ring?"

He held his ring up to her.

"Aye," said Mary.

"This ring represents Darkleigh."

Mary was quite taken aback by this.

"How can it represent Darkleigh?" she said, with a puzzled face.

"Because it is the ring worn by old lords of the manor, passed down through the generations of my family. With it, I carry a massive responsibility even though I live no more and I am no longer the lord of Darkleigh. With this, my abilities shall work for Darkleigh before they work for myself. In this ring, thou hath my contract to that end. My binding honour."

Mary's face had reset with certainty and courage. If that was the case, it wasn't surprising that he'd wanted it back. Mary felt her belief in him grow.

"Sounds like we're in safe hands. But how can it stop whoever comes for us?"

"Thou art. And do not worry, thou shall see," Clarence asserted.

"Despite what other folk do to us though, we've got no voice, us lot. That's the problem. But I must say, Clarence, I feel nice and safe now."

Mary enjoyed the way that what she was experiencing replicated how she used to feel with her father. The pause lingered.

"So, let's shake on it," Mary said, rising up to her new pal.

They were all smiles as they shook hands, and a new type of bond, which neither of them had ever felt before, was established.

Chapter Twelve

So it was. Mary and Clarence's extraordinary friendship gained steam over the next few weeks. The bond became stronger, with Mary coming to care for Clarence, the mighty warrior with a gaping vulnerability. Clarence took his lead from Mary on all things — there was very little he knew of this new world. He felt no embarrassment at all in being guided by a woman. He couldn't remember having been under female care since his mother, but the feeling didn't feel foreign to him. Because of everything she did for him, his admiration for her grew. One thing he came to regard as a treat was the three 'schoolroom' sessions they did every week. In them Mary would come to Castle Hill where he would escort her to the main hall, and she would sit down with one of the volumes she'd smuggled out from her home. These were history books that she treasured, which her father had left to her. Clarence came to understand that Mary was one of only a few people of her station in life who could read and write. This had indeed been a rare privilege for peasants and serfs in his day, but his family had made sure that literacy was shared by all in their lands. The history she read to him from these books gave him some rippling shocks, the kind that came to enthral him. He learnt that later in the century he had died, two rival houses of kings, one of whom he had served under many a time, clashed. He sighed as he heard that a bitter civil war had ensued. Clarence didn't like scenarios when brother turned on brother, but even today he could tell that the country was far from united. The following century's events made Clarence's jaw drop in disbelief. For in that century, a certain king called Henry VIII renounced his faith in the Church of Rome, and took up something called the Reformation, which wonderfully intrigued Clarence, at a time when art and culture was advancing too. He had then established his own 'Church of England'. Clarence was anchored bluntly again though when he heard of the extreme loutishness with the fates of Henry's wives. The turmoil of the sixteenth century, however, proved a mere taster of the rupturing shocks to come for him. For in the century that followed, Clarence was absolutely blasted to hear that a movement, later an army, led by a certain fellow called Oliver Cromwell, had risen up and deposed the king. But they hadn't replaced the king by one they favoured, no. They had actually *executed* the king of their own volition, in doing so committing regicide. England had been ruled by someone other than a king for eleven years thereafter. Thrill after crashing thrill continued to greet Clarence as Mary read to him the history of the country since he had slept. In the century that preceded their own, Clarence laughed with incredulity as he heard of how Scotland and England had joined together to become Great Britain, not through war but via an agreed legal precedent. Unheard of in his day, he took some happiness in that, as despite the many wars fought with them, he had always had a liking for the Scots. Later in that century, the country had experienced the dawn of industry. And in this, coal, cotton and canals had risen to the fore in his native Lancashire. Machines now allowed things to be made in great, unprecedented numbers. More people could now benefit from them and more of them could be sold, allowing anyone with the nous to make such an operation work to become wealthy. Clarence remembered the merchants in his day, but this was as if the whole operation were on opiates. Barges and ships allowed goods to be transported to markets as far apart as one end of the land to the other. Folk had travelled far and wide for markets in his day, but the sheer length and breadth, often of the whole land, that goods and some folk travelled was bewildering for Clarence. In fact, despite everything that he'd learnt, it was this relatively tame aspect that made him feel all the more grateful for Mary's help. For if Clarence had been living now, he knew he would have felt as if the whole world could reach him and become known of his very actions, given the great advances made in transport and deeper knowledge of far-off places. The last history lesson Mary gave him was saddening for her. It was then that she explained that most folk who had flocked to the mills and factories from the countryside were much worse off in their new lives than they had been hitherto. She described the harrowing conditions she and her friends faced in the mills, and at home. A streak of anger grew in Clarence as his family would have never allowed this, certainly not on their estates. Mary described the long, long hours and low, low wages in the mills, which were riddled with temperatures of extreme warmth, or cold, and machines which wore your body literally down to the bone, often causing illnesses and injuries, and all too often, deaths. Clarence came not to think of these places as houses where the goods of commerce were produced, but as sadistic chambers of pain. Mary explained the draught, damp and lack of food that people were faced with, along with open sewage and disease. Although most folk were as house proud as they could be, disease and decay came to impose themselves on the once jovial vills that Clarence had known. Mary summed the whole sodden situation up in one sentiment. That freedom didn't exist, and never had. This industrial explosion had given a few lucky folk, the benefits of economic liberty, but for most, it was just another clever trap, dressed up anew. What compounded the situation of her and her fellows was that they had no voice. Clarence could only listen soberly.

Mary came to delight in the fact that only she could see Clarence. Because from then on, he was her shadow, her companion and friend almost everywhere she trod. Sometimes he hid in the shadows of the mill, peeking out from behind a loom or a pillar, smiling coyly at her. She always giggled when she saw this. In fact, he came to join her on every shift, which made her feel safer than she ever had before. Whenever a callous overseer paraded by, the icy stab of Clarence's temperature kept them going by, without a hint of bother for Mary or her pals. She couldn't remember when she had last felt as secure as this.

Out in the open, at archery practice, she often saw him flying around the club house as a trail of light or a flashing orb. Each and every time she struck the dead centre of the targets, she would look back to the club house and the flashing would be frantic in response to her hit. This delighted and touched her so much that it moved her to tears on one occasion.

They would often play hide and seek together in the castle, like a couple of bairns. Having the run of an old castle was exciting for Mary, and she soon came to forget about the dangers of frivolity in an unstable structure. Sometimes, when Mary thought she had found the cleverest hiding place possible, Clarence would step through the wall and laugh like a villain in a play. After screaming, Mary would squeal with delight and scold him for cheating. Clarence just thought it was fun.

Clarence would as well often accompany her on market days, taking in the sights and sounds of what was to him the newness of his old manor. The accent that issued from the lips of Darkleigh folk hadn't changed, which had comforted Clarence ever since he had met Mary. Nor had their decency of spirit and happy character, despite the horrendous conditions of industry they were subjected to. Industry, Clarence noticed, caused most of their woes. Others were of being at a distance from their extended kin. Had this industrial age divided families? He traversed the streets silently with Mary, and she would nod at the many sights along the way. As the tightly packed brick and slate rows hung over him, Clarence couldn't help but feel like he was in something of a fortress. But whether that was something to be celebrated, he didn't yet know. Ensconced. But for what reason? One thing that delighted him were the cobbles on the roads. They echoed tunefully with the endless steps made upon them. There were so many he wondered where they all came from.

With her in the mills, he came to appreciate the terrible nature of them. It was all just as Mary had honestly described. Eyes strained by dim candlelight to see the intricacies of the looms they had to operate, often through clouds of dust. All this amidst oppressive cold or throbbing heat. Those on-going conditions were punctuated frequently by shuttles flying off the looms and clobbering some poor operator. He saw fingers, hands and wrists get mangled savagely in the damn machinery as well. Looking down helplessly was all he could do, as he was under strict instructions from Mary that trying to communicate with anyone but her wouldn't go down well.

One magic day amidst all this, Clarence was sitting alone in the old courtyard of his castle. Deep in his meditation, he heard a horse neighing. The neigh was known to him, and distinctive. It became louder and louder as Clarence's focus deepened. Eventually, he saw visions of who the neigh belonged to. And it was who he thought it was. It was Azlight, his old horse from life. His emotions burst at seeing her. For Azlight had been a part of his inner circle of closest confidantes, in the same league as John, Tilly and Michael. He saw her mid-brown fur as she danced and dashed about. The tone of her neigh was unmistakable — she was calling for him. He put her in the foreground of his vision so he could study where she was. The wonderfully imposing, surrounding greenery suggested only one place — the hills. Leaving his castle, he swooped towards the north-western hill that sheltered the valley. Tearing up that hill, he was soon on its first plateau, with both its sides raised. Climbing down, he felt a hint of insecurity being on his own in a place where the wind called through it and down the valley. But it was a healthy insecurity borne of excitement.

"Azlight," he gently intoned on the wind.

Then the place's whole benevolence sank through him satisfyingly. Letting the hill absorb him in this way almost meant that it was recognising the respect he still had for the primacy of nature it represented. A moment later, the hill chose to reward this respect, as from behind an outcropping there trotted Azlight, catching sight of her old master and running towards him. Clarence burst into dry tears. Azlight then reached him, and he hugged her and wouldn't let go, his heart rising to comfort once again.

"Oh, Azlight, my darling Azlight. My pet, my friend, my comrade," he said, renewing warmly the wonderful bond which had existed between him and this animal during the time they had lived.

He had travelled England on Azlight. He had ridden her into battle. He had jousted on her. On her he had trodden to every uncharted corner of his family's lands, and together had made a catalogue of adventures. He had nurtured her as a foal from his days as a squire. Her daring had matched her caring for him. This had touched him as very few humans were able to. She had always known how he felt. In Clarence's family, knights never owned horses, but worked with them to achieve their desires. Horses were seen as creatures with some magical elements in them. So for knights to make the best use of them, they needed to win their respect. The bond between knight and horse was sacred and owed much to nature. Clarence and Azlight walked home together that day, and Clarence soon realised that she was, of course, a spirit like he. And she too, knew when to increase or lose her denseness, and had the ability to appear in gloriously detailed full-body form, all the way through to a small, faint orb. When Mary next came round, Clarence mentioned that he had a 'surprise' for her. Walking out from behind the decrepit stable, Mary's eyes widened with shock and delight at seeing such a beautiful animal. Taking her to Azlight, he introduced them.

"Mary, meet my faithful friend, Azlight. Azlight, meet my friend from this new age, Mary."

Mary was in tears as Azlight's muzzle drew close to her, and she gently stroked her snout. Mary loved meeting horses at market, but this encounter was beyond that.

"Shall we go for a ride?" Clarence suggested.

"Will she be allreet with two people on her back?" Mary said with concern.

"Yes, she shall be fine. I wouldst not hath suggested it if I thought otherwise. Besides, she is a spirit and cannot feel our weight."

Within half an hour, Mary and Clarence were streaking through the hills on a flamboyant Azlight, who was clearly glad to be doing what she did best. Clarence felt unbridled joy to be back in the proverbial saddle. Mary, too, was overcome with the visceral experience she thought she would never have. The wind made a tunnel through Azlight's path and Mary screamed with delight as the three of them ascended to a point of sheer joy. But as Mary and Clarence walked Azlight back from the hills that night and stroked her back into orb form so she could rest, there still remained one question circulating with taunt in Clarence's mind. Why had he risen again?

Chapter Thirteen

One Sunday, Mary arrived at the castle with no books. Seating her in the great hall, Clarence asked why that was so. She explained that none were required as what she was going to talk about was taking place at that very moment — in some way. Intrigued, Clarence asked her to tell more.

"Remember how I told you that freedom doesn't exist here? How we don't have a say in what we can do, where we can go? Not just us but most folk?" she asked.

Clarence nodded.

"Well, it was like that everywhere, across Europe, for a really long time. But in the last century, some people thought up some ideas and challenged that. It'd been coming for a while, but things really exploded. They called it the enlightenment."

Clarence didn't understand why, but the way Mary told him this, it was like he was listening to a ghost story round the campfire.

"The folk at the top, the ruling class, they struggled with it at first. They still do in some places, like in this country."

Clarence could feel tension gather around them. Mary's voice had taken on a tone of trepidation.

"But it broke through for some. They changed their country because of it. Changed the way their country was run. Changed their lives forever. They became free."

Mary spoke that last line so fluently and without sensation.

This made Clarence instantly ask, "How so?"

Mary looked him in the eyes, as if revealing an inconvenient truth.

"Basically, they turned their country into a democracy."

Clarence's eyes narrowed at this. He had no idea what that was, but the word echoed within him. It carried a residue of familiarity that he couldn't ignore.

"What is that?" was his next question.

"Well, it's a type of government. You have to get it if you want to be free," explained Mary.

Clarence still felt a bit clueless.

"Well, my father started the practice of freeing *everyone* in our lands. His peers thought he was delirious for it, but he wanted people to be people. The only way he said he could do that was by making them free. And to be honest, our people did deserve that. They lived in the way we had raised them to…"

"Aye, and cheers to your father, Clarence. But the kind of freedom I'm talking about isn't like that. It's not a gift from a member of the ruling class. It's something you have to be born with."

Clarence was flailing at this point. For all his sympathetic nature, he simply just couldn't understand this.

"I mean, being free means being able to think for yourself and make your own decisions about what you feel and why. Then it means doing what you choose because you think and feel a certain way about something. It also means you can leave something that holds you down. Do away with the tyrant's boots."

Mary's voice sounded sweet and lyrical with this. Clarence was whimsical with inspiration, listening to her.

"That's the unwritten part, if you like. That's the priceless picture of liberty, as we say. Something you have to live, and not just talk about."

Clarence was captivated, absorbing these lovely ideals, as if he'd discovered a new liquor, which hadn't been available during the time he'd lived.

"But to do that, you need democracy. You need a change in the style of government so that laws can be made to let you do this."

Clarence was returned to focus again.

"And hath anyone in Christendom done this before?" he asked.

"Aye, they have. In France."

"What happened there?" Clarence enquired.

"They had a revolution."

"Which is?"

"When you overthrow the government by force. With them it was their monarchy. They deposed him and cut his head off."

This mightily alarmed Clarence.

"What! Good Lord! What happened then?"

"They became a republic and then got a dictator called Napoleon, who called himself an emperor. Which meant Great Britain had to step in and sort him out."

"And there are people in this land who want that, are there? Mary, surely thou must know that regicide only ends badly. And it was thou who told me so. Remember with the Civil War?"

"Aye, but we want to do it the legal way, which doesn't harm anyone. We want parliament to reform."

"When I lived, parliament was where thou met the king if thou had enough position. He smiled and nodded at you before doing what *he* wanted," Clarence commented cynically.

"Aye, well, nowt's changed," Mary bluntly said.

"Whose hands is parliament in now?" Clarence asked.

"Well, it's not the king's any more. 'Cause of the civil war. It belongs to the 'well-to-do' aristocracy and some merchants and industrialists. They'll be mates of Shackfield who're in with that lot."

"He owns your mill," Clarence tallied.

Mary nodded.

"The rest of us don't get a smell-in," Mary said with a hint of bitterness in her voice.

The general lull in the room hung heavy over them. The truth was like gravity itself — crushing. Clarence chose to treat his words with sympathy.

"Apart from the king not being in control, my dear, that is the way it always hath been. Right from the very inception of the kingdom, the strongest king hath always ruled. He chooses his best servants to rule over different provinces in his absence, and thou get ones who art bad and ones who art good. But that is the way of things. It is the divine way, my dear, the way the good Lord intended it to be. Sadly, there is no way of challenging this order…"

"What!" Mary was incensed by this. "What, Clarence, are you saying, you're on their side?"

"No, my dear, of course not! Thou know me and my family! This would be abhorrent to us!"

"Then why are you supporting them?" Mary shouted.

"Mary, for thy own sake, curve thy tone! Thou shall do thyself some damage! All I am saying is that God grants the nobles of the land a divine licence to rule. And whether that rule is fair and just is in their hands. Our peers used to hate us for saying this, but in our time, we saw more *peasants* than nobles who would go to heaven. They used to sneer at us, as we were by inference saying that they were destined for hell! It pains me to say what I said about the divine order, but it is the truth."

Mary calmed somewhat. Clarence was grateful.

"And which God is this, Clarence?" Mary challenged. "…'Cause he's certainly not the one I turn up at church on a Sunday to pray to."

Clarence couldn't think of what to say.

"I tell you now, Clarence, that if you believe in God, then there's more than one way of looking at him. 'Vainly we offer each ample oblation, vainly with gifts would his favour secure; Richer by far is the heart's adoration, Dearer to God are the prayers of the poor'. And that's Anglicans who sing that!"

Mary then became more understanding, as, in spite of his virtues, she remembered how far back Clarence was from.

"We left the church of England because they said what you just did. Now, our religion isn't perfect but at least it's given us an opportunity to see the true face of God. And from what he's said to me, he's on the side of the righteous, no matter who they are. When the church jumps in with the government, Clarence, it causes so much harm. I believe in God and Christ, but the way they're always in bed together, it drives me mad…"

"What, God and Christ?" Clarence queried, raising an eyebrow.

"No, the church and the government," Mary said, with a hint of a laugh.

"Ah," Clarence acknowledged. "And thou believe that thou canst be in charge now? That thou and thy friends can stand on an equal footing with the nobles in the land?"

"Aye," Mary confirmed.

Clarence was fearful for her. Mary had, burned into her mind, an angry image of the way she and her fellows were kept at heel, by their 'social betters'. How people of her status in life had no rights, in their *own* land, subjugated by their *own* people. Clarence noticed the anger and realised that he needed to make a move.

"My dear, for all my prowess, I am but a mere spirit, and I do not think that my influence could be felt in matters as complex as the reforming of parliament. However, I was once the lord of this manor. And if anyone still loves it as much as I do, no matter what it hath become, then I canst at least support thou somehow further than what I am doing now, within the bounds of my old manor."

Mary wasn't sure what he was suggesting.

"Who knows?" she began rather sarcastically. "Maybe Darkleigh could become free before the rest of the damn country."

Clarence sensed that Mary had latched on to his suggestion.

"So tell me how I canst help thou with this endeavour?" Clarence said in something of a conspiratorial tone.

Mary smiled as she knew that the bonds of friendship they'd sealed were stronger than old sentiments.

"Well, I don't see how you could, other than what you're already doing."

"Well, I hath lost count of the number of times that my parents and I used to speak to other nobles of our station and higher up. We interceded on behalf of our tenants, who, from time to time, had been caught up in misunderstandings with them. So, how about I intercede in this, my old vill, on thy and thy friends' behalf?"

Mary was now intrigued.

"How so?" she asked.

"Tell me, my dear, where does this squire Shackfield fellow live?"

Chapter Fourteen

Mary bought Clarence a coat for their journey. Although Clarence couldn't feel it, it still enticed him as it sat on his constitution. He gave it a dear look when Mary gave it to him; he was flattered to receive a gift from her, but he knew exactly why she had bought it. It was to conceal suspicion about who he really was when he met Shackfield. With this long coat, Clarence appeared as any member of the yeoman class would have. Shackfield, with all his snobbery, would surely entertain this. For the journey, Mary invited along Bertha, as she didn't want to wait outside alone. Mary watched as she and Clarence shook hands, knowing that Bertha had no idea that Clarence had been the ultimate result of their original jaunt to the castle. Clarence was friendly and made no complex talk in his conversation with Bertha. Despite a few extra chills, it was enough to convince Bertha that he was indeed a solicitor, and a friend of Mary's family, from the villages in the hills. Max would be his name for tonight. They left long before dusk set in, with Mary's mother giving her the usual warnings to be wary at the tavern. From the town's north-easterly edge, Shackfield's residence was plain to see amongst the valley's flat land. It was where he stayed when he was conducting his business locally. And he had been seen in town a few times recently, at a couple of his other mills. So Mary had every reason to believe that he was there. As they left the urban thicket of their town, they looked towards where they could just about make out the outline of a neat mansion in the near distance. Outside the smog, the sky was starting to retreat, casting a majestic sunset of orange and terracotta as it slipped back beyond the hills. They saw Shackfield's mansion reflect in the sunset, cutting sharply across the valley. The mansion's isolated position filled Mary full of excitement, for it was as if she was going to some mystical locale on a quest. But at the same time, she felt oddly sorry for Shackfield, out there on his own, detached from the hub of merriment and fellowship that the town nurtured, in spite of its terrible poverty. And she already knew of one real mystical locale in the town. So they began the trek, over fields and over fences, the odd bumps and brooks in the wide-open ground breaking up their stroll. The walk seemed to take a while and Mary almost forgot about the evening's objective. They didn't lose sight of Shackfield's place though, it was damned impossible to. But the closer they got, the more deceivingly fortified it appeared to be. For there were various lumps and bumps of land which weren't visible from afar, but close up they broodingly halted potential interlopers.

Amongst the crags of land that stuck up as if to angrily barricade the outside world, Mary, Bertha and Clarence searched for the front gate. As they raised their heads they could just about see the top of the mansion poking out from the crags, as if it were keeping a condescending eye on them. Eventually, they concealed themselves amongst the crags which were closest to the ornate ironwork of the front gate. The crags did a good job of shielding the mansion from view. All they could see was a winding strip of gravel which led to the front door. Everything else was obscured.

"Well, this is it," Bertha said apprehensively.

Clarence regarded it. It had obviously been built a few centuries, at least, after he had died, but he had no idea what had led to the ground becoming as ravished as it was. He had no memory of that. It baffled Mary too. (Unbeknown to them, it had been a cannon explosion in the civil war.)

"Ta ra, Max, good luck," Mary called as she took Bertha by the hand to the safety of the shelter of the crags.

"It's a shame we can't go with him," Bertha commented.

"Oh, don't worry, he and Shackfield are good mates. He'll be fine on his own," Mary countered.

"He doesn't strike me as the type of fella who'd be mates with Shackfield," Bertha said sceptically.

"Well, put it this way, when I told him about what Shackfield's done with all of us, he rolled his eyes in despair. Max has been away for years now and he's not been up to date with what goes on. He was really anxious to help us."

"Nowt' like a friend to set you straight, is there?" Bertha asked Mary, looking directly at her.

"Nay," Mary began to reply, but then noticed Bertha was smiling at her off the back of that last thought. The pair ended up laughing.

Clarence, as Max, briefly used his second sight, checking there was no one watching what he was about to do. Satisfied, he walked through the iron gate and made for the front door, observing all he could of his surroundings. He thought about using his second sight again, but he could feel no sense of threat from the house. He saw the immaculate lawns and neatly finished square mansion. The windows were dark and private, with none on what must have been the ground floors. The door in the fawn and light brown mansion was surrounded by a platform with curved, oval steps and neo-classical pillars. Walking up to the door, Clarence looked vacantly around and knocked on it. After a stretched moment for him, it was answered by a quizzical servant.

"Yes?" she said bluntly.

"Hello, I am here to speak to Squire Shackfield. I have been looking forward to this meeting all week."

"That's strange, the master's not expecting anyone yet. And if he was, he'd be in the drawing room, ready to entertain them."

"Really?" Clarence said, eyebrows raised, trying to look confused.

"Aye, and you'd have come in round the front."

Clarence glanced up, slightly taken aback by her last sentence.

"Why?" he said, maintaining a raised eyebrow.

"Because that's the front. I'm surprised you got in at the back."

Clarence was on the spot. Suddenly he felt vulnerable, simply at the thought of being caught out.

"I... I am sorry. The gate was open so I just... I did close it when I was in," Clarence salvaged.

He knew it had to be good enough to convince the servant. She rolled her eyes.

"Oh again," she sighed. Then a smile spread across her face. "Come in, sir."

Clarence smiled as she conducted him inside.

Clarence was led through a long, darkened hallway, which almost shunned activity. At the end, the servant led him through a narrow door and into what Clarence recognised as a foyer.

"I'll tell the master you're here. Oh, by the way, who are you and what is it you want?"

Clarence smiled.

"My name's Max Walmsley. I'm a solicitor from Hazelthorpe, just up the road. It has come to my attention from certain sources within the law that the various properties of Squire Shackfield may be at risk of being trespassed upon. I've come to offer my legal advice."

"Oh dear, I see. I should think the master will be very keen to see you then. Do wait here."

The servant disappeared up the broad flight of stairs that dominated the foyer. Their whiteness cut a crisp contrast to the dark browns and navy blues which coloured the walls and polished floors. He again thought about using his second sight to glimpse the inner warren of Shackfield's lair but decided against it again. He still didn't feel the spike of any threat. He'd allow Shackfield to feel brave on his home turf. The servant re-appeared at the top of the stairs.

"Hello, sir, yes, I'll just show you to the drawing room. The master's only too keen to see you. He says he's glad you called."

Clarence nodded. He was surprised by how easy it had been to blag his way into this fortress. Maybe he should've tried the Trojan Horse approach on sieges before, and ignored his commanders. The servant guided him to the ornate drawing room, which overlooked another fine lawn and elaborate gardens. Clarence absorbed as much of this as he could. Castles were all very fine, but he knew it was the labour of Mary and her friends which was paying for all this. The servant said that Shackfield would be with him in a few minutes. He nodded again and waited. It was in this time he decided he would use his second sight, if only to a slight degree. Closing his eyes, he entered a shallow meditation and waited to see what there was, now eager to glimpse the inner sanctum of his friends' enemy's lair. Behind the large double doors of the drawing room, he was then distracted by a rather flustered presence making its way through the space behind them. The presence, who Clarence sensed represented Shackfield, got closer to the doors, so he exited his second sight and sank back into character. The doors opened and Shackfield stepped through. Dressed in his evening gown, he entered, surrounded by an air of supremacy.

"Good evening, sir. Max Walmsley," Clarence said with a small bow.

He immediately strode towards Shackfield with purpose, hand outstretched.

Seemingly impressed, Shackfield replied, "Royston Shackfield. Glad to make your acquaintance, sir."

The pair shook hands. Clarence went to work straight from the off.

"Squire Shackfield, may I compliment you on what a wonderful hall you keep. I have never seen such elegance, such high regard for aesthetics. Such artistry moulded with decorum. A gentleman such as yourself merits a home befitting of his stature, and you, sir, have done yourself proud, if I may say so."

This initial volley from Clarence clinched its objective. Assaulted by compliments, Shackfield reeled with embarrassment.

"Oh, sir, sir, I pray you; such a fine taste for architecture has surely provided for your insight."

Clarence felt gleeful inside.

"Wendy tells me you have some news for me regarding incursions on my property?"

"Indeed. And it pains me to call under such grave matters, sir."

"Oh, don't worry. Do sit down."

Shackfield motioned to a table and the pair went and sat.

"Squire Shackfield, I have received word from the local magistrate that several, shall we call them… strange beings, have unfortunately been sighted on your property."

"Really? This one?"

Clarence nodded his head.

"Good Lord, I'd have hoped the local magistrate would've come down here and told me himself! Oh, no offense, Squire…?"

"Walmsley, sir. And none taken. The reason why the local magistrate is not here himself is because he thought that this news might have been told better by me. Given my experience in such matters."

"Such matters?"

Shackfield raised an eyebrow.

"Yes, sir. These *strange beings* we fear, although it may sound ridiculous to the more enlightened of us, we believe are ghosts."

Shackfield was somewhat sceptical at this. But Clarence pressed on.

"The remit of magistrates is confined to the law, sir. However, despite my legal qualifications, one thing I tell only a privileged few souls is that I am, in fact, a necromancer. No pun intended."

"A necromancer?"

Shackfield's eyebrow was at a sharp angle now. He moved backwards in his seat.

"Yes, sir. I commune with and, if necessary, invoke ghosts and spirits, to persuade them to cease their hauntings and move on."

Shackfield had resorted to a blank stare by then.

"Some local ladies reported the sightings, as they were concerned for you, sir. However, when our magistrate examined the details of their reports, it seemed that it was best to refer the matter to me, given what these intruders most likely are."

"I see," Shackfield said, looking down and lost.

Clarence tried to resist enjoying seeing Shackfield scared. Mary had told him a lot about this fellow — none of it good.

"So what's to be done, sir?" Shackfield's disturbed voice asked.

"Fear not, sir, I have several good years of experience in these matters. Trust me, when I get to work, the ghost's days of haunting are numbered."

Inside, Clarence was laughing at the hilarious irony, knowing that this was something he himself had evaded so far.

"Well, no doubt I'll be in your debt," Shackfield stated.

"Ah well, on that point, sir. It has also come to my attention that a certain matter would benefit greatly from your input. I would be grateful, sir, if you could see your way clear to resolving this, as it will act as my only fee."

Shackfield was enthusiastic.

"Please, sir, tell me more."

Clarence was more serious.

"It has come to my attention as well that a number of ladies and gentlemen in your employ are struggling daily."

"Well, that is the price of survival in this world. Struggle," Shackfield countered.

"Well," Clarence continued with a reluctant graveness, "I am told on good authority that there are a number of ills on your premises. These concern violence and harassment from overseers. Some ladies even claim that rape is an ever-present threat. I hear that there are children in your mills, sir, who shimmy under great carriages on machines to remove excess cotton. For them and for your operatives, I hear grievous injuries are common. Along with illnesses brought on from the dust, sanitation is poor and temperatures extreme. And also, I hear they work twelve-hour days, for six days a week. And the pay is barely enough to keep them alive."

Shackfield, who had been stunned by what he saw as charges laid before him by Clarence, shot to his feet.

"I beg your pardon!" he exploded. "How dare you come in here and insinuate such rubbish! I hope your legal qualifications stand you in good stead, Walmsley, as with all that, I should be seeing you in the white court of Lancaster Castle for defamation!"

Clarence simply raised his hands.

"Sir, sir," he calmly intoned.

This had the immediate effect of quietening a rage-pulsing Shackfield.

"It was not my intention to come here and accuse you. All I am saying is that I have these statements on good, trustworthy authority."

"Those insolent bloody fools will tell you anything to make me look bad. They don't understand commerce. And in commerce, it is the inherently clever who call the shots, sir, not the undeserving, as they are..."

Clarence looked up with a face that brought Shackfield to silence again. It was a face that sported animal like focus. This primal look locked Shackfield's outrage away.

"Sir, do not think that I am here accusing thou. For I am not. Mills everywhere, far and wide, practice these terrible things. For you, sir, are not the problem. How could thou be? Thou are a fine example of a merchant. A credit to us. The problem lies in the state of the laws of this land. There is no equal footing between the good folk of every station in life. The laws allow for what you, sir, may have overlooked. Not out of neglect, but out of the need for you to attend to other matters. You and so many others, that is."

Shackfield was standing there, with his hands on his hips, and a disbelieving smile on his face.

"I don't know who's been telling you what but it's all bloody false! Those protesters, what do they call themselves? Reformers, that's it! They're trying to overthrow us all. And they'll say anything to slander…"

"I understand that you may have forgotten yourselves, sir, thou and thy colleagues in commerce. Art thou born of these hills, sir?"

"Yes," Shackfield abruptly conceded.

"Born of these hills, like thy workers," Clarence said, his voice starting to take on a mesmeric quality.

Shackfield's anger faltered, as he found himself succumbing to the words of Clarence.

"Is your lineage embedded in these parts, Max?" Shackfield questioned, for no reason he could fathom.

"Oh yes, indeed. My family have been yeomen going back several generations, with many small holdings in the northern villages of the hills," Clarence convincingly assured. "And ye?"

Shackfield nodded. "We started off as artisans. My great-great-grandfather used to have a stall on Darkleigh market. He was always there, a real fixture. He was at most of the local market towns."

Clarence nodded in an impressed fashion.

"Then, when things moved forward a bit, my father put all he had into the mills and we took off. Careful investment in the right technology, Max, that's what it is."

Shackfield was by now staring wondrously into an empty space ahead of him. Clarence stood up and put on a relaxed posture. Smiling warmly, Shackfield evidently noticed the chill in the air, along with Clarence's eyes, which although they looked young, stared through the centuries.

"Yes. At one time, there were only ye merchants, and the lords. We yeomen saw ye rise and fall together, with us. No matter what ye have all come to be now, we witnessed it," Clarence's voice illustrating with honey what Shackfield was coming to see in his mind.

At that moment, Shackfield felt a part of something that existed between him and this newcomer he had only met minutes ago. And the other felt the same. Clarence took silent satisfaction in this, as he could feel Shackfield's true nature circulate between them. The monster described by Mary had flaked away.

"So, what is it you ask of me, sir?" Shackfield eventually asked when free of the wonderful haze.

"To repair what is wrong in thy mills, and to pay and care for your workers in the proper way," replied Clarence.

"Right," Shackfield acknowledged, after a long moment.

Clarence had shed Max completely by now. His own voice had returned, his own demeanour, standing tall and precious as the lord of the manor, even though that status had left him. A nourishing cold rushed through the room and made Shackfield groan with relief. Clarence pretended not to notice. But for him it was confirmation that his influence was being felt, from beyond the grave. He felt he was doing what his family had always done best — tending their flock.

"Right, well, yes, it's been a pleasure to meet you, sir," Shackfield said, still quite affected with the feelings which had just riddled him.

He offered his hand to Clarence, and Clarence shook it with a not-too-devious smile creeping across his lips.

Shackfield didn't notice it, saying, "Forgive me, but I have another appointment soon with a very distinguished fellow."

"With which I wish you good luck," replied Clarence.

He nodded and went to leave.

Before Clarence opened the door that he'd came through, Shackfield shouted back to him, "Care for my workers in the proper way." Turning, Clarence nodded.

"And repair the ills in your mills, sir," he repeated.

Shackfield waved, and Clarence nodded with a smile, before leaving.

After Clarence had left, Shackfield was on his own in the drawing room, Clarence's words echoing through his mind, bringing gravity to him. 'Repair the ills'. 'Care for our own'. He didn't even seem to notice when a servant came in.

"Sir," he said, noticing that something was off about the mill owner.

"Yes?" he eventually replied.

"Shall I show the guest in?"

"Yes, yes," Shackfield answered, waving his hand around impatiently.

The servant left and was back in a minute with the next guest, who was standing in the shadows.

As the servant nodded to him to step in, he announced, "His Excellency William Hulton, Esq." and promptly closed the doors.

"Hello, sir," Shackfield greeted, spinning around.

"Hello, Squire Shackfield," Hulton replied with some warmth.

"Thank you for making the journey, sir, I hear you have some enquiries to make of me?"

"Yes, yes, I do, sir," Hulton said. "I gather you are having some trouble with members of your workforce. I was wondering if I could support your efforts to resolve this?"

"Oh, I'm sure you could, sir. But why my workforce in particular? I ask because with respect, every damn workforce in this county gives their employer problems, it seems."

Hulton sighed, knowing it was time for a convincing reply.

"Yes, well, sir, I was wondering if I may assist with the unfair troubles your workers provide as a means of repaying your possible kindnesses."

"My kindnesses, sir?"

"Yes. You see, I am after information. Information regarding some very strange transgressors which my sources tell me have been operating in this locality and may be tied in some way to your mills."

Shackfield remembered Clarence's warning regarding the ghosts.

Trying to conceal his realisation, Shackfield responded, "Really, sir, tell me more!"

"Tell me, Squire Shackfield, have you ever seen a medieval knight roaming round here?"

***

After leaving Shackfield's residence, Clarence entered deep contemplation. Of course, he found no leads to unravel the omnipresent question he had. So instead, quite randomly, he called out,

"I hath made friends. I am fashioning my abilities well. But what now?"

This had the effect of making Clarence feel better at having expressed his conundrum.

"Well done, young squire," echoed Michael's voice, as if having travelled from a distance.

Clarence looked up.

"Michael," he said, with an expectant tone that anticipated something new.

"Thou art succeeding. Thy patience for the folk of today and thy willingness to learn and adapt thy greatness is granting thou success," Michael's celebratory voice came again.

"However, now, thou will soon take part in a great encounter. Then thou shall journey to Lancaster. Answers will abound there," Michael concluded.

This time, Clarence didn't bother to question his old friend. He just smiled, feeling in control for the first time since he'd awoken.

All he said was, "Thank thou, Michael."

Chapter Fifteen

A week or so after Clarence had been round to see Shackfield, he was on the balcony of his old castle, locked in his second sight, staring out over Darkleigh. He noticed that this was the first time he had actually enjoyed using this capability. For, with time, he had discovered that it had many uses other than to effectively spy on people. With time, his second sight had adjusted to allow several important functions. These included using the roar of the wind and the hum of the mills to mould into a voice with its own, unique call across the valley, which sounded as sweet as music. It also allowed him to blend the darkness and fog almost at will, which, he noticed, created a mysterious notion of security across the town. He saw listless squares of vague yellow light fill the on-going sea of windows in what Mary called the terraces. Focusing on them, he saw characters leap from the light and act out a hundred dramas, which could reek of tragedy but taste of glory. When all these things culminated, he realised what his old manor had now become. It was a bastion of belief in something greater than themselves, and what, together, they could become. Enjoying this vision, he stood tall, and clinched the hilt of his sword underneath the long coat which Mary had spent much of what little money she had on. He enjoyed the replicated feeling of being the lord of the manor. Now, he was beginning to understand his old manor more and more. And he was now seeing far beyond the filth, the choking smoke and the harrowing conditions in the mills and dwellings. Now he was seeing a new version of what he'd known. And he adored it.

A few minutes later he heard Mary's footsteps climbing the stone staircase. She entered the great hall and the pair met with affectionate salutations.

"You know, I am proud of you," Mary beamed.

"Proud?"

Clarence needed more information.

"Aye. You put Shackfield in his place."

"Yes, I did. By joining thy needs and his together." Clarence subtly smiled.

"We could do with someone to do that for most mill-owners," Mary mused.

"Well, my dear, when my influence is felt, even in a small area, which was once my jurisdiction, then I hath had a noble effect. And to hath a noble effect was always our main goal."

"Oh, you've certainly had that, Clarence. It doesn't matter that it's just been a pin prick, it was in the right place. One that could make the rest of the buggers sit up and think," Mary proudly stated.

"How hath things been?" Clarence asked.

Mary beamed again.

"Things have changed. Pay hasn't gone up yet, but he gets some folk from outside the mill to tidy it up every day when we finish, and before we start in the morning. The loos are fine and all. They don't smell and they're damn cleaner than the floors. Folk are happier."

"Well, let us hope that the current of my negotiation carries on until balance is gained," Clarence said triumphantly.

"Aye, let's," Mary agreed.

There was a pause of satisfaction between the pair.

"Now, this meeting that I'm taking you to tonight should tell you how we plan to do what you just said everywhere. I know how you feel about tackling the establishment, Clarence, but maybe if you listen to what the speakers say, you'll come to see what we mean."

Clarence could only nod willingly. In truth, he was sceptical about the aims of Mary and her friends. But Mary was his friend and he had admitted to himself by then that he was intrigued by this movement she was a part of. He remembered during the century of his birth, the Peasants' Revolt had ended badly. This sobering thought gave him a backdrop to tonight's meeting. At the same time though, the prospect of going was tantalising for him, given what his second sight had been showing him. But niggling away on top of this was still his secret desperation to sleep again, this time forever. For he hadn't told Mary this, but it was in a spirit's nature to crave it. All he had told Mary since his last communication with Michael was that eventually, the next step on his proverbial ladder would be a journey to Lancaster. He was unsure when this would be.

Mary hadn't reacted to this, other than smile. But restoring his focus back to the moment, he said to Mary, "Right, shall we go?"

Mary nodded enthusiastically and linked Clarence as they left the castle and then the woods.

Walking into the dark over-hangs of town, Mary and Clarence said nothing to each other. Clarence could tell Mary was pleased though.

"Where are we going?" asked Clarence.

"You'll see," Mary assured.

Entering the ginnels behind the workshops and blacksmiths, which were still chattering away, Clarence used his second sight to try and spot unwanted persons before they became too close. But it was a quiet night. Mary led him through various dark, narrow ginnels, and Clarence came to know definitely that Mary's movement was clandestine.

Compounding this was when Clarence began to ask about the meeting. "Mary, my dear, what is on the agenda for to…"

"Shhh," Mary responded in an understanding but prompt way.

Second sight always present, Clarence heard various different conversations as they passed by the backs of taverns, workshops, the backs of shops and people's houses. None of them on the topics which Clarence and Mary had spoken of, especially not on this issue of Reform. Traversing the ginnels as they were, Clarence felt that he would have been truly lost without his second sight. That, he thought, was probably a good thing, given the nature of the event they were going to.

It was around then that Mary gently squeezed the denseness that represented Clarence's right arm, and told him with sensitivity, "Clarence, you need to disappear now. I'm sorry but you do. I wish I didn't have to ask you. They might get suspicious and come after you if you don't."

Clarence heard the remorse in Mary's voice. He knew that if she brought him in, folk would ask questions. Any inspection of him, (which he had been told was necessary for all newcomers), would result in his ghostly status being discovered. God only knew how they'd react to Mary after that. So, Clarence nodded and vanished into an orb. Resting on Mary's shoulder they changed direction sharply. Going down a new ginnel, a back gate was open and one bloke stood there, casually leaning against the wall. He caught sight of Mary. Mary smiled and he smiled back.

When Mary got to his position, he greeted her, "Hey up, Mary. You on your own tonight?"

"No, me' sisters came with me. They're in the tavern," she replied.

"Nice of them to walk you down the darkened ginnel, eh?" he said with sarcasm.

Mary frowned.

"It's not far," she said.

The fellow smiled and ushered her inside. Clarence had by now let go of his second sight, knowing they were there. He wanted to feel the raw excitement of the random direction they were going to take. He could see the rear of the building they were entering was covered with a makeshift roof, one which had been added at haste, it seemed. Mary pushed the door at the building's rear and went in. There was a plastered hall lit by candles. About half way down another fellow stood over a trap door, which lay open.

"Mary." He nodded.

She smiled back as she descended the trap door. At the bottom they came out into an expansive room. At that point, Clarence sensed they were underground. There were a lot of barrels about. Clarence realised that they were in a tavern's cellar. Laura Duckworth was standing there. Mary's face lit up on seeing her.

"Hello, Mary, on your own tonight?" Laura greeted.

"'Fraid so, Laura, but both my sisters are in the tavern."

"Ah reet. You know what to do."

Nodding, Mary raised her left hand and spoke the words "Rise again when there's nowt' to even rise for. Compadres of Reform live in me."

"Good enough for me," Laura chuckled.

She nodded them through. Mary smiled warmly as they made their way in between the barrels. Clarence felt the excitement build in him. Soon, they came to where around thirty other folk, of both genders, and of different occupations were deep in conversation. The expressions on their faces suggested that they were in serious conversation. A sight well known to Clarence from meetings at his old court leet and before battles, he remained invisibly perched on Mary's shoulder, as she found Bertha and sat down next to her amongst the barrels, wooden beams and stone floor.

The hum of conversation dissipated once Joe Duckworth stood up, trotted past the candles and lamps and clapped his hands.

"Reet then, folks. Good evening, thank you all for coming. Once again it's grand to see all my people here tonight in support of the cause of liberty."

Embedded deep within his orb, Clarence rolled his eyes. He respected these people for the principle of what they wanted, but Joe sounded a lot like Mary which told him that he would be in for a long night.

"Aye, liberty, fraternity and equality. Three priceless tenets of the Reform movement. Not criminal, not treason but what all people born in the eyes of God, are naturally entitled to. When we achieve this, and are living our lives as the free-thinking individuals we are, we'll remember what brought us there. And that was each other, the spirit of us, of our collective raising each other from degradation. For our affection for our fellows is what underpins a healthy nation, the love of the Lord running through us with a common streak."

Those assembled entertained the flowery words of Joe, knowing that although he had fallen in love with the project, he strove to mean every word he said. Some hung on his every word, but Clarence was cringing by then.

He continued. "As many of you know, there has been a mass meeting proposed, to take place in Manchester. I'm firmly in favour of this, as only a town the size of Manchester can sustain the numbers that many believe will attend. Although it will be a very serious day, it will also be one of excitement and merriment, given that a picnic is being suggested as well. So bring your glad rags, 'cause it's kind of going to be a fun day out. You might want to wear your garters, Laura," Joe finished, winking at his wife, who raised an eyebrow as some laughed. "But to tell you all about it, we have with us here tonight quite a famous gentleman, who's dynamic in the service of liberty and Reform. He hails from Middleton, which is much closer to where the action's going to take place, so he's much better informed at the moment than we are. I'm sure he needs no introduction amongst the more aware ones of us, so please welcome Sam Bamford!"

The people clapped, and up stepped a modestly smiling young fellow wearing boots and a tail coat. Clarence sensed nothing in him. Then he spoke.

"Good evening, friends of Darkleigh," he began.

Clarence noticed the warmth and sincerity in his voice as it floated through the air.

"Our comrades in Middleton send their regards."

Middleton. A famous vill. Clarence knew it for Thomas Langley. This made him twitch within his orb. A sound of acknowledgement for Sam rang out.

"It's wonderful to be here," Sam continued. "Whenever I see a flourishing Hampden Club or Union Society, I see hope. Even when there's no one there after hours. As long as I know it's flourishing and that there'll be many people at its next meeting, then I feel hope, reaching out with us all into the future. And the fact that this meeting is evidently well-attended tonight is proof that Reform is alive and well here in Darkleigh. That means it's safe for me to assume that the many mill workers of this town, including all others from all stations amongst disenfranchised folk, feel the same way as we do in Middleton and indeed the rest of the Salford Hundred and beyond."

Clarence noticed Sam Bamford's celebrity, as the poise and facial expressions of all there indicated that they had much respect for him. Clarence was entertained by his eloquence.

"Sometimes, perhaps cruel rumours abound that folk from the towns shallow in the Blackburn Hundred are ignorant to Reform. When Joe and the committee invited me here tonight, I knew for sure then that such rumours are made by two kinds of people: agent provocateurs wanting to cause disturbance and them who put old bitterness before the need to transition towards solidarity and thus liberty."

Massive applause echoed in the cellar. Joe Duckworth joined in but glanced above to the pub warily.

"Anyway, friends," Sam continued, the applause instantly ceasing, "I'm here concerning what has already been mentioned by Joe. There is indeed a mass public meeting planned to take place in Manchester in the summer."

There was a pause, even amongst the silence, which meant that folk wanted to hear more. Furthermore, drooping jaws and widening eyes signalled it was an issue of great value to them.

"We estimate that it will take place early in August," Sam confirmed.

Cue a cellar riddled with intrigued sounding whispers.

So Sam carried on. "We regret that the exact date and time cannot yet be confirmed. However, the setting is likely to be St. Peter's Field, in the vicinity of the church of that name. And, we aim to get a much-esteemed speaker to attend, someone who is passionate in the cause of Reform. Henry 'Orator' Hunt."

That announcement engendered a gasp from everyone there. They were impressed.

"So, my main purpose now is to invite this Hampden Club to attend," Sam said, pursing his lips.

"Can we have a show of hands please?" Joe requested.

Everyone's hand shot up. Joe and Sam were massively proud.

"Thank you, friends. We will look forward to having you all there," Sam beamed.

Clarence, at this moment, was for some strange reason enjoying himself. There was something reassuring about the mere tone of this Sam Bamford. And it had succeeded in making Clarence feel relaxed to the core. Despite the cynicism Clarence had for Reform, the flavour of speech that issued from Sam's mouth, even though he wouldn't admit it, was leaving his mind fertile to the planting of new ideas.

"One thing I would like to say, friends," Sam struck up again with a serious tone.

Folk's attentions returned with concern.

"I know… I don't have to say this with such fine people as I *know* you all are. But I must insist on certain things preparing for, leading up to, during and even after the date we set for this meeting. Now, a small band of the most ardently passionate ones of us in the past have, as I'm sure many of you will have heard, brought us into disrepute. This has been done via their loud, drunken, impolite behaviour which has added fuel to the flames of our nemesis, the establishment. Perhaps only superficial fuel, but at the backend of the day, we are campaigning for a land which not only deals with poverty severely, but also where peace is in charge, and where its cooling influence is felt amongst us all, so we can reap its benefits. And for us, peace largely means the *prevention* of: damage to dignity, injury, even death. That is why I have to tell this to every Hampden Club in the country I'm visiting. So, on the day of the meeting, I ask that you all make your way to the meeting together, in an orderly fashion, in a sober, friendly and dignified manner, respectful of the dignity of all persons, whether they be taking part in the meeting or not, and this need for respect includes towards the authorities. We want to show that we are capable of having a very large say in the way our country is governed. So we need to show them that our anger towards what they represent, even though it is justified, is restrained. This manner shall last for the duration of the meeting and on our ways home afterwards. Then we can all have a good tipple," Sam finally concluded.

For a moment, everyone paused in respect, admiring just his tone even, which had been a mixture of sincerity and tenderness. The aura around Sam told Clarence that he was a leader, and he spoke with the genuine mark of a leader, just as folk in Darkleigh had heard and seen his father do. Just as the same folk had witnessed with him. Then, applause and cheers broke out.

Cries of "well said, Sam", "no one tells it like you do" and "hear, hear" all rang out.

Grinning with embarrassment at such an enthusiastic reception, Sam nodded and took something of a bow. Although equally happy, Joe then walked to the foreground of where Sam was standing and waved his arms about, followed by a gesture to the ceiling. Folk then made their cheers much milder! Clarence was by now thoughtful about all he had heard. He wanted to come to full-body form and join in the cheers. Despite being unseen and unheard, he felt once again that he was a part of something. It was also interesting to experience this feeling without himself as leader, as he had been so used to in the local scheme of things. The way Sam had described how they should approach the mass meeting had taken him back to what his family had done for years. Approaching a problem with diplomacy, working it out on behalf of their people, the way true nobles did. Except now his people were leading themselves, moving in that direction together. A streak of excitement rose again at this point in time to experience this.

He whispered in Mary's ear, "Canst I meet him?"

All Mary could do was nod, but it was a nod which told him plainly that she *wanted* him to.

Chapter Sixteen

Slowly, the people who had been at the meeting filed out in silence, into the pub from the cellar. Mary knew which pub it was, but Clarence was surprised to find that it was *The Phoenix*. For some reason, he hadn't recognised it. Maybe using his second sight would have been a good idea after all. They entered the main pub in dribs and drabs, so as not to raise an eyebrow. In the darkened hallway they waited, and Clarence, still an orb, came out with Mary and Bertha. Being greeted with the throbbing light of the pub felt rewarding. They had attended another secret meeting without being detected by prying spies. Yes, Clarence thought, this was surely *The Phoenix*. Clarence looked at the stone floors, wooden beams and the walls decorated with farming tools and animal horns. Memories of old customs filtered back to him. As did many other happy memories, stemming from good times he had enjoyed with his people in there. But the beaming orange light reflected by the walls served to remind him that there were things to do; so he whispered in Mary's ear that he was off to the loo. Mary smiled to herself in acknowledgment. Off he shot in his orb to the loo, his second sight telling him it was at that moment deserted. Shooting cleanly through the thick plastered wall, he hovered for a second or so before regaining full-body form, increasing his denseness. Sensing there was no one outside the privy, he stepped casually through the wall. Mary then promptly walked up and offered him his trench coat which she had worn since they'd turned the corner which led to the back entrance of the tavern. Smiling, she motioned him towards the vault. Following her, he saw all the different ornaments on the walls, and had to stop himself from engaging with the emotional attachments he had to them. Resisting the indulgence of memories, Mary walked him through a thick crowd of people who were invigorated as they spoke to each other. They had been at the meeting. Eventually, Mary stopped as the folk gave way to Sam. He and Mary greeted each other warmly and then Mary whispered in his ear. At this, he looked up anticipating meeting someone; Clarence met his eyes and he smiled an intrigued smile.

When he reached the pair, Mary said, "Max-Sam, Sam-Max."

Mary, in the hope of it being good for Clarence's confidence to be left to talk to Sam alone, excused herself and walked back to Bertha and a couple of other mill girls.

"Pleasure to meet you, Max," Sam said, offering his hand.

"And you," Clarence replied quite awkwardly, as his alter-ego.

"Mary tells me you want to chat a little about, *sensitive* matters?"

"Yes." Clarence nodded.

"Well then, in that case, follow me." Sam smiled.

Sam led Clarence to a darkened and unfrequented part of the vault. It was familiar to Clarence but he got the feeling that they weren't strictly supposed to be there. As Sam's speech had progressed in the cellar, something about him had become more and more apparent to Clarence. Something innate, which he recognised, without even the aid of his second sight. So, he decided he would examine that first.

"Sam, before we talk about *sensitive* matters, do tell me something of thy history; thy origins and perhaps something of Middleton."

Although not thrown by this question, Sam hadn't been expecting it. But in any case he obliged.

"Yes, of course, Max. I was born to Daniel and Hannah in 1788. I originate from the old Bamford line of Thornham. My great-grandfather was in line to inherit Bamford Hall at one point, but allowed it to pass to another relation. It was in our family ever since the Anglo-Saxons settled the land. My grandfather was the first of my own line to live in Middleton. His house was the first in the town to welcome Methodist preachers — including John Wesley himself. I myself have had several courses of employment in my lifetime hitherto, ranging from being a sailor to a warehouseman. Lately, I have returned to being a hand-loom weaver, which is what I was raised on. I saw it in my family's own dwelling before mills, when I was growing up. And I dabble with a bit of poetry, now and again, like. Other than that, I have lived in various places during my life, including the east coast and Manchester, but chiefly Middleton."

Clarence enjoyed the summation.

"Thy family's line goes back a long way, sir," Clarence said with impressed tone.

Sam was pleasantly affected by what he thought was the supreme quaintness of Clarence's words.

"Indeed. I grew up hearing accounts of my ancestors striding to meet with the old lords."

Sam's face grew reminiscent at this point, as if he were recalling personal experiences.

"Aye, the days when folk weren't that far. When talk tended to bring swifter resolutions to problems. The days when Englanders were Englanders and gents were gents," Sam said thoughtfully, staring into a void.

Clarence stared up, feeling himself reach out to Sam.

"Of course, not everything resolved itself that simply. Forgive my idyllic portrayal, as there were some tyrants about, like there are today. But on meeting with a fair lord, as often as not, you could resolve even their wickedness. Aye, I know of the last old Sir Ralph Assheton. Ah, he was the cream of the calibre I'm talking about. A model lord. He died before I was born, but my parents couldn't speak highly enough of him. But now all that is largely gone. Land may be owned by the same folk in some places, but the machinations of industry have removed people from the close bonds which once united them. Families, people and lords alike. No lords to look out for us now. We have no voice now to make the terrors of this industrial age known, and, most importantly, done away with."

Sam's tone remained warm despite being tainted with the conspiratorial.

"And that's why, dear Max, we have the radical Reform movement."

Clarence looked up again. This time a hint of realisation sparked inside him.

"I meself have been involved with radicalism for about four years now, Clarence. I'm secretary of the Middleton Hampden Club — big honour, that. Aye, it's time for us to find our own voice, 'cause this country can't move without it. They need us as much as we need them. And the best way to do that is by parliamentary reform. You know with the advent of the civil war, the king lost his absolute hold on the country, of course?"

Clarence nodded.

"Well, more folk gained more rights because of that. More people, not many, but some more, gained a bigger say in how the country were run. We can make that circle complete, Max. Simply by striding together, with no anger in our hearts or malice under our lips, but declaring by noble example the ills of our present land and the remedy. No greater service can be given from one person to his fellows, surely."

The moment that followed crystallised for Clarence. For in that moment, his realisation fell perfect; these were his people, come of age. And they moved with the same pride and entitlement that he and his father once used to. However, he was coming to understand that they didn't need lords, they needed independence. His attitude changed, he shook Sam's hand.

"Sam, all I can do I'm afraid is wish ye fair luck. I am due to leave my village in the hills soon, as I have some important work to attend to a good few leagues from here. But if I am asked to describe my support for thy movement, I will answer that it is absolute and unshaking."

Sam smiled gratefully.

"Thank you, sir, just please, don't mention our names," Sam replied, with some nerves in his voice.

"Thou hath got it," Clarence reassured.

They then left the vault to find Mary.

When Sam saw Mary back at the bar, Sam stopped by her and said, "Your friend Max is extremely entertaining."

Mary smiled, knowing that meant the conversation had gone well. Sam melted into the throng of chatting punters, many of whom had been at the meeting. Now chatting away about trivial subjects, Clarence walked up to Mary with the biggest smile she had ever seen on his face. She knew a transformation had taken place.

She noticed the light in his eyes and said, "Sounds like you had a good time?"

Clarence nodded.

"Now I see, Mary, now I see. Why it is that thou and thy friends think the way ye do."

That was all Clarence said, as he knew that all talk of Reform was to be kept secret.

"I'm so glad," Mary said.

"There is one thing I must ask you though."

Clarence's more serious tone grasped Mary.

"Mary, I feel now the time is right to progress in my journey. As I hath said, the place I must go is Lancaster. With thy help, I hath amassed I believe more than enough knowledge of this modern world to be able to face it. And more importantly, thy assistance hath provided me with such courage to do so."

Mary's face now exploded with happiness.

"Ooh great, Clarence, wonderful! I'm so glad that I've been able to help you!"

"Yes, but there is, as I say, one thing which I need to ask thou."

Mary suspended her joy to wait for Clarence's request.

"Will thou come with me to Lancaster? I wouldst feel so much safer with a friend there."

Mary's reaction hung in the ether for a long, long moment. She tried to speak, and Clarence decided to wait for her to reply, rather than try to persuade her.

"Clarence, I... I can't. I mean... I've got a living to make. I'm a weaver, and that's what I'll always be, like it or not. I can't come to Lancaster with you. And then there's me' family. Me' mam and me' sisters. I can't leave them."

Clarence had suspected this answer. And he accepted it. He wouldn't try and mangle her wishes. What with liberty and all.

"Very well, my dear, I understand."

Clarence's tone was resigning, and this upset Mary, as she knew her very unique friendship was soon to come to an end. Not only would Clarence leave for Lancaster, but he'd sleep again forever sometime after he got up there. But still, it had been good being a knight's lady! There was strong fondness between them, as from now the time between them was precious. Above the deep hum of natter in the bar, Mary and Clarence heard calls outside, and let them blend in with the comforting sounds of the tavern. Clarence didn't consult his second sight, he was determined to enjoy the moment. And it broke between them when Joe Duckworth came along.

"Anyone fancy a drink?" he said, feeling triumphant due to the meeting.

"Yes please, Joe, I'll have a pint," Mary promptly replied.

Joe reached into his pocket. Breaking the jovial atmosphere, the ancient oak door of *The Phoenix* swung open. Folk looked round, as the abruptness of it surely heralded something. James Hartwell staggered in, bent over, labouring to speak.

When he did, he said, "Top Hat's on fire... they're all stuck on the third floor. Shackfield and all."

Several folk ran to James and helped him to a chair as a huge gasp went up, followed by a few screams, as many of those assembled in the tavern had family who were at work at Top Hat, on the nightshift. Everyone ran outside, with Clarence, Mary and Joe amongst the first out. Clearly illuminating the night sky in the town's centre, there was indeed what looked like a bowl of fire. And standing in it was the unmistakable shape of Shackfield's No. 1.

Chapter Seventeen

On the third floor, folk were clamoured. They were beginning to feel the heat. Anxiety was reaching a sharp summit. On one side were the workers, of whom many were Reformers. On the other side stood Shackfield with the overseers and his reluctant wife. Around sixty people were all on the same floor, a distinct divide between them. They knew the first and ground floors were on fire, including the corridors and stairs. Every exit was blocked by the fire. They knew what was imminent. Some were at silent prayer, overseers and workers.

"So it should come to this eh, Squire Shackfield?" said Arthur Wainwright, a tackler.

Shackfield looked up, resentfully.

"After all we've been through together, it looks like we're all going to burn to death."

The volume of Arthur's bluntness matched the cynicism shown by his employer, even as they faced eternity together. Some started to cry.

"Arthur, for God's sake!" Ellen Lake scolded.

"I'm just saying how ironic it is, love. We've tried everything with this great entrepreneur of his age, and it comes down to this. All sharing the same fate."

"Aye, but reet now, Arthur, we need to be thinking of other things, like how to get out of here," Roger Harris reminded him.

Arthur raised an eyebrow.

"Aye, let's get thinking," he said mockingly.

"Sir, how about we try that shoot you installed for all the muck last year? I'm afraid you'd be sliding down there, but it's probably our only hope," suggested Obadiah Gerring, a milder overseer.

"Certainly, Squire Gerring, you can try," Shackfield obliged.

Gerring nodded at a couple of the tacklers who ran to a remote corner of the floor with him and started fiddling frantically with a hole in the wall in the corner.

"Aye, look at them three. Now that's the way it should be done all over. They don't care what side of this petty border they're on," Elizabeth Cronckshaw said astutely.

Shackfield raised an eyebrow.

"Hmm. And you would have us work like that all day every day, would you? No distinction between those who're chosen and those who aren't?"

"What the hell do you mean?" Elizabeth returned.

"Oh, come on now, Lizzie, I'm talking about the divine order. Those who have property are chosen to rule. I have acquired property through my excellence in commerce, therefore…"

"Don't think that bloody tripe will wash any more, Shackfield. Look at where we are, what's happening. All you can think about is that old tripe about God giving you a licence to do what you bloody want," Elizabeth shot in.

Shackfield's wife responded, "Yes, darling. Look at where we are, what's happening," her tone trying to supress her anger at her husband.

"Darling, I know these are dire circumstances, but I'm just trying to remind Lizzie who's in charge here," Shackfield replied.

"In charge! Well, tell me, dear husband, what exactly have you done to lead us out of this mess? Why aren't you at the windows, making bloody hand signals at least!" his wife exploded.

Shackfield didn't know what to say.

"I am working damn hard, dear! I'm trying to keep order before help arrives, by quelling this ridiculous rubbish she's coming out with!"

"Well, at least that ridiculous rubbish offers a way out of this mess," Shackfield's wife said, storming off to help Gerring and the tacklers.

Elizabeth was now staring straight at him.

"What are *you* looking at?" Shackfield snarled.

"You know, in just a couple of weeks, we've seen a little of your decent side, Shackfield. Them loos you installed. Very reasonable. The extra space. We appreciated it. Nice when you can breathe."

"Good God, what is it you want off me?" Shackfield bellowed.

"You'd started to answer that question yourself. Tell me, when we get out, will we still have a job at one of your mills?" Elizabeth asked.

"Look, Lizzie, why do you always dump your woes on me? I don't control the damn markets! *They* dictate whether or not you can have a job! My hands are tied! I can't march into parliament as you would wish to do yourself, no doubt, and demand what you want, can I? No, I'm just a merchant!"

As soon as Shackfield mentioned parliament, Lizzie in that moment understood Shackfield knew what she was. She had been exposed. Everyone there knew. But she didn't care. Time was now short.

"Can't you? How about you speak up for us to your mates? You know, the ones on the select committee? Or your *friends* in parliament? You could've been great you know..."

"What, I don't have a damn clue what you're talking about! How dare you insinuate..." but Shackfield was drowned out by the sound of screams from outside.

Some moved to the window. An anxious huddle developed as the sole remaining divide was one of life and death.

Clarence, Mary, Bertha and everyone from the meeting, including Sam and Joe, ran all the way to Gaynor Street, to the main entrance of the mill. They joined the crowd which had formed on the street. The whole town had assembled in alarm.

"What happened?" Bertha asked.

"A loom caught fire apparently," someone answered.

"Oh no," Bertha shrieked.

"We think they're all trapped on the third floor. We hear the fire started on the ground floor but spread to the first. And it'll be too hot for them to get to the second," someone else explained.

"Aye, and all the gates are locked!" another added.

Clarence looked around, something brewing in his mind. He took Mary aside.

"Mary, is the town well still in operation?"

"Not really," she replied, distressed by the futility of it all.

"All right, listen. I am going to retire into the darkness. Just try to keep everyone as calm as thou canst. Oh, and it shall be helpful to pray. See if thou canst get something going," he instructed.

"Oh, Clarence," Mary exclaimed, rolling her eyes.

Nodding to her, he made his way into the safe, anonymous darkness of the ginnels. Mary turned to the crowd.

"Reet, folks…" she said with her loudest, most commanding voice. Some of the folk assembled turned to the town's local hero.

Many others were clinging to buckets of water brought from the brook at Castle Hill.

Back up in Top Hat, both workers and overseers were now at a window, staring down in terror. Shackfield remembered his recent pact with Hulton. Hulton had given him assurances that the indiscretions of his workers could be savagely dealt with, in exchange for information on the knight who had recently attacked a special constable of Manchester. Hulton hadn't told him how his wayward workers would be dealt with, but Shackfield was beginning to regret the pact he'd made with him. Shackfield's wishes were now coming true thanks to an exploded loom — and taking him with them.

Clarence had backed off into the safe anonymity of the shadows on the other side of the street, which the terraces cast. He looked up and surveyed the roaring, angry fire. He entered his second sight and saw that it was indeed dominating the first floor. Checking the rest of the mill, he also came to see that everyone was grouped together on the third floor in an agitated huddle. Exiting his second sight briefly, he pondered the possibility which had arisen in his mind ever since he had left *The Phoenix* and saw the fire. Closing his eyes, he prayed he had enough strength to summon that possibility in his mind. He wasn't even sure whether his second sight's capabilities extended as far as he needed tonight. So he prayed.

"Dear Lord, for the sake of my people trapped inside this mill tonight, please grant my endeavour success. For although I may not be their lord any more, they art still my people. And for tragedy to happen would be a wicked cruelty. Lord, please lend me thy power here tonight. Amen."

From there he went back into his second sight and remembered one of its marvels. It was the ability to orchestrate the mixing of the mist and darkness which descended on the town. He had strayed away from this particular ability though, given that he felt it wrong to interfere with what was natural. But now he made his prayer. He had asked not just for God's approval, but his support as well. So now, in the midst of his second sight, he looked up towards the clouds. There were few about, so he had to fix his focus on one of them in particular. Then, he reached out through his second sight, towards this cloud.

He spoke, "Over to Top Hat, dear friend, over to Top Hat," over and over again in a series of tender whispers.

Outside, the fire intensified, shooting out across the yard. Folk screamed. Mary paused in amongst the small group of folk she had managed to recruit to prayer. She felt questionable of Clarence. However, she noticed that everyone had remained deep in prayer. The weavers, the spinners, the shopkeepers and the artisans. She was impressed and felt inspired to carry on herself.

Slowly but surely, the cloud began to move, despite the lack of wind that night, toward the mill. It crept towards them like a shy animal, like the steadily encroaching movement of a trebuchet. Clarence repeated his whispers over and over again, with patient tone. Outside of his second sight, no one noticed the cloud as it came to rest directly over the mill. Clarence nodded in gratitude.

Then he changed his uttering to, "Become a great cloud, swelling with thy product."

Outside of Clarence's serene second sight, folk screamed in terror and desperation as they heard the fire roar up to the second floor, one below where all in the mill were gathered. Debates raged within the crowd about what could be done. Someone had fetched an axe for the gates and folk were chasing to the brook to get more water. Again, with the progress of slow degrees, the cloud padded out. Bigger and bigger it grew, until it was twice its original size. And it now occupied a brooding, swelling presence in the sky above the mill. It was eager to release something. Nodding with thanks again, Clarence opened his eyes. As he unclasped his hand, a great torrent of rain then fell from the cloud, absolutely drenching the mill and shocking those who had been standing around it with the abruptness of its arrival. The volume of rain was like nothing anyone had seen before in that town, and rain was something they were well acquainted with.

The fire seemed disturbed by the way it reacted to the rain. The infinite little pellets overpowered it, and beat it down relentlessly. The fire soon shrank in size, and it was no time before it was contained just within the mill itself. Closing his eyes, Clarence returned to his second sight.

"Strike with intelligence my friend. To where it is required" was Clarence's final command.

The cloud responded almost immediately. It had become hooked on the sensation which Clarence's prayers provided. Its downpour increased, but this time the rain seeped rapidly into the cracks of the mill's lower floors. Instead of falling randomly, it found its way into the mill any which way it could, gushing into it at speed. It moved as if seeking out where the flames were, ripping them down. All three floors affected by the fire were deeply saturated for around five minutes. The flames resisted with arrogance, but their efforts were soon stifled. When the five minutes had expired, each and every one of the flames had been snuffed. The mill, leading up to the second floor was now dripping wet. The abnormality of the rain had caused the crowd to gaze on in absolute shock, the way it had gone straight to the flames. The people assembled had turned from being horrified to captivated.

Of course, the crowd became jubilant. Relief, gratitude and joy reached a feverish tumult within them. Too preoccupied with their friends' and families' deliverance, they hadn't noticed the irregular behaviour of the cloud itself which had now shrunken and retreated back towards its original position in the sky. They had been preoccupied with its effect. Mary and her group finished praying. They stared towards the mill, astonished.

It was impossible to hear their words but the movements of their lips revealed one sentence: "Thank you, God".

Clarence opened his eyes, sighed deeply and left his second sight. He could feel his ghostly energy depleted. He was much less dense. He found it hard to increase his volume. He didn't feel tired and knew he didn't need to sleep, but he felt less capable of doing something significant now. He felt like going back to orb form. The prayer he had just made had taxed his constitution. Looking to the cloud responsible for his people's deliverance, he bowed and thanked it from the bottom of his heart. It was then, albeit with steady progression, that the folk who had been trapped came pouring out of the mill. They didn't let the puddles and the muck register as they ran across the yard to where folk were gathered, clamouring in front of the gate. Shackfield himself unlocked the gate.

Two streams of people collided to embrace their loved ones, friends and neighbours without even noticing Shackfield was there. He was relieved and even his wife had begun to look on him with some pride again. Clarence took stock from the fact that he had helped prevent tragedy. But what left him reeling in silent amazement was his collaboration with nature to do this. One on a greater scale than simply mixing darkness and fog. Now he had concern about his own abilities. Right then, he felt unable somehow to carry on appearing in full-body form. Then he was approached by Mary, who proudly linked him.

"What did you do, Clarence?" she asked.

"I shall explain what *we* did," was his only reply.

They marched, along with everyone else, to the square. Its space for revelling would come in handy. As would *The Phoenix* for tonics to calm the nerves!

As the crowd entered the town square, bound for the taverns, Mary looked Clarence squarely in the eye.

"I have faith in you, Clarence. But I never thought you could do anything like that," she said, the admiration pouring from her.

"As a spirit I am able to collaborate with the Lord. And with the elements," he smiled.

Mary was quite in awe.

"I want to see more of this. I want to be there with you when you rest again. 'Cause if there's more like that, which involves helping folk like, then you've got me."

Clarence was unsure of Mary's meaning. But he didn't respond at first, given his thought that Mary meant something courtly.

"I've changed me' mind about Lancaster. What an adventure!"

Clarence lit up, the boldness of his spirithood returning.

"Mary, my dear, I am not sure just how to express my thanks," he said, oozing gratitude.

Mary happily hugged Clarence. He knew he was going to Lancaster, and felt well because of it. He felt even better because now, two close friends would be with him.

Chapter Eighteen

The following morning in the town square, a few ale stains adorned the cobbles. It was a weekday, but it didn't feel at all like one. Today felt more like wakes week, a festival or a Sunday. And this feeling was no more prevalent than in the mind of Mary, as she popped her head out of a ginnel to inspect the scene. The much lighter hum of the other mills, the stillness in the square, the astounding lack of fog, and the brilliant blueness of the sky all conspired to make this day feel quite unreal, and unique. Mary had just come from Gaynor Street, where Top Hat had been shut. Visible were the faintest of smoke trails, and the padlocks and chains had returned, as if the mill was embarrassed to be seen. She and Bertha returned to see what was left of it. They saw massive dark singes where the fire had been. Many of those who worked at Top Hat were enjoying rare lie-ins as there were, of course, no jobs for them that day. Despite their escapes from the fire, they knew they would have to seek employment elsewhere, unless Shackfield were to offer them new jobs in his other mills. The loss, albeit temporary, of Top Hat would be felt. By him and by the whole town. For many, last night would carry feelings mounted on both edges of the proverbial sword. Mary had heard some good stories about last night's events though. She knew folk were talking about it, and morale in the town was on an upsurge, amongst everyone. She remembered Clarence's fabulous skill in saving them from the fire. And to her, he could be a diplomat and a warrior at the same time. Then she remembered the prayer group she had got going and felt a flutter of pride at it. She knew that it had lent to Clarence what he had needed to accomplish what only someone in his position could. It was as if he had petitioned nature, and won its support in saving lives. It was time to go home and pack her things. Her sisters worked in different mills and her mother would be out on the fringes of town, swapping ornaments she'd made with produce from farmers. So she would have time to slip away alone, and leave a note.

Back in her family's rooms, Mary opened her travelling bag and shovelled in all her clothes from her box. Then came her bow, quiver and arrows. Finally a spare pair of clogs. She decided not to take any books her father had left her as they were of sentimental value and would be safer at home. However, she did read a description of Lancaster in one of them before she left:

The county town, Lancaster is one of only a few ancient towns still standing in the county. Home to the great castle, base of the House of Lancaster during the Wars of the Roses, the town has seen many a great battle. Now the county's main judicial centre, it has a reputation for resolute justice.

Mary had heard all about Lancaster being the 'Hanging Town', and she knew what she was walking into. But equally, she was excited reading that Lancaster was still quite a medieval place. She wanted to see what her county had been like before industry. And she was sure that Lancaster would give her a glimpse of the ancient genesis that her county had been originally crafted with. She imagined a castle like Darkleigh's but bigger and more 'grand'.

Finally ready to go, Mary picked up her bag and turned to the corner where the door that led to the steps was, only to be confronted abruptly by her mother.

"Where are you shooting off to, lass?" Georgina asked her with suppressing tone.

Mary surrendered the truth; it was her mother after all was said and done.

"I'm going to Lancaster, Mam."

"Oh, you're going to Lancaster, are you?" Georgina said rhetorically.

Mary nodded. Georgina then let out the loudest, most ridiculing laugh Mary had ever heard. She knew that she would have to gather every determined fibre she had within her, right now.

"Reet, and you're going on your own, are you?"

"Oh no, definitely not. I'm going with a friend."

"Who's this friend?"

"Max Walmsley."

"Do I know this Max Walmsley?" Georgina asked with a raised

eyebrow.

"No, Mum, you don't."

This volley of questions Mary knew was borne out of her mother's desire to protect her, but it didn't stop Mary feeling that she was being put down.

"You know, love, there's a name for young women who take up with blokes they hardly know," Georgina said with mocking disbelief.

"Oh no, it's not like that, Mum. He's just a friend and I've known him for about three months now."

"Three months!" Georgina exclaimed. "So you don't *know* him then, do you?"

"Aye, Mum, I believe I know him enough to trust him."

"Trust him, with what?" Georgina asked with greater suspicion. "I can see your bag's packed, so you're definitely serious, aren't you? I just can't believe you're even thinking about leaving us like this! It's beyond daft!"

Mary let her mind tumble for a few moments, hoping she would find words in its fall. Then, much to her surprise and relief, they came.

"Mum, Max is involved with the Reform movement," she said, her voice sounding like she was owning up. "He was at the meeting last night and he told me that he's off to Lancaster to persuade the authorities up there to listen to Reform. He's a very clever bloke, Mum; if you'd have just heard the way he said he'd explain it to them, you'd have loved it. He reckons if we can get the support of the county on our side, then more folk in power will listen to us. They're our people, Mum, despite all their brass. They'll be surely interested in what we want, which is fair. Believe me, Mum," Mary pleaded.

"Lass, that's no place for you. Aye, I'm reet proud when you do what you can for them, but this is going too far."

"Why, Mum, 'cause I'm a woman?" Mary said with some anger.

"Aye!" Georgina confirmed.

"It's all men's work, is it? Trying to make sure we can live as long as we can? Trying to make sure that one day we'll go to work and not come home with diseases? Trying to make sure that we're recognised by the government as people with real talents and personalities, not as performing peasants!" Mary protested.

"Yes, love. Because it's too dangerous for women. You can't hold your own in circles like that."

Mary's face creased with anger at that notion.

"Mum, I'll be with Max. He'll take good care of me."

"I'd like to meet this Max, stealing you away like you were some sort of whore," Georgina said venomously.

"He's not like that, Mum. I might not be as old as you, but I'm a damn good judge of character. And he is *not* that sort, in fact, he's the opposite."

Georgina was speechless.

"Remember Dad, Mum," Mary told her.

Georgina was confused.

"Mary, lass, you're staying here. I don't know what's given you this silly idea. Maybe it's been you slipping away with them books your father left you. Enjoyed reading them with this Max fella? We've noticed, you know."

Mary's shoulders sagged.

"And if your father was here he'd back me up to the hilt," Georgina added.

Mary was cornered. What did she say to her mother now, a person she loved with passion, but who was trying to stop her great adventure? It so happened though that then a mysterious figure from the past materialised in the room. At first, Mary thought it was Clarence and was bewildered. But then the black silhouette assumed a shape familiar to them. Georgina watched in disbelief as the silhouette formed. Mary was conditioned to this by now. Georgina was utterly confused but not at all scared. Then Mary recognised it from that time in the mill not so long ago when she'd been approached by a nasty overseer, just before she'd met Clarence. Mary, by now, knew it was a spirit. They both recognised the feelings that this spirit was bringing on. Feelings of being loved and security. Mary knew who it was and moved close to Georgina. Georgina wanted to say who it was but couldn't.

So Mary said, "Mum, it's Dad."

At that exact point, the silhouette looked up, straight at Mary. The blackness of his form disappeared and standing there was indeed Frank, Georgina's late husband and Mary's late father.

"Hey up, there!" Frank cried jovially, as he had done in life.

Georgina couldn't bring herself to speak. Her hands were cupped over her mouth and tears came streaming down. Mary held her comfortingly.

"Hey up, Dad!" Mary greeted with a huge smile. "I knew it was you, thanks for that spot of help at the mill" Mary said brightly.

Frank nodded.

"No problem, lass," he said in his characteristically down-to-earth manner.

He moved closer.

"By heck, is this real?" asked Georgina, wiping tears from her eyes.

"Of course it is. Never left you," Frank confirmed, taking his wife's hands.

Georgina gave her husband an astonished hug.

"It's good to see you and all," Frank returned.

"Ooh, Frank, there's so much I want to tell you," Georgina cried.

"And you will, love, all in good time," Frank said with a mild, reassuring tone. "But one thing I want you to know now is that Mary's safe where she's going. And I know you don't know this young fella Max she's going with, but believe me, I can vouch for him. She's in reet good hands."

Georgina's tears stopped as she looked her husband in the eye and found his legendary sincerity.

"Aye, they've got an important job to do up there, and they'll do reet well. Promise."

Georgina said nothing but eventually nodded. The three of them enjoyed a good few minutes together. Both Georgina and Mary felt the denseness which made up Frank's spirit. It had a renewing quality which afterwards made Georgina feel not only safe but happy too. Frank explained that it was time for him to go, but promised he'd be back again soon to speak to Georgina. Mary gave her mother a bag of coins she had collected to help keep them firmly in their rooms till she returned home. Handing her key over, Mary asked Georgina to give her sisters her love. She then left the home she had known all her life, content that her mum and sisters had peace of mind. So did she.

Back in the square, Mary was greeted by Bertha and Clarence.

"Oh, Mary, there you are. Max tells me you two are off to Lancaster. You're going to show them big-wigs what for, aren't you?" she said.

"Damn right," Mary said with conviction.

Clarence smiled.

"I'm so glad, but, by heck, I'm going to miss you," Bertha inevitably added.

"Course you are, just natural, isn't it?" Mary replied, hugging her friend.

"But I'm made up you're doing this, so get on before I start crying," she quipped.

Mary laughed. "Oh, before I go, any word from Shackfield?"

"Well, his wife spoke to us all outside the gates of Top Hat today."

"His wife?" Mary queried, raising an eyebrow.

"Aye, he weren't there, but she were. I think he knows his wife'll have the better effect on folk. Clara her name is. She says they want to get some sort of relief fund going. To keep us all aloft before the mill gets re-opened. Aye, she's a good woman, she is. Something's told me that about her ever since she started being seen with him. At first I thought she were just his brassy trophy, but everything he isn't, she seems to be. He doesn't know how flaming lucky he is. She were warmly received."

"Typical though, isn't it? Him not being there. When the rot sets in, they're nowhere to be seen," Mary commented.

"Aye. God, it were scary after though, wasn't it, last night? But then it were like a miracle happened!"

Clarence remained a picture of focus, knowing something Bertha didn't.

"Aye, it were amazing," Mary agreed, noticing Clarence's silence on the subject.

"Any road, best let you get off," Bertha said.

She hugged Mary again, and waved to Clarence who returned with a warm smile.

From half way across the square, she turned back and shouted, "Ecky thump, Mary, I'll be thinking of you. We all will! Take care up there, you hear!"

Bertha turned back to her walk, almost in affectionate tears. Mary waved, blowing a kiss at her old friend.

"Love you, Bertha!" she cried.

"Thank thou so much for this, Mary. It means a great deal to me. And thou shall be safe with me, I promise. And so shall the town," Clarence said, gesturing to a standard flying atop the Guildhouse.

Mary looked round and saw it carried Clarence's family crest.

"When I lived, it meant no one, no other noble could enter our lands without our permission," he told her.

Mary just was completely enchanted. Even with just a standard for proof, she believed fully that Clarence's words were true. Then from out of a ginnel, there trotted Azlight. Greeting her affectionately, Mary and Clarence mounted her and quietly made their way out of town, turning for the North Road.

Chapter Nineteen

Mary couldn't remember most of the journey up to Lancaster. She and Clarence rarely spoke on it. He was too busy studying the countryside and Azlight's unholy speed blurred the greenery around them. Mary was grateful and pleasantly intrigued by the fact that not once did she feel sick because of this. Clarence, despite his mind's near lock on where they were going, still connected with Mary at various points throughout the journey, making sure she was secure. One thing Mary did remember was the stop they made in the Forest of Bowland. At that point, they were far from home, for sure, but still far from famed Lancaster. They had stopped by a brook, which riddled along pleasantly through the forest, before retreating to the redeeming shade of a long tree line.

"I think we shall camp here for the night," announced Clarence.

He then dismounted Azlight and helped Mary follow suit. Then, with some tender words whispered in her ear, Azlight's eyes drooped and she gradually faded until she became once more a tiny orb, resting on the grass by the nearest tree. Clarence stared after her, with the thoughtfulness of a father watching his children retire to bed.

"I thought thou must be tired, Mary," he explained.

"Oh aye, I am," she yawned.

Clarence worked out that for someone living, travelling aboard a spirit horse had an obvious effect.

"Well, let's get thy bedding out and find thee something to eat," were his next words.

"Aren't you going to have something with me?" Mary asked.

"No, I am afraid not. I hath no need of food, being a spirit," Clarence subtly reminded her.

"Oh aye, sorry, I forgot," Mary said promptly, a little embarrassed. "Just habit."

Clarence smiled a forgiving smile.

"Not to worry, my dear."

Mary reached inside her bags she had unloaded from Azlight. Out she took some bedding, and to Clarence's amazement, some bread and a pie.

"I see thou hath travelled prepared," he said.

"Ooh aye, no hunting needed for me," Mary quipped.

It took Clarence a second before he felt he could laugh.

Under the trees, Mary ate while Clarence talked about the many festivals that he had attended and presided over in his lifetime. The rich, lovely flavour of the food blended with Mary's wonder at having the colourful past of her home town related. For a while, she forgot why they were actually there. The sun set was now down over the horizon, and Mary experienced a fine feeling of peace swell within her. This gave her the courage to ask Clarence something they had only hitherto skirted around.

"Clarence," she began, "I'll understand if you don't want to talk about this but is it true what they say about how you... died?"

Clarence looked over to her. At last she had finally asked.

"Well, I think it's you they mean," Mary added.

"What hath thou heard about it?" he questioned in turn.

"Well, the legend says that you made a heroic last stand before your enemies burnt your castle. You..." Mary hesitated with regret at telling a friend what she thought was his own tragic story. "It says you put up a really good fight but were killed in the battle, taking lots of your enemies with you. It says the sky rained fire that day."

Clarence laughed at the last detail. Mary didn't know whether to be embarrassed or relieved. The facts of that day had been twisted by someone into a much lighter metaphor. In that moment, it was as if he was staring down a long tunnel through history.

"Well, there was no fire rain, I am afraid, Mary dear. That was added, I am sure, by colourful bards!"

They shared a laugh at this.

"Does thy legend give any more details, for instance who I was fighting with and why? Who was there with me?"

Mary shook her head.

"I think it just said you were being attacked by a jealous enemy," she offered.

Clarence laughed again at that.

"Yes, that part is at least correct," he confirmed.

Mary's eyes widened, feeling that she was on the brink of the truth being opened to her and only her.

"Canst thou remember any other details from the legend at all?" he asked her next.

"Ooh aye. It says you and the garrison at the castle had to hold off about a thousand of your enemy's warriors," Mary added with some renewed enthusiasm at the telling of a story.

Clarence laughed once again, this time with a tone of ridicule. Mary frowned, confused.

"Well, my dear, I think the kind bard who sung that legend was aggrandising me somewhat there!"

Mary realised that the version of the story she had heard was stretching the truth. She rolled her eyes in realisation.

"So do you want to talk about it?" Mary asked sensitively.

Clarence paused.

"With thee, Mary, yes. Thou hath been a great friend to me in my condition and I would like thou to know the truth."

Mary fixed an understanding gaze on him. When he was ready, he began.

"Well, some of the story thou hath heard is true. Indeed I was attacked by a jealous enemy, savage in his character and the way he went about all aspects of his life and business. Indeed some of us and I did make a last stand."

Clarence looked ahead of him, into the water of the brook, with hollow, melancholy eyes.

"The story of how I came to die begins with the story of my greatest triumph. One which I thought would end my family's great mission."

Mary felt bad. She knew he'd be unearthing something extremely saddening for him. Maybe sensing this, Clarence smiled to put her at ease.

"Thou art familiar with the wonderful and unique relationship my family enjoyed with our tenants, art thou not?"

Mary nodded.

"Well, when my parents passed away in 1416, I became lord of the manor when I was twenty-two. And being gullible I wanted to make the biggest impact I could in the shortest time. So, I set about freeing *everyone* in our lands. Continuing my father's practice. I hath mentioned this before, hath I not?"

Mary again nodded.

"Well, as I'm sure thou know already, there were many lords who thought of their tenants and lesser nobles not as people but as objects to be used in their quest for power and influence. Such nobles looked upon us as peculiar for the way we dealt with *all* people. One such was a character called Lord Dalbern. He was a noble, but only in name."

"Reet, he were a baddie, I take it?" Mary asked.

"Dalbern was the most evil nobleman in England at that time. His greed was notorious. Power, status, prestige. All those grand trappings he desired. And he would do anything to seize them. He was the nemesis of our family given that he believed that all those beneath him were there to be used, abused and then disposed of."

"Sounds like nowt's changed," Mary commented cynically.

"Yes indeed," Clarence scoffed.

"Dalbern wasn't anything new. Neither are the likes of Nadin or most of the mill-owners from what I hath seen. But he was the wicked figure of his age. He once lined six women up on the gallows, raping them first and then hanging them, the scum bag. Used to ransack vills for whatever reason he thought right. Burnt towns, murdered rivals. Thou name the crime, he was guilty of it. Kept getting away though because of his position."

Mary's face turned from horror to anger.

"Did someone do something about him?" she inquired.

"Yes. My family. We put him down time after time after time. We asked the king to intervene on several occasions, but Dalbern was extremely crafty and left little evidence. He did end up in court a few times, but his underlings threatened the judges. I remember once I was called as a witness at one of his trials, but he escaped. His thugs smashed the window with a catapult, allowing him to flee. And, of course, there was his family influence."

"Aye, nowt's definitely changed on that score," Mary said again.

"Yes. Dalbern was just a plain wicked character. The one of his age.

But we were able to halt his vile activity. Which meant that we became rivals. And when we defeated the bulk of his forces, he knew his days were numbered. After that, he chased me all over England until I found my way home and ordered my manor to be evacuated. So the people were safe but I knew that he would arrive soon. And arrive he did, with around sixty, not a thousand!"

Clarence paused to smile at this point. Mary returned it somewhat. "He wanted revenge so we picked off his warriors and I fought him to the death. And I won, but the castle collapsed on us after his forces had laid siege to it."

"Oh no, and that's what killed you?" Mary said with remorse.

"I am glad it did, my dear. I had to win. I had to make sure, terrible as it sounds, that Dalbern died. For if he had survived our little duel, then he would hath surely escaped and raised another large force to pursue our people. So I was glad we went down together. I may hath sacrificed, but I did so in the knowledge of reward in heaven, and that Dalbern would be defeated once and for all."

Clarence concluded that story to a Mary who was now open-mouthed and staring into the growing darkness out in the trough. Mary let the pause settle before asking her next question.

"Why are you going to Lancaster?"

"Because my old friend Michael, the rector of St. Darren's in my day, told me to. It sounds like there I shall find peace."

Then Mary remembered Clarence had mentioned communing with an old friend.

"The one who told you to claim what was yours?"

Clarence nodded.

"Well, can't he come with us and help you?"

Clarence shook his head this time.

"Alas, for him it doth not work like that. My instinct regarding his spirit is that, unlike myself, he is only permitted to appear on the Earth for a short space of time. God hath appointed his mission that way. As I say, he comes and goes."

Mary's shock compounded. All she could do was raise her eyebrows in tandem acknowledgment of something which was for her getting more and more unbelievably astounding.

"Do you know what's going to happen when you get there?"

Mary's new question was invasive. Clarence hesitated slightly before replying.

"I do… I do not know, I am afraid. But I know that I shall find some means, any means which shall enable me to sleep again. Michael hath directed, and so I shall find what I am looking for."

Clarence's tone picked up with courage there. For a few minutes, they just looked out at the darkening trough, the lushness of its greenery becoming dense darkness as daylight gave way to the elegant blanket of night.

"I'm sorry you had to go through that," Mary said at last.

Clarence turned to her. He didn't feel like admitting it, but he was touched. It was a genuine piece of sympathy that he hadn't received from someone close to him for what he now knew was four centuries. Mary had been a friend for a while but this had landed like a trinket out of the sky. Smiling at her, he felt emboldened to be inquisitive with her in kind.

"I knew that I wouldst lose everything that day, with Dalbern. But at the same time, I knew I wouldst win. Mary, my dear, hath thou ever lost something that meant the world to thee?"

Mary felt saddened by that question, but she nevertheless answered.

"Aye, I have. It were me' dad. He went when I were about six. I can't remember much of it, but me' mother says me and me' sisters cried for close on a day when it happened. But having said that, I've got a lot of memories of me' father. Good memories. Ones which sparkle like jewels in your mind. And I know he's doing some good now."

Mary paused thoughtfully with that last point, remembering the encounter she'd had before starting the journey. "You know he were the one who got me doing archery?"

Clarence was impressed.

"Really?" he said, excitedly.

"Aye, I remember going to the club with him for the first time. We used to go to the fringes of the woods on Castle Hill to practice. Little did I know, eh?"

Clarence smiled as Mary gazed happily into the darkness.

"Thy father sounds like a truly inspirational man."

Nodding, Mary said, "Aye, he were."

The flowing flavour of reminiscence relaxed them both to sleep that night, having felt the bond of mutual trust and favour between them grow even stronger. It was good timing, as in Lancaster they would need it.

Chapter Twenty

Walking through the corridors of William Hulton's Mount Street residence, Joe Nadin maintained his customary pretence of brooding anger. He had an angry frown, his demeanour sloped as if he couldn't care less. The great thug who proudly wore the licence of King George was, however, underneath outward impressions, quaking with fear. For today, he was going to face his political master again. He was though, taking quiet pride in the fact that he was managing to supress this fear so well (years of practice). When he reached the elaborate door where he knew Hulton would be expecting him, he stopped, gathered himself, and the hint of vulnerability in his eye faded as he prepared to 'go on stage'.

Knocking on the door, Hulton's voice came, "Come."

Nadin, with as much of an air of grace as he could manage, opened the door, entered and closed it behind him.

Turning to face his master, he said, "sir" leaving Hulton to speak first.

Unmoved, Hulton motioned him further in, and Nadin came to a respectful stance a few feet away, hands behind back as if awaiting orders.

"Nadin, I trust you are well?" Hulton began.

"Not too shaken, sir," Nadin coolly replied.

Hulton laughed somewhat.

"Very good, Deputy Chief Constable. Yes, the reason I needed to speak to you today was to inform you that there has been a change of plan regarding the situation with Darkleigh," Hulton said, moving towards the window and pouring himself a brandy.

Nadin's heavy-set features sagged.

"Sir?" he responded, the disappointment evident in his voice.

Turning around to face him from the window, Hulton seemed sympathetic, given that he knew Nadin, of all men, had been genuinely scared by what he had recently experienced in the town.

"Yes, I'm afraid the extra resources I allowed you are now having to be withdrawn."

"B-but, sir, please. I haven't even had a chance to use them yet," Nadin appealed.

"Oh no, no, Nadin. Do not worry. It is not because of discontent with you at all. No, no. Come, come," Hulton said, motioning him towards the window.

Nadin followed with haste, still anxious.

"Nadin. My scouts in that odious town have reported to me some very strange goings-on there. Similar incidents to what you reported. Ones which occurred after you reported what proved to be the first. So fear not. I am wholly assured of the courage and capabilities of our greatest asset in the field," Hulton explained, raising his glass to a Nadin quivering with grateful relief.

"Yes, aside from strange noises, and running into objects where there should be none in the mills, there was very recently an incident whereby a cloud of rain put out a large, raging fire. It was reported that the rain moved with the intelligence only reserved for human beings, as we would understand it, to the source of the fire, having jettisoned its usual character of random falling."

By now, Nadin was bamboozled. Hulton didn't give it away, but he felt amused because of it.

"My guess is that this boggart-come-knight you had an unfortunate encounter with is the source of this strange activity. Which is why I think it is time, Nadin, we reasoned that our jurisdictions as select committee chair and deputy chief constable must end here, and that the office of another, more capable fellow must assume this task forthwith. One who is more versed and powerful in dealing with these matters."

Nadin was still puzzled.

"*We* can cause any mortal man to retreat splendidly in fear. However, these are only men. Not the creatures that oppose heaven. The type you and others have reported in Darkleigh."

Nadin returned to relief.

"From now on, Nadin, all expeditions to Darkleigh are terminated until I authorise otherwise. That will be all," Hulton commanded.

"Sir," Nadin said as he exited the room.

When Nadin had left, there came another knock on the door.

"Come," Hulton said.

In came a servant. Hulton motioned him over.

"Get me the Reverend Ethelstone," Hulton said in a low voice.

The servant nodded and left.

Chapter Twenty-One

As they left the Forest of Bowland, the three of them thundered together towards Lancaster. Traversing a rolling hill, they found themselves charging across a moor. As the moor dipped the town came vividly into view in the near distance. As it did, Mary set alight inside. For she could see, perched on a hill at the crown of the town, the famous castle which she had heard so much about, good and bad. Its silhouette was quite stark, and even from the distance they were at she could make out a flag fluttering in the wind. Next to it on the hill, she noticed a large church. That seemed unusual compared to what she had been used to in Darkleigh, with its two separate hills for church and castle, respectively. For Mary, even though she knew it existed, there was something quite fabled and romantic about the castle, and actually seeing it for the first time was a visceral experience. Desire ignited. She wanted to get closer. She'd heard about all the grisly things that went on there, but despite them, there was something massively, strangely compelling about this one building that dominated the skyline. It was there the earls of Lancaster had lived and had been the base of the House of Lancaster during the Wars of the Roses (or so she had been led to believe). Oh, what great spectacles Lancaster must have seen. But, as well in Mary's mind, it represented the genesis of her whole county. This was the source of her county. This is where it was founded. She thought that every town in her county must surely have a little piece of Lancaster's essence embedded in it somewhere. And here it remained today, at the top of the shire, a real living relic of Lancashire's medieval past, amongst a county which had become absorbed in the deep brown robes of industry. The town was becoming enshrined this way, as a relic of yesteryear, in Mary's mind. In that moment she made the decision that just coming to Lancaster had been a good idea, something she was glad she had done. But first and foremost, she wanted to assist her friend until he found peace. As they approached the outskirts of the town, they passed through a village where the moderate breeze abated; the wind they'd felt just a few minutes ago didn't seem to be effecting the trees there, nor the tavern sign. In fact, there was an odd stillness to the place. Not only were the trees still, but the whole village was devoid of movement, and activity. Not a soul was about. The village just stared statically at them, waiting for them to pass through. Clarence remembered where they were. To the east of the village, they passed some grassy steeps topped by a few scant wooden remains. He didn't bother telling Mary where they were or what the steeps had been. Possibly even what they still were. But to him the broken wood on top of the steeps suggested they had relinquished the role he had once known them to fulfil.

Out of that village they came and into the fringes of the town where Mary was impressed again by a cute assortment of cottages, some thatched, some with slate roofs. Cue her vague memories of thatched cottages in Darkleigh. And, of course, she was tickled to see the roads and ginnels lined with a sea of infinite cobbles. They were different, larger and rounder than what she was used to in Darkleigh. But nevertheless, they warmed her heart as a link between her home town and her county town. Clarence spotted an inn about five hundred yards along the road and slowed Azlight to a jogging pace, taking to the ginnels. Bringing her to a stop, they dismounted Azlight and with a gentle stroke from Clarence, she again faded into a tiny orb, coming to rest on Clarence's shoulder. Clarence explained to Mary that staying on the outskirts would suit their purpose better as it would be a quiet place for both of them to retreat to, if something monumental were to happen in the town. He and Mary then hatched a story as they walked hand in hand to the inn called *The Deft Swan* — they would be a newly married couple from the countryside. The inn-keeper raised an eyebrow as Mary handed over the money, which was enough for a stay of two nights. Their room was long and relatively narrow, but it was a different kind of room to what Mary had encountered before in her life and she instantly liked it.

Thanking her warmly for paying, Clarence joked that he had never had a lady of the manor, and now he knew why. "I could not find one kind enough!" They both roared with laughter.

After Mary had unpacked and Clarence set his armour down, they noticed something out of the window. Dribs and drabs of folk were walking briskly, some apprehensively, in the same direction towards the town. Clarence noticed the looks on their faces; some of them were alight with excitement, others wore ominous frowns. This intrigued him and he alerted Mary.

"Mary," he said, "hath thou any idea what this could be?"

Mary looked out of the window.

"Probably a hanging. Not a big one though, there'd be more people," she estimated.

"There are quite a few now," Clarence commented. "Let us see more," were his next words.

Mary rolled her eyes. They slipped out of their room and locked the door. Out of the tavern and onto the street they went, joining the trickles of folk inconspicuously. Focusing on the trail of folk meant that they didn't notice the sumptuous low cottages become tall, narrow sandy-brown terraces, the like of which neither Mary nor Clarence had seen before. They just followed the crowds. Clarence didn't bother to use his second sight. He knew if there was a hanging on, then it must be so for a good reason. He had seen his fair share of hangings in his day. They were usually for serious crimes. This would surely be no different. He had always looked on with great regret at hangings, powerless to stop them, when they had been necessary, same as any violent punishment. But he also knew the value of trusting the judiciary. After a short while walking, they came to a place Clarence recognised. Market Street, in Lancaster. And it still had the well in its centre, as it had all those centuries ago. This delighted Clarence, but it was short-lived as he noticed that Market Street was enclosed by a building new to him. It was not as wide-open a space as it had once been. He could see into the building at ground level. There was something of a market going on.

From within, someone shouted, "Pound of cheese, half price for today's hanging."

Raising an eyebrow, Clarence snorted at such perversity. That was something new. In his time, no trader would have enthusiastically announced that their produce was cheaper because it was a hanging day. On they went. Crossing over where three streets intersected, the crowd made a sharp right turn at the bottom of a hill. Looking up, Clarence saw the great castle of Lancaster, sitting as it always had done atop its hill.

Just seeing it again made him feel dizzy. He didn't know why. It had been the sight of many a legal exchange between him and the crown, and the scene of various trials which he had been a juror at. Perhaps it was the sight of a castle still complete, unlike the dilapidated state of his own. Seeing a castle still set so mightily in this modern world was somehow comforting for him. He looked at Mary. She was mildly trembling with awe. For her, the day was like a living ballad. Following the crowd, they skirted round the castle, closer to the ring of recently built terraces which surrounded it. As they reached the back of the castle, Mary and Clarence spotted a smooth, sloping piece of land which descended down from the Priory church to where the castle was. The crowd was at its most dense close to the castle, with massed ranks of folk steadily accumulating, and filling the space provided by the slope between castle and Priory. Mary and Clarence turned to face the back of the castle. Yes, definitely a hanging. The gallows were clearly visible, in a space between a tower and a curtain wall. Above it was the beam and the noose, dangling forebodingly. At various points on this natural concourse, there were four bored red coats. Clarence couldn't remember any hangings taking place actually *at* the castle, though. In his life, they had always been on Lancaster moor (near the village of Golgotha, the first place they had ridden through when they had exited the Forest of Bowland. But Clarence hadn't mentioned this to Mary for fear of spooking her).

"Should we stay here?" Mary asked, not wanting to witness a spectacle.

"No, not if thou dost not want to, my dear," Clarence answered.

Then he noticed a chalk board set astride from the gallows. It read 'Today's hanging: Emmanuel Grifforth of Bryn, notorious bread thief. May God have mercy on his soul'. These words instantly disturbed Clarence. Bread thief? That hadn't even been a capital offense in his life. Bread thievery was penalised with a spell in the stocks, at worst a gentle tanning. At least in his family's lands. What compounded his bad feeling about the situation were the comments he heard around him.

One bloke said, "I love a good hanging me. This one's small but it'll warm you up for the big ones. By God, they're fantastic days. You just wait till there's a murderer up there. Or when a whole host of criminals get hung together. They'll be a riot."

One woman said, "I wonder if his tongue'll spill out!" before laughing sadistically.

Others responded as Clarence and Mary did, with both sadness and disgust. Clarence felt shock creep round and grip him, wanting to set in. It succeeded in stopping him from making a move. Mary was worried. She didn't want to witness this. Then, the prisoner was led out. Massive cheers and jeers enveloped the space the crowd occupied. Clarence grasped Mary's hand.

"Follow me, my dear. Trust."

With reluctance in her eyes, Mary followed Clarence to where the crowd was at its thickest. The gaol chaplain and a magistrate followed the prisoner onto the scaffold and stood closest to the door they had all just emerged from in the tower of the castle. They put on a pretence of looking dignified. The prisoner was frightened and forlorn. Sweat dropped from his brow and when he saw the noose his eyes bulged with extreme fright. Shifting him into position was a dishevelled fellow, who Clarence guessed was the gaoler. Clarence noticed that he had a similar demeanour to Nadin. He was loutish and rude, but he hid smugly behind the gravity of his office. Clarence regarded the prisoner, Emmanuel. He felt no malice from the poor fellow. Looking back at the board, which announced his crimes, he couldn't help but question the fellow's true guilt. He then heard some folk at the front of the crowd, nearest the scaffold, remonstrating with the magistrate for mercy. Their crying pleas were obviously being ignored as the gaoler shooed them away mockingly. Clarence reasoned that they must have been Emmanuel's family. He felt helpless. He knew not what to do. Guilt began to make its blunt edge felt now as he remembered urging Mary there. Resentment at the law's evident harshness now rose in him. Looking straight at Emmanuel, he closed his eyes and entered his second sight. At first, he just saw through the scaffold and into the castle, but he brought his focus back to Emmanuel. Then pictures appeared, clear as life, so real that Clarence thought he could reach out and interact with the events going on in them. There in the pictures was Emmanuel. He was surely in his local tavern, playing the violin and enjoying a sing-a-long with friends. Their kindly looks towards him somehow told Clarence that Emmanuel was known in his locality for bringing cheer and joy to others. If that locality were to lose him, how would it fare? The image faded and was replaced by another showing Emmanuel, a woman and several children, obviously their own. Clarence was entranced by the feelings of love and affection he felt there, which emanated especially from Emmanuel. It was clear to Clarence at this point that he was a loving husband and father, as well as a beloved musician in Bryn. Then, the images changed tack. His wife and children were sitting at the table in front of the range looking drained and sad. Emmanuel looked back at them, worried. This was followed by Emmanuel enjoying his work, knelt by a horse, gently talking to it as Clarence did with Azlight, winning its trust. He put a horseshoe on splendidly and with maximum care for the animal. Both he and the horse were clearly pleased at this endeavour. Then, his gaffer approached him. Clarence couldn't make out what was said, as he couldn't see the gaffer's face. But Emmanuel's sagging features were enough to illustrate what the gaffer had to say. A quick image of Emmanuel walking away from the stables utterly downcast followed. He had evidently been laid off. The image then changed to Emmanuel crouched behind some bushes with a couple of other fellows. They were looking crafty and pleased by it, but Emmanuel was looking reluctant, tearful even, as a plan appeared to be being hatched. As the threesome emerged from behind the bushes, they eyed activity at the local market, in particular a luscious bread stall. The next image saw them all grabbing as much bread as they could. Making off, the two blokes who had been with Emmanuel got away, but Emmanuel's guilt had slowed him down, which meant that the local constable at the market was able to catch him. The next image was of him being carted off to Lancaster, his wife and children screaming for mercy. Next up, he was in the dock, trying to explain to the judge that he was deeply regretful for his crimes but that they were necessary given he and his family had to eat. The judge raised an eyebrow at this. Upon that, the images ceased, and Clarence received a strong feeling to open his eyes. Which he did. He focused on Emmanuel, who was now looking up to the skies, reciting what Clarence could tell was the Lord's Prayer. With a firm intent behind his new glare, Clarence then looked upon him with the focus of a wild animal staring down its prey. Emmanuel finished his prayer and looked out across the sea of faces, who were either dreading or impatient for what was to follow.

"You should be pleased. There's a lot turned out for just you," the gaoler snarled at him.

Then Emmanuel noticed Clarence and his rigid gaze. Emmanuel found himself suspending his dread, given he was, at first, quite confused by how powerfully Clarence had locked his eyes on his. Then he felt a streak of comfort and reassurance, even in the face of a sickly ceremonial death. Emmanuel made a half-smile at Clarence who returned with an animalistic grin. Still confused but nonetheless newly relaxed, he stood still on the scaffold and breathed easily, his whole constitution resting in neutral. The officials on the scaffold didn't seem to notice, for Emmanuel was but an entry on their documents to them. Emmanuel's family were taken by his fresh calm, reminding him that they loved him, shouting up to the scaffold. He looked down to them, with another half-smile. Then he looked into the distance.

"Hath thou got thy bow?" Clarence asked Mary.

"No, I left it at the inn," she replied.

Clarence gently fiddled about in someone else's coat pocket, with a deftness of hand that they didn't even feel.

"Here, use these instead," he said, handing her a couple of apples.

"What are these for?" she asked, slightly alarmed.

"Canst thou aim at the officials? The ragged one and the one on the far right?"

"Not the vicar?" Mary exclaimed in a whisper.

"No, not him. The other one," Clarence confirmed.

"Probably but…"

"Very good, my dear. When I cough, throw them at those two characters. I shall conduct the rest of the endeavour."

Mary didn't want to do this, but her protestations mellowed into silence, as something inside her dared her to trust Clarence again. They made their way deeper into the crowd, so they were closer, but not too close, to the scaffold. Clarence and Emmanuel exchanged views, and for a few moments, the noise of the crowd seemed to mute completely. An invisible, raw understanding bonded between them, and it was now. Clarence coughed. Mary screwed her face up into a defiant expression and threw the apples towards the gallows with a wickedly quick arm.

They both landed on the magistrate and the gaoler who exploded with surprise and anger at having been taken unawares.

"Run," Clarence whispered, and Mary ran from the crowd, pushing her way through it and running up the hill into the churchyard.

Raucous laughter rang out.

"After her!" the magistrate whaled.

The handful of red coats present sighed and two of them ran after Mary. Emmanuel twitched, not exactly having expected that. Then Clarence knelt in the forest of folk that were gathered and threw his hood on, reached under his coat and drew his sword. No one noticed as he leapt up into the air, out of the crowd and onto the scaffold. A stunned hush ran amok amongst the crowd and the officials. Then Clarence brandished his sword, as if showing it off before the crowd. This hailed a tense moment, the kind which precedes great rushes of activity. Then he set to work. Jumping behind Emmanuel, he sliced the ropes binding his hands and told him to bend his legs. Then with a push, Emmanuel jumped off the scaffold and landed in amongst his family who cushioned his fall.

However, no sooner had this happened, than the gaoler was on top of Clarence and the magistrate was shouting, "For God's sake, guards, do something!"

The remaining red coats, freshly painted with shock, waded through the crowd towards Clarence's position.

"Ned Barlow, 'Old' Ned Barlow. Pleased to meet you, vagabond," the gaoler hissed in Clarence's ear. "Don't you worry, we'll have another noose out here in minutes, my lad. We'll get him back, and when we do, we'll have him dangling with his would-be deliverer," Barlow followed up with.

However, Clarence let him speak to gauge what he could about the man's personality. He didn't bother to retort, instead he simply allowed his ghostly constitution to lose density, which allowed him to walk through Barlow's ineffectual grab. Turning, Clarence broke the hold which never was before slapping Barlow across the face with his left and striking him with the flat of his sword on the head, causing Barlow to fall down, out of it. Turning towards where the vicar and magistrate had been, he saw they had left, retreating back inside. Clarence wasn't surprised. Looking to the heavens, he let out a piercing whistle and, across the concourse, came racing the magnificent Azlight, complete with barding. The space where her legs would have been was occupied by a white mist. On seeing this, the crowd screamed and ran. Cue a mass exodus from the concourse, which was clear in around a minute. They had forgotten about Emmanuel, as the drama that afternoon had just taken a turn for the unexpected. The sound of echoing screams and feet running trailed off into town. Using his second sight, Clarence saw Emmanuel and his family running to a main road which led out of town. His family were throwing him onto the back of a cart, immediately taking pains to conceal him under a tarpaulin. They then boarded it themselves, sporting what Clarence was glad to see were their best blank faces. The only three living people left on the scene were a dazed Barlow and the two remaining red coats. The shocked soldiers desperately fled. Then Clarence sensed Barlow had recovered. Lunging at Clarence, Clarence side-stepped. He knew he had to end this soon if he was to get away, so he sheathed his sword. Barlow swung for him, but Clarence neatly ducked, tripping Barlow and using his own momentum against him, to throw him into a window in the tower's door. Barlow groaned, plainly signalling to Clarence he was not getting back up. At least not today. Using his second sight once more, Clarence could see that Mary was now well clear of the other side of the Priory church, running through a field. He also clearly saw that the other two red coats were in quick pursuit. Whistling again, Clarence hailed Azlight, who came ripping back along the concourse and came to stop at the gallows. Clarence duly mounted her and sped off, above the churchyard. Clearing it, they saw Mary in the field behind it. Diving in, Clarence put his hand out for her.

Mary strained a little but pushed herself when she heard the chasing red coats shout "Good God!" in surprise at what they were witnessing.

The two hands clenched, and Clarence did his best to thrust Mary up, who spread her legs in an undignified fashion as she mounted Azlight. (Not that that mattered to her though, as escape had been her most pressing priority!)

"I'm damn glad to see you two!" said Mary, stroking Azlight. "That were a smash and grab!"

As Clarence nodded his agreement his mind flooded with what would happen now, as a result.

"Sometimes, impetuous courage hath its place" Clarence said.

The two red coats could only stutter to a stunned halt as they saw the wingless horse fly out towards Morecambe Bay, and away.

Chapter Twenty-Two

The carriage rumbled into Darkleigh square, in a hasty manner which suggested that it was late. Onlookers had that sentiment confirmed when the driver's mate jumped off the front and quickly opened the door. Out the Reverend Ethelstone stumbled, in a humorously unceremonious way.

"Good lord, is this where I have to deliver the word of the lord today?" he remarked.

"Darkleigh, sir," the driver's mate added.

Ethelstone spotted hiding in the corners of the square, which would soon be a throng with folk, two dark uniforms which denoted special constables. They had come last night and were to be his personal escorts for the day. Their presence had to be conspicuous, however, to make the populace of the town believe that this visit from the reverend was not at the behest of the state.

"We'll be back for you at six, sir," the driver's mate called as he jumped back on the carriage and it turned away.

Ethelstone trotted over to the box which had been placed for him outside the Guildhouse with an annoyed air about him. The special constables watched him closely as he took the stand. Some folk had come into the square and were talking to shop-keepers who were outside smoking their pipes. Ethelstone briefly acknowledged the presence of the constables and sighed, knowing it was time to begin.

"My friends," he began, satisfied with the echo it carried across the square. "I, the Reverend Ethelstone, as your friend in the lord, bring you all greetings from Manchester. It is a fine pleasure of life to be able to come and bring you all the teachings of the lord this day. However, along with these teachings comes grave news which I am duty-bound to communicate. It has come to my attention, as a servant of the lord in this county, that this very fine town has had the misfortune to have played host to the worst work of the devil I have heard mention of in my entire career. That is why, my friends, I have come before you this spring day."

Some people were aware that he was a magistrate in the select committee of Manchester and Salford. Others, though, weren't. They thought he was just a colourful travelling preacher. Either way, folk were only half-listening.

"The light of the lord shines upon your endeavours. He sees your great efforts and feels the sheer courage of your labour as you build the prosperity of your town. However, I have recently been made aware that a phantom has been sighted amongst you. One which will, no doubt, seek to perform noble tasks to serve your needs. One which would otherwise be a source of commendation from the Church of England. Phantoms such as these often have spectacular abilities which ensnare our attention, thrilling so many of us. And it is these which give their true purpose away. Yes, my friends. Sad as I am to say, these great abilities they exhibit can only be granted to them by the devil."

Some folk looked up or turned round at this point in the speech.

"For God grants us all gifts, but he would never grant anything so extreme as to be unhealthy. Which is what the abilities of this phantom likely are. *For I hear, my friends, that recently the weather in this town twisted in a vile way. It conspired with someone to deliberately go against its natural will. The only thing attributable to this phenomenon is a disciple of Satan.* My friends, do not be fooled. He will enjoy displaying these abilities for all to see. But it will be but a ruse, to gain your trust. When he has it, he will be preparing with great glee the schemes of Satan in this land, and this town. Heed my advice and turn him away from your doors, public and private. Shun him now you know his true colours. Make a bold statement against Satan!"

Only several people were taking notice, and even they were not rattled as a result of Ethelstone's impassioned warning.

"He speaks the truth," came a desperate-sounding voice advancing from a corner of the square.

Ethelstone turned towards it and saw it belonged to an actor he had seen at the theatre. Ethelstone's glance became one of puzzlement. For the young fellow walking up to his position was dressed modestly and carried a bible. Why was this actor backing him up?

"Yes! Heed his advice, friends, for the condemnation of this satanic imposter is shared by every Christian denomination. The Reverend has spoken on behalf of the Anglican Church. Now I speak for the Quakers."

This young 'Quaker' raged with the conviction of truth. It was this alone that caused quite a few people now to abandon their normal activity in the square and start to gravitate towards where Ethelstone was standing.

"It troubles me to agree with everything the Reverend has just stated. Not because we are from opposing denominations, but because the painful suggestion that a disciple of the Devil is surely walking amongst us here in Darkleigh is the truth. Turn him away, don't trust him! At first sight of him run and alert any member of the local clergy. They shall alert the Reverend here and he shall be spirited to us to vanquish this monster of hell who pretends to like you, to do you favours and be your friend. Who walks amongst us as one of us! For the sake of you and your loved ones, shun him!"

The fellow then slumped to the ground, one hand over his face, clearly making out that he was overcome with the words he spoke. Folk eyed each other with concern. Then, still undecided, they turned and resumed their business, having been suitably chilled. When the people were far enough distant, Ethelstone waved over one of the special constables who came and raised the fellow to his feet.

"Oh, Reverend!" he cried dramatically, still in character.

The constable brought him over.

"How did I do?" the fellow asked, with a streak of delight.

"Good lord, man, what did you think you were doing?" Ethelstone demanded.

"Better than you, evidently," he smugly returned.

"Yes, well. How did you find out about this?" was Ethelstone's next question.

"About our little Trojan horse? Squire Hulton hired me. We've known each other since he went to see Hamlet last year."

"Yes, well, I thought I recognised you from the theatre. But a Quaker, what was the reasoning in that?"

"Well, there'll be plenty of Anglicans around here, sir. They'll also be a lot from these newer denominations. Some of whom do tend to side with these, what are they called? Reformers. Now if we can show that all branches of the faith are united against whatever pantomime character's been parading around here, then they are more likely to believe us rather than..."

"Yes, yes, I understand. More than the band of stuffy old Anglicans who rightly rule them, who they're campaigning against."

"Quite so, sir. Ingenious, isn't it?" the actor said, resuming his smugness.

"Yes, quite a well. We need to leave here," Ethelstone prompted.

The special constables guided them away and out of the square.

Back in Manchester that evening, Ethelstone reported back to Hulton. In his elaborate reception room overlooking the street below, Hulton surveyed all before him.

"Ah, Reverend," Hulton said without turning. "How did our little ruse go today in Darkleigh?"

Trying to compose himself, Ethelstone replied, "It was very... theatrical in the end, sir. I did my best to warn of the interloper in the name of the Church of England. However, it was the skills of a certain young squire who won the day in part, as it were. Pretending to be one of our *non-conformist* brothers."

Hulton laughed with pleasure.

"Yes. Horace and I agreed the brief before he went out. A surprise for you perhaps, Reverend? Given that he did not travel with you?"

"Sir, I could not travel with anyone who I even *thought* was from outside the Church of England!" Ethelstone said with an affronted tone.

"Quite so. Which is why I had him travel separately," Hulton explained.

"How did the populace seem to react?"

"Some were quite taken, sir. Others did not even bother to listen."

Hulton stared thoughtfully to the corners.

"Hmm. I think perhaps we have scored a proverbial hit amongst the credulous people up there, Reverend. However, we need to show them our full broadside to stimulate a substantial reaction. I think maybe a measure more subtle, but none the less effective, will suit our purpose better. Using, of course, the same theme you and I invented."

Hulton's calculating mind turned over as he poured a couple of brandies.

161

Chapter Twenty-Three

That night in their room in the *Deft Swan*, Mary went to sleep very soon, and the orbs of Clarence and Azlight rested by the window ledge. The activity of that day left little room for discussion or reflection on what they'd just experienced. Clarence, though, knew he needed to get to the bottom of why Michael had directed him there. He was now worried that his task, whatever it was to be, had just become harder, given their heroics on the first day. When they woke the next morning, Mary had breakfast on her own. This again caused a raised eye from the inn-keeper.

"Will your husband not be joining you?" he asked.

"No. He's feeling a little tired."

"Aye," agreed the inn-keeper. "A lot of folk are today. It must have been them ruffians who stopped the hanging yesterday. Folk didn't stop talking about it last night. They said that a flying horse were involved as well. That I very much doubt! Too much beer on hanging days, and that's the result."

Mary had been listening intently to this. However her poise maintained that she was just lending a polite ear to his conversation. It was, of course, material that was of great interest to her and Clarence.

When it came time for them to leave for the town, they donned different clothes to what they had worn the day before. They both had hoods, to conceal their faces from anyone who may have been present at the hanging. Azlight remained resting on the window ledge, alert, even in her waking-slumber, to answer her master's call if need be. Hand in hand, there was a solemn nature in the walk of both Mary and Clarence as they came into Lancaster again, and this time, both of them were taken by it. They had been too focused the previous day for sight-seeing. The thatched cottages leading down the hill from their lodgings gave way to a square, which was completely unannounced. In the middle stood some buildings which looked as if their origins went back at least a couple of centuries.

Upon seeing this, Clarence said one thing, "The Friary".

Mary didn't quite know what he meant, so decided she might ask later, if she got a chance before he found what he was looking for. Mary herself was immediately reminded of the square in Darkleigh, which revealed itself like a great mystery after one had navigated the narrow streets and ginnels which converged on it. The neatness of this square, however, lent an air of grace the likes of which she had not experienced before. Not to say that Darkleigh wasn't graceful within its own character, but it was refreshing to her to see a place that adopted an elegant slant. They walked down a wide, round cobbled street next, and turned right onto another. Walking down it, Mary was this time taken completely by the tall, sandy-brown terraces which lined the street. Despite them having something of a regal quality, Mary felt welcomed, not dismissed by them. Looking round, Clarence admired the architecture too.

Though the only words he uttered were "Burgage plots".

Again, Mary smiled, stifling a giggle as she again didn't have a clue what he was talking about. Then they came to a wide opening which they both recognised (Mary from the previous day, Clarence from centuries ago). They were again at the bottom of Market Street. Looking at each other, their grips on each other's hands tightened and they made their way up. As today was a market day, there were an absolute plethora of stalls bustling with activity. The hum of a thousand conversations rose as they entered, and Clarence's second sight picked out the details of some of even the quietest. They mostly centred on normal topics for market day, such as the weight of goods and bartering. Trivial it seemed, but in an existence which had brought him such shocking truths thus far, it was good for him to hear the care-free conversations of others.

"So what now? Are we going to look around?" Mary inquired.

"Yes. Remember the plan?" Clarence whispered. "We art both on honeymoon."

Mary nodded. At first, she perused the stalls acting the part. However, after a few minutes, Mary noticed something about the market, which pleasantly affected her. Like Darkleigh's market days, it was a warm and close affair, but the calls of the market traders in Lancaster echoed from yore to eternity, with what *felt* like a centuries' old call.

Something strange then pervaded Mary. She started to see pictures in her mind again. The kind of pictures she had seen most recently in church. But these were especially vivid and relevant, as if they were happening now. She looked around all the stalls, some selling exotic items amongst the usual provisions. Amongst the sugar, rum and rare animals from the Lakes, the calls of the traders whisked her into the deepest halls of Lancaster. There she saw a panoply of different figures, themselves calling with the same vocal powers as traders. Some with noble and mighty tones, some with just mighty. The locales she was shown were old and brown, fuelling with each moment Mary's fantasy of Lancaster as the capital of her corner of England. These figures were compelling and diverse; some reminded her of wizards, others of the greats of Arthurian legend. They were evidently figures from days of yore. A parade of these characters ran its course through Mary's mind. Some were demanding what were theirs by rights, others were demanding a halt to something. Some tones plainly indicated evil goals, and others were obviously standing in their way. Then, something made sense to Mary. These folk were the antagonists and protagonists of Lancaster. Then she remembered a line in one of her father's books. 'Time honoured Lancaster' as Shakespeare had once said. Sense crystallised in her mind, and the visions ceased. Mary wondered if what she had just experienced was like Clarence's second sight. More so, where had it just come from?

Clarence was engaged at a stall with leather products, pretending to marvel at their wares. Lifting his head to survey the rest of the market, he noticed at its far end, a lass of about eighteen. She was standing a few yards away from the building which now enclosed the square. Moreover, she was looking straight at him, in the way that lasses sometimes do when they're aggrieved. Clarence, even without the aid of his second sight could make out a smooth, pale face, with neat oval-shaped eyes, and a long, curving nose. She also had the longest and shiniest black hair he had ever seen. She was poised in a slightly brooding fashion, albeit without even a hint of anger. Even though she was at the other end of the market, the movement and the hum of conversations slowed and became muted to Clarence. It felt like she was getting closer without even moving. Clarence looked away and looked back, and there she still was, the unreality of the previous moment having diminished now, with her still not having moved from the spot he had first seen her at, moments ago. She was wearing a long robe, with the hood down. It was grey and tarnished with what looked like many years of wear. She lifted her hand from a sleeve of her robe and Clarence saw an elegant if sharp set of fingers. One of them sported a ring, which featured a phoenix — like his manorial ring. Twisting her wrist, the ring caught the light and the taint of its light shot across the square at him. She then headed up the street, in the shade of the building which presided over the square.

"Mary," he said, newly ignited.

"What?" she replied.

"This way," he followed up, making his progress quick without breaking into a run.

Through the market they went, continually careful to avoid running, so as not to arouse suspicion. The lass Clarence had spotted didn't run, but she moved fast, as if to glide. Up the street she went, in plain view, though no one other than Clarence and Mary seemed to notice her. Past the presiding building she went, past another street that snaked round its back. Soon, she stopped at a break in the long terrace of shops and turned to look back at them, daring them in. With that, she disappeared into the gap. When Clarence and Mary got there, there was nothing but darkness.

"Looks like some sort of ginnel," commented Mary.

Then she noticed a sign above it, written in swirling font: Music Room Passage. Mary was tantalized by this.

"Hmm. Wonder what a music room is?" she mused.

Clarence closed his eyes and entered his second sight. He was now good at summoning it at will. Through the ginnel he saw a courtyard, quite open, and in the middle was the girl waiting there.

"Come on, let us go," he said brusquely.

Running through the darkened ginnel, they soon came out into the open, but the girl was nowhere to be seen. The courtyard was more like a square than a courtyard, however. The dominant colour was white and offered a distinct feeling of tranquillity. The square was neat and well-kept but it didn't lack features. For in one corner there was what looked like, a two-storey tavern. The ground floor dispensed drinks, as they could see through the windows. The upper storey had a balcony, and two fellows were at play: one playing a bass, the other a violin. Again the merry chatter of folk gave rise to the wonder Mary had just experienced minutes ago. A waft of sweet music drifted towards Clarence and Mary. Looking over to the fellows, Mary was intrigued that they were ensconced completely in their music; they hadn't noticed Mary and Clarence run into the square, or so it felt. The musicians' eyes were closed, their heads bobbing deftly to their beat. Mary was taken by this pleasantly eerie circumstance, but Clarence was frantically looking around, trying to spot the girl. But before he could use his second sight, the violin player pointed down one of the ginnels that led off the square. Mary wondered whether he was pointing after the girl. He pointed again, with his eyes closed, not even looking at her. Somehow Mary felt like this was trustworthy.

"Clarence, this way," she said, grabbing his hand and leading him off down the ginnel.

As they neared the end of it, someone stepped out from behind the buildings that stood onto the front of a new street. It was the girl, who only half acknowledged that there were two people chasing her. She duly set off again. She glided again this time, but at a faster pace. Downhill she went, towards the coast where Mary and Clarence saw there were several ships moored. As they ran, causes for concern entered Mary's head. Firstly, the girl had been waiting for them at the street at the end of the ginnel. The slight glance over her shoulder demonstrated that there was no surprise that they were still chasing her. This told her that she wanted to be chased. (Like a lot of girls, she thought.) Secondly, that violinist had pointed the exact way to her. He hadn't even opened his eyes but he knew she and Clarence had been there. And he certainly knew where the girl had been. Did he know something about what was going on, Mary wondered? But then she transferred her thoughts back to the pursuit. The girl was by now on a road which ran parallel to the water's edge and had turned left. She was chasing towards St. George's Quay now, and Mary wondered what alarm they'd raise running through an area riddled with cargoes being inspected. However, the girl was headed in the direction of the bottom of the hill, where the castle stood. This perplexed Mary and Clarence. Now she was making for a tavern which stood close to the bottom of the hill. But she didn't bother to open the front door, which was heavily bolted. No. She walked through it, as ghosts do.

"I knew it," rasped Clarence.

When they themselves reached the tavern, there were next to no folk about, which was fortunate.

"What now?" Mary said, stumped.

Closing his eyes once more, Clarence enjoyed the fluent use of his second sight. The girl was nowhere to be seen, but there were a few people upstairs, tending to the barrels. After exiting his second sight, Clarence rolled his eyes at the fine curiosity of seeing a tavern where the barrels were kept upstairs.

"What now?" Mary said, with some impatience.

Winking at her, Clarence replied, "Be very quiet."

Lowering the density in his hand, Clarence reached inside the door, to where the lock was. With a few smooth touches, he unlocked it. Mary was impressed. Smiling back at her, they went inside, with total concert in their silence. Clarence pushed the door to. Delving into his second sight again, he looked down. Upon doing this, he caught one last sight of the girl, as she looked up at them from the cellar. Her expression was self-evident to Clarence. She knew exactly where they were standing, despite there being a thick floor separating them. She moved towards a non-descript box in a corner of the cellar and vanished. Leaving his second sight, Clarence smiled with cunning. He gently prodded Mary and gestured towards the bar. Mary had been taking in the delicate ambience of the tavern, no doubt where many adventurous sailors had drunk down the years. The panes of mottled glass in the windows glinted thoughtfully down onto the dark wood which made up the floors and chairs, making them seem all the richer in the stories they no doubt could tell. However, she obliged, and moved with Clarence behind the bar, ducking under the lid in the counter and going into the back. In the back there was what was clearly a door leading to the cellar. Again, Clarence reached inside the lock. With a quiet pop, the lock undid itself and they both climbed in as silently as they could. Once in the cellar, Clarence didn't need his second sight to see where the girl had vanished. Gently locking the door they had just entered from, he faced the corner she had disappeared into.

"Clarence, I can't see a damn thing," Mary whispered.

"Not to fear, my dear," he replied without any hint of worry.

He guided her to the corner.

"Can you do something with this?" Mary asked, with Clarence able to see her holding a candle through his second sight.

Clarence willed the candle to be lit, which it duly was. Mary was delighted.

"Forgot I had this" Mary grinned.

Clarence smiled as they stood over a large box they found themselves with.

Here they now were in the cellar of a tavern they had entered through false pretences. Mary wanted some justification or explanation. "Second sight lead us down here?"

Clarence just nodded.

Mary managed a laugh. Clarence then swept old covers off the box, and Mary held her candle close to the bare wood. The top of the box was actually a locked door. But, shockingly for Clarence, there was also a phoenix painted on it, which covered most of it. Reaching down into the lock again, Mary stopped him.

"Wait!" she said firmly.

"What are you doing? How can you be sure that that girl isn't leading us to something bad?"

"Mary, my dear. Occasions like this call us to have faith. I shall not pretend to thee, I hath no proof. However, I do hath the warmest feeling of faith. That today is the sole source of my courage."

Mary remained unconvinced.

"And what if there's many a terrible thing down there? Robbers, smugglers? Which there will be in a port town like this, bless it. Or worse, what if she's not friendly, what if there's monsters, boggarts or demons stuck down there?"

Clarence couldn't help but understand Mary's apprehension. However, the strength of his own conviction outstripped any cause for fear he had. During his life, he had always waited patiently for that process to happen. When it did, he was never disappointed.

"Mary, my dear. All I canst say is remember what Lancaster means to thee. Thou hath told me before that Lancaster is a guardian of the medieval county, which was when I lived. Because of that, it is surely a town of wonders in thy mind. All I ask of thou is to give those sentiments a chance as thou journey down here with me. And, of course, I swear on my honour that I shall die again before thou art harmed. And when hath I ever let thee down?"

Mary knew what Clarence said was true. She had been absolutely correct with the concern that vagabonds hid out beneath the cellars of a port tavern, but Lancaster played host to her fantasies of what a medieval town would have been like in her part of the world. Because of that, she wanted to give it a chance. She wanted a greater sample of adventure from it. For already had they caused an almighty stir. Clarence then finished with the lock and flung the door open. It led down to a wide space below ground. Her candle seemed to barely illuminate it. Mary gave Clarence a quick hug, all sincere. Down she went. Clarence happily followed her down. Closing the door, they abandoned themselves to the darkness.

Chapter Twenty-Four

Down the tunnels Mary and Clarence went. At first, their pace was quick given that they thought it necessary to keep up with the ghost girl who had led them there. But as they progressed in the darkness, courtesy of Clarence's second sight, they soon realised that she had vanished. The girl had been a cause for concern, even for Clarence. For questions were burning at the back of his mind about her, despite his massive impulse he'd had to follow her. It scared Mary more, because as suspicious as she had been of the girl, they now had no guide. Holding Clarence's wrist as firmly as she could, they went on. When Clarence said they needed to duck down, they ducked down. When he said they needed to be careful underfoot, they were careful. At one point, Mary whispered to Clarence, asking him whether he saw, heard or even felt others down there with them, living or not. He replied that he didn't; however, something was brewing with passionate energy somewhere, but that was all he could tell, and he didn't quite know what that was. Soon after, they came out onto another tunnel, which had a light source at its end. The rectangle some three hundred yards ahead was filled with a pastel shade of peach, which made them nod to each other in the darkness. At the end of the tunnel, Mary entered the rectangular opening and was rendered speechless. For she had just walked out onto what reminded her of a corridor. And she could clearly see that the light was coming from *two lamps* half way down it.

"Clarence," she said, pleasantly surprised, "look at this!"

Clarence had exited his second sight in the previous tunnel, turned onto the new corridor and indeed he too became surprised as well.

"Yes, my dear, what a wonder," he exaggerated, snatching at humour to relieve their tension.

Giggling, Mary led now. She and Clarence walked down the corridor, both knowing (but not saying) full well what the lamps meant. They were on their guard. This proved to be quite a long corridor, and

Mary, perhaps involuntarily to quell their nerves, started a conversation.

"Clarence. You mind if I ask you something, love?"

"Not at all," he replied.

"This friend of yours, what were his name? Michael?"

"Yes," Clarence confirmed.

"Did he tell you that something was going to happen up here, so that you could sleep again?"

"No. He only told me to come here. He said I wouldst sleep again as a result, but he did not tell me what wouldst bring that about."

Mary was frustrated on Clarence's behalf.

"Bet you thought you wouldn't wind up down here?" she said with some sarcasm.

"Hmm. He did not giveth me a lot to go off, didst he?"

Mary picked up some mutual frustration, which was new for the highly composed Clarence.

"But I must say, there is something endearing about these cosy tunnels. I dost not know about thou, but I feel a sense of involvement here. A feeling that we art alive in the town's very essence, despite being perhaps a mile underneath it!"

Mary, amused, rolled her eyes. But what Clarence said rang true with her, even though she daren't admit it. Mary re-steered the chat.

"Here's the big grand question: do you trust him?"

"What, Michael?" Clarence replied.

"Aye, Michael. Do you think he's sent you here for a good reason?"

Clarence looked directly at her.

"Oh yes. A very good reason."

"How's that?"

"He wouldst not hath sent me here for nothing. Believe me, I knew him all my life. Not only was he wise, but in our manor, he truly was closest to God. But despite that, he never let that give him a feeling of loftiness over our tenants. Folk sensed that humility and respected him for it. And most importantly, he was a good friend."

"Aye, he must have been for you to just come up here on his say so," Mary pointed out.

"How do you feel? About being close to God?" Mary next inquired.

"Yes. I hath always been close to him. But when I re-awoke to spirit,

I must admit I didst question him. But answers came. They always do when thou pray."

He didn't see the subtle smile on Mary's face.

"How about thou? How close to God dost thou feel, dear Mary?"

"I feel him, the God I recognise, every Sunday when we go to church. You come out feeling so fresh, redeemed like. Sometimes it's difficult, I'll admit, waiting for prayers to be answered. Some say weavers spend half their lives doing that. But I remember Sam Bamford, who you met after that meeting we went to. When I've spoken to Sam in them meetings, he's always said what we need to change everyone's lives, them being our rights, aren't the establishment's to give. He says that God gave them to us when we were born. And I like that, that's the God I believe in."

Mary paused, and looked thoughtfully upwards, as if towards open sky.

"Maybe he'll send us an avenging angel, who knows?"

Something about Mary's concluding sentence caused Clarence to look up. As masterful timing had it, as he did, a blue pulse, clearly visible to him, shot through the corridor, going past them and away.

"Ooh, it's a bit chilly," Mary said lightly, not having seen or heard the pulse.

The pulse had come and gone, but Clarence's attention had been grasped. For further down, he noticed murals on the wall.

"Mary," he said. "Look."

Gesturing ahead, Mary's eyes narrowed with intrigue as they darted down the corridor and came to regard the first of these murals. The first one they came to gawp at featured a hill which depicted a thousand knights in armour, and surely as many archers. On the left side of the painting, there were many banners, featuring a myriad of colours and designs. But the largest at the back of the massed ranks featured a phoenix! Despite this, however, the most intriguing feature of the mural was the figure which hovered above this army, surrounded by a yellow glow. Although without wings, he was definitely hovering there like an angel. Sword drawn in one hand, sceptre in the other.

"Is that a king or summat'?" a confused Mary asked.

"I do not know," answered Clarence, equally mystified.

He then noticed that both armies in the mural didn't look ready for battle at all. In fact, they were tremendously at peace. Strange, but nonetheless impressive, Clarence thought.

Grabbing Mary's hand, he said, "Come, my dear, the light shall guide us. Let us see if there art any more of these, as we move to where we art meant to be down here."

They made off down the corridor.

Down there, time didn't seem to apply. It became a redundant concept. Their minds became entrenched at a banquet of food for thought. These included the likes of more lamps, but yet no folk, and more murals. The latter alternated between the extremely beautiful and the eerie, even ominous. At one point, Mary did ask how long they'd been down there, but Clarence assured her that the day had not yet expired. His feeling was that it had merely become stretched.

Shortly after, they came to a junction within the dusty tunnels, barely illuminated by a single lantern in the centre, dangling from the ceiling. Leading away from this circular junction were five other tunnels, in darkness.

"Cross-roads," Mary commented.

Above each tunnel were painted symbols. A ship, a castle, a cross, a hay bail and, above theirs, a tankard. However, the most intriguing was one with a phoenix. They both approached it to get a better look. Fully gripped, they tried to navigate why phoenixes, well known imagery in Darkleigh, were popular here too. As a symbol at this strange junction, it wasn't easy to speculate as to what it was.

"There it is again," Mary stated.

Deep down, Clarence felt more and more light fall upon Mary's earlier question regarding whether Michael had sent him there with good reason.

"I feel we should continue forth, on the same course as we were on," Clarence said.

"Phoenixes. Like in Darkleigh. That's four times now. Do you think we're being told something here?"

Clarence was feeling too vigilant to answer. Instead he started down the tunnel with the cross painted over its entrance. Mary reasoned that by now, Clarence was feeling very holy. Sighing, she groped along in the darkness with him again, as there were no lanterns to light the way this time. After passing down a long tunnel, Mary felt a satisfied feeling rise within her, the same she felt after archery competitions. Today, it was tinged with the satisfaction of involvement in something she desperately wanted to call an adventure. She had only felt that in her life when she had been to the hills with her archery pals and Bertha, or on the rare occasions when she had visited the coast with her family. Descending a flight of steps, which seemed purposefully narrow so as to put folk off descending them, they came to a flat, level area in which the walls were quite far apart and the ceiling was higher than those of the tunnels. In front, there was what both of them recognised as a rood screen. Its middle sported an opening to pass through but it was obscured by a thick curtain. Clarence tried to use his second sight, but for some reason it was reluctant to help him see or hear beyond the curtain. He decided to get a second opinion.

"How dost thou feel about this, Mary?"

"Honestly?"

"Yes, honestly."

"Excited," she firmly stated.

Grinning, Clarence then instructed, "Well then, brace thyself."

Pushing the curtain aside, there in front of them was a little chapel. The altar was no more than fifteen feet away, with small pews either side of the nave. In the nave were rushes, which indicated a recent festival. On the altar was an assortment of *lit* candles. Behind the altar were murals, obviously from the same hand which had painted those in the tunnels. Though this time they depicted Christ. On the altar there was a cross, mounted highest in the centre, and a chalice and plate on either side of it. Beneath it was a curious dark box. Clarence found himself drawn to this, yoked with a chord of familiarity.

"Well, by heck," a male voice said abruptly behind them.

Mary and Clarence spun round, with the readiness of battle.

"Not many get this far, if any," the voice followed up.

Mary and Clarence could just wait as the owner of the voice came into view, courtesy of the candles. There was a woman with him, and they were both wearing patchwork clothes. Clarence noticed Mary twitch into a state of preparation.

"I think you'd better come and see the chairman," the bloke said, with authority.

Clarence and Mary stuck very close together as they were led out of the chapel and back into the tunnels, ready to pounce if needs be.

Chapter Twenty-Five

The couple led them all the way back to what Mary had called the 'junction', where they paused before taking the passage under the phoenix icon. During the walk, Mary hung close to Clarence in case she needed him to guide her in the darkness. But she retained her independence by not linking him. Clarence thoroughly appreciated this by now! The couple didn't speak as they led Mary and Clarence through several tunnels and passageways in that mysterious underground labyrinth. In fact, there was a strange calm about them which suggested to both Mary and Clarence that they were used to doing this. Indeed, Mary and Clarence had taken heed from the bloke's only comment so far that they had done well to get as far as they had done. Clarence did not make it known who he was; in any case a spirit would not carry jurisdiction in the living world. Both of them had a damning feeling that they had been trespassing. Clarence was cursing himself in his mind for not having been more attentive to the dangers of gallivanting down underground tunnels — especially those which lay close to Lancaster Castle. There had been a host of evidence — the lanterns and wall paintings, but his excitement and zeal had overtaken his reason, which now provided the most grinding feeling. He then decided he would use a silent whisper to communicate with Mary. He had done it before but as a general rule refrained, as this, as a form of communication, did have a startling effect on the living. Looking toward her embarrassed face, he spoke the words in his mind and then casted them off to her, like smoke from a candle.

'Mary. I feel that we art trespassing. I do not know where these people art taking us, but I shall try to find out. I feel no malice or ill-intent from them, but continue as thou dost, to remain close to me'.

Clarence noticed Mary's initial reaction, of somewhat shock, hit her, and then dissipate almost immediately after it had arrived. Clarence smiled at this. Mary was becoming better able to repel certain things. Mary looked back at him with a look that plainly illustrated that she felt very unsure of what was to come, but that she trusted him at the same time, nevertheless. Clarence made prayers of gratitude every day for this, which was an on-going theme in their relationship. A feeling then met Clarence. It suggested, through no indicator the tunnels or their guides provided, that their journey was nearly over. Clarence tried to use his second sight but couldn't. They had avoided getting too close for comfort in the tunnels with these two folk, following them from a short distance away. There was nowhere to run without getting lost, so the couple didn't need to be too vigilant. There had been no uneven floors, no holes, no low ceilings, and no traps, nothing which would have necessitated the physical help of their 'guides' to be able to negotiate. Lamps placed at intervals were also a massive help. But even so, Clarence was still sinking his mind toward the possibility of a confrontation, one which may involve the use of his sword, concealed under his coat. He was busy reckoning Mary's position in relation to his and how that would inhibit his defence of them. He was also, by slow-burning degrees, preparing himself to enter a state of battle, which he did to some extent before every kind of fight he was in, battlefield or being attacked by ruffians. The images and intended fate of Emmanuel had done this for him yesterday, but here, he had to summon up raw reserves of battle emotions to enable this. However, he maintained a surface expression of contrition, of course, to misguide whoever they would soon come face-to-face with. His feelings were right. They eventually came to the end of the tunnel they were in and found themselves standing in a lobby. In front of them was an oak door, reminiscent of the ones found in castles and old churches. Clarence for one, of course, recognised this, as did Mary, a moment after. The bloke had stopped at the door and turned round to face them. Behind them, another set of doors bolted, which took Mary and Clarence by surprise. The bloke said one thing, which made for a disappointing climax.

"Now don't get any daft ideas, like legging it," he warned, in a voice which was sincere but amiable.

This grabbed the attention of Mary and Clarence in an unexpected way. For then, both their guides unlocked this great oak door in front of them, and pushed it open, ushering them in. Staying close by each other, Mary and Clarence went in, closely followed by their guides, who immediately closed and bolted the door after them. Mary and Clarence were much taken aback when they entered what was clearly a very well-lit hall. One that was in the midst of a feast, and a merry feast at that. The first thing that imposed itself on them was the multitude of people sitting at long, wooden tables. Conversation and joviality raged amongst them. As they sat there, enthusiastically eating and drinking, they didn't even notice that Mary and Clarence had arrived. Laughs and cheers rang out, the kind that reminded Clarence of his own court during the time he had lived. And they were the most curiously eclectic collection of folk Mary and Clarence had ever seen in one place. Both genders, from every age group were there. Mary noticed some dressed in the typical garbs worn by mill workers, followed, quite surprisingly, by some wearing tall hats and cravats. But it was Clarence who noticed some others who added particular spice to the broth. For it was he who at first saw, engaged in normal conversation, a lady who he sensed clearly was a witch. With a face flanked by long, shiny black hair, she also wore a long dress embroidered with eye symbols. That is how many witches dressed in his day, and Clarence was privy to the happy truth about them. But it was the subtleness of her gazes and her insightful poise which gave her away. He had known witches to be great custodians of those particular traits. Elsewhere he had to restrain a gasp as he saw a painted man, wearing beaded jewellery. He had heard descriptions of this, passed down from those who had travelled on the crusades, but he himself had never actually seen this, when living or as a spirit. Others wore colourful costumes and sat mock-regally, as if aping the disposition of queens and kings. If the body of folk sitting before them were the main source of surprise and intrigue, then it was well complimented by what they saw on the walls of this 'great hall' they had entered. Its walls were adorned with many more murals, which Clarence recognised were depicting scenes from what had evidently been events in Lancaster. But as well there were, as nobles had had in their great halls, drapes and banners. Most of these sported a phoenix. Because of this, a pang of certainty arose in Clarence. There were also pieces of armour hanging up. But if what they had seen so far had presented some favourable questions for them, then it was what they would see at the back of the hall atop a stage that would invade the pleasantly colourful picture, twisting its presence rudely into focus. For sitting at the back was another table from which one fellow sat on his own. He was tucking into a meal and had a book open next to him. But to his right stood a young woman who took Mary's breath away and caused Clarence to recoil in amazement. For it was the same girl who they had chased through Lancaster to reach the tunnels. She caught sight of them and gave them a satisfied smile, knowing that she had led them to exactly where she wanted them to be. But an even greater surprise for Clarence, one which involuntarily chilled him even as a spirit, was the shield that hung above this stage. For it had been one of his own, a yellow background with a red phoenix clearly rising from the ashes of a castle. There was no doubt it was his, given the distinctive hole at its top. Clarence remembered catching an arrow from a cross-bow in France there. Seeing an actual possession of his threw him. He grabbed Mary's hand this time, disturbed and mystified by where they were, who their 'hosts' were and what exactly all this meant. A myriad of possibilities, both good and bad, paraded through his mind like a carousel. Mary, noticing it too, held him close.

"Don't worry," she said. "Remember how you felt before battles."

"Wait here," their female guide instructed as she and the male guide approached the stage.

Still the jovial talk went on, not even seeming to be aware in the slightest of the interlopers, which Mary and Clarence now knew they were (even if they had been lured there). Their guides approached the fellow sitting on his own respectfully and after a few seconds, he looked up. He was as delightfully good-natured as the party it seemed he was presiding over. The male guide whispered something to him. It was at this point that the ghost of the young woman vanished, still wearing her devious grin. The fellow on the stage turned his head towards where Mary and Clarence stood. He stood up to see them. Still mystified, Mary and Clarence looked back at him. With a welcoming smile, he raised a mace. Banging on his table three clear times with it, all conversation and merriment ceased with a crystal-clear abruptness. All heads turned towards the stage. Silence was now a clear canvas on which this fellow would speak.

"My friends. We have guests."

All heads and eyes then turned in Mary and Clarence's direction. With all gazes fixed on them, they had to resist becoming unnerved with all their determination.

"Your names, please?"

"I'm Mary," Mary spoke.

Clarence had to make a choice between Max Walmsley and his true identity. He chose.

"I am Sir Clarence de Darkleigh," he stated plainly, choosing not to enshrine his name with his former position.

Somehow, when he told them who he was, the silence in the room seemed to deepen. The looks on the faces of the people there assembled went from either welcoming or playful to as shocked as Clarence had been moments ago when he had set eyes on what he was certain was his old shield. The fellow on the stage laid down his mace gently on the table.

"And is there a way you can prove that claim, Sir?" was his next question.

So, Clarence took a ghostly glove off and held up his hand, with his fingers sporting two rings: one his knight's ring and the other his manorial ring, which Mary had returned, complete with an impressed image of a phoenix rising from ashes of a castle.

"Sir," the fellow began again with sincerity, "can you treat us to a demonstration of the famous mark to begin a feast with?"

Clarence's countenance froze at this. Not only did these people have his shield, but they knew about his legendary trick with his sword to begin festivals and feasts with. As lord of Darkleigh, he had gone to the square or Guildhouse with his retinue and someone had thrown an apple across at him. He had then proceeded to perform one of his spectacular jumps, slicing the fruit in half in a way which caused it to land into the palms of two folk attending. *How* did this fellow know about that? Clarence knew exactly what he wanted. So, he nodded. In turn, the fellow nodded to someone who was sitting down, and Clarence's mind began running through the drill to perform the feat. Someone stood up and threw an apple high up in the air, which sailed across the room, almost hanging there as a multitude of eyes watched expectantly. It reached its highest point just before it reached Clarence, who in one smooth, stunning movement, jumped up into the air while drawing his sword, and sliced the apple cleanly in half, sending both halves to land neatly in the hands of two folk who hadn't even been expecting it, with two splattering sounds. The assemblage regarded Clarence almost as if he were an idol. This was followed by a pause, which both Mary and Clarence could sense was digging deep, ready to erupt. And erupt it did, in colossal cheers that consumed the hall. A joyous mobbing from the crowd followed. Still very unsure, Mary and Clarence were somewhat distressed by this response, which saw people hugging them, crying frantically and chanting relentlessly in celebration.

Their chants took the form of "He's back, the phoenix king!" "The great redeemer returns!"

They would have felt the cold composition of Clarence, but their unbridled joy pushed them through it.

"Clarence, what the…" Mary started, but stopped when all he could do was look back at her with an equally bemused face.

This went on for several minutes, and during this, Clarence looked towards the stage where an equally delirious threesome was trying to make their way down. Eventually, they made it.

"Allreet, allreet," the fellow who Clarence had by now worked out was the leader said. "Give them some air!"

Mary experienced some relief at the irony of this, given where they were. The crowd soon recovered some calm and parted their ways to let the three from the stage through. Those who had sprung up from the tables continued to look at particularly Clarence, with suspended mania. When they had waded through the mass of folk, the leader greeted Mary first.

"Hello, love, nice to meet you," he said, hurriedly shaking her hand.

Then he turned his attentions to Clarence. The leader's face was red with happiness, as if it were about to explode. Shaking his hand with both of his, he made something of a bow.

"Oh, Sire, Sire, my Sire. What an honour. What an honour! At last, you've returned! We knew it would be some time soon, but we weren't expecting you today!"

Clarence was more comfortable now, but his eyes still narrowed with his continued confusion.

"I am expected?" he questioned.

"Oh aye, yes, well, you are..." the leader said, beginning to backtrack. "Aye, of course. I'm sorry, Sire. In our great zeal we've forgotten that you may not know who we are, or what we do. Sorry, aye... excuse us. We're just overjoyed! Follow me, Sire, and I'll tell you and your friend *all* you need to know about us!"

A cheer went up again, and Clarence and Mary found themselves being shoulder lifted towards the stage, where a door concealed in the wooden boards opened up for them promptly.

"Music if you please, good friends," the leader ordered.

Merry spirited music struck up and the frolicking continued around them. Mary and Clarence eyed each other again, but this time it was a look of mutual relief.

Chapter Twenty-Six

Clarence and Mary were taken under the stage at the front into an underground cavern. It had been carved out in the same ways as some of the tunnels had. However, it was a large, oval space. And it was quite a cave of curiosities. Mary and Clarence found themselves down there with four others: the leader, the couple who'd guided them there, and the ghost who had lured them to the tunnels. With the door to the hall now bolted behind them, they could still hear muffled cheers and fast, eager conversation.

The leader began. "I believe you've already met Alison," he said, gesturing towards the ghost who did a curtsy.

This time, there was a look of sweetness on her face as she vanished.

"Aye, she's our home ghost. A bit shy at times. One thing she's always been good at is bringing visitors here who we're expecting," explained the leader.

Mary and Clarence exchanged blank looks, then projected them back at him.

The leader heeded their bemusement and continued. "Aye well, before I go on, my name's Richard Overfield, chairman of this society. This lovely couple are Josiah and Caroline, two of us who patrol the tunnels. We'd be lost without them!" he laughed.

"And exactly *what* art ye all?" Clarence spoke.

When he did, Richard, Josiah and Caroline were enthralled by every word he said.

After a resulting pause, Richard said, "Aye yes. We, Sire, are the Society of the Phoenixes. And we have lived underneath Lancaster for four hundred years!"

Clarence noted the similarities to his own circumstances in this.

"Our job as a society has been to care for folk, whoever they are, wherever they're from, who are unwanted. And, of course, vulnerable folk who've ended up here."

183

The three of them smiled proudly at this. Mary realised that they were something akin to a charity.

"Like whom?" she asked, wanting confirmation of her theory.

"Well, all sorts, my love. In the first century of our existence we cared for sick people, mainly. When they couldn't be cared for by anyone else we were there."

"Ooh reet, you must've helped a lot of warriors then, from the battles?" Mary added.

"Er no, that came later," said Richard, confused himself for the first time.

"But what about the Wars of the Roses?" Mary protested.

"There must've been casualties in all the battles that were fought here?"

"Well, no, my love. The Wars of the Roses didn't happen here, really. They passed by here but there was never any great battle. Things were relatively quiet."

Mary felt stumped. A major part of her fantasy of Lancaster had just been dissolved by someone who seemed likely to know what he was talking about.

"In the next two centuries of our operation we became something of a shelter for monks at the Reformation. Then as well it were priests, different folk from outlawed faiths, and many witches as well. We sheltered them, took them in and gave them lives and meaning again here. Aye, many's a time we'd snatch them off the gallows, them and us gone in a mighty puff of smoke!"

Clarence and Mary were at the point of being inspired, but still they wanted to hear more.

"And aye, in the mid-seventeenth century, we were able to take in some soldiers, my dear. Mainly ones who were disgusted and disillusioned by what had happened around them," Richard explained.

"You mean the civil war?" Mary realised.

Richard nodded.

"We repeated that again when the Jacobites came to town, the second time with Bonnie Prince Charlie himself. They found that a lot of folk in Lancaster supported them, you know. Anyway, we've never been political, but we saw some of our own discontent in theirs. During that same century we had some runaway slaves. But here, they didn't only find refuge, but their true identity, free to be who they once were, back in Africa. For years now we've been saving lives and trying to put reet what's gone on on the surface by our clever agency. Things go missing in Lancaster a lot from tables, mainly the excesses of our noble lord justices. This is where they end up, only to be sorted and given back to the neediest folk around. Aye, we've saved countless lives, many who've stayed with us. And we've set a good few free and all, who were passing through, like."

"I bet you're well busy at the moment, then" Mary remarked.

"How very noble. But how on God's fine Earth do we fit into all this?" Clarence asked.

Richard made a motion towards him.

"Oh, Sire," he said, affecting a reverent tone. "Oh, Sire. We were founded in 1419 by Michael Snudworth."

At this, the whole of Clarence flooded with understanding. His features sagged too, reflecting this.

"Your priest in Darkleigh came here after you defeated Lord Dalbern and started a new life for himself in the county town. It was here he wanted to put the money bequeathed to him by your parents to good use, so he used it to carve out these tunnels, and begin the society with."

'Of course', Clarence thought. This was a typical endeavour of Michael's. He had used the legacy of all he had been in Darkleigh and had continued on Clarence's family's old creed of honour. Something started to form inside him. Mary felt his temperature rise slightly. Worried that he would disappear to orb form, she decided to question further on his behalf. Clarence was finding it difficult to bring himself to words.

"But how does Clarence actually fit into that?" she asked.

"Well, oh well. Sire, one of the founding tenets of this order has been the belief that you will come back. As you have. We were expecting you in a blaze of glory, which is of course the least of what a great man like yourself merits. But I'm sure we can have another two-day, nay three-day feast in your honour if you like?"

Clarence had become speechless.

"Aye, well. That will be decided. But as I said, we have always lived in the belief as Michael had foreseen, that you would return in exactly four hundred years," Richard explained with great zeal.

He then motioned them over to a series of tapestries on the wall. The first one depicted a priest leading his people outside Lancaster Castle. The priest was making a gesture into the air as if he had just thrown something skyward. Above the castle in the air was what Clarence knew to be a phoenix, leaving a cloud of ashes in its wake. The next one was of the hill the castle was built on, with a layer of earth lifted away in the picture to reveal a number of tunnels with the hall at its centre. A variety of different colours represented the body of people who made up the order in it. Lastly, Richard showed them a tapestry which depicted the town of Lancaster, with a great array of townspeople assembled, marvelling with clear awe at something in the sky. Casting his eyes up the artwork, Clarence immediately recognised it as himself. He was there in full armour, tabard on. But two things caused whatever had tried to form within him to fuse all the tighter: a glow behind him and, most startlingly, an amulet which caused him to gaze with familiarity at it. Clarence lifted his hand, wanting to touch the tapestry. Richard looked on gladly, as he saw Clarence gaze with stunned amazement at what he hoped he would now recognise as his destiny.

With tact, Richard now said, "You see, Sire. We've been praying for your return for four hundred years now. And now here you are. Our lord, our hero."

Clarence looked back to him, lips parted.

Slowly, he said, "Dost thou know why I hath come back?"

Richard nodded. "Let's get you sat down, Sire," he said.

In the centre of the room, Clarence, Mary, Richard, Josiah and Caroline all sat down.

"Sire, if I could offer you something in the way of refreshment, I would. But I'm guessing you can't..." Clarence shook his head to confirm.

Richard then looked across at Mary, but she also declined.

"Sire, Michael left us some of his manuscripts. We believe them to be an assortment of prayers and treatises upon the nature of the Lord, from which we have learnt much," Richard began with.

"Thou shall hath done. For the true nature of the Lord brought such wonder and happiness to Darkleigh. Not one Sunday went by when thanks to Michael I didst not feel the Lord's true presence in my life," said Clarence.

The countenances of everyone lit up at this, the first sure words Clarence had spoken since he had announced his name. They had come so bold, with Clarence almost speaking them through a mist that surrounded him, into infinity.

"Yes, Sire," Richard nodded.

"Yes. He also left us letters. Many of which were designed for our education. Perhaps the greatest we have on permanent display, in the great hall, is one in which he promises that one day you will come back, and the reason why."

Clarence, although he didn't realise it, was leaning forward in his seat, conditioning his whole being towards receiving the information which would crown his visit and cancel his confusion with one blow.

"It says that you will return to liberate us."

At the mention of the word 'liberate', Mary's eyes widened, as it was the type of word she coveted a lot. Clarence dipped to a silent state of disbelief.

"You will come back to set us free, and to help us take our place amongst them on the surface. You will reign, and we, the Phoenixes, will be free. Safe in the knowledge that we shall never be cast aside or forced underground by them who don't understand us. It's time for you to take your place once again, Sire, at our head."

For what seemed a highly elongated moment, Clarence, nor anyone in the room, said anything.

"And then of course there's the amulet," Richard added.

"The amulet?" Clarence returned.

"Ah yes, the Duke of Lancaster must have what's his."

"Pardon, didst thou just say Duke of Lancaster?"

"Aye, Sire," Richard answered, eyes bulging with enthusiasm.

They knew who Michael was, they certainly knew who he had been. And Clarence was in no way surprised that Michael had come here, building a safe haven from his family's gift for his loyal services. And what a dynasty of his own he'd founded. It was quintessentially de Darkleigh. In fact, it was quintessentially Darkleigh. Clarence felt as if the whole of his old manor had been supplanted here. But, now this fellow, who he had met minutes ago, was now referring to him as the duke of Lancaster.

"Thou art saying I am the Duke of Lancaster?" he asked again.

"Aye! That's what that amulet you're wearing on that tapestry entitles you to," Richard explained, pointing back to the wall.

"How so?" Clarence questioned.

"It was made by monks from this county, for someone worthy. They gave it to Michael for safe-keeping. Dalbern wanted it, which is one of the reasons why he chased you," Richard explained with sensitivity.

Clarence was suddenly stunted. If this amulet was one of the reasons why Dalbern had been pursuing him, then why hadn't someone told him? He hadn't even known it was his. Then, Clarence remembered his feelings on seeing it on the tapestry and somehow sensed its significance, despite never having come across it in his life.

"What importance doth it hath?" was Clarence's next question.

Richard's head turned with anticipation.

"Oh, Sire, you should read that book over there," he said, nodding to a book open on a lectern. "You wouldn't believe what it says," he said with an overwhelmed undercurrent in his voice.

"But that is surely fantastical! The Duchy of Lancaster was never created for a noble of my level. And in 1399 it merged with the crown. A fine medallion made by monks cannot contradict this, they hath no power to form duchies. Only kings do," Clarence said, stating his confusion.

"True, Sire. But it was the desire of the monks that the holder of the duchy the amulet would represent would indeed hail from this county, and not be stationed distant from it. It was to be given to only one that was worthy. Who cared for his people as a shepherd cares for his flock. Michael received it from them with you in mind. There's two duchies now. The one founded by kings of yesteryear and the one the amulet can sustain. Except the amulet lies dormant."

At this point, Mary had been lost in the truth of the moment. It was like they were a part of an olde legend which was demanding its next chapter be told. Clarence was plainly overcome.

"And how exactly, without a writ from the king, doth that very finely crafted amulet deem its holder duke? What doth it hath to enforce its power?" was Clarence's next question.

Something cataclysmic stirred in Richard, with Josiah and Caroline looking on in awe of what Clarence had asked.

"Oh, Sire. You should read Michael's writings. What they promise," Richard explained. "It's been handed down through generations of our society. Of course, we've never been able to use it ourselves, for it is in a tightly sealed box. The amulet however would be useless in our hands anyway, for its power only arises when worn by our true sovereign duke. Which is why it would never serve the crown. It would simply be an ornament in their hands."

His tone then changed to a deliberate, bold enunciation.

"But in your hands, Sire, the power of heaven, an authority higher than any mortal king, will open up. That is what the monks forged it from. That is what gives you rights in our county. But only one thing is required for you to use it in that way. That is a key, something which we have never been able to procure. For it is buried, Michael wrote, in a secret location somewhere in this town. That is well though, as another of Michael's prophecies stated that when you came to free us, the key would find you."

Richard finished his profound narration. Clarence was mystified, but with a dash of excitement.

There remained though an issue, one which for the sake of honesty and his own self-respect, Clarence knew he couldn't omit from the conversation.

"Richard," Clarence reluctantly began. "A few months prior to coming here, I awoke in Darkleigh. For the first day of my return to this earth, I experienced Darkleigh as I had known it centuries ago. Albeit devoid of life. Then, the cruel truth set upon me that I was a spirit. And this happened in the rudest of ways. I realised that Darkleigh was now gripped by a beast known as industry, in the same way as many places in our county and further afield are. If it had not been for the support and guidance of my good friend, Mary, here, I would hath made a determined dive into the realms of madness, haunting at the remains of my family's old castle any fool who ventured into it for a merry jaunt."

Mary rolled her eyes with irony, remembering her foolhardy

expedition to the castle, which had raised Clarence in the first place.

"Because of that, it has become my most sincere wish to, as soon as possible, rest again. That means that I want my soul to return to heaven, which sadly means that I hath no desire to continue to haunt this earth, even if my presence allows for only good and noble occurrences."

Even Mary was deflated at this. Josiah and Caroline too, were deeply disappointed. The poise of Richard's drooping mouth was suspended in motion, trying to retain composure.

"I see, Sire. Aye, of course it is your wish to sleep again, which must be respected." A long, defeated pause followed. "But until you find the means to bring that about, please, let us entertain you. Which means that from now on, you can, if you wish, be our guests."

"Thank you," Clarence replied.

Richard rose to his feet, still with a demeanour of delight. He then guided them all outside, back into the hall.

Out of the chamber they came, back onto the stage, as the Phoenixes regarded their every move with admiration. Motioning Clarence forward delicately, Richard picked up his mace, which Clarence eyed, and tapped the stage firmly with it three times.

The whole congregation of Phoenixes knelt, and Richard shouted, "Sir Clarence de Darkleigh, our deliverer, has returned."

"Hip hip…"

"Hooray!" the whole body of Phoenixes thundered back. "Hip hip…" "Hooray!" they cheered, rising to their feet and swamping the stage with cheers.

Chapter Twenty-Seven

That night, Mary and Clarence went back to their inn on the outskirts of Lancaster. Night was setting by the time they got back and they went straight to their room, knowing full well that they needed a good deal of rest to meet whatever they were going to do the day after. Clarence went into their room and noticed Azlight still on the window sill as they had left her. He himself sat next to her on the window sill and began to disappear to orb form from the legs up. Mary noticed this, and made sure the door was locked. She wanted to speak to him before they both retired. They had seldom spoken on the way back.

"Well, that were a surprise. I were expecting pretty big stuff when I came up here, but nowt' like that," she opened with.

"Hmm" was the only acknowledgement Clarence could offer.

Mary decided she'd have to mount something of an offensive.

"Clarence, now all that's happened to us, I can't believe it! Them people... are just like us. Just like the Reformers. I mean, they're a bit different, 'cause they've been waiting for centuries for their lord to come and rescue them, which isn't a bad thing, but they want to be free like us. And like us, they're forced to do it underground! Even though we don't actually go as deep as they do. Finding them's like a sign, a message, isn't it? Shows we're on the reet track!"

"Hmm" was again all Clarence could manage.

"Don't you think they're great? You must be well impressed, the way they've waited faithfully for you. And kept what were yours. And you've got your answer now for sure, haven't you? You know why you've come back!"

Again, Clarence only responded with a vague "Hmm".

Mary sighed. "It's obvious you're not impressed," was her next comment on the situation.

"Oh no, I am very impressed with them," rebutted Clarence. "Humbled into silence."

"So do you think they're worth fighting for?" Mary said, resuming her probing.

"Oh yes, they art well worth being fought for by someone," Clarence awarded.

Mary's face sagged with disappointment.

"But not you or I," Clarence admitted.

"But why?" Mary protested.

"They hath not a saint in hell's chance," Clarence asserted.

"Of what?"

"Making it work."

"What?"

"The whole thing."

"Why?"

"Thou know why."

Clarence was being closed in his answers. Mary rolled her eyes.

"Why, is it because you think that whoever rules over them on the surface has some daft divine right to, Clarence? Like what you said about Reform? Come on. I saw your eyes when you spoke to Sam Bamford about it. I *felt* your understanding of us grow in that cellar, in that meeting you came to. Don't tell me that there's any difference between what we want and what they want!"

"Mary, my dear, if I or anyone else were to help them, to go to the mayor, or to the magistrates, or the sheriff, who rule over not just the town but the whole county, and explain to them that there is a group of people living beneath them who hath been the scourge of them and the town authorities for four centuries, and that they now demand their liberties, how dost thou think those people, those ruling classes will react?"

The ensuing long pause of silence told Clarence his point had been received, even though Mary didn't say it.

"Couldn't you protect them?" she finally said.

"What! We hath caused enough trouble as it is, in Darkleigh and here. We art criminals. The red coats and constables hath our faces. When they see us again, they shall pounce. They shall deploy however many of them it taketh to subdue us, and while I might escape as I cannot die twice, thou, my dear, shall hang. Dost thou think I want that on my conscience till I find eternity again?"

"Clarence, you saved me from Nadin. You protected our people in Darkleigh. You pledged to protect Darkleigh forever if there were a backlash from the authorities if that's what it took! You stopped that hanging yesterday — that were amazing! And you just went and did it, you didn't think twice, you just took to it. Why would helping them be any different? Is it that the stakes are higher now? Are you scared? 'Cause if you are, don't worry. You've got me to help you now. You really inspired me, Clarence. Now when you fall down, I'll be there to prop you up. Just like you've done for me. It's not like it's something whimsical that we're doing for fame and fortune. This is about so many folk, Clarence. This is something that actually matters, something well important."

During this, Clarence had taken to boring a hole into nothing with his stare, affected by the rousing words of Mary. All he could do was agree.

"I know, Mary. I know," he finally conceded.

Mary was relieved rather than satisfied. However, she still sensed that Clarence was holding back about something.

"Then, Clarence," she said in a soft voice, "what's stopping you?"

He turned to face her completely now, his upper torso starting to vanish.

"Thou art right, Mary. I pledged to protect Darkleigh forever, forsaking resting again if needs be. And that shall remain the case forever. I gave thou my word and bond. And I will rise for Darkleigh as its guardian if needs be when I find rest again. But if rest I canst, I want that to be forever if it can, Mary. Desperately. There is a difference between me protecting my beloved manor and doing so for the whole county. Not just that, but today I hath found out that I am heir to something which my best friend who knew me from birth did not even see fit to tell me about. Dost thou know what the Duchy of Lancaster is?"

Mary shook her head.

"It was a position created the century I was born. Dukes of Lancaster, who hath been the king from 1399, hath separate rights to tax folk in regions which fall under duchy jurisdiction. That includes the county palatine."

"Palatine?" Mary said with a raised eyebrow.

"Yes, the palatine. If the rightful duke so wanted, he could make separate laws for our county. Laws which would only apply here."

"Well, that's amazing, Clarence. If we could make our own laws here then that could do so much good. If you were the duke, Clarence, you could end this conflict between us and the establishment. At least in our county. They'd love you for it. You could pass laws which could give us the vote. You could make laws which could force the mill owners to make conditions better..." But she trailed off when she saw the grave look on Clarence's face.

She waited for him to explain.

"And now this instrument which I never knew about is being offered to me as Excalibur was to King Arthur. An instrument which could allow me to rule over the county in the same way a living duke could, if what that Richard said is true. Believe me, protecting Darkleigh eternally will be enough for me. And as I explained, Mary, my sole goal as a spirit, deep down, is to sleep again. I hath no true desire to mess with such great positions. Surely those art the affairs of the living?"

Mary found herself slide comfortably into realisation. She nodded.

"I understand, Clarence. That's the reason we came here, isn't it? So then, aye, it's up to you. Completely. If you want to sleep soonest, then you're entitled. You've lived once already. It's unfair of us living folk to ask you to do our own earthly work for us. But until we find a way for that to happen, them people need help, all the help they can get. Which is why I'm going to take his offer and move in with them. I can't make you follow me, but I hope you do," she concluded. "I'm either staying or walking home. I spent the last bit of money I had here," Mary stated, gesturing about the room.

Clarence went downcast. He had dragged her there. He had led her into this. Now he didn't know what to do. He hastily vanished into orb form and joined Azlight in her resting state. Mary went to bed.

***

By now, Clarence had got used to the fact that spirits didn't really sleep. He could take confidence that he was an orb and not haunting, inactive as it were; however, during this state, spirits didn't really sleep. They stayed in what Clarence had identified as purgatory. He experienced what he called 'light dreams' every night. Mostly, they were lonely affairs, where he would just sit in the hills, which went on for ever and ever. Spirits never got tired, so he used the time to meditate. It was time well spent, with his mind and reason becoming as sharp as the blade of a broadsword. But tonight, however, the familiar landscape he once again walked, was gold-tinted, swamped generously in a rich, autumn-like sun. He decided he would walk for a while, to experience as much of this pleasant sensation as he could and because the newness in turn invited his curiosity. However, it wasn't long before a hooded figure began traversing the hills, on a course bound for him. He knew this was the closest thing to dreaming he could experience, but he retained total control of himself in spite of this. So Clarence prepared to react in whatever way he needed to. But no sooner had his preparation begun than he caught sight of a beaming face he knew all too well under the hood. It was Michael. Clarence lit up, seeing his old friend in spirit, once more. Clarence moved towards him, initiating a handshake. Michael met this with enthusiasm, taking his hood off.

"Michael," Clarence greeted.

"Sire," Michael returned.

"It is truly good to see thou, especially at a time like this," Clarence declared.

"The pleasure is always mine, Sire." Michael winked.

An amused Clarence rolled his eyes.

"How dost thou feel now thou art in Lancaster?" was Michael's first question.

"Well, I hath achieved certain things. Which are well. And a myriad blessings to thou, for doing what thou didst with the Phoenixes," Clarence congratulated.

Michael smiled.

"Thank thou, Sire. That was my project. The best way I could honour the memory of thee and thy family," outlined Michael.

"Thou didst well," Clarence praised again.

Michael nodded humbly.

"But something plays cruelly on my mind. Michael, I cometh here to sleep once more. As thou recommended. But now demands hath been placed on me. This strains me, Michael. For as a spirit who doth not take any delight in haunting the living, my main purpose is to return to eternity, to sleep forever. As a spirit I am completely redundant in this world, in any meaningful way. Now I hath a whole body of albeit good folk treating me like a saint and expecting great things from me. I do not see it as my place to interfere in the affairs of the living," Clarence concluded with a grave air.

Michael's focus was unshaken.

With the slightest of nods, he softly spoke. "Thou art right, Sire. Thy ethics in wanting to distance thyself from the living is the right and noble course for a spirit to choose to take. Thy attitude deserves commendation. And thou will, Sire. Sleep again. However just because thou art a spirit, do not make the mistake of thinking that thy purpose on this Earth is completely redundant. Thou may think that thy achievements since thou arose in Darkleigh are but tokens of thy gallantry to a people who were once thine."

Clarence's nod confirmed this.

"And because of my reluctance I am worried that my friend, my only friend on Earth is starting to lose faith in me…"

"She is not losing faith in thee, Clarence, neither is she thy only friend," Michael interrupted.

"Michael, thou told me that to sleep again, I should come to Lancaster. Which I hath done. Now I hath the answer to my conundrum. I know why I hath arisen again. Though now it contradicts my desire. The desire I hath a right to, surely."

Clarence's frustration was starting to get the better of him.

"I also told thou, Clarence, to claim what was thine. That way thou *shall* sleep forever, sooner than thou canst imagine."

Michael then gestured to the silent sky, where a red rose had appeared.

"My dear Squire, it is, and shall always be thy choice," Michael said with a neutral tone of voice. "All I canst say is that image we gaze upon represents thy destiny — to sleep again. It also happens to be a licence from God. One which he grants only to those he is sure will wield his power with the absolute greatest responsibility. Trust me, my son, thou art not redundant on this Earth."

With this, something registered in Clarence, something he recognised deep within. A castle and a phoenix appeared above the rose. He was taken with wonder at this. A red cap suddenly appeared on the phoenix. His wonder deepened still.

"Each other's destiny," Michael whispered to Clarence as he patted him on the back and slowly faded from vision.

He put his fading hand out to Clarence. After a short hesitation, Clarence shook it. Michael laughed then vanished completely. Left back in the golden-tinged green landscape, Clarence stared up to the heavens. Inside he was deep in wonder.

Chapter Twenty-Eight

That night in the cellar of *The Phoenix*, Joe and Laura Duckworth were preparing for another meeting. Between them, they carefully moved barrels and kegs to the periphery of the room and arranged the benches.

"You know, Joe, I'm reet proud of these benches," Laura stated.

"Aye, they represent very fine craftsmanship," Joe agreed.

"Aye, but I meant the way everyone sits down together on them. Men, women. Catholic, Protestant, Methodist and the rest. Whoever they are and whatever they do. It's priceless what we've got, you know."

For a moment, Joe paused in his work. He came close to his wife.

"Oh, Laura, you can always see the treasure underneath," he said softly, stroking her shoulder lovingly.

"Aye, not just me but certain bobbins can as well," Laura pointed out.

Joe was unsure of her metaphor and was confused.

"A government spy would love to blow us open, wouldn't he? Finding us all here would be like winning big at a card game!"

The true subject of Laura's conversation caused Joe to sigh and roll his eyes.

"Laura, my dear, I've relaxed admission for a reason. We need as many folk as possible to come with us to Manchester. And that happens in just a couple of months' time. We're not going to boost our numbers by being overly secretive. The more people go, the more the establishment will react. Trust me, we'll need all the support we can get."

Laura understood her husband's logic but nonetheless her reservations persisted.

"Besides, my best guess is that all the spies will be in the towns closer to Manchester. I doubt they'd come up here. Too many hills, too much wind and rain."

Laura smiled and fell into Joe's arms, satisfied with his reassurance.

About an hour from then, folk started merrily streaming into the pub.

They had been told either at work, by door-to-door or via word of mouth that there was a Reform meeting on that night in *The Phoenix*. The general vibe of all persons attending was good-natured and eager to explore what was for many a new proposition that Reform entailed. They were mainly folk from the mills but included in their numbers many other folk who performed various trades from around the town. There were even a good share of shopkeepers, solicitors and doctors from the hill villages attending. This multitude of people made Joe smile, recalling his wife's words from earlier. There was one individual Joe noted who wore a golden rose in his hat. Taking an extra breath, he knew exactly what this denoted: a revolutionary. But all were welcome, even though the Reformers had no designs on instigating a revolution. Joe prayed the fellow would be won round by the methods of the Reformers, which would be discussed in detail during the meeting.

The meeting went well and a huge applause was received by Joe and Laura. They had hosted a fine meeting, and various local figures involved in Reform, including Joe himself, had spoken eloquently. There was a positive flavour of conversation in the bar and vault afterwards, both of which had been taken over by folk who had been to the meeting. Joe knew that they were speaking openly about what they had just been to, and he enjoyed the sense of enhanced courage he felt due to this. Then, he was approached by the fellow with the revolutionary's hat.

"Hello, sir," the fellow greeted, immediately offering Joe his hand. "What a fine, fine meeting. It's been a massive honour for me and my friends to attend," he said, nodding over to two other fellows at the bar, who warmly acknowledged Joe.

Joe was pleased.

"Could we go and talk privately, sir?" the fellow enquired.

"Of course. But first, I must know your name," Joe checked.

"Ah yes, of course. Forgive me. I'm Walter Sixsmith, sir, of the Revolutionary Brothers' League, as are my two friends there."

With his smile masking his apprehension, Joe showed Walter to the tavern yard, where they took shelter under the canopy.

"This is the most private location during nights like this," Joe explained.

"Ah, thank you, sir," Walter warmly thanked.

"You said you were from a Revolutionary Brothers' League?" Joe opened.

"Yes. Indeed we are. However, tonight I must say how impressed I was with your reasoning and methods. Let me assure you they are sentiments shared by most of us in the league. However, there is an element which has gained a reputation for extreme tactics in bringing about what we both want, I must concede. I'm sure you'll be well aware of them?" Joe nodded.

"Well, let me go back to them, sir, and repeat everything I've heard here tonight. Regardless of their beliefs, I swear they are good men and they will see sense, your sense, because of this."

Joe was suitably reassured.

"However, sir, as a brother of change, I would be failing in my duty of care to you and all who have attended tonight, if I did not mention the terribly pressing matter of an outside force which threatens to tear us *all* apart. Someone, or rather something, who could exploit our present situation in pursuit of his own ends."

Now Joe was concerned, if vague.

"You saw my friends at the bar, sir? Well, the one on the right was a minister. A radical minister but also a champion of peace. He was so glad when he heard there was a meeting at Darkleigh tonight. Because that gave him the perfect opportunity during the day to investigate evidence of..." Walter looked sick at the prospect of what he had to say.

Joe was starting to worry. Walter managed to salvage himself.

"The activity of Satan which many people from outside the town have heard of."

Joe's face creased with slight objection, as he wasn't sure what Walter was referring to. Walter noticed this.

"The knight," he said bluntly. "He's a disciple of the devil. My word on it, Joe. My friend went to Castle Hill today. And for sure, there is a beautiful atmosphere in the woods there. But the castle, or what's left of it, plays host to the most wicked of things. People have been using it for satanic rituals, Joe."

"By heck, how do you know that?" Joe questioned.

"By the evidence, Joe, by the evidence. Apart from pentagrams and pictures of the devil, there were as well pictures of the knight, with verses from the Satanic Bible written in Latin. I can't tell you what they said. My friend did the deciphering. I regret it's too much for me to repeat them."

Walter looked sick again.

"Joe, my friend, do NOT trust him. If he should come back, lock yourself and your loved ones away. Instruct all your fellows in your Hampden Club to do so as well. Do not shelter him, for he shall cut you all down with the contempt the devil shows all good Christian folk. Shun him and alert the clergy. For he is not a friend to you, me or anyone in personal terms. Nor is he a friend to our cause. I swear it to you. All he does is for the benefit of the devil. Please, Joe, heed my words," Walter concluded, offering his hand.

Joe shook it, not quite sure what to believe as Walter went back inside. Joe looked up into the night sky. He felt neither scared nor dismissive of Walter's warning. This was the first he had heard of any knight. But Walter's desperate tone was surely based on the testimony of eye-witnesses. And how else could an old medieval warrior have come back? Joe felt polarised by Walter's words. He continued to glare at the night sky as Laura came through.

Back in the tavern, Walter nodded his friends over and they left. Walking out onto the moon-lit cobbles, Walter's face changed from serious to sly.

"Gentlemen. Mission completed. I think the mines have been well and truly laid."

"The mines of doubt?" one of his friends asked.

"Indeed. Though they may take a while to explode. But, like a fine wine, things reach their finest quality in time," Walter quietly laughed.

His two accomplices shared the laughter as they strolled off into the night.

Chapter Twenty-Nine

Clarence and Mary walked down somewhat briskly back into Lancaster. As the thatched cottages and cobbles of the town became thicker, Clarence noticed Mary's enthusiastic stride. She was very much looking forward to reuniting with the Phoenixes and embarking on whatever adventure she foresaw. Clarence, on the other hand, was undecided. Despite the appearance of Michael in his light dreams the previous night, he still had strong reservations about what the consequences would be for aligning themselves with the Phoenixes. He, of course, would take an interest in Mary's welfare: their friendship was too entrenched for him not to. But he knew he would have to divide his time carefully between tending to Mary in whatever way she'd let him, and finding someone who could help him return to the grave. He needed a necromancer of some kind, perhaps even a clergy member, to help him rest in eternity, this time permanently. They would perform whatever ritual they needed to. Then he expected he would vanish slowly after having a final conversation with Mary. It would be difficult to avoid the Phoenixes in all this. Clarence once again considered what they had told him about why he had returned, and marvelled once again at its lunacy. The title 'Duke of Lancaster' was, whether they were capable of comprehending the contradiction or not, a distant office held by the king. There was no way he could challenge that. Even if he were to help free them, then what would happen after that? Where would he and they go from there? In the newly industrialised world, they would surely find that liberty was something of fantasy, their buried constraints being replaced by those in the great castles of industry.

As they walked across the grounds of the old friary, and towards Stonewell, Clarence made a cursory glance through the town with his second sight. It went as far as the docks. His face crinkled in confusion as he saw being marched down from Castle Hill, a convoy of people, marshalled by red coats. They were all in chains and looking forlorn. He ended his vision.

"Mary," he said with concern. "There appears to be a long line of folk being led down in chains from the castle towards the quayside."

Clarence's words carried a questioning tone. Mary immediately reacted.

"By heck, they'll be being transported!" she exclaimed.

Clarence's eyebrows dipped with confusion.

"To the colonies! That'll be what their sentence is. I've heard of that happening, but I've never actually seen it. Come on, let's go."

The tempo of their walk increased, passing through the safe darkness of the ginnels, which allowed them a few shortcuts.

They were soon at the quayside, leaning on a disused cargo crate. Despite trying to affect an image of being at rest, they were very much engaged in observing the disturbing scenes unfolding several hundred yards away. The solemn procession neared the quayside, bound for a cargo ship. It was marshalled by a squad of troops and featured at the front the odious Ned Barlow. He was clearly enjoying himself, whistling merrily, wanting all and sundry to know that he thoroughly enjoyed each and every aspect of his work. When the convoy reached the quayside, Barlow stopped in his tracks, abruptly turning to face the prisoners. He was clearly preparing to give them a grand speech before they set off for whichever far-flung part of the globe they were destined for. As with the hanging, which never was, the previous week, the families of the convicts were there. They were crying and bidding their loved ones farewell. Final hugs were being made, and the horrified screams of wives and desperate cries of husbands rang out across the quay.

"Ha ha, right now, ladies and gents. Say your goodbyes, 'cause this'll be the last time you'll get to see these people who we've let turn up here today. That is unless they can pay their passage to Australia sometime in the future," Barlow sneered with his usual sadism.

"Australia, oh, God, no!" one woman cried.

Her child next to her innocently asked, "How far away's that?"

His mother could only eye him in horror. Clarence felt something rise in Mary. It was the need for action. It was stirring and reaching its climax. Then Clarence turned his focus on himself. He felt a strange mixture of reluctance and anger gather in him, the thickness of which made the decision he felt approaching him very difficult. Then, Mary turned to him.

"Clarence, we've got to do something."

A shard of a moment passed after Mary made that statement before their attentions were distracted by a number of folk climbing over the quayside and jumping silently off the waiting ship. With such silent ease of movement, they approached the line of convicts and the next thing Mary and Clarence knew, there was a crackling sound as a huge cloud of red dust arose, engulfing the convicts, Ned Barlow and the red coats. Clarence recognised Barlow's voice in his cough. The red coats buckled and hit the ground, which was all Mary and Clarence could see of what was happening. Clarence entered his second sight again and studied the mysterious folk who had intervened in the brutal practice of the law. His mouth sagged in shock. For he recognised all of them as being Phoenixes, including the couple who had brought them from the chapel to the great hall.

"What is it?" Mary asked.

"It is them," Clarence replied. "It is the Phoenixes.".

Mary looked on with surprise. The red dust cloud was now starting to clear, and the red coats were recovering. Ned Barlow was still on his knees though, coughing as if seized by a wicked illness. Mary could just make out a prisoner being freed from his shackles by Josiah, who had been picking at his chains with a fashioned string of metal. A 'click' sounded and he was free, embracing Josiah with enormous relief before running off down the quayside. A breeze came in off the Lune, which caused most of the cloud to travel rapidly away from where the convicts had been and up towards the hill. It revealed the former prisoners running or being carried down the quayside together with their families, assisted by most of the Phoenixes who minutes before had entered the fray. But there were some Phoenixes who remained there, including Josiah and Caroline who had been engaged in picking away at the convicts' chains. They stayed composed in the face of their nemeses, but Clarence sensed they were now at a loss.

"Dost thou hath thy bow?" Clarence quickly asked of Mary.

"Aye, but it'll take some time to get it set up," she said.

"Do not worry," he said, as he flung his cloak aside and drew his sword.

The red coats, fresh with anger at how their authority had been undermined, growled as they trained their muskets on the six or so remaining Phoenixes, who appeared frozen in time. Cocking followed, and the people who had been awaiting Clarence's arrival now rested between focus on the moment and the certain death it was now to provide. That was until a dark blur passed between them and the red coats and terminated its morbidly fast progress in front of them. They were relieved when they saw it was Clarence whose reassuring presence now separated them from death. Three red coats fired, but Clarence moved with wicked pace to intercept the musket balls in the air, slicing them down with the blade of his sword.

The only thing he said was "Retreat".

Instead, the red coats gave off a regimented battle-cry as three of them charged at Clarence. The rest ran towards the Phoenixes, with the aim of arresting them. By now, Mary was enclosing from their rear.

"Do as he says!" she instructed the red coats.

They spun round and one shot at her. The musket ball missed her, but Mary collapsed as if hit. But just before she reached the ground, she shot an arrow at her would-be assailant. Hitting him square in the sternum, he went down. His colleagues had turned back to the Phoenixes they'd attempted to arrest. Fists flew, muskets twirled and struck at the Phoenixes. At this, the Phoenixes had drawn their cudgels and started hammering at the troops through the gaps which their muskets in close quarters left. Clarence quickly spun his sword through a series of defensive manoeuvres designed to hem back the troops who had ascended on him personally. This sliced their muskets with no bother, rendering them ineffectual. Their reaction was to flee, after exchanging shocked looks.

Mary had returned to her feet and was shooting again at someone who was trying to get a clear shot at her amidst the brawling chaos. This red coat was hit in the shoulder by one of her arrows, which cancelled his progress in battle. With that, some of his colleagues turned to see Mary bearing down on them, like a ghostly figure in a dream which moves towards you, with you being unable to move. Clarence brought the tip of his sword to rest on the musket of one of them, as if in warning.

The fighting untangled and ceased. The stunned red coats could only then watch as Mary ran round to group with Clarence and the Phoenixes. Escaping, they all ran off, following their friends down the quayside.

A cruel and inappropriate punishment had been thwarted, and each and every one of the Phoenixes knew it. The satisfaction they felt was matched only by the swelling sense of triumph they felt at the accomplishment of their task. The transportation of petty criminals had been prevented. Josiah's delight was moderated by the exertion he had been subjected to.

"We got them all out, Sire," he commented.

"Aye, and *we* all got out as well," Caroline put in.

Secret feelings of heroism rose in Clarence. In that moment, he felt something else within him come full circle. It reached its summit and gave him a clear message. One which told him why he was feeling so heroic. This was how he was meant to feel. This is what he was to this body of people, whose society had waited for him for four centuries. Now he felt greater heroism than he had *ever* felt in his whole lifetime. His appetite had been set. He said one thing as they all descended down a secret trap door in the quayside wall.

"Josiah, I am sorry it hath taken something of a battle for me to decide this. But I am thine. I will campaign on thy behalf to secure thy freedom. On that, my heart is set."

The width of Josiah's smile increased. Now he felt even greater for hearing Clarence's words.

"You don't know what that means to me, Sire. You don't know how much it'll mean to the society," he said with a tone that glistened with gratitude.

Chapter Thirty

So Clarence, Azlight and Mary moved in with the Phoenixes. They adjusted well to their new life underground. Mary deemed it both exciting and cosy! She went onto state that she had never felt such an intense sense of belonging. It had happened in the mill, in her family and at the archery club, but it rose to a new and unprecedented level there. Azlight enjoyed herself, running through walls, and then through the Phoenixes themselves who adored the fun of it all — and her! Clarence soon came to feel the same bond between them and him as he had had with his tenants back in the day. Having been won over by the symbols Michael had shown him in his dream and the brave actions of the society on the quayside, he told everyone that he would be more than happy to be their 'Duke' — a decision which received massive cheers when announced. Clarence was convinced that wherever he was being led, it would ultimately gratify his desire to return to eternity. But as with all desires, attainment of it would be preceded by a quest. He had seen this pattern occur numerous times when he had lived. And Clarence trusted the wisdom of Michael, even from beyond the grave. He knew he would have to lance some fiery hoops to get there, but he would endure it.

Before long, the Phoenixes didn't just become friends, but family. Such was the feeling of closeness between them. Many great feasts and dances were enjoyed in the great hall, with Clarence choosing to place himself at the tables rather than on the stage. For a deliverer in their eyes he may have been, but he was no one's living lord any more, despite pledging to be their duke. Because of this, the stage became redundant as Richard joined them too. In this environment, Clarence faced an endless stream of good wishes and questions, all of which bolstered the way he thought of himself. He was only too happy to answer each and every question in detail. Treatment like this made him feel truly heroic. And truly wanted.

A number of varied 'sorties' followed. The first involved silently moving through the shadows of the Lancaster ginnels just before dawn arrived. This had the purpose of allowing them to assist drunks who had been thrown out of the taverns and inns before the town authorities got to them when light came. However, that morning, there were few drunks about. But as the party of Phoenixes, including Clarence, Mary, Josiah and Caroline, moved silently down Bashful Alley, they witnessed an ejection of another kind. A door crashed open and a young woman was pushed out. She was then followed by a burly fellow who shouted at her.

"You're no good here. You can't perform, you silly mare."

"How dare you treat me like this!" she protested.

"You're a lying chowder-yed! You told me I was going to be a dancer!" she shouted.

"Dancers do more than dance in a place like this," he snarled, slapping her down.

She fell across the cobbles, almost prostrate. Gestures were made between the Phoenixes. Suddenly, there was only the silhouette of Clarence at the end of the tunnel-like alley.

"Hey up," he said.

The brute looked up, confused. Out of the darkness, Mary's bow crashed through his lower legs, knocking him to the floor. Then, she stood guard with an arrow ready as Clarence came down the alley and put the whore-master in a lock, politely but firmly instructing him to find a new course of employment. And to acquire some morals in the way he treated others. Josiah and Caroline helped the young woman out to Market Square, where she hugged them with gratitude. She stated that she was indeed a dancer and she had been lured there and was threatened with beatings if she didn't provide 'certain other' services as well. But she was glad as she could now go back to her family and dance safely in taverns once again.

Another day saw the four of them with a party of other Phoenixes chance upon a pair of young merchants in Sun Square. They were crying. When they asked why, they were told that they had been refused entry to a conference in the Assembly Rooms, an oh-so fashionable place in Lancaster, for not having the right boots. This infuriated Mary in particular. So, with some comfort to stem the flow of tears, Clarence marched them back to the Assembly Rooms, with the instruction that they would not take no for an answer. On the journey, the pair had told of how their enterprise was aimed at cutting costs for folk who couldn't afford what the merchant classes could. All the Phoenixes grinned with pleasure. On the door, the two over-sized fellows found their stern looks melt as Mary raised her bow, and the rest of the group their cudgels. They fainted as Clarence actually walked *through* them, followed by the two astonished merchants.

Approaching the organiser, he said, "Thou would do well to listen to these two fellows. They art setting the standard for how business should be conducted in our shire."

The stunned organiser had no choice but to welcome the two merchants in, who doffed their hats to Clarence and his party as he left.

When patrolling the tunnels with Josiah and Caroline one night, Clarence and Mary came to realise that they were close to the *Carpenter's Arms,* the tavern where Alison had led them to the tunnels in the first place. Using his second sight, Clarence related that there was a secret meeting taking place in the barrel- less cellar. Its topic — smuggling corn, which was to be sold cheaply to the people. The decent-hearted smugglers were treated to a heck of a shock when Clarence rose through the stone floor, offering his assistance. But with his kind smile, they soon listened to what he had to say. A wonderful rapport soon sprung up between them which included a warmly received suggestion made by Clarence that the corn should enter Lancaster parish via an opening at the end of the Phoenixes' quayside tunnel, before being distributed to needy folk. The measure was seized on and was a success.

Both Clarence and Mary came to feel the greatest they had ever felt thanks to episodes like these with the Phoenixes. They loved the Phoenixes, and the Phoenixes most certainly loved them! The Phoenixes basked gloriously in their work, which had increased in its volume since Clarence and Mary's arrival. They had their duke and they were revelling in it, every day and night. They felt part of the epicentre of something which brought such depth and vivid purpose to their lives. They felt, though they were two pious to say, that they were now part of legend. One of Clarence's questions about himself had been answered, but by then he didn't even want to ask the other one any more.

Chapter Thirty-One

One night during that early summer, Richard decreed that a party should take place to celebrate the recent successes of the Phoenixes, with their great hero-duke at the helm. Clarence was bashfully delighted by this, but nonetheless took to the celebration with great enthusiasm. He enjoyed sitting as their 'Duke'. By now he had been absorbed by the role.

At one point, Clarence said confidentially to Mary, "Thou know, I think I may tell them my proposal tonight. The mood is fair."

"What's that?" Mary asked, unsure of what he meant.

"Well, thou said to me thyself, dear Mary, that the purpose of this body of folk is almost identical, other than in name, to that of thy Reform comrades."

Mary's face lit up with excitement.

"By heck, you're going to ask them to come down to…" Clarence nodded rhythmically.

Mary felt very pleased. However then she noticed Caroline and Josiah slip out, strangely dejected. Concerned, she decided to follow them, putting into practice some of the skills she had learnt since being involved with the group. She followed them through the tunnels which led away from the hall and dormitories. When Caroline and Josiah reached the junction, they chose the tunnel which had the ship painted above it. Mary knew this tunnel led to the quay, from where they had smuggled the corn. After about half an hour, Mary noticed in her tailing of her friends that she could hear the labour involved in the hauling of cargo faintly permeating the earth which lay between them and the surface. She reasoned that this must be a shallow tunnel, which, certainly if a large volume of persons were travelling along it, would require much silence to avoid detection.

She had been travelling down this new tunnel for around ten minutes when, completely unannounced, Josiah turned round and said with no surprise, "You know, if you'd have wanted to come, all you needed to do were ask."

Mary's progress halted instantly. She was shocked.

"How did you know…?"

"You forget, love, we've been doing this longer than you," Josiah chuckled.

Mary attended to her embarrassment with a conceding smile. Within about another ten minutes, the three of them had reached what Caroline called 'The absolute marvel'.

"You've not seen it like this yet, have you?" she asked Mary, who shook her head.

Opening out the trap-door, Mary was astonished to see the most amorous sunset she had ever seen set over the bay. There was no room for chairs but enough to sit comfortably. Which all three of them did. Looking out from this 'balcony' Mary, even with daylight ebbing away, could see right up the River Lune, right up until its mouth. And the sky above it was glazed with such sublime tones. Mary sighed as she saw this, and Josiah and Caroline smiled at each other, remembering their first time witnessing the sight.

"Welcome to the best seats at the quay," Caroline said.

"By heck, does everyone know about this?" Mary asked.

"The sunset? Oh aye, but we're the ones who come here the most," explained Josiah.

"Many folk come here to do their thinking," Caroline followed up.

Mary nodded. She'd had many moments in Darkleigh where she'd just wanted to escape the cheers or woes of those who'd surrounded her. Despite this understanding, she still felt a need to ask questions.

"I noticed you left the hall when the party started, is something up?" Mary opened with.

"It's a place we'd rather not be when it's like that. Well, not tonight," Caroline, perhaps cryptically, answered.

"Oh," acknowledged Mary.

"Aye, tonight's a bit of an anniversary for us," Josiah added.

"Reet," Mary acknowledged again.

She thought it wise to allow what information was coming to drip through in its own time. By now, Josiah and Caroline knew there was enough trust as their friendship with Mary had grown strong since the episodes where she had become one of them.

"Aye. Today's the day when we got married," Caroline began.

"Oh, reet," Mary responded. "I didn't know you two were married."

"Not many do. To most of them in there, we're just two friends who are the best at patrolling the tunnels," Caroline continued. "But aye, we are actually married."

Mary didn't know what to say. But she sensed there was nothing to celebrate tonight.

"Should I wish you a happy anniversary?" she asked.

"Aye, you can do if you want, love, but…"

"We lost our home the day we were married, Mary. You see, we're from Bowland, originally. We had a farm up there. All our own holdings and all. Then came the war," Josiah interjected.

"Aye, and the government offered us a deal. They wanted to buy us land holdings in exchange for a contract where we could provide food for the army. It sounded fair at first, but then we checked the contract. It said that it involved us selling the lands of our own sub-tenants, who'd be turned out in the name of the war effort. And them people were our friends, so we said no, firmly. We told the government where to shove it. About a week after we went to the church in the nearby village, had a lovely day, and a lovely reception in the tavern there too, didn't we?"

Josiah nodded, his nostalgic eyes slowly moving to tears.

"'Course, come the evening it came time for us to go back. Which we did. But then we saw something we'll never forget. Our house, our home, our friends' homes, had been ransacked. Crops trampled, livestock killed, and all. It were the worst thing I've ever seen. And there's been some terrible stuff up here in Lancaster. Then I ran back to the gatepost and saw that a letter had been nailed to it. Had 'GR' and a crown on the top. Said that this land had been requisitioned by his majesty's government to aid the war effort. So we scraped the last bit of money we had together and came up here. Took all our documents to court at the castle, shire hall. We wanted advice before we took the matter to York, but they said that our legal rights to the land were now forfeit. They turned us out, penniless, unemployed and homeless. But then the Phoenixes appeared, literally out of nowhere."

Caroline laughed at the conclusion of the story she had just told with frankness. Mary by now was devastated. Josiah had tears in his eyes.

"My God, I'm sorry," was all Mary could say.

"Aye, we've been here for six years now. But it's been six well spent, hasn't it, love?" Caroline nodded.

"Aye, it has. It helps put right the mighty wrong we had done on us, helping folk out, whoever they've been conned by."

"Richard were worried about us at first. Being married. Said if something happened to one of us, the other wouldn't cope. Then we showed him how we work together and he changed his mind. Calls us the 'Tunnel double', " laughed Josiah.

"Aye, but we told him not to let on about us being married. For the same reasons as he was concerned for," told Caroline.

"By heck, they're at it in the countryside as much as they are in the towns," Mary sighed.

"What's that?" asked Caroline.

"Well, conning you. They just want you over a barrel. Same old," Mary said grimly.

"Oh aye. A lot of folk think that just 'cause you live in the countryside you're safe from the ruling class and the government that works for them and them only," Caroline agreed through a bitter tone.

"Aye. Believe you me, if they want what you've got, they'll find a way. No matter how clever or wicked they have to be, they'll find a way to make it look like they were justified," commented Josiah.

"Don't you think folk are starting to see through that though?" Mary raised.

"Oh aye. Folk see through it well enough. There's just not enough folk who are united behind something to stop it. And that's what they play on. Folk are too busy scrambling about, trying to make ends meet to be able to come together and do something about it, like. They've got us divided. When you think of the Yeomen doing their own thing, the minor aristocracy doing theirs, and the folk cooked up in the factories. Good Lord!"

Mary shielded her face as she smiled a devious smile which would have told her friends that she knew otherwise. But she didn't want to seem clever in doing so.

So she innocently said, "Have you folks heard of the Reform

213

movement?"

"No," was their reply.

"It's really big in the south of the county especially. Has lots of followers."

"What's it about?" Josiah asked.

"They want to change everything about the way the government's run. So everyone else as well as the big-wig landowners can have a smell in. They want to make sure that everyone can have a vote. That way we'll be able to elect folk to parliament to make laws to protect us in the factories and make sure that we can have a bit more than what we have. Well, I mean, not many of us have an eye on grand mansions or owt' like that. But so we can make sure there's always going to be bread on the table, clothes on us backs, work to keep you going and money for you to go and see the quack. Stuff like that."

Caroline and Josiah were intrigued by the end of it.

"And you know about it, do you?" Josiah inquired, taking his intrigue further.

"Aye. I've been one myself. Been to a few of their meetings in Darkleigh and all. Handed out bills for them."

"Does Sir Clarence know about this?" Josiah then asked.

"Ooh, aye. He's been to a Reform meeting with me once and all."

Caroline and Josiah were taken with this. Mary noticed and took things further.

"Later in the summer there's going to be a big mass meeting in Manchester. So I've got to go back down for it. It's going to be a big demonstration, a big statement, if you like, telling the government and them who rule what we expect to happen in the future. So, I'm going to try and get the Phoenixes to come. 'Cause I see us lot in the Reformers. I see us in my friends at the mill. And I see them in us lot."

For the first time in the weeks since Mary had met them, Josiah and Caroline were genuinely surprised.

"You're both invited, of course," Mary offered.

"Reet. Well, it sounds good, lass, but I doubt… well, have you told Richard about this?" Josiah pointed out.

"Oh well, no, not yet. But I will. He'll be great to have there as well, of course."

"Well, that'd be your next port of call," advised Josiah.

Mary nodded.

"Though good luck with tearing him away from this lot. He's not the arrogant type, but this is his pride and joy," warned Caroline. "You might have a bit of a battle," she followed up.

"Well, I must say when I heard that legend about Sir Clarence I thought it were just an old legend. A great symbol, if you like, but nowt' else. I'm so glad I've been proved wrong. Don't get me wrong, I've always known ghosts exist. You can divine them like you can make fire, there's nowt' spooky about it. But then his spirit shows up and then I learn about this! All that praying has paid off, Caroline," laughed Josiah.

Mary didn't like Clarence being referred to crudely as a ghost but was glad she'd raised the *spirits* and optimism of her friends. If she could persuade Richard to let the Phoenixes travel down to Manchester, and for him to come with them, she knew deep within her that she would have achieved something she was born for. The three of them stared out into the fading sun, cascading its riches over the Lune valley. The magic of the moment merged benevolently with the lavish glory of their dreams.

Chapter Thirty-Two

Returning to the great hall, Josiah and Caroline were happier, and Mary took quiet satisfaction in having helped them back to the party. Taking their seats again, they were soon enveloped in chatting to everyone on their table. Although they weren't displaying unbridled feelings of joy, it was obvious that their warmth of feeling had increased and was now radiating round their table.

Sitting back down next to Clarence, Mary greeted him by saying, "Good things are happening tonight, Clarence."

Clarence, who had up until a minute or so ago been engaged in a conversation with two former miners, was happily intrigued.

"I am glad," he replied.

He didn't question her comment, and this pleased Mary, given that she didn't want to be faced with having to deny Clarence knowledge of something very personal she had just learnt about Josiah and Caroline.

"Now, my dear, I am going to strengthen their understanding of the existence of hope in the outside world, a hope which mirrors theirs."

Mary nodded with anticipation.

"Then I'm going to ask them if they shall accompany us to Manchester for the great meeting, which shall be taking place there."

Clarence had hit the bedrock. Anticipation turned to sheer excitement in Mary's mind. Nodding, Clarence rose from their table and jumped up onto the stage, a place he was seldom seen. Cue a sudden hush in the hall. Richard waited for his sovereign to say something profound. The look of pride in his eyes was evident. Adoring faces turned to him.

"Good evening, friends," Clarence began. "Art ye enjoying thyselves?"

A good-natured roar of agreement followed.

"That is well. We work hard to perform all the good deeds which our county town requires, do we not?" Another roar followed.

"And tonight, we art celebrating our wonderful achievements

accordingly, art we not?" By the third roar which followed, Clarence realised the Phoenixes were almost worshiping him.

He let the adulation drench him for a few moments nodding with pride at them. Then he knew it was time to begin.

"The change in the attitudes of many who dwell on the surface towards ye hath been something I know ye hath long desired. And rightly so!" Clarence opened, with a resounding, thundering tone.

That encouraged another cheer.

"Ye hath wanted thy liberties to be respected by the state who shunned ye! Ye hath wanted the priceless notion of being able to look all others on the surface in the eye and receive the same respect that ye would pledge to offer them!"

That last point engendered the most rabid cheer heard that night.

"It is not right that ye should be spurned from the land that gave ye birth. The land ye no doubt love."

Folk nodded their heads with vigour and many called "aye".

"Thy crimes art non-existent. All ye hath done is care for those wanting to pursue peacefully their own faiths, give disillusioned warriors a new cause to campaign for, free the enslaved, protect young women whose only transgression in life was to have children out of wedlock, and to bring strength and comfort to those who hath been tainted by vulnerability."

Now a wave of applause washed through the hall. Folk rose to give Clarence a standing ovation.

"But, my friends,", he began again with the applause ceasing, "believe me when I tell ye that there art some folk whose permanent homes art on the surface who share thy grievances. Folk who take issue with the many injustices that hath developed over four hundred years. Folk who believe, as ye do, that NOW is the time for change. They art called the Reform movement. They may hath their meetings to discuss the changes they seek in secret, many underground like us. But they live and work on the surface, each day staring boldly in the eye the tyranny that in turn tries its utmost to stare them down."

With that last point Clarence was subtle in his tone, so as not to sound critical of the Phoenixes.

"How are they wanting to change things on the surface?" Molly

Walhurst called.

"They wish to reform parliament. They want to see an end to the likes of the corn-laws, which starve us. An end to borough-mongering which treats the seats in parliament as if they were personal property. And that is just to begin with. They want each person to have one vote, so that their representatives can be elected to make laws to protect them on their behalf. In short, they want this land to become a democracy, and with it, a free nation. They go hand in hand."

The Phoenixes were still absorbed by Clarence; they had each become enchanted by what he had described. Everything the Reformers wanted stood like jewels on a hillside, sparkling in the sultry twilight. And, despite not fully understanding what it was yet, they crucially saw their own purpose in that of the Reformers. Most, if not all, sensed a connection between their discontent and that of their surface counterparts. Furthermore, they sensed a connection between the *changes* they both sought. Clarence sensed this as well, and was pleased. Mary was ignited by excitement and hope. Josiah and Caroline, in line with what Mary had just told them, were optimistic as well. Then someone asked an inevitable question.

"Sounds great, Sire, but how do we fit into it all?"

Clarence unleashed it.

"My friends, this is where I must ask ye to join with us. Join with the Reformers and make a stand."

Some were mildly confused.

"In the town of Manchester, this very summer, there will be a mass-meeting, attended by thousands of people. There they will listen to a renowned political speaker proclaim their rights. Then there shall be a picnic. The vast number of people there is intended to persuade the ruling classes, which have our land in their palms, to see the point of view of the Reformers."

Clarence looked down at Mary for confirmation he had got everything he had said right. Mary nodded with proud vigour. Glad of this, Clarence made his great invitation.

"So, what I and the Reformers ask of ye, my friends, is will ye all come down to Manchester with us this August, to lend thy support to our brethren at the mass meeting?"

With that, the atmosphere in the hall went flat. The Phoenixes were still Clarence's captive audience, but they had, unbeknown to Clarence, reached a thick curtain wall which they believed they were not capable of breaching. Clarence sensed the new atmosphere, as did Mary. Josiah and Caroline were surprised, wondering if their comrades would go with him. The confidence the Phoenixes had showed during Clarence's impassioned address to them was now evidently flaking away. They were looking to each other now, wondering if someone was going to voice their support of Clarence's proposal. But none came.

"Speak to me, friends," Clarence implored.

"Sorry, Sire, we…" someone started but the flustered chattering that ensued swamped him.

With a reassuring hand raised, Clarence jumped down from the stage and into the ranks of the society, to try to determine what the matter was. Mary waded in amongst them, her melodic tones of appeal blunting somewhat the worried debate. It was then Clarence noticed Richard slip out of the hall and towards the tunnels. Concerned, he naturally followed him.

Chapter Thirty-Three

Clarence shadowed him all the way to the chapel. Richard took his seat in one of the pews. Clarence entered shortly after and sat down opposite him.

"Thou know, this could be what ye hath been waiting four centuries for, Richard," Clarence sensitively began. "The Phoenixes. Eventually part of the liberation of all in this land. Maybe that is why I came back now. A friend I brought here had knowledge of something that I wouldst not hath understood otherwise. Maybe this is what that prophecy was about. The day the Phoenixes emerge and take their place amongst their compatriots, and perhaps win their liberty."

Clarence had been calm and matter-of-fact in his tone, so as not to patronise Richard. But he needed to make a bold point regarding what an opportunity this was to be. Richard turned round to Clarence. He was on the verge of tears, though had not the energy to cry.

"Sir Clarence. My lord, I have been chairman here for twenty years now, and a Phoenix for thirty-five. I found myself here because I believed I was the receiver of a curse. I come from a farm, where we used to breed horses. When I was a lad, I had the time of my life. I helped my father breed horses, my mother feed them. All my life was spent around horses. Now, when all the mills and factories sprouted up, a lot of my pals took off to the towns. Said they were going to seek their fortunes there. That were at best. At worst, they said things would be so much better in the towns. Better standard of living, like. And, of course, as I'm guessing you'll have witnessed with Mary, the other side of the coin told a different story. They absolutely pleaded with me to go. But nay. I were happy on the farm with me' parents. And I had a darling fiancée, too. But one day I visited my friends in the nearest town, see I wrote to them, like. They invited me over to stay for a few days. So I went. And, of course, I then saw what life were really like for them. But in the midst of all that bloody grind, I felt something. Something I'd felt in the countryside.

Something which didn't give up on me, or them. It were strange 'cause it made life more than bearable. It made it worthwhile. Something like a beacon."

Clarence didn't admit it, but he knew exactly what Richard meant. He had felt the same presence in Darkleigh.

"And it were that that kept me going throughout the visit. We had a great time when we could. In all the taverns, having dances and the like. Often, bailiffs of the landowners called round, shouting that my pals hadn't paid enough rent. But they were honest with their excuse — they didn't have enough money to pay the landlord, given that they needed to eat to get to his stinking mills to work in to get what they had. 'Cause I were an unknown quantity in them parts, I were dressed in my country outfit, and pretended to be a country gent. So I declared that my friends were under my protection and beat the bailiffs off. I did it so well they stopped coming. With help from my pals, of course. It were almost like I'd given them hope. So one day, there were a big to-do in town. My pals called me there, everyone were saying that the landowner whose bailiffs I'd been kicking were there. The landowner were meant to be kicking off himself. When I got there, I were ready to fight. I were younger then and daft like that; the way things are at that age. But when I got there, I got the shock of me' life. 'Cause none of us had ever seen him, like, no one knew who he were. I saw who the landowner were."

There was a grinding pause, tears straining in Richard's eyes.

"It were me' father. He'd been told that there were a young gent from the country who were championing the folk who were imprisoned on his land. When he saw me, his face were red with rage and blue with disappointment, at the same time, like. I still remember it now. My mother were looking on, from a distance, crying, like. And I remember me' friends looking at me, shocked, knowing who the landlord were. They had no idea what I were going to do. Fight for them or fight me' own father. Talk about the devil and the deep blue sea. Well, I didn't know what to do. So I fled. I never returned to that town and I never saw me' friends again. Though I did get back to me' parents' farm. My father had always been a good bloke. I just couldn't understand why he'd allowed all the people of the town to have all that squalor imposed on them. It were then I found out that me' fiancée had moved away, went off with someone else, 'cause I'd been having a reet grand time in the town. She'd got tired of waiting for me. Of course, me' parents arrived back soon after. Me' father gave me an hour to pack and then sent me away for good, saying I'd undermined and humiliated him. Disowned me, he did, me' mother were in tears. I've never seen or heard from them since. Then I found myself up in Lancaster where I'd taken to drinking. They were going put me in the pillory for that, but then the Phoenixes rescued me and the rest, as they say, is history."

Clarence was rendered speechless. Clarence had lost his parents when young, but not in such sad circumstances. He didn't know what to say.

"Richard, my friend, I am so sorry," was all he could offer.

"You see, Sire, the Phoenixes gave me hope. Just like Christ does. Perhaps not the same as that, but I was led to believe that we were waiting for something, nay, someone who would return and save us all from the ills imposed on us by society. Now, of course, Sire, you must do as you will. You're the revered one here, not me. Not us. I know you mean the best for us, inviting us to Manchester. But that day in the town I made a decision. A decision I really should never have had to have made, I know, but it were the pin on which the rest of my life turned."

In a bad, bad moment, Clarence felt the pang of being accused touch him.

"What exactly art thou saying, Richard?"

"Oh, forgive me, Sire, forgive me. I'm not making any statement against you, but I'm just not sure what to believe now. Everything Michael said would happen has happened. And I just don't understand what good will come of going to Manchester. You see, this society, these tunnels, are all a lot of us have known for such a long time. For some of us, they're *all* we've ever known. Asking them to go to a big strange place like Manchester, well, God only knows what effect it'll have on them. And what'll happen when it's over? Will things change? Will they just come back here? Our existence could well be exposed to the authorities down there and up here! And then what? Will they come after us? Ransack the tunnels? In so many ways it could be the end of us. Sorry."

Richard got up, bowed to Clarence and left. As he was on his way out, Mary came rushing in.

Composing herself before entering the chapel, she whispered, "Clarence!"

Turning round, Clarence got up, seeing the look of urgency in her eye. He went over to her.

"What is it?" Mary explained that there was a gathering going on right outside the castle as they spoke.

"What's it about?" Clarence asked.

Mary said she wasn't sure, but the word which was being passed along the ginnels and through the taverns of Lancaster was 'Reform'.

Chapter Thirty-Four

Up on the moors and hills north of Manchester, mill-workers and Reformers alike took obvious delight in practicing drilling. Although their paces weren't too formal or militaristic, it had been agreed that skills learnt in military life could be helpful when marching to the meeting that was to come. Re-appropriated by the Reforming marchers, it would be a gracious and powerful demonstration of the discipline that they wished to convey to the establishment. The sincerity of their cause would surely help to leave their opponents floundering. Supervising the drill were veterans from the recent wars with Napoleon. They wouldn't admit it, but in seeing their own people move with such form and pride brought tears to their eyes. They felt the old feelings of military comradeship burn deep within them. But this time, the cause was different. The battle was to be won by oration, they hoped. The proverbial field of battle was to be the peace of St. Peter's Field in Manchester. Their army were their friends and colleagues from the mills and other walks of life which felt or detested the deep bite of tyranny. Armed only with decent disposition and the united belief that there were remedies to what blighted the great lives they wished to lead.

Arnold Varley, a former sergeant, shouted with warmth, "Alreet, ladies and gents! By the flag, quick march!"

"What does that mean?" one of the marchers shouted.

"It means when he starts moving, you move!" Arnold laughed, having the best time in a long time.

The flag bearer, a tackler named Joseph Shaw, turned round and said, "You see, reet important me!"

The marchers laughed.

"Alreet," Arnold shouted. "Let's have you along…"

The wind rolled over the moors, causing the masses of grass and reeds to wave, bringing a cooling influence to the zest that a dense body such as themselves had created.

In Reform societies and Hampden Clubs all throughout the radical towns, there was a constant flurry of activity. Aside from the mills, more time was spent at the clubs than was spent at home. Great and elaborate banners were made, using leftover bits of textiles from the mill and from their homes. Words and slogans were sewn on to them, as were motifs and badges. Everyone offered their help with this. From the burliest of tow path men to young bairns, true joy radiated in moments when finished banners and flags were raised. A variety of colours, they carried messages like 'No Corn Laws', 'No Borough-mongering', 'Equal representation is our right', 'One vote for all' and the bold, blunt 'Liberty or Death'. As the month of August drew nearer, the confidence of the Reformers grew. This led to them handing out bills at fairs, inviting all to the mass meeting in Manchester. Engaging with folk out in the open was something they took to with such a pleasant manner, one which made their clubs and each other proud. The responses were varied. Some snorted and walked away. Others needed some explanation. Others were chuffed at being invited to the rumoured meeting which they'd heard whispered about in taverns. Either way, the meeting was set to attract a crowd far larger than the thousands of Reformers put together. This encouraged some to make brief speeches in the open air, espousing the virtues of Reform and painting a lovely picture of the day in Manchester in prospect. One thing that was mentioned was the presence of the speaker, Henry Hunt. He was going to take the chair at the meeting and deliver a fine speech indeed. Hunt was lauded as a true radical and the best speaker in Britain. Fusing these two aspects amongst the cotton folk of the North-West was akin to offering free beer on a feast day.

On Castle Hill, Joe Duckworth and several of his close friends from the Reform society pushed their way through the branches of the trees which now constricted the space around Castle Hill. He noticed the hole in the lower outer wall Mary had made, and he shovelled himself down and through it to the other side. His friends followed suite. Joe and they had grown up with stories about Castle Hill, (for it was a fixture in local folk lore), as Mary had. However, awareness of the remains of an actual castle had escaped their consciousness. Standing up in the courtyard, their awe was short-lived as the business of their visit needed to take centre-stage. Looking around extensively, they found not a scrap of evidence corroborating what Walter Sixsmith had told Joe.

Snorting some mirth, Joe announced, "Aye, petty scare-mongering, lads. Best watch out for them in future."

"Aye, they won't be coming to any more meetings, I tell you now, Joe," one of his friends agreed.

"Cheers, Alan. Scare-mongering we can laugh off though. Borough-mongering, well, that's a different matter."

They all grinned in agreement.

All over the radical counties, the radical presses were deep in their work. Newspapers were flying off at an alarming rate, their front pages were adorned with information about the mass-meeting in Manchester, which was to take place. Activity was reaching a peak. The rupturing fault-lines of change were starting to shudder. And everywhere that demanded it were feeling them all the more. A land's destiny was fast-approaching.

Chapter Thirty-Five

The day after the disappointing reaction to his announcement, Clarence found himself on the moors again. It was an accommodatingly warm day and he was staring out to the bay, in a light meditation. Mary was lying behind him, amongst the trees which lined the top ridge where the county gallows had once stood. She was enjoying a pleasant snooze. He hadn't spoken to Richard or anyone else since yesterday, as he was starting to feel a hint of rejection. It was after all, they who had proclaimed him as some kind of returning hero when they had found out who he was. Then, when seeking to empower them, their reaction had been quite stale. Then a thought entered the pristine canvas that stood in his mind. He remembered Richard telling him about the key which would allow him to open the box and wear the amulet which gave him extraordinary powers which not even living dukes were privy to. Yes, the key. Clarence wondered where it could be. He had indeed read in Michael's scripts that it was buried somewhere in Lancaster, in a secret location. Clarence steadily ended his meditation and entered his second sight. His first natural choice was the castle so it was into its fabric he began to pierce, his mind's eye intent on finding the key which would hopefully call to him. However, it was something else which did so. The subtlest of tones caused him to abandon his pursuit of what would bring him primacy.

It called in despairing fashion, 'Marvin... Marvin'.

Clarence was given the impression from this call that there was someone in peril there and that things were at stake for whoever that name referred to. It was coming from the Well Tower. Clarence then let himself drift through the air, off the ridge, towards the castle in the near distance. As he did, he progressively took on orb form.

Within his orb form, he began exploring the Well Tower, searching for someone who that name echoed with. Checking dungeon by dungeon, it didn't take long before he caught sight of a fair-haired young fellow who was chained to the floor. He was clad in what many mill-workers wore. He was fidgeting about, used to another kind of blunt barbarity than the chains that held him in place. He was frustrated and resentful. Levelling up in front of him, Clarence was not yet visible to him as an orb. Despite this, he delved deeper in his second sight to perform the same feat he had done with Emmanuel, when he had first arrived in Lancaster. A contrast of colours blew across his second sight, along with flashing pictures of the fellow he took to be Marvin. Clarence already felt a connection, however. As soon as that thought crossed his mind, these colours gave way to more vivid pictures complete with echoes. There he saw a town square, different to Darkleigh's, but what he was able to faintly recognise as Rochdale. There he saw who by now he was sure was Marvin giving a speech before a crowd, something Clarence now knew to be a staple of this era. This was followed by a new image of Marvin using empathetic and persuasive body language in a tavern's backroom, causing many heads to nod. Behind him was a banner which said 'Rochdale Golden Shuttles Reform Society'. The elongated drawls of several words, including 'Forthright action' and again the name 'Marvin' could be heard. Clarence knew for sure he had the right person. Exiting his second sight, Clarence steadily began to leave orb form, gradually appearing to Marvin in full-body form. Marvin didn't know what to be more perplexed by: the compounding dip in temperature in his cell or the mist which was solidifying as a figure before his very eyes. When Clarence had fully formed, he was grateful that Marvin was able to resist the temptation to scream. He just stared up at Clarence, gawping in shock.

Marvin spoke first. "What are you?"

Clarence grinned.

"Remember the de Darkleighs?" he gloated, aware now of his family's legendary reputation in the ballads of Lancashire.

"No," Marvin replied, still perplexed.

Clarence smiled at his own bantering audacity and approached the point.

"Young squire, I am Sir Clarence de Darkleigh. Seventeenth lord of Darkleigh. Thou must be Marvin?"

Marvin nodded enthusiastically.

"It seems that thou art in a bad predicament?"

"Aye," Marvin agreed.

"Marvin, thou art safe to admit this to me. Art thou a Reformer?"

This time Marvin wanted some validation.

"Why, who are you working for? Are you a spirit?"

"I work for the Phoenixes, a body of fine folk who make it their business to protect those who get left behind in the county town. And, yes, I am a spirit, well-reasoned. I hath no connection with the authorities, especially those who run this castle," Clarence concisely informed him.

This explanation, and how Marvin had seen Clarence materialise before him — like no living being would do, satisfied him that there was now enough mutual trust between them. Especially as Clarence seemed to be sympathetic to his predicament.

"Aye, I'm a Reformer. We came up from Rochdale, asking that a petition we had signed by all of us could be used at the next election. You know, when they elect MPs for the county. You see, I'd put meself forward as a candidate, like. Said I'd be here, on the hustings. We asked that all the signatures acted in lieu of us being here. 'Cause they're not going to be able to make it, when the next parliament's called. They took the petition, alreet. Said they'd use it as evidence. When we asked what the hell they were talking about, they arrested me and threatened the rest of us with their muskets. I mean, by heck, they apply the law in daft ways in Lancaster, don't they? I'm on trial Friday and all," Marvin explained.

"What for?"

"They've not said yet."

Clarence raised an eyebrow.

"That was illegal when I lived. To imprison someone without charge was ridiculous."

"They've suspended Habeas Corpus. You know, the one that says you can't be locked up without charge?"

Clarence was disgruntled. Marvin looked up at him, slightly awe-struck.

"Are you a knight? A medieval knight?"

"Yes," was Clarence's matter-of-fact reply.

"Wow," Marvin said.

Clarence wanted to talk more at length about his origins as it would allow for a greater dialogue between him and Marvin. But time belayed him.

"Listen, Marvin. I am going to get thou out of here. Trust me. Thou and thy friends exhibited a peaceful, respectful disposition, didst ye not?"

Marvin nodded vigorously.

"Of course we did."

"Then they hath no reason to hold thou like this."

Clarence wanted to help him get out now. But to do so would require Mary's help and the help of several other Phoenixes. Maybe this would be a welcome distraction for all of them. Clarence took some bread from a pouch on his belt.

"Hath this. And remember thou art not going to come to any more harm during thy stay in the county town. Thou shall certainly not be found guilty. We will not allow it. Dost thou understand?"

"Aye," Marvin replied, sounding hopeful while navigating his way through Clarence's old way of speaking.

"The guards shall not bother thee again, if only to give thou some food," Clarence promised in addition, removing some ectoplasm and leaving it on the wall of Marvin's cell.

"They will not like that. But for thou it shall be an oddly endearing smell," Clarence promised.

Taking his hand, Clarence gave him a firm handshake for emphasis. With that, Clarence jumped through the grey stone wall and was off. Marvin just sat there in his cell, a devious look freshly streaking across his face.

As Clarence set off back towards the moors, an impulse struck him. It came completely unsolicited, and from his naked mind, rather than his second sight. It was a strange feeling of familiarity — with Marvin. Clarence had no memories of this fellow, just an instant rapport and understanding, which wasn't unnatural for folk in his county. However, Clarence had connected with others in the same way and not felt this impulse. He couldn't help but think that he'd met Marvin somewhere before. But he couldn't have, because his store of memories were completely devoid when presented with him. Furthermore, it was impossible to have had any memories of him anyway. For Marvin was a young fellow who would have been born relatively recently — centuries after Clarence had lived! And Clarence would definitely have remembered any encounters with him since he awoke that horrible day to find Darkleigh in what he thought was a warped state. As Clarence flew as an orb, back towards the moors, he was assailed again, this time by his second sight along the way. It was the first time in a long time that it had just spontaneously put itself upon him without having been bidden. For it showed him a sight which disturbed even him to the point where he recoiled into cringing. Around the castle of Lancaster, many, many crimson monsters appeared, their fangs formed slender and hideous like sabres. They proceeded to swamp the incline which led to the gatehouse, pouring in as well from the streets and ginnels in hungry, snarling fashion. They took over the concourse at the rear of the castle between hanging corner and the Priory church. Like blots falling from the sky they came to dominate Clarence's vision, until the whole scene ended as quickly as it had begun. Abruptly being dragged from his second sight, Clarence felt the absence of breath in his lungs, as he always did. But the feeling of being short of breath was for the first time in a while, snatching at his conscience.

Chapter Thirty-Six

The military ring around Manchester was getting tighter. So tight it was desired by the establishment and loyalists that it would choke the wicked activity of sedition which Manchester and its surrounding towns were rapidly becoming famous for. The great knot was ready to tie, all that was needed was the slightest of pretexts to pull it through. In Manchester itself there were six troops of cavalry and seven companies of infantry stationed there. Bolton, Oldham and Ashton had two troops of cavalry each. Rochdale was marked with the presence of two companies of infantry while Stockport enjoyed that of four, in addition to a troop of its county's Yeomanry cavalry. Five more troops of the latter were stationed in Altrincham. And all these units, whether regular or militia, were deep in the business of scouring those towns for loiterers who could turn into a mob; merry gatherings in the backrooms of taverns which could be celebrating more than the likes of a Christening; odd activity amongst those going to and from work or church. Or so they had been briefed.

In many a workshop, sabres were sharpened for the use of the cavalry units. Those entrusted with the sharpening were glad of the few guineas they would make. They took to their work like demons forging their sabres in hell. Knowing full well that they were for military use, they could be forgiven for their ignorance in that the bitter fruits of their labour were being used to keep their own people at bay, besieged by the shadows of both the mills and the militia. Elsewhere, in the many stables the militia used, horses were freshly shod. Saddles replete with military livery were being fitted upon the horses. The military, whether regular or Yeomanry, was making its presence felt, digging its heels firmly in as the months approached.

In Manchester, Joe Nadin and his special constables were making enquiries in every public house they could imagine would host seditious activity. Every and any scrap of information that merely hinted at a Reform meeting taking place or that there was a resident Hampden Club at the establishment was chased up. Nadin continued with his infamous approach, vigorously encroaching on the licensees, demanding information. But even he left each one satisfied that there was little, if anything, to be gained from them. In the same town, Reform bills advertising the meeting were scornfully whitewashed by loyalists.

The 'great' spy Walter Sixsmith returned to Darkleigh to spread more of his fantastical suggestions. However before he did, he made the grim mistake of calling at *The Phoenix* tavern. On a quiet day, he ordered a jug of the town's legendary pale ale. The landlady frowned as he asked for it without any hesitation, in the early afternoon. Quaffing away, Sixsmith didn't realise the greatness of the ale's effects. Although registering its fine taste, his unaccustomed palate couldn't cope with what happened next. With a groan, he soon felt the need to go outside. When out in the square, he looked up into a quiet day in said square and was met with a great host of boggarts, spooks and knights palavering around with the silliness of a hundred bairns.

Captivated by what he saw and heard, he began shouting to passers-by, "knights!", "spirits!", "ghouls!"

They rolled their eyes and said one thing, "Pale ale. Best leave him to it."

For Darkleigh folk knew that those unaccustomed to that kind of beverage could not be reasoned with.

In Manchester, William Hulton received a letter from Sixsmith within days, accounting for the rumours of there having been a knight in Darkleigh who had interfered with the process of the law (upon meeting Nadin). Sixsmith had had it explained to him that his experiences when having drunk his chosen pint were in accord with the notorious effects of the town's pale brew. Hulton afforded himself a sly laugh. Then he remembered the livery Nadin said the knight had carried. Then he connected the image of the phoenix rising from the flames of a castle with the tavern Sixsmith had purchased his chosen beverage. Then he imagined, unsurprised, Nadin drinking away in this tavern the day he claimed to have been set upon by this 'knight'. Sense had been made and Hulton put the whole issue to bed. As the month of the great meeting approached, he decided quite rightly that he had things of much vaster importance to attend to.

Chapter Thirty-Seven

With Marvin's impending trial, Clarence pondered. He didn't mind the condition but when it left him no closer to being able to discern his next move, then it left him feeling rudderless. Tomorrow, Marvin would be up in the assize court. What Clarence would do now was anyone's guess. He knew that Mary and he would go to the meeting, with or without the amulet. And, if necessary, he would speak for the Reformers to those who held them down. But 'what now?' he thought. What now at this very moment?

Sitting on the steeps again, he gazed out to the hill again at the centre of town. Out to the glimmering bay and beyond it to the luscious and mighty fells. The rush of wind passed by unmolested, plainly delivering him the feeling that he was on his own. And he didn't mind. In fact, he felt deeply comforted by the sensation. Moments later though, it was pierced by footsteps he knew. Two pairs — Mary and Richard. He hadn't spoken to Richard since the harrowing conversation with him in the chapel.

"Good day," Clarence greeted, not abandoning his gaze out to the landscape.

"Hello, Sire," Richard returned softly.

There was a moment of silence.

"Clarence, Richard's told me everything. I understand why he's not jumping at the idea of walking down to Manchester. But there's something he wants to say," Mary explained.

Clarence turned round to them and nodded, not losing his composure.

"Sire," Richard began. "What you offered us was an opportunity capable of making our lives. Of fulfilling the role our society has always had. No-one wants to turn it down. More importantly, no-one wants to turn you down. But, I just feel they need something, Sire. Some proof, some reassurance that they're going to be safe. That after the meeting down there they can come back up here and there'll be one of two things waiting for them. Either the tunnels, shielded from the outside world, or the welcome of them who live on the surface. 'Cause as I said, the first one's all many of them have ever known."

Clarence understood. The Phoenixes needed their own safe-tower, either way.

"What about courage, faith?" Clarence asked.

Richard bent down to him.

"Oh, Sire. Sire. They do have it in them. I swear to you. If you asked for their help, and asked them to follow you into hell, they would *want* to follow, regardless. But can you show us courage and faith? Can you inspire us?"

Clarence looked down to the field beneath the steeps.

"I need that key for the amulet, do I not?" he said.

"Aye," Richard confirmed.

"Could ye find it for me? For if it is heaven sent, then who knows what the scope of our achievement could be?"

"I'll have them search for it immediately, Sire!" Richard promptly answered.

The smiles between the three of them, despite the speculative nature of Richard's pledge, suggested that they had reached some kind of accord. But immediately after, there came a loud whisper from the centre of the field that lay beneath them.

"Thou art not taking *my* legacy," it said.

Mary, Clarence and Richard looked down to the field and saw a solitary figure standing in it with his back to them. Clarence sensed it was a fellow spirit, as he felt not the same feelings on regarding him as he usually felt with the living, but that was it. They saw that he was wearing armour and a tabard, and the words which had drifted across from him had been carried by a smoothly rasping, continental voice.

"I would prefer to speak French, but I want your friends to hear this," he said again, quite resentfully.

At that point, Clarence noticed that the likely-spirit was wearing a crown. A possibility occurred to Clarence. Then the spirit turned and it was confirmed. His tabard was as Clarence had seen it in portraits: the royal arms (Quarterly, France ancient and England) differenced by a label of three points ermine. This plainly denoted the Duchy of Lancaster. However, more than this, it was the almost regal energy which arose from him. A duke who was a king in all but name. Clarence was affected by that in particular.

"Thou know who I am, no?" was his next question.

It was Clarence's instinct that told him for certain who the spirit was.

"John O' Gaunt," Clarence said to a stunned Mary and Richard.

"Thou wish to call thyself the duke of Lancaster, but thou art a common knave compared to me. The duchy of Lancaster exists for the use of high nobles. It is for their benefit and their benefit only. That is the way it hath always been. That is the way of the Lord," John sneered.

"Wrong on both counts. But I used to think as thou do," Clarence said, assuming a dynamic stance which showed he was ready for a confrontation.

"Thou think I shall let thou usurp my legacy? If this amulet is as powerful as they say, then it belongs in my hands!" John intoned, drawing his sword.

"Take shelter," Clarence instructed to Mary and Richard.

"Let us talk," Clarence remembered, as he moved his hand to his hilt. As he found his hilt, his hand paused on it.

His expression offered Gaunt a truce. But John was not interested. He made a spiralling jump up to the steep Clarence was on as his friends ran for cover. Clarence drew his sword within the space of a moment and halted Gaunt with an abrupt slice of his blade on his, and a fierce duel ensued.

Moving backwards and forth with their own attacking flurries and series of blocks, Clarence decided he would use distraction.

"So, how didst thou come to hear of what I hath inherited?" he asked.

"Thou think thou art the only spirit between heaven and Earth?" John shot back.

"Thou art surely arrogant. We art everywhere. We hear and see everything!"

Clarence laughed defiantly. "Our cause could well win the help of spirits."

"Their help! What is it ye art doing? Staging another Peasants' Revolt!" John dismissed Clarence's prize concept.

"Oh no. *We* are rising to what God hath truly assigned us all. The brotherhood of choice, my friend."

A few slashes later, Gaunt peered from behind his blade. On each side his face wore disgust and confusion. They jumped down onto the field, the frantic speed of their swords clashing with elaborate patterns and furious, constant frequency.

"Thou know, I could summon a thousand warriors at arms if I so wished." Gaunt said, attempting a taunting.

"So, thou take what thou want using raw power. Shame! I shall not let that happen with our shire."

"But dost thou not see? That hath always been the case. Fairness hath been a redundant concept with us. Nobles acquire. At the expense of who lies in their way," Gaunt stated, with frankness.

"So then thou admit it?" Clarence asserted. "Ye art barbarians who rob from the people ye swore to protect!"

At first, Gaunt didn't answer and the duel continued. The open space helped. It helped them cancel out each other's widest and most sweeping attacks.

Then, in the midst of one attack, Gaunt asked, "This new duchy of thine is made for someone who knows these fine folk campaigning for their liberty, is it?"

Clarence suspected a rouse, given his opponent's sympathetic tone of voice.

"Yes," was all he answered with.

Then John parried a slash from Clarence. Clarence stayed anchored in his stance to avoid being taken by surprise with a new move. But one did not follow. Instead, John took a step back, lowering his sword so that its tip pointed down to the ground, suggesting he desired a rest in battle.

A kindly smile spread across his face.

"Thou know, I only spent nine days here in my entire life. Probably why I hath been given this job to do."

Clarence still thought John was trying to lure him, given his new gentle approach.

"There is little doubt that the prince regent who shall inherit the living title 'Duke of Lancaster' hath no interest in this county. But if thou were to become a new kind of duke, Sir Clarence, will thou throw thy borders open to *all* those who sought shelter, from high and low?"

Clarence nodded. "What is thy purpose now, John O' Gaunt?" Clarence said, sword raised back, ready to pounce if needs be.

John gestured and his sword and scabbard vanished.

"To give thee this. Well done, champion," John said, handing Clarence a glowing golden key.

Overcome, Clarence's concerns dissolved as he felt mutual regard grow between a colossal nobleman of his day and himself. Accepting the key, Clarence now knew what was his. With a handshake, John disappeared.

But not without saying, "I'll see thee again, Clarence. My work here as a spirit is done."

Clarence looked up to the sky, nodding his regards. Looking back to the steeps, Mary and Richard were looking on, still stunned but also now enjoying a bold sense of triumph.

Back in the tunnel chapel, Mary and Richard looked on in awe as Clarence carefully inserted the key into the box where his amulet was said to reside. Gently opening the box, Clarence removed from it the amulet. Putting the gold chain it was set in, round his neck, he turned to Mary and Richard who gasped the greatest gasp of their lives as the ruby-red rose-shaped jewel in its centrepiece glowed, then flashed with appetite, knowing it was finally being worn by its rightful wearer.

In the main hall, Richard called the Phoenixes together to witness Clarence. Now truly their duke. On the stage Clarence appeared, and the sharpness in his eyes, along with the whirling, cascading blue pulses shooting out from the amulet, caused the evaporation of all their fears, including that of going to Manchester. Their rampant cheers confirmed this, as a pulse of light from the amulet exploded, darkening the room for a second as it reacted with lamps. Then a shower of red roses followed. It was time for a celebration.

Chapter Thirty-Eight

Many of the Phoenixes had drunk a few pints the night before, and they, along with the lighter drinkers, were fast asleep come daybreak. It was early in the morning and the dominant sound was that of snoring. They had had another celebration to honour their duke. Richard had nodded with certain belief in the ability of Clarence to keep them safe from anything in Manchester. The rest of the Phoenixes had made their changed feelings felt with wave upon wave of cheers. They had seen with their own eyes and heard with their own ears, and felt with their own hearts, the great spectacle of the previous day. They had made a new pledge — to follow their duke to liberty wherever they were required. Their confidence had been won, and a relieved Clarence had modestly received the celebrations. He emerged from his nightly meditation and Mary, Josiah and Caroline rose as quietly as they could. For they all knew that today was Friday, the day of Marvin's trial. However, there would only be four who would be involved in the rescue of Marvin that day. They knew they had to rise to yet another impossible occasion. But what Mary and Clarence had come to appreciate over the last few months was that that was a speciality of the Phoenixes. Today though, in the wake of celebration, they would need an attitude of complete belief, fuelled by defiance. In another room, by candlelight, Clarence spelled out the plans with no grand speech to inspire. Inspiration flowed freely through these three living people he had come to be as close to as Tilly, John and Michael.

"When we art directly under the castle's foundations, I shall flow through to the Well Tower to release Marvin. Then, ye shall come up through the shaft which leads through the foundations of the castle and position thyselves at intervals in the courtyard. There ye must keep watch for guards. There shall be few at this time in the morning but the stealth and silence of our agency today shall prevent what there is from being alerted to our presence. When I emerge from the Well Tower with

Marvin, we shall all return here in the tunnel ye entered from."

Mary, Caroline and Josiah smiled at him, satisfied that they were going to be successful. The Phoenixes had completed daring sorties akin to this in the past, but only infrequently. All four of them braced themselves, but with it came a zest of excitement. Not to mention defiance.

Assuming orb form, Clarence pierced the Well Tower's inner wall and made for Marvin's cell. Mary, Josiah and Caroline had made for the tunnel which led to the castle. It took all three of them to lift away the large oak door which provided the entrance to the shaft. Once inside they immediately ascended it. As their climb progressed, the silence got less dense the closer they came to ground level. Soon, Mary was able to carefully agitate the cover in a wall next to the Well Tower, which separated them from the open courtyard, and neatly lift it away. This gave her the opportunity to look around. As Clarence had predicted, it was deserted. Looking around, Mary wanted to sigh as the aesthetic of the castle so appealed to her. From a different shade, she thought of the castle as a mythical locale of romance, as she always had done, sitting grandly at the top of her shire. The way the light of the early hours coloured it now, her admiration was at its peak. For the neatness of the castle and the faceted sides of its courtyard was so peaceful. The greatness of the castle rested in the solace of the early morning. But one glance at the railed off section for the prisoners across the courtyard reminded her of its deadly and oppressive purpose. Off the back of that last thought, she turned her focus back to Marvin. Helping her friends out, they silently replaced the cover of the tunnel and spread out in the lower courtyard. Mary stayed close by to the Well Tower. Josiah and Caroline stood either side of the gatehouse. The next part of the sortie involved them waiting for Clarence to emerge with Marvin. Which was the hardest part.

Clarence arrived in Marvin's cell. He didn't need his second sight to see that Marvin wasn't there. The cell was empty. Clarence was pitched into instant confusion. Trials, he knew from the Phoenixes, never took place this early. He noticed the meagre remains of a meal on the floor and remembered calling in on occasion throughout the week. He had brought Marvin some good food in these visits, and some reassurance. Clarence knew by his mere reaction that Marvin loved his visits, enshrining them with gratitude. Entering his second sight, he peered through the walls of the Well Tower, across the courtyard and into Hadrian's Tower. Peering into the assize court, he could clearly see a reluctant Marvin being tried. Oddly though, there were very few people about, other than a couple of guards, the judge, the prosecutor, the dastardly Old Ned Barlow, and despicably, no jury. Clarence readied his whole constitution to fly right across to Marvin's position, but then remembered his friends down in the courtyard below. If he could get across to Marvin's position, help him he could, but his friends would be on their own. If the castle woke up, then they would be detected, and more guards would come. Then his friends would be arrested and he would have four people to save from the noose. He needed to lead them there, to the assize court, in rapid time. Jumping out of the Well Tower, he landed next to Mary, who spun round to meet him. She was expecting an update.

"He is not there," Clarence quietly reported.

Mary's mouth began to sag.

"He is in the assize court. With no jury."

"They must be doing this on the quiet, so as not to draw attention to their illegal dealings," Mary whispered with venom.

Gesturing over to Josiah and Caroline, he called them in. Explaining the situation in very hushed tones, Clarence asked how many guards they had counted.

"Two," Josiah replied. "They're looking out over the town. They haven't seen or heard us."

Clarence nodded. Then he delved into his second sight and peered beneath the courtyard. He saw another tunnel sprouting off from the one his friends had come up via, which led almost to the assize court.

"This way, my comrades," he commanded, leading them back to the tunnel they had emerged from. Mary, Josiah and Caroline were confused, but inside, they knew he was making things work.

Once back inside, they shimmied as quickly as they could towards the start of the other tunnel Clarence had detected but that they had missed. Deep below that old gaol castle, they ran as fast as they could behind Clarence, desperate to find and rescue Marvin before his time was up on the scaffold. Clarence didn't bother to use his second sight as he could remember vividly the path the tunnel took. Within minutes, they were there. Clarence checked his second sight again. Fortunately, there was no one about. Quickly and in concert, they lifted a very heavy door away, after Clarence had agitated its lock. Then they were in the deepest bowels of the castle. Re-securing the lock, they then ran down the dimly lit corridor. Their sole intent on reaching the court, or the drop room, before Marvin was led out onto hanging corner. Within moments they reached the assize court where Clarence had seen Marvin. Kicking the door through, the four of them tore into the court — only to find it empty. Save the judge, who hadn't even noticed them. Not looking up, he was reading a broadside in a leisurely fashion.

"Marvin Coviash! Where is he?" Clarence demanded.

The judge looked up, casually confused.

"Marvin Coviash? That young fellow we sentenced today?" the judge asked in innocent tone.

"Where is he?" Clarence boomed again.

The judge straightened up in his grand seat at the head of the court.

Dipping an eyebrow, he said, "Why are you so intent on finding… the likes of him?"

By now, Clarence knew the judge was trying to stall them. But before he could try and penetrate the judge's mind, the fellow had gestured to the exit on the right of the courtroom. After feeling no purpose in staying in the old, heavily wood-panelled court, Clarence led them out, re-entering his second sight.

Booting down the door to the drop room, the four Phoenixes ran in. Greeted with silence, there was only the coffin in the room, waiting dreadfully for Marvin. They all knew what this place was, but the four of them this time, not just Mary, noticed its odd tranquillity. However, there was no temptation to bask in it, as a chilling sense of defeat was peering out from behind the thick veil of the walls separating themselves and hanging corner. A gentle, cooling breeze blew into the round stone room, and for the first time since entering, they noticed that the window-come-door to the gallows was open. They dashed outside, onto the gallows. And, of course, there they were. Marvin, the gaol chaplain, a magistrate and Old Ned Barlow were standing there. Marvin was pinioned, and standing directly behind the noose, which was eerily still. Clarence and his party could see the concourse between the castle and Priory church now and was surprised to find it completely void of people. The officials on the gallows then turned to face them with calculated, slow movement.

"Well, well, well, well," the magistrate began. "They say a good hanging brings out the finest folk. Shame about the ill-attendance for this one, but it was necessary to bring it forward to this early hour."

Marvin turned to face them now, his face stained with tears of desperation. Clarence and his friends raised their weapons.

"Oh, I would refrain from that if I were you," the magistrate said smugly.

For then, from the north-east side of the castle from Church Street, there came the brooding crunching of boots.

"Oh, Lord," Mary said.

Josiah closed his eyes, as if preparing for a final ordeal. From both their left and their right, upwards of two hundred red coats marched promptly into place, filling the concourse. With that, they could see their escape routes firmly barred. A lonely set of steps croaked up from behind them. Turning, they saw a red-coat officer regarding them blankly, adjusting his sabre. 'Good Lord, what is this?' Clarence dashed in his mind. Then he remembered the vision, and inside, he sank. He cursed himself for not having seen this coming. Clarence knew he could take on armies of thousands and still come out victorious. If he so desired, he could pitch himself like a wizard into the swelling ranks of the red coats in front of him. Then he could spend all day deflecting their fire and making sharpening tools of their bayonets — before he despatched them, or before they all fled. But he was not alone. He had three folk, all close friends, to consider. Whatever he did, they would be at the mercy of the troops. His retaliation could mean their deaths. Then a tinge of anger entered the tangled fray. Did Marvin inform them that they would be here? Was he partly responsible for this? But given the ruthless reputation of Lancaster gaol, Clarence's desire to blame him soon dried up.

"Keep close, friends," was all Clarence said, under his breath.

"I swear, Sir Knight, I breathed no word to them," declared Marvin.

"It's true," Barlow confirmed. "You know how long I've been working in this castle? Long enough to know that castles have ears," he sadistically sneered.

"Indeed. As does the whole of Lancaster. We thought we would wait till today to catch you. That way we could spoil your greatest endeavour and add prison-breaking to your charge sheet," the magistrate craftily added.

"Aye, there may be no-one here today, but come next week, there'll be thousands for you — promise!" Barlow said, saliva falling from his mouth in anticipation.

The four of them stood shoulder to shoulder as best as they could. All four of them wanted to scrutinise exactly how the establishment had found out about the rescue. Clarence had no wish to lay down in front of his enemies, but neither could he initiate a battle. They looked out ambivalently to the sea of red coats. The red coats looked back at them, waiting for a reaction. Clarence took pleasure that the whole encounter felt like a stand-off, which would otherwise mean that he and his friends retained some power. Somehow, a feeling of power rose inside him, a spring from nowhere. It helped him keep his composure, allowing for God to provide whatever solution he could; if it was their destiny in his eyes to survive that day. Then, the wind rustled the trees at the rear of the concourse, giving the scene some noise at last. Followed by folk abseiling down silently from them. The four of them focused on the mysterious tree folk, and recognised each and every one of them. Smiling, Clarence told the four of them to raise their hands. Which, with devious grins, they did.

Barlow and the officials hadn't yet twigged. They were just taken with their capture. Some of the red coats were confused, others smugly satisfied. Others saw the penny dropping. The rear ranks spun round as the first wave of Phoenixes pierced them. They did so with a great battle cry. Taken from the rear, and by surprise, the red coats wavered in disarray. The officers were disturbed as all eyes then gazed up to the top of the priory as a bell sounded. But it wasn't the church's bell. Its shrillness split across the concourse, snaring everyone's attention. Clarence, Mary, Josiah and Caroline, as did all the rest of the Phoenixes, knew who the unmistakable figure was. It was Richard.

"The hand's been forced, comrades! To battle!" he shouted down to them.

Then, the great struggle began. Leaping down to join their friends, Clarence dived into the melee, the red coats by now feeling their dominance molested. Richard's announcement to them all had allowed the red coats some time to recover. But that simply heightened the resolve of the Phoenixes. Cudgel and stick were now clashing with musket and bayonet. The limited room meant that neither side was really able to fire anything, yet. But the second and third wave of Phoenixes ensured that their attacks retained the element of surprise. They dropped subtly from the trees, and Clarence noticed this, just as he had done when they had fallen off the ship to rescue the convicts on the quayside. Red coats fell like flies as the Phoenixes leapt in deeper into their ranks, taking them out from above. Josiah and Caroline flung the magistrate and chaplain back into the drop room, throwing them into the now-dithering officer who had barred their way before. Bolting the door shut against the rest of the troops who were now running to the drop room to join the officer, they grinned at their speed of thought. As the ranks of red coats began to clear under the pressure of what Clarence was sure was the whole society, some muskets were fired. Mary winced with horror, and responded by taking out each soldier readying their musket or aiming them in space. Richard suddenly appeared next to her.

"Damn good job, Mary!" he said with more than a dash of pride.

"Aye, we weren't expecting this. Ta," she returned.

"Yesterday, Sir Clarence rightfully showed us the way. We feel the woes of so many. Now it's time for us to rally to their side as he has to ours."

"For Sir Clarence and liberty!" Richard shouted at the top of his voice.

A massive cheer arose, which affected Clarence, fighting off officers sword to sword at unearthly speed. He paused for a moment and his whole countenance was seized with passion. Passion that lent itself to what he had already unleashed against those who had come to kill his friends. For the cheer was the kind of cheer that resembled a roar of approval. A roar that was primal. The kind of roar he had heard on many an old battlefield in his life. That was the cheer of warriors. Elsewhere, Richard chimed the bell again, with just about enough force so as not to disturb the progress of his fighters.

"Surrender, red coats! Surrender and we can end this."

"Carry on, troopers, disregard this brigand!" an officer ordered to them.

Richard had a fair view of the carnage that had taken place and that which would follow.

"No, do surrender. Keep your lives!" Richard countered, with more appeal in his voice.

Clarence had been necessarily pre-occupied with the battle and only remembered Marvin mid-way through a sword fight with a puffed-up captain. Kicking his feet away, Clarence looked back to the gallows to see no one there. He jumped back onto them and moved his sword through a series of patterns, designed to repel in-coming fire. With that accomplished, he entered his second sight and searched for Marvin. He didn't have to look far. For Marvin was being led through the last remaining clumps of red coats by Barlow. The troops surrounding them were very unsure, their only purpose now being to retain a felon. He also saw that Mary, Josiah and Caroline had jumped down onto the concourse at some point and were now burying themselves in the pockets of fighting still going on. Mary was now using her bow to slap their enemies across the chins. With wicked speed, Clarence jumped across to where Marvin was, over the red coats. By the time he reached Marvin though, Barlow had taken out a pocket-knife and was holding it to Marvin's throat. Grinning with unique menace, Barlow thought he had it won. Clarence placed his sword down and raised his arms calmly. Barlow dragged Marvin away, up the concourse. Clarence closed his eyes and spoke through his mind to Mary's.

'Mary, Barlow has Marvin. Get into position, my love.'

Mary heard the words as soon as they were spoken and immediately terminated her fine slashes. Clarence checked the position of Marvin with his second sight and saw that Barlow still had him alive, and was getting well away from the fighting. Mary ran up the concourse towards Clarence's position. She ignored the nick that a musket ball made on her shoulder and pressed herself through the pain. Then Clarence spoke through his mind to Marvin.

'Thou shall be right, dear friend.'

Clarence's echoing voice reached Marvin, and he resolved to remain calm, feeling the comradeship. Mary could only just about make out Marvin and Barlow through the clusters of fighting that raged between her and their position. The expression on Barlow's face told her that he hadn't noticed her. Mary pulled back on her bow, only then realising that this shot would make her life. This shot was the only thing that counted. All the competitions she had ever won ebbed forever from her mind. She remembered her father and her mind synched. Letting loose, all noise drawled into the background and time itself paused to witness the single most important shot she would ever make. It sailed quickly, and for Barlow unexpectedly, through the air, down to him and Marvin, gaining momentum with its descent, and from nowhere embedding itself in Barlow's shoulder. Recoiling grotesquely in pain, Barlow's arm became loose, and Marvin seized the moment. Stamping on Barlow's feet and pushing his arm away, he made for it, bolting back to Clarence. However, it was Mary who eventually greeted him. For Clarence dashed with his magical speed up to Barlow, whose firm grip on his knife had been lost. Barlow sneered at Clarence with utter malice, before drawing a pistol. But with one swipe of his sword, Clarence knocked it from his hand. Barlow staggered back, his hand now numb from the phantom strike. With the knife, Barlow made a couple of vicious swipes at Clarence. Clarence dodged these neatly and then ran Barlow quickly through. Barlow instantly fell down with a grey storm in his eyes. Defeated. Clarence whistled a distinctive whistle. Through the concourse Azlight trotted, *through* Phoenixes who cheered her arrival, and *through* red coats who screamed as she gathered pace. Everyone, even Mary, was surprised as Azlight had appeared from nowhere.

Rushing precisely to Clarence's side, she halted abruptly, and Clarence smiled to her, "Azlight, my dear, take Marvin back to his friends and return to me."

Azlight neighed in acknowledgement, and Clarence helped Marvin onto her.

"I... I don't know what to say. Thanks, I suppose..." Marvin was clearly overcome by what had happened.

The efforts of the Phoenixes and Clarence had rendered him speechless.

"Do not worry. Your task now is to return to thy hometown and prepare for the meeting, which we hope to see thou and thy friends at," Clarence said warmly.

"Well, there'll be thousands there, but aye, I hope to see you too," Marvin smiled back.

Nodding to him, Azlight drew rapidly away, carrying Marvin back to Rochdale. Clarence and Mary hugged in triumph, saturated with the satisfaction of their latest sortie to defy tyranny. But the colourful fog of euphoria almost instantly faded as they turned back towards the battle which had taken place on the concourse. It brought them back to the sickening reality of what the cost of their triumph would be; the red coats were retreating now, and the Phoenixes were simmering in confidence as the biggest victory since their founding was upon them. But strewn across the concourse were defeated red coats, some dead. Clarence grimaced. Mary was remorseful. As well there lay some deceased Phoenixes, which sourly grappled with the emotions of Mary and Clarence, being worthy distractions. Clarence decided there was one last manoeuvre of battle which needed calling. Jumping high up into the castle grounds, and onto the keep, he held his sword aloft, and peeled off his tabard to reveal the amulet. It glowed in delight.

"Warriors below. Our battle is won. Now ye shall either rejoice or retreat."

As he said this, a great cheer sounded from the Phoenixes once again and the last of the red coats left the concourse. But not before blue lightning radiated from Clarence's amulet. Both fearful and inspiring, the Phoenixes paused in sheer amazement, before cheers erupted once again.

Chapter Thirty-Nine

An overwhelmed silence descended over Lancaster for the rest of that day, and night. The next day was exactly the same. Everyone in Lancaster knew what had taken place.

In a deeply moving ceremony, the Phoenixes had burnt their dead on the steeps of the moor. In a drastic role reversal, they provided a greatly peaceful place to release the souls of their comrades to heaven. Where not even twenty years ago, they had been a place where lives had been brutally ended with twisted ceremony. As the hazy fires reached for the skies, Richard, Clarence and the rest of the Phoenixes felt their tears and their hearts go with their fallen friends. Although utterly saddened, their motivation now increased. Now, the memories of their friends made them want to go to Manchester all the more, to lend their fire to justice.

After, for the first time in centuries, the Phoenixes rose to venture out altogether, in broad daylight, in full view of the townsfolk. The fear and encumberment of many centuries they knew had been washed away the previous day. For today, there was only the fluent, flowing feeling of freedom which ran amok through them. So strong was this current of glory that the reaction of the townsfolk didn't provide any source of even concern for them. Their mission in Lancaster had been fulfilled, and their duke had led them to their birth right. However, it so happened that the reaction they received was, at first, nothing short of neutral in its characterisation. Folk came out in dribs and drabs to witness the 'citizen walk' of this rumoured, mythologized, secret society of people who had up until yesterday inhabited the tunnels under their town. They watched in silence and with drooped jaws as the Phoenixes, led jointly by Clarence and Richard, marched through Market Street and into the square in a modest, forgiving manner. More and more folk came out. As the Phoenixes arrived at the castle, they turned to see that the whole town had turned out to greet them. In the space of a moment, their silence peeled away — giving way to cheers. Not cheers of approval, but cheers of gratitude. With corresponding feeling, the Phoenixes bowed to the townsfolk as if they had just finished a theatrical performance. The red coats who had survived from the previous day maintained their positions as outsiders, tending to their normal civil duties but looking to Clarence for some kind of permission. Their presence had not escaped his mind. Allowing them the same fondness he normally reserved for civilians, his nod gave his assent for them to carry on their duties of keeping order and maintaining the public peace. But from now on, it would be under his fair terms, his gentle rule. That was clearly what the people of the ancient county town wanted. Within moments of the cheers increasing, the Phoenixes stepped down from the hill and mingled with their new brethren in Lancaster, who welcomed them as if they were returning family members. Triumph had arrived in the county town. What remained was for Clarence to take up residence.

And so it was. He chose the white court, which was a semi-circle in the way it was assembled. It fitted the most people in and he commented that it was akin to the round table — or half of it. This humour went on to characterise the next few days he spent there; settling disputes amicably, hearing people's grievances and cases where someone had been unjustly accused. But Clarence didn't lord over them like many dukes would. He instead made his power felt by the subtle humour which gave the gravity he was capable of instilling into any situation a complementary flavour of trust. Because of this, crowds gathered outside the castle, cheering his name. They knew from his actions on the battlefield that he was sincere in his convictions. But when he went out to greet them from the battlements, he spoke to them as one of them. He had no reason to do otherwise given who he was. His natural warmth made people trust his authority and they saw, heard and felt themselves in the character of this fellow who called himself their duke. He wasn't distant or drawn from distant stock; he was here, with them. He epitomised them. He was them. Clarence's court sat down to discuss the all-important matter that Mary had put on the table. She had been asked to pick one topic, and she chose one of the Reformer's prize goals: universal suffrage.

"Reet," Clarence said, putting quill to paper. "Now, this bill shall guarantee that every person over the age of twenty-one shall hath the right to one vote each in this county palatine. It shall be a secret ballot and there shall be no record on the bill they use to cast their votes. Totally anonymous."

Striking his mace down on the table in front of him, he then said, "Reet, that makes it law round here. Not just round here, but in this whole county."

At this, the court rose up and cheered, applauding Clarence, saturating him with adoration.

"Right. Now what remains is for us to journey to Manchester for this big demonstration. We shall call in on Darkleigh first and garner their support."

Mary and the Phoenixes immediately got up and got ready.

Clarence explained in secret to Mary that although the establishment didn't see him officially as duke, he had the power of the amulet. This could protect any law he made from being overridden by anyone. Mary grinned, basking in the safety and surety she felt. At one point as her last night in Lancaster came, Mary looked out over the town from the walls of the castle. In all directions she sighed, not being able to comprehend what she and her friends had achieved there. Summer was now entrenched and the evening sun highlighted the town where she had truly become the person she had always dreamed of. Her potential had always been there, but in the mills, there had never been the platform. Now she could return to her home town to share the new found independence she felt gushing through her. But not before she looked out on her county town once more, not in the way she used to do. For the way she used to do had been the understandably naïve perception of a young woman who had enjoyed the sensation of being haunted by a legend. Not that there was anything wrong with that, but now Lancaster served a higher, nobler purpose in her mind. She looked across to the moor, then to the cobbles, thatched terraces and tall brown tenements back up on the hill she stood on. She saw the Priory, then across the bay before finally looking out to the Fells, which represented a kind of hope for her. They were beautiful and tantalizing. They were the unknown but the unknown had lost its fear element. Now there was just her and her friends who had made Lancaster a new genesis of her shire — one which was them through and through.

Chapter Forty

On the seventh of August, the select committee of magistrates for Manchester and Salford were gathered at William Hulton's Mount Street residence. In the darkened room they all sat, there were but a few objects on the table in front of them; a jar of brandy, twelve glasses (one for each of them), a lamp lighting the immediate area and a copy of the *Manchester Observer* newspaper. There was an angry tone to their conversation, and none of them seemed in the slightest relaxed. Hulton surveyed his magistrates. He knew this kind of situation well. This was the kind of rapid, incensed conversation that followed the favourite getting beat at the races. Then he regarded the room, and how reassuringly cosy it felt. It reminded him of various rooms at his ancestral residence at Hulton Park. This was the kind of setting he and his friends had indulged in when they had just got in from riding on his estate. They too had brandy, which quelled the invigoration engendered by traversing the woods and rolling fields. But he wasn't in Hulton Park. He was in Manchester. And the topic at hand was something deadly serious as opposed to frivolity. Moving towards the table, he read on a page of the *Manchester Observer,* which was open.

A requisition having been presented to the Borough-reeve and Constables of Manchester, signed by above seven hundred inhabitants, requesting them to call a public meeting 'to consider the propriety of adopting the most LEGAL AND EFFECTUAL means of obtaining a REFORM in the commons houses of parliament', and they having declined to call such a meeting, therefore the under-signed Requisitions give NOTICE that a public meeting will be held, on the area, near St. Peter's Church, for the above mentioned purpose on Monday 16th instant. The Chair to be taken by H. Hunt Esq, at 12 o'clock

After having read that, Hulton remained composed, concealing his inner defiance. Knowing he had not the power to ban meetings such as this as they were not strictly illegal, he maintained his arrogant air. The frenzy of disturbed conversation continued, his colleagues not even noticing he was there.

"H-hmm," he intoned.

The conversation ceased and all heads were turned towards him. In his matter-of-fact tone, Hulton began.

"Gentlemen, thank you all for coming so quickly. As you are no doubt all aware, there is a very serious matter which we need to discuss. As you can see from the newspaper in front of you, the seditious element in this town and those surrounding it have made their intentions clear. They intend to meet on the sixteenth of this month to have their little soiree. There will be a speaker, the 'renowned' Henry Hunt. The fellow with the white hat."

Hulton's attempt at humour did nothing to reassure his colleagues. He sighed a meagre sigh in response to this.

"Yes. Well, our job as magistrates is to keep order, of course, and make sure that such meetings do not contain any message, especially when spoken to a great number of persons, which could be deemed treasonable."

"It's treason in itself, a meeting like that," Ralph Fletcher cried angrily.

"Quite so," Hulton calmly agreed.

"So we should best make sure that sufficient numbers of militia are present nearby on the day, to save the country from those who would eat it away from the inside!" Fletcher emphasised.

Hulton didn't agree nor differ. He simply remained composed and said nothing. However, there was a general sound of enthusiastic agreement at Fletcher's statement.

"Perhaps but it should be remembered that we do not have any actual powers to disperse meetings such as this. Neither can we legally deem the action of such a meeting taking place as treasonable."

Hulton knew someone would eventually say that. In this case it had been a fellow magistrate called Wright. All looked round to him. Some out of silent admiration that he had told it how it was, others who were desperate to accuse someone of siding with traitors, to satisfy their fears.

"And you would have us do what, sir, in response?" Fletcher shot back abruptly.

"Gentlemen, what I am saying is that these people, these Reformers as they call themselves, are responding to certain conditions that have been imposed on them through no fault of their own. By all means, station militia nearby to intercept any sign of insurrection. But bear in mind, these are our own people. We have tended to them for centuries now. This meeting they're calling could be a good opportunity to listen to them, and for us to understand their mere feelings. For when we do that, we know what action we may be able to take to assist them reasonably. This will then allow us to take the sting out of what their ghastly philosophy of Reform is demanding. When we tend to their needs, all talk of Reform will fizzle out. There will not be the need for it. That will mean that we have prevented any change they propose. Certainly, the talk of revolution will be gone.".

No one in that room had any response to Wright's logic. Fletcher was chattering away, silently resentful. Then the Reverend Ethelstone spoke up.

"Good grief, man! It is they who should be eating out of our hands, not the other way round!"

There were some cries of agreement.

"What view would the Lord take, sir?" Wright asked.

"The lord would surely teach us that benevolence is a virtue. However, that benevolence is dispensed according to the wisdom and discretion of those closest to him. And anyone who seeks to undermine God's authority by seeking to depose their social superiors appointed by him are not worthy of the scraps from beneath our tables," the incensed vicar shot back.

Hulton had heard enough.

"So, what are the specifics of these military arrangements we have mentioned, gentlemen?" he asked.

"Well, of course, the Manchester and Salford Yeomanry Cavalry are at our disposal, sir. Along with the Cheshire Yeomanry," Fletcher answered.

"Jolly good. Make sure they are on hand on the sixteenth," Hulton ordered.

Cries of "Aye" rang round the room.

"And of course the special constables will be ever-present,"

Ethelstone added.

"Very good, very good," Hulton acknowledged.

At that moment, a knock on the door came.

"Quiet now, gents," Hulton told them.

"Come," he shouted.

A servant entered and presented Hulton with a letter. Hulton nodded and the servant was gone. Intense debate was raging between two parties who had sided with the principal speakers in the conversation from beforehand. As this was happening, Hulton read the letter. A smile crept across his lips. A sly smile which went unnoticed by his colleagues engaged in debate. Hulton inserted the letter in his pocket.

"How much time have you spent with these ragged peasants, Squire Wright?" Ethelstone taunted. "Are they growing on you, sir?"

"I would caution you, Reverend, against such foul jests, lest you want a duel!"

"Ooh!" Ethelstone and his faction cried like bairns.

"Gentlemen, there is no need to impugn each other's characters. Do hush. Though I must say, Wright, you do seem to be taking this nonsense a little too far. We are the masters, they the..." All looked at Ralph Fletcher before he said what he wanted to say.

That led him to stop, given that he didn't want to admit what his own people were.

"Yes, they the subservient ones," he substituted.

Hulton lifted his glass of brandy. The rest of the committee knew he had reached a decision when he did this.

"Gentlemen, discipline. When this meeting is over I want to see all of us shaking hands, is that understood?"

"Aye," all of them spoke.

"So it is agreed. The two Yeomanries shall be on hand, ready for our use after the riot act is read."

All nodded.

"As well I can reveal, gentlemen, regular units including infantry and Hussars amongst others shall be present as well," Fletcher smiled.

"Reverend Ethelstone, I'm giving the responsibility of reading the riot act to you, sir," Hulton stated.

"Oh, thank you, sir," he responded, with enthusiasm that was only genuine on the surface.

"In the meantime, we shall have our legendary toast!"

The whole committee raised their glasses.

"Down with the rump, up Church and King!"

The whole committee cheered in agreement.

"That will be all, gentlemen," Hulton said after.

The whole committee broke up into civil chatter from there on in. Wright approached Hulton.

"Sir, one thing I was reluctant to raise there was the issue you informed us about at the last meeting. The delusional behaviour regarding the inhabitants of Darkleigh."

"Ah yes," Hulton agreed. "The supposed ghosts from yesteryear who blaze the banner of revolution?"

Wright nodded. "What will be our course of action regarding that particular town?" Wright quizzed his master.

"I understand, of course, why you have approached me about that matter now. And I am glad to say that that little matter has resolved itself. I doubt we shall be hearing any more of the very fascinating ghosts of that town. Whoever has been stealing armour from the local church and riding through the town with a pretence of power has recently curtailed his activities. Worry not."

"Very good, sir," Wright said, wondering why Hulton had become so relaxed and reassured about the matter, seemingly out of the blue.

"It seems that the recent indulgence the populace up there has for spotting ghosts is down to nothing more than the fine liquor the town is known to produce. A liquor that has been tried by our own spies, and its effects subsequently witnessed."

Wright nodded, desperately trying to hide his scepticism as Hulton moved amongst them. At the back of Hulton's mind were the incredible reports from Lancaster. However, he simply refused to believe them. He did have a vast militia on hand, stationed throughout the county to quell this band of two hundred or so rabble who had supposedly overthrown the castle and had been dispensing law up there as if it were their own city-state.

Chapter Forty-One

The great day was almost upon the many, many folk who intended to make themselves heard, one mighty voice which would lay down a gauntlet to those whose yoke had expired, and to those who continued to hold them down under the stone of sheer malice. In Middleton, the famous Sam and Jemima Bamford prepared with a silent zeal what was to be their pride and joy. In *Ye Olde Boar's Head*, banners had their finishing touches added, and the marching order was finalised. In Saddleworth, Dr Healy tended to his patients as usual while going straight to his Hampden Club later. His presence injected even greater morale amongst his friends. In Manchester, the town's Female Reform Society was bonding well, and this suited their compassionate leader, Mary Fildes, and also her no-nonsense secretary Susannah Saxton. Shy ladies and those with the most active gobs had grown more and more sisterly by the day. In Darkleigh, Joe, Laura and the rest of the town's Reformers were making their final preparations. They looked down the square of their little town, which everyone, Darkleigh folk and outsiders alike, noticed stood with fierce independence. It had surely grown from being self-contained on its own in the hills, isolated considerably from its comrade-towns. Reform was enjoying increased support in the town, which had already been quite substantial. It probably generated this thanks to the practice marches in the square they'd been having. Their smiles and enthusiasm for their forthcoming venture had affected the townsfolk. In their droves folk had pledged to join the town's Reform society in attending the meeting. They loved a cause to rally round, one which warranted the blazing of the town's banner.

Clarence, Mary, Josiah, Caroline and the Phoenixes had had a long, long walk from Lancaster back to Darkleigh. Azlight had rode alongside but as an orb, given that Clarence was now in his heart a Reformer — and a Phoenix. He hadn't wanted to ride on horseback with his people, as he felt it best to reject any practice which promoted himself over them with regards status. But he felt Azlight's affectionate essence with him and responded to her with equal care and tenderness. All the way from Lancaster, the merry and enthusiastic conversation had continued non-stop. There had been no complaints regarding distance, or the lack of food and drink. In the two days and nights their brisk walk had taken, the benevolent feelings had busily circulated around their party. On their journey, they had stopped off in the same part of the Bowland Forest where Clarence and Mary had stopped off at on their journey up. The Phoenixes had been affected by the sheer scale and natural majesty of the place, many staying up late to watch the sun descend beneath the legendary trough. And now they approached the hills which sheltered Darkleigh. Mary and Clarence knew their shape ten miles away.

They had pointed them out to the Phoenixes and had said, "You see them hills there, there's us home!"

At mention of that, eyes had lit up. Many were already perceiving it as a promised land, of almost biblical proportions. One which could house the gateway to the liberty they sought, and that of others. Certainly for those who fell into Clarence's new-founded jurisdiction. The breeze picked up as they neared the gap in the southern hill which would lead into Darkleigh. Excitement and anticipation were gathering. Mary knew it, but she knew it was mild compared to what was to come.

"How we feeling, Caroline?" asked Mary.

"Aye, reet fine," she replied.

"Can I ask how you felt going through Bowland?" Mary gently questioned.

"Aye. It were more what I didn't feel that surprised me. I didn't feel like I wanted to cry. I didn't feel upset. I felt for our old friends and neighbours. But I saw them living in the forest, healing. Strange but true. Then I felt us passing through it together. And I felt brave and reassured. Backed up. Like I were on a crusade," Caroline told.

While Caroline had been saying this, wonder had flared up in Mary's eyes, happily astonished at her friend's description of passing through her old home. Into the shade of the gap in the hill they went.

"Feeling well, Josiah?" Clarence asked.

"Aye, like I could take on the whole world," he replied promptly and proudly.

Clarence laughed an encouraging laugh.

"I know the exact feeling," he agreed. "What about thou, Richard?" Clarence asked.

Richard's face was soaked in pride.

"Very good, Sire. Very good," he nodded.

Clarence shared in his feeling.

***

The sun was in the process of setting that day, August fourteenth, 1819 as Mary and Clarence's party entered the square of the town of Darkleigh. Mary had decided she would visit her mother and sisters later. First, she would introduce everyone to her comrades in the Hampden Club. The two hundred or so of them stopped outside *The Phoenix* and Mary went inside, so she could get Joe to come out. Surely enough, she found Joe in there, in the snug with the central committee. They were clearly deep in their planning of the event coming up on the sixteenth. Mary was surprised and impressed by the fact that they weren't doing it in secret.

"Hello, Joe, hello, fellas," she greeted.

Turning around, all of them were obviously glad to see her.

"Hello, sweet," they returned, buoyed up by her return.

"Oh, love, where've you been? Your mother said Lancaster?" Joe asked.

"Aye, Lancaster. And I've made a good few friends, too," Mary said, gesturing outside.

Curious to see what she meant, Joe and the committee followed her outside and were quite overwhelmed to see around two hundred folk in the square.

"Friends from Lancaster, these gents are the central committee of Darkleigh Hampden Club. Gents, these good folk bring greetings and salutations from the county town and are eager to rally to our cause and attend the protest on Monday," she emphatically said.

After that, the Phoenixes burst into applause and the committee gratefully waved their hats in the air. Cheers followed. Joe raised his hands, appealing for calm, despite the good-natured cheers.

When they abated, he said, "My, you have been busy, Mary. Recruiting these fine folk from *Lancaster* of all places! Come in, come in!"

The Phoenixes noticed the tavern sign and paused before entering in realisation. They were in Darkleigh. Home of their conquering hero. Where Mary had come from — the woman who had helped them find the courage to ascend to the surface. As they filtered into the pub, the barman's face was a distinct mix of gratitude and apprehension! He was glad of the custom but had never seen so many folk in a tavern at any one time! Still, drinks were bought in a relaxed manner and a good time was had by all. Laura, who had been dancing in the back came through and said she'd see to the Lancaster party's accommodation for the next week or so. None of them could be grateful enough. Clarence milled around, speaking to different huddles of folk, making his assuring presence felt. He had told them en route to Darkleigh not to mention him being Sir Clarence de Darkleigh or that he was now a duke of Lancaster. There would be a time and a place for that if required within the near future. Despite this useful modesty, the amulet nestled happily underneath his tabard. He had decided that right now, all momentum should be with the Reformers and the spectacular story that they needed to tell, rather than his achievement.

At one point, Joe took Mary aside and they agreed on the subject of the occasion being a very welcome surprise, and a happy one at that.

"How's your friend Max? Bertha tells me you went with him to Lancaster."

Mary wondered why Joe was asking about him. However, she knew him and she knew that it was highly unlikely that Joe would be suggesting something about her character, asking her why she had agreed to travel some distance away with a bloke, her being unmarried.

"Oh, fine thanks. We had a fine time in Lancaster. It were great being a solicitor's assistant. Helping with litigation, like. You know, we spoke on behalf of people at the castle and all."

Joe smiled finely at this.

"Glad to hear you had a fine time," Joe stated.

But then his tone changed tack in a slightly graver direction.

"Mary," he began. "Damn, we've got courage, we have. But... while you've been gone, there've been rumours round here, of a knight being spotted. Which of course are completely daft."

Mary nodded; her face conjured up an innocent look.

"But as well similar rumours have come from Lancaster, of a knight disrupting things, albeit for the better in the eyes of many."

Mary felt increasingly apprehensive.

"It can't be true?" Joe asked.

"All we did were sort things out at the castle for folk. And these who we've brought back were the poor folk of Lancaster. Folk who see the remedy of their problems in what we do with ours."

Joe seemed relieved.

"The thing is, we've read in the radical press recently that Henry Hunt wants us to bring no weapons. And I've got to respect that. We need to show them establishment blokes that we have purely peaceable intentions. And he's right. We did want to take some sticks and brickbats just in case *they* kicked off, like, but he says we can't. We want to discredit them who say we have a liking for violence, which is ridiculous anyway, but we need to demonstrate it. Which is why we can't be seen to be harbouring a knight-at-arms in our ranks!" Joe laughed.

Mary shared his laughter. Mary told herself that for the good of everyone there, and for the march, which was to come, she was telling the truth. This helped her to close down most of the guilt she felt from having to modify it. The main thing was, Joe was convinced.

Smiling at her, he said, "Reet. Sounds grand then."

Mutual warmth swelled round them, and they were both grateful.

Looking on from behind wooden carvings, Clarence felt even more gratitude towards Mary. She had helped steer him when he had only despair in front of him. She had been before the Phoenixes his only friend. She was a firebrand of change and justice, from this confusing era he had been launched back into. She was in his eyes a legend. He knew all too well that that was the way he and his family were regarded in these parts. However, Mary and her comrades deserved to go down as greats as well, more than he. In the next moment, he felt a long stretch of peace, as when warm colours are painted across a canvas to represent a landscape, with nothing there but them. Then his second sight took over, unprompted again, giving Clarence the message that something impending was afoot. He didn't wrestle with it as he had done before, rather he rolled with it. He allowed the vision to come and pass in its own time, descending to calm as the buoyed-up conversation continued around him. But what Clarence saw was an approaching whirlwind. One that didn't bring excitement or challenge routine, but one which brought chaos and tragedy. One which tore through with jealousy the lovely vision before him. One that warranted immediate action. Then the vision left him, quicker than it had come. He mulled around for a few minutes and Mary came and found him.

"Hello, Clarence!" she greeted.

"Hello, Mary," he warmly returned.

"Canst I speak to thou outside?"

Mary nodded and they went outside, into the square.

Clarence spoke first.

"Mary, I want thou to know that our friendship hath been one of the best things I hath ever experienced. In life or as a spirit. Thank thou. Thank thou for everything thou hath been to me. Having haunted with thou as my friend hath been a great, great honour. I never knew of anyone like thou when I lived. Even amongst the greatest of knights."

Mary giggled with embarrassment.

"It is true, my dear. Thou art the jewel in the crown of all I hath accomplished as a spirit on Earth. Thy friendship, and then what we hath forged together."

"Oh, Clarence. You might not realise this, but you're all my dreams come true. You rescued me. Even lasses like me like to be rescued, from time to time. You were with me on our adventure, too. It was a pleasure helping you with everything, Clarence. No one has ever made me feel so safe since me' dad. You helped me to find the courage to do things that no other mill girl's ever done before, surely."

For a moment, they regarded each other with such deep admiration. Clarence knew he had to say what he needed to. Mary was just lost in the moment, gazing at him.

"Mary, dear, there is something I need to attend to. And it is something which shall make me say something I do not want to."

Disappointment was starting to filter into Mary's gaze.

"Mary, I cannot come with ye on the march to Manchester. I am sorry. There is something colossal which I need to do. But trust me, it is for the highest good of all. Of everything we stand for."

Mary was on the verge of tears as she shook her head.

"But, Clarence, you're the duke of L— Your people need you! What about the Phoenixes? What about the folk from Darkleigh? What about me?"

Clarence tried to calm her down with hand gestures.

"What's brought this on? What's so big you can't be with us?" she demanded.

"Oh, but I will,"' Clarence stole in. "I will, Mary, believe me. Ye might not see me, but I shall be there. Trust."

Mary was disgruntled now, trying to hold back her anger. Her arms were on her waist.

"Clarence, them people have put their trust in you. They've had faith in you. I've had faith in you. And now you're just going to disappear, at this time, without so much as an explanation!"

Mary was massively incensed. The contrition on Clarence's face reached an extreme level. Clarence gathered his speech.

"Mary, my dear. I need thou to do the leading on Monday. Thou art in charge of the Phoenixes in my absence. Lead them in that strong, noble way thou dost, and all will be well with them. Richard will understand. Now, I need to go. Please break this to them as best as thou can. Tell them their duke hath their best interests at heart…"

Mary was shaking her head as this was going on. Clarence took her wrists.

"But I shall be there, Mary, I shall be there. I swear to you."

Letting her wrists go, there was a brief pause before their hug. Nodding, Clarence made off into the shadows. Mary reluctantly went back inside, heavy with what she had to tell folk.

Chapter Forty-Two

The next day, August fifteenth, Clarence rode through the hills and over the moors on Azlight, who thundered along. Since his vision in *The Phoenix* he had become single-minded. And his single mind centred on one objective: the raising of an army. Because the *real* Duchy of Lancaster was his. And he knew he had to underline that. He needed to parade the strength of his cause, to make the modern 'nobles' who had robbed from and usurped his people think again. Certainly, the establishment had all the official entitlements on their side. But in their heart of hearts, they knew they had no right to use anything to lord over folk who they should be protecting. All thoughts of the meeting had left Clarence's mind. They had been replaced by the building of his ultimate destiny. To do this he needed an army of warriors, who he intended to reward after the battle. One by one, he made his way to the towns of Salford, Blackburn, West Derby, Leyland, Preston and Lancaster itself. As hosts of their hundreds, he rubbed his amulet at each one of them, and entered his second sight. In it, he saw great beacons created, flaring up spontaneously. These beacons carried standards and spun at incredible speeds, seeming to shed their energy in all directions, so to cover all of each hundred they were placed in. And their traces landed on the graves of many an old noble family of Lancashire, slowly enticing their spirits to rise. And rise they did, when they heard from the story the energy told that they had a new duke, who was truly one of them, and was one with the same earth they and their ancestors had trod on for centuries. Amongst the small army that rose, to constitute their new duke's retinue, there were the spirits of the Asshetons of Ashton and Middleton, the Bradshaws of Haigh, the Chaddertons of Chadderton, the Byrons of Clayton and Rochdale, the de Grelleys of Manchester, the Radcliffes of the Tower and Ordsall Hall, the Norrises of Speke, the Andertons of Lostock and Euxton, the Hoghtons of Hoghton Tower, the Towneleys of Towneley Hall, the Tunstalls of Thurland, the Hollands of Upholland, the Molyneuxs of Sefton, and the Shuttleworths of Gawthorpe, to name just a few. The rich panoply of old Lancashire nobility rose with passion from the Mersey to the Duddon.

Yes, *the* duchy was his. Now, Clarence needed help to secure it. Which meant a meeting in his new castle at Lancaster that day. All who Clarence had raised crammed into the white court, Clarence biding them a warm welcome. They waited expectantly, intuitively. Thanks to what they had been shown by the beacons, they needed no explanation as to who Clarence was and what his aims were.

"Thank ye all for coming so soon, my friends," he began. "Some of ye I know, others I do not. Some of us hath come from years far removed. But I wish ye all to know that I value ye, all of ye. I hath recently passed laws by virtue of my office in the shire which I require to be enforced. And, yes, to do this, I need thy help. But more so, I need thy passion for our terra firma. Ye know this land as well as I. It will be that love for it that will give us our desire to succeed. This county can fulfil its true potential now my office is in place. And hath no fear, those who may accuse us of treason are the true traitors, having betrayed the very essence of what we are. For I myself am unstoppable. Now just imagine what all of us united could achieve, my friends."

The whole of the white court was enraptured in cheers at this. The old noble warriors of the shire were unanimous in rallying to Clarence's banner.

"But I wish to stress that in return for thy assistance thy place in heaven will taste all the sweeter, and the glory surrounding ye on Earth will increase beyond all recognisable scale," Clarence concluded, and another huge cheer went up.

Chapter Forty-Three

August sixteenth came. And what a beautiful, peaceful day it was. No one went to the mills that day. In fact, no one went to work at all. In the mills, the owners and a few overseers had remained to enjoy the sedateness. The atmosphere in each of them was akin to that of an empty cathedral. They thought of their mills in a different way now thanks to this new found sensation. Though it was a significance that didn't originate with them, but from those who worked for them. The looms were silent, and the only movement was the dust which shone thanks to the sunlight pouring through the tall, narrow windows. The mill owners stood in awe of that feeling.

Everywhere, the Reformers rose, ready for their big day. Ready to walk to Manchester in good-natured processions, listen to the speaker and show the country that they wanted change. Also, they were quite looking forward to the picnic! The sun shone everywhere, and the moderate heat provided a good feeling. Not too warm but not too cool, conditions conspired perfectly in the Reformers' favour. And, of course, Mary rose in Darkleigh, once more from her bed in her family's rooms. She saw the light massing behind the curtains. Excitement set in. Today would be a massive day and she arose in the same way she did on Christmas morning. She had to gently wake her mother and sisters up, as they had expressed a desire to come as well. As she put her summer dress on, a sad truth of the day came to her. She needed to tell the Phoenixes that Clarence would not be coming. This made her sigh and threatened to undermine how she felt about the day. But she composed herself with some deep breaths. She had been used to disappointment as a weaver, but she convinced herself that today she had nothing to be disappointed about. For a mass body of her people were going for a day out in Manchester. There they'd have a picnic and listen to a speaker. All this would help them celebrate how they felt about Reform. This would be noticed and respected, hopefully, by those in power. She closed her box on her bow and quiver. She knew she couldn't take them.

"Reet, I'll see you in the square at eight. I'll come and say hello before we set off, because, as you know, I'll be leading them who've come from Lancaster."

Mary's mother and sisters took this well and were happy as they waved Mary off. But not before Mary asked whether her father had been to see them in the intervening months. Georgina, her mother, looked up and the glint in her eye and the subtle nod of her head told Mary that her father had been making his remarkable presence known. Mary left her family's rooms and walked down the stairs through the doors and onto the street. It felt good for her, her delicately cobbled street being furnished with sunshine.

One by one, she called at the houses where the Phoenixes were staying, and soon, they were all following Mary to the square. Many folk came out and admired their merry procession. When they reached the square, Joe was hanging about, striding hither and thither like an expectant father. There was already quite a number of people there.

"Morning, Joe," shouted Mary.

"Morning, Mary," Joe responded, looking up.

He was greeted with upwards of two hundred folk behind her, and the impressive scale dawned on him of how many people she had brought.

"I see Max isn't with you?" Joe remarked.

"No," was Mary's short reply.

Joe didn't take it any further.

"Aye, well, I think if you form up there, that should complement our ranks really well," he said, gesturing across to the other side of the square.

"Sure. I just need a word with them," Mary said.

Joe nodded and continued about his business. Mary clapped, signifying that she wanted the Phoenixes to huddle around her. She knew what this meant. She was now their leader, along with Richard. It felt good but also strange without Clarence. Josiah, Caroline and Richard were the first to her side.

"Reet, folks, good morning," she began. "I'm so glad and so grateful that you all chose to do this. I've made such fine friends of all of you, I hope, since we met in Lancaster. And I know you'll hear and see today what we've spoke about many times before. Your cause is our cause. You'll witness that today. I'm not going to bother running through the rules — you already know what they are — and I know you'll abide by them to the letter. One thing though I need to tell you about which you'll find reet disappointing as I did... is that Clarence can't be with us."

Richard, in particular, was disheartened with disbelief. Looking around, Mary saw the countenances of everyone drop, mostly in confusion, others in plain disappointment. "But I'd ask you not to let that affect our spirit. 'Cause everything he is, everything he stands for, is with us today. He can't come for good reasons. Reasons that he can't talk about, but reasons that are aimed at helping our safety."

Folk had been listening to her with drooping mouths.

"OK?" she asked at the end of it.

"Well, no, not really, Mary!" Caroline said with restrained anger. "Everything we were told about him, the way he promised us he'd be there for us. That were what won us round! Now we're told he won't be there! I'm feeling lied to!"

It wasn't hard for Mary to sense that this sentiment was felt by almost everyone there. For most, confusion had turned to shock with the sudden news.

"Friends, friends, I myself am astounded by the situation. Hearing that our one... true leader won't be with us has left me floundering. Today of all days. Mary's job has been to report that to us. That means that she and I are now leading our party down to Manchester. Whatever the reason for Clarence's absence, I'm sure as she says, it's with our well-being in mind," Richard reasoned.

Caroline was sceptical.

"Reet now, we need to be glad of being here. Excited about what we're about to do," Richard added.

Some said "Aye", some mildly, others more resolutely.

The Phoenixes were too loyal to feel betrayed, but their morale was sinking, fast. Mary felt she'd reiterate Richard's welcome intervention.

"Friends, please. Clarence might not be with us, but we on our own still embody everything about him. Everything he stands for, we stand for. All our voices tally with his. And his with ours. But with that in mind, think what so many of us *can* do today. The difference we'll make. We'll go to Manchester today and join up with thousands of other folk who want the same things we do. So, in a way, Clarence will be there. But trust me, friends, he's not gone away 'cause he's selfish. He's gone away because he needs to, for all of us. Surely you trust him to believe that that's true."

Mary concluded her speech and it was followed by a long pause of silence. Then the Phoenixes erupted in cheers of agreement.

One of them shouted, "Here's to Mary and Richard!" and more cheers followed.

Mary was proud and relieved. She felt she had done something significant as a leader in talking her comrades round. She felt the relief flow, having conquered the idea that they were nothing without Clarence. They were all Clarence anyway, and he all of them.

In Manchester, the proverbial stage was being set. At eight in the morning, the town surveyor was out, clearing St. Peter's Field of stones. With his official position, he took quiet pride in his work, knowing that he was helping to back the cause that day, one which he had admiration for. The bill-posters had been out. There were two kinds of bills to be found. Those which warned folk to stay in and make sure their servants did the same and ones which welcomed the marchers, thanking them for their fine conduct. A distinct line lingered in the Manchester air that day. The sun poured down, allowing for a pleasant feeling of warmth. All the streets and ginnels of Manchester lay silent and still. Before the arrival of the thousands of folk, St. Peter's Field, the venue for the meeting, emitted a dramatic quality, basking in the tranquillity before the monumental event it was to play host to. However, the machinations of the establishment were also turning. At nine, the magistrates gathered at the *Star Inn* on Deansgate. And, as discreet as they possibly could be, up to one thousand five hundred troops quietly filtered out onto the streets of Manchester, concealed. Like a silent but deadly gas they assembled. One troop from the Manchester and Salford Yeomanry formed up on Portland Street. Another troop of their colleagues waited on St. John's Street, along with a troop of the 15th Hussars and the Cheshire Yeomanry. Another group of the Hussars and a troop of the Royal Horse Artillery were stationed in Lower Mosley Street, along with two six-pounder field cannons. Companies of the 31ˢᵗ and 88ᵗʰ infantry regiments found themselves forming up on Brazennose and Dickinson Streets, respectively. They clung silently to the shadows, away from the display of the main thoroughfares. Later at the *Star Inn*, a significant number of the Manchester and Salford Yeomanry were spotted by innocent passers-by drinking copiously. They too wanted it to be a monumental day.

In Middleton, Sam Bamford moved to the front of his contingent, to address his people.

"Reet, friends. We all know what today is, don't we?"

"Aye," the collective cry went up.

It was an 'aye' of enthusiasm.

"Today's the day of the meeting. The meeting that could well change all our lives forever. And so many others across the country. Today *will* be the day when we drag this country out of the dark ages and into the enlightened age proper. In other words, we're going to make the transition into liberty. But you might be thinking that we're serfs, bound to our lords, like in the olden days. Well, that's just bloody daft. You see, we're all free. We all have the same rights. 'Cause we were born that way. We don't have to justify our freedom to the establishment, to them in power. The conditions we've had imposed on us, are just a reflection of their fear and ignorance. Of what *we* could achieve. And what we could make this country achieve with liberty. What we suffer isn't a reflection on us. We're free, we're dignified. They just can't see that. But they will. Which is why we're going to Manchester today to say it proud. God-given rights, thousands of them, shining on Peter's fields."

Cheers went up. But they were disciplined cheers. All throughout Sam's speech, people had been thoroughly absorbed, hanging on his every word.

"And, we're going to deny violence as a means to achieve this. Which is why we've got no weapons. We can rise above the need for them and show them in power we trust them. We trust them which is why we've brought our loved ones to the meeting. We trust them as our countrymen, and they'll be forced to see the reason in that. I'm glad to see you've all brought just yourselves and your reason. And I can tell, I can see it in all your eyes, that you are keen to better the bigotry of our enemies with the finest behaviour possible. Thank you."

Sam finished with a nod and the rest nodded back in admiration, before cheering.

"Reet, let's go!" Sam said, and the Middleton contingent set forth.

In Manchester, the Manchester Female Reform Society readied themselves. Dusting off their bright white dresses, almost all of them sported delighted, happy smiles. The big day had arrived. For a good long while now, they had been preparing for this. Although their leader, Mary Fildes, wouldn't admit it, the society was her pride and joy. She felt that bond with every member and the strength of the bond was amplified collectively. Walking out into the street, they formed up, without the need of Mary's say-so. Over the past couple of months, they had grown tight as a unit. The varied (and sometimes gobby) collection of women had come to share a mutual respect for each other brought on by their shared interest in Reform. They were determined that liberty was something for all. It appeared to many as a bounteous fruit hovering in the distance. A glittering concept created by men perhaps but understood by all. And Mary Fildes was living proof that women understood only too well what liberty, comradeship and equality were. If that great power existed in their minds, then that understanding was the only warranty they needed to be a part of it. Positioning herself with her secretary, Susannah Saxton, in front of the crowd, she spoke.

"Sisters," she intoned, sounding both trustworthy and assertive at the same time. "Today's the day. Today, we're going to walk to St. Peter's Field. And this walk will be the walk of our liberty."

The group cheered.

"And when we get there we'll go in with our heads held high."

A second cheer went up.

"'Cause we may be doing something that many members of our own gender even think is wrong for us to do. But we know much better, don't we, sisters?"

The biggest cheer came.

"Sometimes it may feel like we're charging through a storm. We are. But at the end of it, when it dies down, people will see us and what we've done through eyes of friendship and respect. This will be because we'll have given them the courage to be who they want to be. Neither us nor they will be bound by expectations that have hitherto downtrodden us.

And that process starts today, sisters, on St. Peter's Field."

A massive cheer went up again. The ranks of the MFRS broke for a few minutes as its members went to hug Mary and Susannah. After that joyous moment, they filtered back into line.

Lifting their banner, Mary said boldly, "Right then, sisters. Onward!"

In Saddleworth, Dr Joseph Healy finished with his last patient for the day.

Herb used, he said to the young fellow whose blisters he had just painlessly removed, "There you are, young fella. They're reet fine now."

Folk from all walks of life were proud of their herbalist hero. The young fellow smiled his gratitude, not being able to bring himself to speak, given his astonishment. Then, he put his boots on and followed the doctor from the field to where his contingent was assembled on the road to Oldham. With a stout face he stood at the front of his contingent with their banner which featured the slogan 'Equal Representation or Death', along with two hands shaking, underneath a heart. He didn't bother to give a grand speech. They would come later, for sure. And he as a prominent figure of Reform would delight in his.

"Reet, friends of Saddleworth, Lees and Mossley Union, forward!"

The cheers sounded as they made their enthusiastic way forward.

In Darkleigh, the square was bristling with folk, and bustling with activity. The huge Darkleigh contingent was formed up, with folk chasing around, making sure they had items for their picnic, helping to raise banners here and there. And there were some impressive banners. The central one was the biggest and held up by several folk. It had on it a picture of Darkleigh nestling peacefully amidst the hills. When Mary saw it, she knew that Clarence would have adored such a sight. His people, together as one. The banner said 'Darkleigh Reform Society. Liberty must await'. Flanking the inset picture of the town nestled within the valley, there was a red rose to its left and a phoenix to its right. Dotted amongst the crowd were other banners and flags which carried messages like 'Liberty or Death', 'No borough mongering, no corn laws, no taxation without representation, no more'. She looked up at the Phoenixes' banner. A landscape, which obviously represented Lancaster, was its centre, with the castle and priory clearly visible in the middle. At the top there were the words 'The Phoenix Society of Lancaster...' and beneath it the statement 'supports Reform. We are unconditional friends of the movement'. And below that there was, unsurprisingly, a phoenix. Mary felt a curious sense of completion at taking all this in. The sights, sounds, even the smells helped stimulate that priceless feeling within her. Walking round her contingent again, she made one last check to make sure that all were happy. They were ready and willing to go. She went over to her mother and sisters who were going to march with the main Darkleigh contingent.

Embracing them in a hug, Mary said, "You'll be alreet today. Promise. Like you've always said, Mother, there's forces up there that know and do better than us!"

Georgina smiled warmly. Her wisdom said that her daughter was right. Mary's sisters squealed with excitement. As she returned to the head of her contingent, she saw Joe Duckworth jumping on a crate in front of everyone. The square quietened.

"Reet, good morning, folks. Great to see so many of you here. Thanks for coming!"

Applause rang out. Nodding in acknowledgement, Joe continued.

"Today is the day. We're off to Manchester to proclaim what we know for certain is true. And it's going to be a massive day in all our lives. So let's enjoy this day together!"

A cheer of agreement went up.

"I'm not going to remind you of the need for good behaviour. Good folk don't need that. And besides, you know the score."

Cheers and applause went up again.

"So let's go and say how we feel!"

And with that, Joe turned towards the main road which led out of town and began a brisk walk forward. With a cheer, the Darkleigh contingent steadily streamed out of the square in precise order. Mary had been expecting something deeper from Joe but reasoned that today he probably thought that all those speeches had already been made. Today it was surely more important to get to the meeting on time. When it came the Phoenixes' turn to go, she strode forth proudly, as Mary Rishworth leading her friends. The same Mary Rishworth who had always dared to do things that weren't meant for women, like archery. And the little town of Darkleigh had come to love her for it.

As they passed through the gap in the southern hill, Mary felt more and more as if she were part of an epic legend. Looking around from the cover of the shade, she saw all her friends, old and new, characters in this great, noble tale. Her zeal of excitement rose but remained manageable thanks to the discipline involved in their undertaking. It was a truly fine feeling. The shade of the hill both refreshed and invigorated them, which added to the good nature of what they were doing. Coming out onto the moors, the breeze augmented the sun's generous rays and mirrored their goal: stating their demands while respecting the rights and dignity of those who opposed them. Around six hundred folk from Darkleigh walked across the moors. Two hundred of them were the Phoenixes from Lancaster. From afar, they would have been quite an awe-inspiring sight. Like an advancing army whose weapons were reason and a desire to lead those who kept them at bay, rather than wipe them out. The vast, sweeping green moors stretched from horizon to horizon and the waving grass bade farewell to the ranks of heroes going to support their compatriots at what would be the greatest event in history hitherto.

Around eleven o'clock in the morning, the first contingents started streaming in. At around this same time, the magistrates moved as conspicuously as they could to number six Mount Street, their usual lair. As they did, folk at work looked on ambivalently. Some shops closed. Then they joined the Reformers or bolted themselves in their cellars. But those who arrived indicated plainly that they were glad to be there. Some even felt a frivolous sense of pride at being first! Though they soon came to regard conversation and creating an atmosphere of good feeling as greater things to achieve. Half an hour later, two to three hundred special constables entered the fray, descending upon the field like territorial magpies. They proceeded to form an avenue three ranks deep on both sides between the hustings, and, somewhat alarmingly, six Mount Street.

On Lancaster Moor, where Golgotha Hill was, Clarence, the Duke of Lancaster by virtue of his right to the mysterious amulet, climbed to the upper steep. The spirits of a few hundred Lancashire nobles of yesteryear and some of their retainers watched him, smiling gladly. But this time, there was to be a new goal, one which he would require the help of other folk from heaven and purgatory to achieve.

"Reet then. Art ye ready? To claim what's ours, from those who hath no business carving up our precious land?"

A huge cheer went up. Looking out towards the Fells, he took his mace of office which Richard had given him. Then he lifted it up and regarded it reverently in front of his face. Then he thrust it into the air and screamed a primal scream of battle. All the noble warriors assembled followed suit.

Chapter Forty-Four

As the colossus of Manchester drew closer, Mary and her pals thought that they were reaching something of a city of enlightenment. As Manchester's great funnels of industry were that day inactive, there swirled on the currents of the rejuvenating breeze a sense of peace and enticement. These allowed folk to feel that Manchester was, that day, not merely a gigantic centre of production defined by its function, but a citadel which held promise. The massive box-like structures of the mills and numerous chimneys came to denote that promise in the minds of the folk from Darkleigh. Instead of the oppressed feeling of the dreary, daily grind they usually heralded, they announced that whoever was pouring in there that day were coming to friends. In Mary's mind, she likened their steps to those taken by lost knights seeking Camelot, or deposed nobles seeking solace and friendship in Sherwood Forest. Or the folk from Marseille when they were approaching Paris. Manchester loomed large.

Contingents poured in from all over and seeped like liquid gold into Manchester, heading for St. Peter's Field. There were mixed reactions from those clustered outside taverns. Many shouted words of encouragement. Some even set down their drinks and joined. Others were plain clueless while some even shouted taunts of derision at the brave marchers (which were ignored in line with the spirit of the day). The Darkleigh contingent arrived at St. Peter's Field around one o'clock. There was already a huge crowd there. In fact, the crowd was damn massive. It seemed that over half of Manchester was there, not to mention the thousands from all over. Sixty thousand folk were gathered on St. Peter's Field or in the vicinity of the streets surrounding it. Darkleigh (including of course the Phoenixes) joined at the rear from Peter Street. Mary knew they wouldn't be the last to join. More marchers closing in on them from the rear confirmed this. Mary took a long breath in. She felt and heard her heart beating, even amidst the conversation of sixty thousand folk. In that moment, euphoria came to gather in her. This was the proudest moment of her life. Her heart was drenched in the knowledge that she was a part of something that truly counted. Something which would bring the most basic human relief to her people then, and for generations to come. Liberty. They were the tip of the wand of that cause in this country, and it was about to weave its magic. Just about visible from their position were the hustings at the rear middle of the field. Standing on them were some high-profile Reformers. Mary saw them and knew that amongst them there would be people like John Knight, John Johnson and Richard Carlile. Not to mention Mary Fildes as well, a big draw for the fairer-minded gender. All great names she was never sure she'd even see in her lifetime. Looking around her, Mary saw an absolutely comprehensive collection of banners and flags. Many of them were adorned with the expected slogans. Some had a skull and cross-bones on them, with the motto 'Equal Representation or Death'. She giggled, calling them 'peaceful pirates' in her mind. Another featured a red heart with two shaking hands, with the slogan 'Unite and be Free' above them. They were two of the larger banners. What also struck Mary was the diversity of towns surrounding Manchester which were there. Banners and flags announced that they were from the likes of Ashton, Oldham, Saddleworth, Bury, Bolton, Wigan, Leigh, Stockport, etc, etc. There were even some from Blackburn and Preston there. Although Mary wasn't aware of their presence, the meeting was being attended as well by pockets of good folk from all corners of Britain. Mary thought about their long journeys there. Then she thought about how Clarence would love a sight like this. All his people assembled as one, claiming what was theirs by divine right. Where was he? Then she returned her focus to the glorious feeling of the moment. The sun beamed down, and folk were handing out pieces of bread, which had been coveted for the occasion. She saw a banner some distance ahead of them from Rochdale. That made her think about Marvin, and if that was his contingent, and if so, was he standing there the same as her? Was he thinking about them? She looked to Josiah and Caroline. They were evidently pleased to be there. They were standing close, like married couples do.

She spoke across to them. "Hey up there, you two! How are you?"

"Feeling damn good to be here," Josiah promptly answered.

"Aye." agreed Caroline, who looked lovely in her long, flowing dress.

"Just sad about Clarence. He'd have loved this," Caroline pointed out.

"He's here. In spirit," Mary said, half true.

"Aye, dead or alive, he wouldn't miss this for the world!" joked Josiah.

Caroline tutted before joining the laughs.

"Eee, you do look reet gradely, love. Just like our wedding day," Josiah told Caroline.

She returned with the most affectionate of smiles.

"How's you, Richard?" Mary asked of her co-leader.

Richard couldn't stop smiling with pride.

"Overwhelmed," was all he could manage.

She squeezed his hand warmly and shared his rich feelings. With his other hand he held Alison's, her imagination gripped by the scale of what she was a part of. Mary looked through the Darkleigh contingent and saw Bertha, Anne and Unity happily chatting away. That made her smile.

The time passed amicably until about quarter past one. For then, a carriage passed through St. Peter's Field with none other than Henry Hunt standing in it, waving his distinct white hat about by way of a greeting. Folk clapped en masse and huge, good-natured cheers went up. The civility of the greeting was reflected in the pride and gratitude in Hunt's smile. With him there was Mary Fildes and various journalists, keen to spread the news that would be made that day. Mary Fildes waved the banner of the Manchester Female Reform Society about. Behind the carriage followed her sisters of that movement. They were all clad in white dresses which dazzled everyone. Mary likened it to a biblical scene. The carriage came to rest at the hustings in the middle of the field, where all its passengers disembarked and climbed onto them. The carriage departed and the cheering and clapping continued. The enthusiasm of all assembled was immense and could not be silenced. All the while though, they sprinkled their passions from a jar of respectfulness, just as had been asked of them. Masterful.

At No. 6 Mount Street, the select committee had been watching the assembly gather with trepidation. All of them were doom-ridden and the debate which had stretched through August raged amongst them still. Fifty loyalists were gathered in the garden behind them on Mount Street. They had approached the magistrates to make their distress known at the number of people assembled. William Hulton, however, was as composed as usual. A servant approached him. He took two notes out of his pocket and gave them to the servant who then vanished.

"Good grief, look at the women. All decked out in white!" one of them said.

Another remarked, "They have been marching onto the fields there since nine o'clock this morning, in military fashion. For crying out loud, what is happening?"

Wright and Fielden stood together at another window and Wright said, "Yes. I've never seen anything like it. The discipline, the intricacy of such a body of people in peacetime."

"What in God's name are we going to do about it?" Colonel Ralph Fletcher demanded.

"Gentlemen," Hulton said as if announcing something.

All chatter ceased. He approached the table where most of them were crowded round. He placed a writ in the middle of the table.

"A dear fellow called Francis has signed this. A good loyalist fellow, painful in his service of the king. Now we can arrest these miscreants. All that remains for us to do now is to read the riot act. Reverend?" Hulton said brightly, to a nervous Reverend Charles Ethelstone. "Your place nearer to God is likely to persuade our friends outside."

Outside, Mary had joined with Joe and Laura and were busy chattering over whether everyone on the hustings would be allowed to make a speech.

"Of course, Henry Hunt's going to be the main one, probably. They don't sing his name for nowt'," Laura said.

"Aye, but I'd be surprised if Sam Bamford doesn't speak. He's a big draw for a lot of folk, too. No disrespect to Hunt, but he's been at the grindstone, hasn't he?" Mary added.

"Aye, well, with Hunt's eloquence and Sam's passion they'd make a formidable duo. Anyway, today shouldn't be about popularity. Today's about finding us justice, isn't it?" Joe said, balancing the issue.

"Aye," Mary and Laura both agreed.

Mary felt well, ready to receive the unprecedented proclamations. A local lady by the name of Sarah Jones gave her warm-up speech, which bolstered Mary and the wider crowd's spirits. Then she heard something being shouted faintly from a good way behind her, but she couldn't make out what it was for the life of her. All she could tell was that the voice sounded quite desperate. Its tone was the only thing which was carried to her. Evidently, no one else could hear it, given their expressions. Then, the leaders on the hustings waved to the crowd with smiling faces, signalling that it was time for the speeches to begin. An instant hush spread over the crowd. Sixty thousand souls on Saint Peter's Field, Manchester, waited so patiently that a drop could surely be heard. Stepping up with dignity, Hunt began to speak.

Chapter Forty-Five

"Good afternoon, my friends, what an honour it is to see you all here today. Thousands of my compatriots stand here before me in what will be a towering day in history."

So Henry Hunt opened his fine speech. Although at the back of the fields where Mary and the Darkleigh contingent were, they strained to hear him.

"Oh dear, someone should tell him to speak up," Laura said, irritated.

"There'll be loads of note takers out there somewhere. They'll distribute what was said after. The main thing is we're here," Joe said, trying to push home the good side.

On Cooper Street, masses of folk were vying together to get a chance to see the hustings and hear the speakers. This made them ignore the pace of hooves they heard coming up on them from behind. Moments later, when it was realised that the sound of mass hooves belonged to cavalry, many managed to jump out of the way. One lady, Ann Fildes, was not so lucky. A horse caught her and she went flying, knocking her two-year-old son William out of her arms. She barely had time to gasp as she watched William fly across the street in peril. But what happened next was massive for her, but much more subtle. Someone jumped out of nowhere, it seemed, and caught William, as she broke her fall. Both unscathed, the dark figure returned William and guided them to the side to re-join the crowd. She couldn't utter a word of thanks before this figure ran *through* the nearest wall. Looking on in shock, Ann walked deeper into the crowd and thanked God for their strange deliverer. The commanders of the cavalry rode into Pickford's yard.

Mary did not grow tired of trying to listen to Henry Hunt. That was a curious feeling for her, probably the first time she'd felt like that in her life! Then, she heard Henry's voice trail off, replaced by the sound of many horses' hooves, which instantly changed her mood. She saw heads turning to the east of St. Peter's Field, then a cheer went up. It was a cheer of welcome, which was obvious from the tone. But the sounds which followed were more chilling. Vengeful and disgusted cries were heard as within moments, Mary saw cavalry wade through the crowd some distance in front of her, making for the hustings. Her blood ran cold and her heart stopped. For a long, stretched moment, she couldn't hear anything other than the silence of shock. The inverse of people's prayers was coming true.

Indeed, the yeomanry were ploughing through the crowd, as best they could. The sheer density of the crowd made this very difficult though. This made them compete with each other as to who should be first to the hustings. And all through this, their sabres were flailing about randomly. Most folk were watching in shock. Why was this necessary, at a meeting which had been entirely peaceful and good-natured? Some of the yeomen became entangled in the crowd and permanently stuck, much to their chagrin. The initial reaction of the crowd sections they'd tried to mow through had been to run, but that had been rendered impossible by the onslaught of not just the soldiers, but as well the long lines of special constables, the hustings and the vast masses around them. Confusion as to why the yeomen had come was being replaced as the dominant emotion by horror. The rigid lines of constables heard the encroaching yeomen and were themselves beginning to look nervous. That was all of course apart from none other than Joe Nadin, who was striding down the avenue his constables were just about maintaining, full of his usual over-authority. In his hand, he carried a piece of paper. He and some members of the yeomanry reached the hustings at around the same time. The collection of folk who had been assembled up there were then set upon by swipes with sabres and the constables and cavalry throwing them down by force.

"You're all under arrest! By order of his Excellency William Hulton Esq. Chairman of the select committee of magistrates for Manchester and Salford!" Nadin obnoxiously announced, not even bothering to read the charges.

In an act of both defiance and sacrifice, Henry Hunt threw himself amongst the constables, and in doing so knocked Nadin to the ground. He was then instantly seized by a dazed Nadin and his cronies, who speedily frogmarched him down the avenue and into No. 6 Mount Street. A loyalist with a stick knocked his hat down over his face and he was hissed and pushed by some of the constables.

"Have at their flags!" a member of the Yeomanry cried.

Amongst the Middleton contingent, Sam Bamford stood there, tears welling up in his helpless eyes. His heart slowly breaking, his wife Jemima turned to him

"What's going on, Sam?" she asked.

"I… I don't know, love," he replied, not knowing quite how to even respond.

He knew there was nothing he could say or do, in the face of what was happening. Then, he felt a cold presence gather next to him. He didn't react at first, as he was absorbed by the terrible scene unfolding before him.

"Canst we hath thy permission to intervene, Sam?" someone asked him.

Sam spun to his right to see a curious-looking fellow, but one who nevertheless seemed familiar. He had long, flowing blonde hair and wore a long, flowing blue cloak. Sam felt the coldness of his aura and quickly wondered about the fellow.

"Who are you?" was Sam's question.

"Oh, come on Sam. Surely thou recognise me. They called me the hero of Flodden," the fellow said with a wry smile. "We both know what is going to happen in the next few moments, Sam. Please, let us help ye all."

Sam was transfixed and couldn't respond. Although he wouldn't admit it, the fellow was a welcome distraction. But Sam couldn't speak, so the stranger took this as tacit permission to proceed. He then threw his cloak off to reveal a rugged battle-dress. It was decorated in all the individualistic accoutrements of warriors of yesteryear. But, most shockingly, he also sported an old medieval sword at his side, a bow and a quiver full of arrows. Raising his bow to the heavens, he took an arrow and shot it up into the air, almost vertical. At a height, the arrow up-ended itself and seared down towards one of the yeomen, who had been shouting scathing insults at the Reformers. The arrow hit him square in the chest, and he fell off his horse. But on the ground, there was no blood, agony or writhing around — just a defeated posture, and his eyes now a curious storm of grey. Everyone surrounding that yeoman gasped in amazement, looking about them. 'The hero of Flodden' Sam thought. Then he realised who the mysterious stranger had been. Turning around to speak to him again, he felt perplexed as the fellow was no longer there.

While that had been going on, both the constables and cavalry had grabbed the banners, flags and liberty caps which had decorated the hustings, with wicked zeal. The cynical disappointment of the yeomen who hadn't made it to the hustings changed to vicious glee as they targeted the flags and banners closest to them, grabbing them with one hand and slicing at their bearers with their sabres. They struck in all directions indiscriminately. This engendered an uproar of affronted defiance from the crowd, who did their best to keep hold of their flags, snatching them back or clinging on to them with all they had. This resistance was especially strong at the hustings as well. Of course, all the Reformers assembled knew well that today was supposed to have been a day for respect and tolerance, even in the face of those who oppressed them. The Reformers shouted back angrily at the yeomen and the constables but offered no resistance other than that, in line with the aims of the day. But with this terrible display, their graces and peaceful disposition were rapidly reaching their limits.

Back at the Darkleigh contingent, no one knew what to do.

Laura was distressed. "Oh, my God, what's happening up there?"

"Why are them soldiers up there? I hope no-one kicked off!" Mary stated.

"It won't have been that," Joe said, with a dead certainty in his voice.

Screams travelled from nearer the hustings to their position and by then, the whole surrounding crowd was deep in disturbed chattering.

"Gosh, maybe we should do something to help them," Mary offered.

"We can't do that, Mary, they're the cavalry, look at them sabres!" Laura cried.

"We've not come here for a fight, either," Joe reminded them.

Mary felt so helpless. She wanted to encourage the crowd to move on the cavalry and over power them so they couldn't do any more harm. But she still somehow felt oddly restrained by the day's peace theme. If she hadn't have known the establishment of old, she would be confused as to why the cavalry was now charging. The Phoenixes shared her dual emotions.

"Mary, what the hell's happening?" Caroline asked. "Can we fight them now?"

Mary wanted to say yes, but unsure of what would happen next, she said "Er, no, no. We need to go."

Mary turned, prompting Laura and Joe to do the same.

"Allreet, Darkleigh! Turn around slowly!" Joe ordered.

Everyone did.

"Let's go!" was his next shout.

But as the crowd shuffled forward, they felt themselves unable to move, given the vast numbers now in front of them who needed to do the same as they had to escape. A message travelled through the six hundred or so folk of Joe's contingent, right back to him.

Bertha turned to him and said, "They can't move. There's too many folk in front. Some of them don't even know what's going on!"

Everyone's face, including Mary's, sagged into deep horror. They knew they were trapped. Mary's stomach tumbled into terror.

Then, the Cheshire Yeomanry arrived near to the hustings too. The regular professional unit of the 15th Hussars had charged up Lower Mosley Street and formed up in front of six Mount Street where the magistrates were based. William Hulton was notified and came to the window, his legendary composure on the verge of slipping. The 15th's commanding officer, Lieutenant-Colonel L'Estrange asked Hulton what was to be done. Hulton exploded. The blind commanded the blind.

Gesturing across to St. Peter's Field, he shouted as if stating the obvious, "Good God, sir! Don't you see they are attacking the yeomanry! Disperse the...!"

But then Hulton felt the flat of a blade on his shoulder.

Unbeknown to the Reforming crowd, the other bodies of troops that they couldn't see, who were lying in wait for them, were taken acutely by surprise as from out of walls and even thin air, colourful medieval warriors emerged before them, hissing like wild animals. There was no mistaking their accoutrements, they had all heard of them from books which dealt on the subject of yore. But even after they noticed this, their shock and apprehension was compounded by the ghostly glows that surrounded their accosters. On St. John's Street, the warriors charmed the horses of the remaining cavalry troop there into passivity. This caused their troops to demount and with thick-set anger, confront them. Away ran the horses. Archers targeted the two six-pounder cannons on Lower Mosley Street while billmen covered them, staring down the troops. The infantry companies stood toe to toe with their warrior counterparts. At the front of each body of these warriors, the lead smiled an endearing smile while being poised to rip through them. They also held out a hand to them, half restricting, half almost in friendship. That led some of the troops to feel disarmed already. A part even, of who were ready to be their adversaries.

Mary, Joe, Laura, Caroline, Richard and Josiah had been talking to those surrounding them, trying to arrange for the loudest of them to shout to the folk at the extreme back to leave the field. By now, folk were clinging onto their friends and families, doing their best to provide comfort. Then they heard more horses' hooves clattering *towards* them. For a second, they couldn't breathe in the face of the coming storm.

Chapter Forty-Six

Hulton stood there, frozen. Hugely shocked, he stared out over St. Peter's Field, and down to L'Estrange, who was still glaring back up at him in anticipation. For the first time in a long time, Hulton was stumped.

"Who are you?" he asked the owner of what he could tell was the blade resting on his shoulder.

"I am the Duke of Lancaster. Call thy troops off," the voice ordered.

Behind them, Tilly and John had the rest of the select committee pressed into the opposite end of the room.

"Where's Henry Hunt?" Tilly demanded.

The select committee didn't answer. Such was their level of shock. Then, one of them broke the silence.

"He's in the cellar," said Fielden.

Wright shook his head in agreement.

"Allreet, let's go," John said, gesturing the two of them over to the door.

He followed them out while Tilly and her longbow kept the rest of them pinned back. Their ghostly glows were something never seen by even the clergy of the select committee before.

Outside six Mount Street, L'Estrange was shouting up to Hulton, demanding orders.

"Sir, what is it you want us to do?" he cried, each appeal getting angrier.

No answer came from Hulton. In the meantime, the violent struggling of the yeomanry amongst the crowd was causing injuries. People were kicked down, concussed with sabres and struck with them. Screams and angry cries issued from the crowd. One member of the yeomanry was rucking some space away which would allow him a charge within a few moments' time. Seconds were running thin. Down from the heavens, it seemed, there came a streak of arrows, slicing down with a vengeance towards the yeomanry. Each one of them struck the cavalrymen square in the chest, rendering them as good as dead. For when they were struck, they just limped, faculties redundant. And a number of folk noticed the grey storms which occupied their eyes. On top of the buildings lining Windmill Street, there stood the silhouettes of a group of archers — who had just between them *taken out every single member of the Manchester and Salford Yeomanry*. The blunt noises of the impact of all the arrows had caused L'Estrange and his 15th Hussars to turn and be instantly affected by shock given the sight they saw, of the yeomanry who had moved amongst the crowd, out of action, dangling on or off their horses. The crowd were looking towards the tops of the houses on Windmill Street, relieved, but still gasping with extreme surprise at their deliverers. Some had their heads in their hands, believing them to be Reformers who had ignored the instructions for the day and come armed. Sam Bamford strained his eyes to see, all the way from the thickness of his contingent, and could just about make out the fellow who had spoken to him minutes before — as Richard Assheton. Mouth drooped in shock, L'Estrange assumed that the defeated yeomanry was the work of the crowd.

Forgetting the need for orders, he shouted in command, "Forward, Hussars! Clear the field!"

The commander of the Cheshire Yeomanry, who by now had seen the archers on the rooftop too, had looked over to L'Estrange when he had called his battle-cry. He followed suit.

"Arrgh! Forward!"

In six Mount Street, Henry Hunt was released by the magistrates Fielden and Wright, who inside themselves, were glad to assist. John helped him out of the cellar. When Hunt emerged into the sparse light, he noticed the armour and face-paint on John and was hugely taken aback. But not as much as when he saw Fielden and Wright, grinning at his celebrity.

"Did you let me out?" he asked.

All nodded.

A shocked "Thank you" was all he could muster.

John turned to Fielden and Wright.

"I would seek finer employment if I were ye, now. Many thanks."

Again, the two magistrates nodded and ran from the building, throwing down the back door which had been heavily bolted. Through the garden they ran, where the loyalists had fled from, out of the premises and down Lower Mosley Street, past spectral medieval warriors fighting modern troops and into the cellar of *The Briton's Protection* tavern. The rest of the select committee then came down the stairs where Tilly and John herded them into the cellar, and locked the door firmly on them.

The Hussars and Cheshire Yeomanry descended on the crowd, sabres primed, with the sole intention of mowing them off-field, as merciless as the horsemen of the apocalypse. As the horses met the crowd, folk barely had time to scream when a thunderous, inexplicably fast torrent charged through them, to meet the lines of cavalry that bore down upon them. Folk were poleaxed with shock twice in quick succession. When they were able to look they saw, facing the cavalry head-on in close quarters was an array of medieval knights. They sported different colours and liveries. The lavishness of these warriors was a sight to behold. And they had appeared on what had surely been the crest of a divine wave, to engage their enemies on their behalf, who up until moments ago had been on the brink of striking them down in cold blood. A moment or so later, folk noticed the light but vivid glow which surrounded them all, followed quickly by the deep drop in temperature. Foreign for what had been a warm summer's day. Incredulous comments followed, but for the most part, the crowd of Reformers could just watch with fascination and listen with trembling awe as the knights called to one-another, their battle cries carrying with long, inhuman echoes. The Hussars and yeomanry had been shocked too. Now they had to contend with the sheer ghostly speed of the knights, coupled with the old martial forms their attacks, parries and blocks used. The cavalry had been prevented from attacking and dispersing the crowd, but folk were retreating into one-another, and what had been a crammed space before, was getting even tighter.

By now, Mary and her section of the crowd, who had been further from the hustings, could now clearly see there was no one left on them. The speakers and organisers of the event had disappeared. God only knew where they were. Debate raged incessantly around her. Distressed debate.

Different theories of escape were being tested, but Joe Duckworth just kept saying, "There's nothing we can do reet now. Just stay together. Hold onto each other."

But then Mary's heart froze as she saw a figure materialise from nowhere on the hustings. Whoever it was wore a long robe, much like the illustrations of monks from times gone by she'd seen in her father's books. Mary and her mother, Georgina, were the only people to notice this mysterious figure's coming.

"Mary, who's that, love?" Georgina spoke.

"I... I don't know, Mother," replied Mary, who, quite strangely given the situation, had a note of certainty in her voice.

"But he must be one of us," was all she followed up with.

At six Mount Street, whoever it was who had Hulton cornered allowed him to turn, to the outside of his blade, and back away somewhat.

"Call them off, now!" he ordered.

Hulton was spluttering, but could not bring himself to say anything.

"What in God's name *are* you?" he eventually stuttered.

The figure stepped into the light. Hulton gasped as he saw the orange/bronze armour and the tabard, which he saw displayed a phoenix rising from a burning castle. Not to mention a chain with a ruby-red jewel in its centre. In that moment, he knew that the fanciful rumours had been true — a knight had arisen in Darkleigh. Looking out with desperation to the crowd, Hulton saw the troops he would have commanded, embattled with a long line of armoured knights, (who were surrounded by pale glows) the latter separating the former from the protestors. He looked back to the knight who had him cornered. With mouth dangling, he knew in that moment that he was staring at Sir Clarence de Darkleigh.

"One last time. Call them off," Clarence told him.

Then, a distraction moved up to the balcony they were standing on.

Atop the hustings, a few more folk had noticed the robed figure, whose glow was not visible against the crisp blueness of the sky. Removing his cowl, Michael saw and heard the terrified screams of folk, even though there was no way the cavalry could get at them. More startlingly, he heard the exertions of people who were becoming pressed by the pressure of the crowd. Looking up towards the magistrates' lodgings, he aimed a loud whisper at Clarence.

"Sire, I think we should lead these fine folk off-field."

"A fine idea," Clarence echoed back.

Reaching under his robe, some of the screams turned to affirmative words as Michael produced Clarence's duchy mace. On the balcony, Clarence nodded his assent, and Michael uttered an inaudible incantation before striking the mace rapidly down on the hustings three times. Clarence's amulet flashed with enthusiasm. What followed next led many folk to believe that the world was ending that day, in Manchester. For in amongst the protestors, a large, swirling whirlwind engulfed them, causing further temporary terror. However, it didn't take long for the whirlwind to reach absolutely rapid gyration. Before folks' fears peaked, the storm vanished — along with them. Leaving not a person on St. Peter's Field, other than the troops and special constables who battled their ghostly antecedents.

Seconds later, folk reappeared, but this time they were all congregated around the church of St. Peter itself, and the streets adjacent to it. (None landed in nearby Dickenson Street though, with the warriors of yore rigidly separating the infantry there from the protestors). Stifled screams gave way to enormous relief and thankful giggles. On the church steps, Michael appeared.

"Greetings, friends," he echoed.

Over sixty thousand turned in his direction.

"I see ye art not alarmed. I am pleased by this. My name is Michael Snudworth and I bring ye all the Lord's true blessing. I am here, along with the good Squire Hunt, to proclaim thy liberty!"

The crowd listened with merry surprise.

"Allreet, folks, try to act as we were before the troops came," Mary said to the Darkleigh contingent, as Laura, Joe and Alison chased round to make sure all were OK. Mary then caught sight of Bertha, Unity and Anne, looking about themselves, remembering that fateful day they had all been to the castle.

Georgina, and Mary's sisters, Alice and Ella, were looking around frantically, not having an idea how to respond. But then Georgina felt an anchoring presence grow firmer behind them. All three of them felt the mysterious drop in temperature, but Georgina recognised its source. For it was the same one who had assured her of Mary's well-being in Lancaster. It was her husband, Frank.

"Don't worry, my lasses," Frank deeply intoned. "Just breathe. Let Mary do her stuff and we'll be all reet. You mark my words."

The dithering of Georgina and her daughters ceased with immediate effect. They felt themselves anchor now, into surety.

"Oh, Frank," Georgina said with reverence. They turned around.

"Dad!" the girls exclaimed.

They all ignored the irregular chills emanating from Frank as they embraced him. As Mary held the last hand of one of her contingent's members, with the aim of calming the owner, a whisper from afar reached her ears. Before the first word of it was spoken, she knew who it was from.

"*Mary,*" it said. "*Come and find me at the Quaker House.*"

Mary's whole face ignited. Slipping through the crowd, it was a few minutes before she was able to run down the side of what she recognised to be a Quaker Meeting House. Then, out of a ginnel swooped Azlight, with Clarence mounted, in full armour. Mary's highest hopes since being spirited away from St. Peter's Field were confirmed. Now, she was ablaze with what they stood on the cusp of.

"I thought thou might need these," Clarence said, tossing her bow and quiver.

Grabbing them, Mary strapped them on with the greatest eagerness. Taking Clarence's hand, she thrust herself onto Azlight, and they sped away, back towards where the battle was now being fought.

Chapter Forty-Seven

Towards the top of Lower Mosley Street, the troops who had been guarding the cannons had quickly found that the warriors they faced were relentless, and unassailable. The archers shot at the cannons with their angelic arrows, rendering them useless. The troops who hadn't been cut down fled.

The infantry units in Dickinson and Brazennose Streets heard the commotion on St. Peter's Field, but were in something of a disarray, as no despatch had come with orders. The warriors had heard the cries of battle too, which had echoed through the streets to reach their position. They just stood there though, remaining focused and ready to pounce. The infantry were also now confused by the echoes of Henry Hunt's voice, booming amicably from the area where the church was set, punctuated at pauses by applause and some cheering. This made their officers nod, and they tried to advance. They snarled as they engaged the glowing warriors, muskets at the ready.

The warrior at the front responded by affecting a remorseful face and offered them an option. "Surrender," he said, almost tenderly.

This caused some of the troops to hesitate, but they were soon pressed on by their colleagues. The troops attacked with the regimented violence of their training, and the warriors responded with the artistry of theirs. The main thing on the minds of the latter was though, that these red coats could not, would not, be allowed anywhere near the protestors who were their charge.

Charging back onto St. Peter's Field upon Azlight, Clarence and Mary prepared. Mary made a quick survey of the action, and saw cavalry staggered, out of line, tangled with the luminous knights. The combat was intense, with many of the knights now having discarded their lances in favour of swords, maces, flails, axes and so on. The cavalry were affronted and angry. The validity of what they represented was wearing rapidly thin. The special constables had long since broken up their 'avenue', and were running around, diving for cover with extreme distress. The cavalry slashed about furiously, but their sabres could only bounce off the armour of their ghostly antitheses. With parrying blocks, slick manoeuvring and deft strikes, the knights were causing more and more of the cavalry to fall down, defeated. Mary noticed the blue uniforms of the first wave of yeomanry who'd made the initial attack. They lay motionless on the floor. Each and every one of them had a grey storm raging where their eyes should have been. More and more Hussars and members of the Cheshire Yeomanry were joining them as the minutes went by. Clarence rode through the mounting carnage by the hustings, and dropped Mary off there. She jumped onto them and readied her bow. As she pulled its string back, synching into her legendary focus which had served her so well down the years at tourneys, John, Clarence's old Sergeant-at-arms, jumped up onto the hustings and offered her a bucket in which a silvery liquid swayed about.

"No bloodshed," he stated.

Mary dipped all her arrow heads, in her quiver, into the liquid. Then they exited it with a fearfully flashing solution on them. John promptly left and Mary aimed. Picking up on two Hussars charging for the backs of a group of knights stuck in a knot of fighting, she imagined the path her arrows would take. She made the shots, one rapidly after the other. The two Hussars fell from their horses seconds later. Mary was so glad that her arrows had been treated with what she could only fathom was a magic solution. It was then she noticed another person on the hustings, wearing a robe and holding up a smooth gold weapon in one hand. He had his eyes closed and was twirling his other hand around, quite rhythmically. She noticed that the horses of the cavalry who were without riders responded to this and were heading off field, weaving intricately between the groups in battle. Michael was sending them to the Pennine Hills to begin new lives as wild horses, escaping the harshness of their purpose.

Nadin was tearing around, barking at his special constables to "Hold the line" in an attempt to sound military.

But his orders went unheard, unheeded, ignored. At that moment, some members of the infantry had drifted through from Brazennose and Dickinson Streets, to investigate the rabid screams, after finding their efforts against the warriors providing the barrier to the protestors fruitless. There they were then confronted with life-changing shock. Mary aimed the next volley of her arrows at them, cutting several of them down. The remaining troops saw where they had come from and made a beeline for Mary's position on the hustings, dodging the cavalry and knights as best they could, unable to get a straight shot away at her. Mary continued with her arrows, enjoying the advantage of her raised position. She struck them down until there were only a few left. Some of them were taken with the horses' hooves of their own colleagues. As they closed in, Mary jumped down to the back of the hustings. Nadin saw this and made for her position. The remaining members of infantry left ran to the side of the hustings opposite to the direction of Nadin's run, ready to jump out at Mary. But as they begun to edge round its side, an arrow from an eagle-eyed Middleton archer landed right in front of them, stopping their progress. This allowed Mary time to jump out at them!

"Surrender!" Mary cried as she appeared in an instant.

The troops just raised their bayonets, ready to slice at her, so Mary followed suit with her bow. She swept at the first red coats' legs, then caught his chin with her bow, the quick movements taking him by surprise. Down he went. The next one sliced at Mary's dress with his bayonet, ripping it. But Mary parried and, turning into him, raised her bow between his legs, squashing his vulnerabilities. He too went down. The training with the Phoenixes had stood her in good stead. The third one flung his musket at her as if it were a sword. Mary caught this and twirled it away before decking him on the chin, followed by a stroke from her bow. But then she turned to the side, to see a new squad of troops bearing down on her. She knew that numbers would likely prove her undoing now, and felt herself start to set in shock. However, then she heard a familiar cry. Azlight, with Clarence atop her, cut right past the path of these troops, scattering them in all directions. Mary looked up and nodded her thanks. Returning the nod, he then jumped off Azlight and pushed Mary out of the way. When Mary looked round, she turned to see a frustrated Nadin grunt at her as Clarence stepped in with his sword and shield, barring his path. 'Always there for me!' she thought.

A young lieutenant of the Hussars, William Joliffe, hung back on his steed as his colleagues made charge after angry charge. He had lost the taste for battle. His strategy had been to shepherd the crowd away, given that they were civilians who required a mere dispersal. However, during the battle which had instead erupted, it had changed to staying anonymous within his ranks, making less and less of an attempt to mount an attack of his own. He felt inspired by these archaic warriors, protecting the charge for freedom the protestors were making. At the present moment, he was just sitting there, contemplating in the heat of battle what he was to do. Then, his superior drew up alongside.

"Good Lord, Joliffe, what the hell are you doing! Bloody engage, boy!"

That proved the catalyst for his decision.

"Sir, your services here are not required," he calmly said, throwing his superior out of the way.

Then he opened up at the top of his voice.

"Hussars, yeomanry! Withdraw! Lay down your arms and withdraw!"

This unexpected order turned the heads of many of them. The knights too, moderated their strokes of battle, for a moment. Joliffe may not have been the commander but some seized on his order, relishing the perfect excuse to leave the battle. Which they did, unmolested by the knights. Others sneered at him with disdain. Joliffe then took the greatest decision of his life. Throwing off his red coat, he unleashed his sabre and charged at his former colleagues. Toppling one with some good blocks and counter-strikes, he then ran for Peter Street.

Elsewhere, the challenge of the troops had now almost vanished. The infantry on Brazennose and Dickinson Streets had now either fled or fallen. But some had defected. The realisation of the day the Reformers had designed, supplemented by the super-natural events taking place around them, had caused their hearts to swell with pride. They too now were demanding a greater state to fight for. Red jackets lay strewn on the ground. They, along with some forgiving Reformers, were now consoling their colleagues who had surrendered. Their aim now being to carefully encourage them to renounce and be free. Then, Joliffe arrived.

"Right, let's see if we can get some sort of guard set up, so no one interferes with the rest of the meeting," he said to a sergeant.

The same scenes could now be witnessed on St. John and Lower

Mosley Streets. The support from outside St. Peter's Field was now non-existent for the establishment. Only the civilian loyalists looked on, staring stunned at what was playing out before them. However, as the peace progressed around St. Peter's Field, the medieval warriors who had helped cause the enlightenment of the troops began to fade slowly, turning almost to apparitions of dust. As they vanished, they were all wearing contented smiles.

Clarence had brushed Nadin off, and was now on top of the former hustings, surveying what was around him. The cavalry were dissipating, but so too were the warriors Clarence had recruited to his banner, vanishing all to heaven. This evidently went unnoticed by Nadin, whose mind was set on revenge. For he too climbed the hustings from the other side Clarence had. Dashing straight at Clarence, Clarence turned and caught his sabre abruptly with his sword, halting his run. Nadin then proceeded to slash away with some massive moves. Clarence, close to the end of the hustings, contained these, moving his weapon into place to meet each stroke with the tightest of manoeuvres. Ducking one, he rolled through towards the centre of the hustings and Nadin followed, sabre raised. But this time Clarence had momentum, launching his sword at Nadin in an attacking move. Nadin felt the force of this knight, whose prowess in life he realised was now augmented by ghostly strength and skill. Then he saw the amulet flash fearfully on Clarence's chest armour. Genuine fear was displayed as his mask lifted and he mounted one last, desperate attack. Clarence decided it was time to wrap up the challenge of Nadin. So after a couple of parries, Clarence waited for Nadin to raise his sabre to his outside to swipe again. There was the moment, as Clarence stepped to Nadin's inside, sweeping him off balance at the ankles. Nadin staggered back, and raised his sabre for one last desperate swipe, but Clarence spun his sword into place and plunged it into Nadin before his weapon swung, running him through. Nadin exhaled for the last time, as his body fell still, and seized up. The grey storm swamped his eyes, blotting them out like the sea on a shore. And the true figurehead of tyranny in Manchester, the unjust scourge of liberty, was no more.

Some of the special constables had come out from their hiding places in the shadows, and Mary noticed them looking around angrily for anyone they could attack. She darted to cover, as she was out in the open.

One of them noticed, however, and gestured to his colleagues. Some of them proceeded to chase Mary, others followed in the shadows of the ginnels. But actually, those that remained in the shadows weren't special constables. A trio of them caught up with Mary and raised their coshes. Mary raised her bow in response, but the constables ended up falling down, clobbered by none other than Caroline and Josiah, who had emerged from the shadows. They then threw off their stolen constables' coats and hats. Mary was delighted they had joined the fray. Behind them were a number of Phoenixes, including Richard.

Around him from the hustings, Clarence surveyed the situation again. Everywhere blue and red coats were fleeing, and the echoes of his second sight told him they were fleeing, not just the fields but Manchester entirely. The defeated troops had disappeared, thanks to the workings of Michael. But so too were the knights and warriors he had brought. Their tasks on Earth now complete, they had faded to heaven, ready to resume or indulge in their well-earnt rest. For if the old flower of Lancashire nobility was blooming again, it was to serve what had only ever been its one reasonable purpose: protecting those 'under' them, so that they could emerge as a force united by their own accord. He enjoyed a moment contemplating that, meditating a little as the battle drew to its end.

Then though, he received an alarmed appeal: "Sir

Clarence, help me, Sir, help me!"

Clarence immediately recognised who the voice belonged to and shifted his focus towards the origins of the cry. It had come from the upstairs of six Mount Street.

Chapter Forty-Eight

Clarence jumped right up from the hustings and back onto the balcony of what had been the magistrates' residence. The doors were still open, so he entered the dimly lit room. Tracing the trail of the voice he had heard, he expected the person who called to emerge out of the shadows very soon. But he couldn't feel that person's presence. Moving deeper into the room, taking stock of all the furniture which could be concealing new attackers, he paused and went to enter his second sight. But then the voice came again, this time from behind him.

"Hello, Clarence," it came, with a tone that hinted sly conspiracy.

Clarence turned. There, at the boundary where darkness met the light, stood Marvin. He was gazing out towards the fields.

"Marvin!" Clarence said with surprise. "What art thou doing here?"

"Just getting a better view. Today, after all, will be a towering day in history."

"Yes, but thou art not safe here. Thou need to get to safety," Clarence underlined.

"But thou art here, Clarence. Thou and the ones of us thou hath brought."

Clarence was now confused. Why was Marvin speaking in the old ways now?

"Where is…"

"Hulton?" Marvin finished.

"He's locked up with the others. Useful man Hulton. Like them out there, he serves his purpose. Or at least he will once more when I thank thou for thy amulet," Marvin said in a cunning voice, turning to face Clarence.

By now, Clarence suspected the worst of Marvin. He was surely a spy. That was clear now. He had been deliberately placed in Lancaster to garner information on them. Phoenixes had risked their lives saving him. Many had given them. Anger rose in Clarence, but he measured it on the crest of focus, wanting to discern what this traitor actually was.

"How much didst they pay thou, Marvin? To lure me and our society to you? What didst thou hope to achieve by pretending to be a Reformer in peril?"

But Marvin replied, "They, Clarence? Not they. We."

In a horrible moment, Marvin strode a few steps toward Clarence, and as he did, his Sunday clothes tore off him, flaking away into dust. Then, Marvin's whole constitution warped and transformed into another armoured warrior, one which caused Clarence to frown in disbelief. For it was someone he had known very well. Someone who was well capable of manipulating any establishment, be it old or current. It was Dalbern.

Outside, the fighting was reaching its conclusion, with the field almost clear of the troops. The special constables were getting hammered by the overriding drive of the Phoenixes. A trickle of constables then mounted their escape. Mary and Richard called for them to be left to it, given that the day had begun with a peaceful theme. One which they wanted to restore as soon as possible. Mary noticed all around her that the ghostly knights, archers and sergeants were now disappearing. And they were doing so with the same contentment. This frustrated Mary as she had wanted to thank them. In fact, she had wanted to meet them afterwards and proclaim them as heroes. But the fact that she would never do that now gnarled her. She looked over to six Mount Street, where she had seen Clarence leap up to minutes ago. Her face twisted with intrigue. Now there were five knights left.

"Good Lord," was all Clarence responded with.

"Thou art not the only one who arose after four hundred years. I never forget what is mine by rights, Clarence. Never," Dalbern rasped.

"Now, I want thy amulet. And thy duchy, and thy army will be mine," Dalbern said with slowly demanding tone. "Because then, we can have what we had back, Clarence. And thou canst be a part of it. Those fellows locked in the cellar, they hath just about been holding the old order together. Now it is crumbling. But think, with that amulet, with that power, we canst restore it. Its former glory shall shine! In spite of being my worst enemy, I always admired thou, Clarence. As a warrior, and that gift thou had for nullifying the peasants. Under me, serving me, thou shall hath a prominent position…" Dalbern trailed off with temptation colouring his voice.

Clarence smiled curtly.

"Firstly, Dalbern, there is not, nor was there ever a 'we'. Secondly, there shall never be. Thirdly, thou art a fool if thou think the amulet could serve evil desires like thine. And back then, people never belonged to us. No matter what any document or clergyman said. Some of us thought they did, like thyself, but others, like my family, realised that all we were were their temporary guardians. I am so proud that I hath arisen now to witness our people coming of age and sharing ownership of their land and lives, as sisters and brothers," Clarence concluded with subtle but firm emphasis, against the thug who had been his arch-enemy in life.

"Very well, Clarence. Thy choice," Dalbern said, drawing his sword. "A shame, but thy choice."

Clarence followed suit.

Chapter Forty-Nine

The special constables were now gone from the field, and the sight and hearing of the five knights left extended well beyond St. Peter's Field, well beyond Manchester even. It was this that allowed them to witness the retreat of the constables behind the troops. All felt peaceful on St. Peter's Field now, even for them. They paused within their focus, waiting for their leader. Mary, Richard, Caroline and Josiah noticed the stark peace on the fields as well. The only activity seemed to be the dust, which rose to the skies endearingly, impaled by the sun. Mary then ran in the direction of the magistrates' house.

In the upstairs of six Mount Street, both Clarence and Dalbern raised their swords, a move they both knew signalled the start of a duel. Then it began. Dalbern made the first move, crashing forward with a massive chop before Clarence side-stepped and swiped for his side. Dalbern remembered Clarence's old dexterity from their lives. This made him work all the harder to counter and block the smaller but more lethal moves of Clarence. Then, both of them, perhaps without realising, increased the speed of their duel to vicious pace, cancelling each other out with their moves, which became dead-locked in the middle. Neither of them was able to reach the other's constitution and strike each other down. In the process, the furniture of the upstairs room was torn to shreds as their swords flew frantically. Clarence remembered fighting John O' Gaunt. That had been training. This was a duel which would have a definite outcome. The intent, and the pace, was vicious. And neither Clarence nor his nemesis knew what would happen when either of them was slain. But he kept his focus narrow. Fighting the duel.

"I never knew thou could masquerade as a living person. But the ploy was typically you," Clarence frowned.

Dalbern laughed.

"Oh, believe me, where I hath been, Clarence, many abilities hath opened up for me."

Clarence then unleashed a speedy attack to the top of Dalbern's blade. This caused him to stumble, but at the very second he managed to regain his balance, he swooped round low at Clarence who was now poised to strike him down. Clarence noticed at the last moment and squeezed in a block, moved in hurriedly from the bearing-down position his sword had been in seconds ago. The force of this flung Clarence down and backward. Dalbern then ran at Clarence, sword lowered to cover himself. With time running out, Clarence swiftly removed the amulet and held it aloft. He saw it was flashing. He had come to be able to 'read' its glows and flashes. Now it was as ready to fight as he was. Dalbern stopped short, confused by Clarence's apparent offer.

"If thou truly think the land, nay, the world will be better off with us dominating again, then take it," Clarence said.

Dalbern was still confused but his greed got the better of him. He lunged towards the amulet, but then Clarence threw it into him. Into Dalbern it sliced. And slice it did — right through him. The amulet, which by now was on the other side of the room, had left a hole in Dalbern's ghostly body, shaped exactly as itself. Dalbern just twitched with shock at first, not believing what had just happened to him. Then he looked down on himself, and with shock, back to Clarence. He staggered back, then came to a stop in the middle of the room. The final action of his haunting was indeed haunting as simultaneously, he let out an all-consuming scream and his whole constitution exploded in a giant burst of dust, emanating from the hole Clarence had struck. With a loud pop, the last of the dust flew, and mellowed into nothing. Now, finally now, Dalbern was no more. Clarence picked himself up and went over to the amulet. Picking it up, he looked towards the window where he knew the battle had been won. The silence was almost total outside. Slipping the amulet back on, he left the house.

In the garden to the rear of six Mount Street, Mary made her way to its back door. She had just been set upon by the urgent need to do so. Then Clarence, slightly depleted in colour from the rigours of battle, walked out. She ran up to him, and offered her assistance. He took his helmet off.

"It is all right, my dear," Clarence reassured. "It is good to see thee. Tell me how the battle went."

"By heck, we cleared up with them!" replied Mary.

Clarence nodded a knowing smile.

"They art a fine bunch," he said.

"Who were they?" Mary asked, the shock of the ghostly warriors' instant descent on them still demanding an explanation.

"In their day, they were the noblest families of this shire. And today they hath served many. And serve me well they hath, too."

"Clarence, what's going to happen now? Are you OK?" Mary questioned, switching her concern back to Clarence.

"Yes, my dear. I feel that I must move on now though. God is calling me back."

Mary was grave.

"Oh. Clarence, you can't leave us. You've done an amazing thing for us, and so many other folk. We need to show you how grateful we are. How much we love you!"

Clarence took off his amulet and gave it to her. She was stunned.

"Remember this, and if thou art ever in conflict with anyone again in thy life, imagine you and this other person stood above the rose here. Now imagine both of ye wholeheartedly shaking hands. Tell everyone else that. Do that, Mary dear, and I shall feel thy gratitude."

Mary was utterly taken with the masterful meaning behind Clarence's words. But still she sighed.

"Oh, Clarence. Does this mean that this is the last time we'll ever see you again?" Mary said, starting to cry.

"Only on Earth," he reassured. "But before we see each other up there, we'll hath a good many chats when thou sleep."

Mary was dazzled.

"Who's going to lead us?" she then asked, her voice calmer.

Clarence smiled again. Lifting the chain that carried the amulet, he put it round her neck and winked at her. Mary felt something powerfully wholesome shoot through all of her. Her whole being crystallised as she realised that today represented a beginning. Then the two of them hugged in the greatest hug they had ever enjoyed.

Henry Hunt had finished his speech on the steps of St. Peter's Church. Others had followed, and were now receiving claps and moderate cheers, as many folk had had one ear on the activity back on the fields. Suddenly a voice boomed from that direction, loud and mighty like the supernatural.

"My friends, thank ye for turning up today. It hath been an honour to see a whole host of my compatriots together, marching in peace to claim what is thine. Thanks to ye, I am now enlightened. Now I can retire with complete honour. God speed."

The voice had warped round buildings, and filtered almost directly to the Reformers via the streets and ginnels. That caused the curiosity of folk to be ignited and they slowly turned and walked back to the fields.

As they left the area of St. Peter's Church, via the streets and ginnels, they re-descended on the wide-open space of St. Peter's Field. There they saw the ground littered with banners, muskets, shakos and the like. Their jaws were drooping, their progress slow with disbelief. But they were about to witness one more thing. St. Peter's Field was washed with a breeze, which cooled the warmth of the day. The only folk remaining there were Mary, Richard, Caroline, Josiah, Alison and a few of the Phoenixes. They were staring up into the sky, which is where everyone else's gaze immediately went. For above them was a blossoming flower, of giant size. People braced themselves, stifling a few gasps. But as the flower unfurled, folk were able to tell it were a red rose. The kind worn by so many of yesteryear. Up in the sky with it there came five remaining knights, who bade farewell to those they had served, before disappearing into its centre. Then came the last armoured warrior, who Mary and the Phoenixes knew had been Duke. Heralded by a fresh breeze, Clarence flew slowly across the fields on Azlight, with John and Tilly mounted behind him. He looked to the friends he had made amongst the living, then to the rest of the sixty thousand or so folk now staring up at him in awe. Old met new in a gracious ring, and he was complete. There would be much work to do soon, after a party tonight. But for now everyone, especially Mary, felt the chill of re-birth run through them, as they stared to the outgoing champions of yore. Then, as Clarence and his party met the rose, he waved warmly to Mary. She returned the acknowledgement, and he was gone, to rest, surely forever now. The red rose then vanished itself and then there was a deep pause. Then Mary climbed onto the hustings and an inn-keeper who had denounced his loyalism and embraced the crowd gladly handed her a jug of ale.

Raising it to the crowd, she proclaimed, "Now this is us!"

In response, the cheers of sixty thousand heroes sounded out around the fields. Through Manchester and beyond their echoes were heard, captured in time. These ghostly cries of triumph would echo forevermore to those who sought meaning in the old urban castles.